BREAKING NO-DATES RULE

BY
EMILY FORBES

WAKING UP WITH DR OFF-LIMITS

BY
AMY ANDREWS

MILLS
BOON

It's their last summer of being single!

Off duty, these three nurses, and one midwife, are young, free and fabulous—for the moment...

Work hard and play hard could be flatmates Ruby, Ellie, Jess and Tilly's motto. By day these three trainee nurses and one newly qualified midwife are lifesavers at Eastern Beaches hospital, but by night they're seeking love in Sydney— and only sexy doctors need apply!

Together they've made it through their first year in hospital, with shatteringly emotional shifts, tough new bosses and patching together broken hearts from inappropriate crushes over a glass of wine (or two!)

Read on to meet the drop-dead gorgeous docs who sweep Ellie and Jess out of their scrubs. And if you missed Ruby and Tilly's stories

CORT MASON—DR DELECTABLE
by Carol Marinelli and

SURVIVAL GUIDE TO DATING YOUR BOSS
by Fiona McArthur

are available from www.millsandboon.co.uk

BREAKING HER NO-DATES RULE

BY
EMILY FORBES

MILLS
BOON®

First published in Great Britain 2011
by Mills & Boon, an imprint of Harlequin (UK) Limited.
Harlequin (UK) Limited, Eton House, 18-24 Paradise Road,
Richmond, Surrey TW9 1SR

© Emily Forbes 2011

ISBN: 978 0 263 88608 5

Harlequin (UK) policy is to use papers that are natural, renewable and recyclable products and made from wood grown in sustainable forests. The logging and manufacturing process conform to the legal environmental regulations of the country of origin.

Printed and bound in Spain
by Blackprint CPI, Barcelona

Emily Forbes began her writing life as a partnership between two sisters who are both passionate bibliophiles. As a team, Emily had ten books published—and one of her proudest moments was when her tenth book was nominated for the 2010 Australian Romantic Book of the Year Award.

While Emily's love of writing remains as strong as ever, the demands of life with young families has recently made it difficult to work on stories together. But rather than give up her dream Emily now writes solo. The challenges may be different, but the reward of having a book published is still as sweet as ever.

Whether as a team or as an individual, Emily hopes to keep bringing stories to her readers. Her inspiration comes from everywhere—stories she hears while travelling, at mothers' lunches, in the media and in her other career as a physiotherapist all get embellished with a large dose of imagination until they develop a life of their own.

If you would like to get in touch with Emily you can email her at emilyforbes@internode.on.net, and she can also be found blogging at the Harlequin Medical™ Romance blog—www.eharlequin.com

Recent titles by the same author:

NAVAL OFFICER TO FAMILY MAN
DR DROP-DEAD-GORGEOUS
THE PLAYBOY FIREFIGHTER'S PROPOSAL

Did you know these are also available as eBooks?
Visit www.millsandboon.co.uk

For Sophie Grace, one of my many gorgeous nieces.
This book will be released as you celebrate
two major milestones, your eighteenth birthday
and the end of your school days. This is my gift to you
as you enter the next stage of your life;
I hope it is everything you've ever dreamed of.
Wishing you every success and happiness,
with all my love, Auntie K

PROLOGUE

THE old gate at 71 Hill Street squeaked in protest as Ellie shoved it open. The noise went unnoticed by her as she was intent on getting inside, getting home. Tears blurred her vision and she struggled to fit her key into the front door. She was mortified. She wanted to climb into bed, pull the covers over her head and hide from the world.

Finally the door opened and she stumbled through it. She felt physically sick and she got to the bathroom with seconds to spare before she vomited. She leant her head against the cool surface of the tiled wall as she waited to see if her stomach had emptied itself of her dinner. The rich meat she'd ordered didn't combine well with the nausea that rumbled through her following Rob's announcement. She'd been so nervous throughout dinner she'd barely tasted her meal and now she wondered why she'd bothered eating at all.

Physically she felt better once her stomach was empty, although emotionally she felt battered and bruised. She rinsed her face and brushed her teeth but the minute the toothpaste hit her stomach she felt herself start to gag again. With one hand she quickly gathered her blonde hair into a ponytail and held it out of the way as she vomited a second time.

* * *

Jess and Tilly left the hospital together after their late shifts and walked down Hill Street to number 71; home. Heading straight for the kitchen, Jess put the kettle on and searched through the bread bin for penicillin-free bread. Someone really needed to get to the shops she thought, they were living on takeaways and toast and if they didn't shop soon ther wouldn't even be any toast. She found a couple of slices of bread that looked edible and slid them into the toaster.

From the bathroom the girls could hear the sound of running water followed by vomiting.

'Is that Ruby?' Tilly asked.

Jess shrugged. 'No idea.' They'd arrived home together so she knew no more about what was going on in the house at the moment than Tilly did. And with four, and some-times five, people sharing a house, there were plenty of things happening. Despite the colour-coded calendar in the kitchen no one could be expected to keep up to date with all the action.

Tilly went into the passage and knocked on the bath-room door. 'Ruby, is that you? Are you okay?'

'What are you doing?' Ruby's voice came from behind them, startling them both.

Tilly turned around. 'We thought you were in the bath-room. We could hear vomiting,' she explained.

Ruby came down the stairs, shaking her head. 'Not me,' she said with a shrug. 'But Adam's back. I heard him come home and he had company.'

'It could be Ellie,' Jess said hopefully. She didn't want to think of Adam's company.

'Ellie's supposed to be having dinner with Rob,' Ruby replied.

The bathroom door opened and Ellie emerged, white faced and shivering with black smudges of mascara under her eyes. Tilly, Ruby and Jess stepped back, enlarging their semi-circle to make room for her.

'What are you doing home?'

'What happened to dinner with Rob?'

'Are you sick?'

Ellie looked from one friend to the next as they each asked a question. She opened her mouth but no sound came out.

The girls could see Ellie's lips moving but there was nothing to hear. 'Something's wrong,' Ruby said to the others. She took Ellie's hand and led her through to the lounge where she sat her down. Her hands were like ice. 'Someone grab a blanket, I think she's in shock.' Had she been in an accident? Ruby searched Ellie's body for clues but there was no sign of an injury—no scratches, no blood, no bruises. 'Ellie, talk to us. What happened? Are you hurt?'

Jess returned, carrying a box of tissues and the quilt from Ellie's bed. She draped the quilt around her shoulders. 'Was there an accident?'

Ellie shook her head. Physically she was unharmed, but how did she explain the night she'd had? None of them knew that when she'd gone out to dinner with her boyfriend of three months she'd been expecting a proposal. None of them knew what she had been wishing for and none of them knew how her world had been totally turned on its head.

The girls took up their positions on the couches surrounding her.

'You look terrible,' Tilly said in her usual no-nonsense fashion. 'What's going on?'

In a house of four women, and one, often-absent, male, there weren't many secrets. Ellie didn't intend withholding the story but she didn't know if she was capable of sharing it tonight. She gathered the corners of the quilt in her

hands and pulled it tight around her, seeking comfort in
its warmth. She looked at each of her friends in turn. Her
voice wobbled when she spoke. 'You'll say you told me so.'

'Of course we won't,' Jess said.

Ellie kept her focus on Jess. Tilly and Ruby had never
really warmed to Rob and therefore Ellie thought Jess
would be the most sympathetic. 'Rob asked me to dinner
tonight and I was sure he was going to propose, but he had
a different surprise.' She paused as she reached for a tissue
and blew her nose. 'It turns out he's married.'

'What?'

'He's married?'

'That bastard,' Tilly fumed. 'I always had a bad feeling
about him.'

'That's not helping,' Jess said to Tilly, before turning
back to Ellie. 'Start at the beginning, tell us what happened.'

Ellie sniffed and reached for another tissue. 'Rob invited
me to dinner and I was sure it was going to be a turning
point in our relationship. You know how he doesn't like to
go out on dates, he prefers to stay home, always saying he
wants to relax after his long days at work and doesn't want
his private life made public at the hospital.' The girls were
nodding, they all knew Rob. He was an orthopaedic surgeon at Eastern Beaches Hospital where they all worked
as nurses.

Ellie had accepted Rob's reasons as legitimate but now
she wondered how many of them had been for convenience
and deceit. 'I thought that because we were actually going
out tonight it meant he was ready to go public with our
relationship. I thought it was a good sign and I was all
ready for a proposal or at least for him to ask me to move
in with him. But he had an even bigger surprise. His wife
and daughter arrive from the UK next week.'

'He has a daughter too?'

'And you had no idea?'

'Of course not,' Ellie protested. 'Do you think I would willingly have a relationship with a married man?'

'No,' Ruby said as she shook her head, 'but how do you keep something like that hidden?'

'Easy,' said Tilly, 'you keep them in another country.'

'But surely he'd have photos of them, take phone calls from them, stuff like that,' Jess mused.

'I guess with the time difference and his hours at the hospital it was easy to make sure he never spoke to them when I was around,' Ellie said. 'There was nothing to make me suspect he was anything other than what he said. There were no phone calls, he didn't wear a wedding ring and there were no family photos, not one.'

'Did he say why they're coming now? He's been here for months.'

'They were waiting until the end of the school year.'

'How old is his daughter?'

'Dunno.' Ellie shrugged. Getting all the details hadn't been high on her list of priorities. 'Old enough to go to school, I guess.'

'So he's just been killing time, fooling around with you, until his wife gets here?' Ruby sounded horrified.

'I always knew there was something suspicious about him.' Tilly sounded as though she'd like a chance to tear Rob to pieces.

'Well, you'll love the next bit even more,' Ellie told her, thinking it would give Tilly further reason to dislike Rob. 'He seemed to think I'd like to keep the relationship going once his wife arrived.'

'You're kidding! I hope you set him straight.'

'Of course. I actually created quite a scene. I didn't think I had it in me. I think that's why he orchestrated to have the conversation in a public place—I'm sure he thought there'd be safety in numbers.' Thinking back to her reaction, Ellie was rather pleased she'd shown some fight. Even if the whole experience had left her feeling embarrassed and nauseous, at least she'd had the last word. And, as depressing as the evening had been, she did feel marginally better once she'd shared the saga with her girlfriends. 'I can't believe I've been such an idiot.'

'It's not your fault, Ellie. Rob lied to you,' Ruby tried to console her.

'God, his poor wife,' said Tilly.

'Who cares about his wife! What about Ellie?' Jess was outraged.

Tilly just shrugged. 'Ellie is better off without him. His wife isn't so lucky, she's stuck with him.'

'But you guys know how much I want to belong to someone,' Ellie said as she reached for yet another tissue. 'I had all my hopes pinned on Rob and he's played me for a complete fool.'

'Rob is the fool, Ellie,' Ruby interjected. 'Don't waste your time crying over him. You'll meet someone else, someone who deserves you.'

Jess agreed. 'Your soul mate is out there and he's worth waiting for. Then everything will fall into place. You'll have your happy ever after.'

'I thought he might be "the one".'

'Trust me, Ellie, he's not. You'll know when you meet "the one". You won't be left wondering.' Ruby had found her true love in Cort and she was convinced everyone else should, and would, experience the same happiness.

'I feel like I'm running out of time.'

'For goodness' sake, you're only twenty-three.' Tilly spoke up with the wisdom her few extra years gave her.

'I know, but I want children. You know I was an IVF

baby—what if I have trouble getting pregnant, like my parents did? I want to know sooner rather than later.'

'If you want my advice, I wouldn't advertise that fact. It's likely to scare most men away.' Tilly was her usual pragmatic self.

'If they don't want children then they're not the man for me, are they?' Ellie responded.

'But wanting children doesn't automatically make them right for you and I don't think you'll find most men putting kids at the top of their to-do list, even the decent ones.'

Ellie could feel tears welling up again. 'Rob said he wanted kids.'

'Now you know why. He's already got one.' Tilly in particular didn't keep her opinions to herself. Ellie loved Tilly dearly but she was definitely a person who saw the world in two dimensions—right and wrong—and unless you agreed with her you were obviously wrong! This made her a very good person to have in your corner but you didn't want to be on her bad side. She hadn't liked Rob and it turned out she'd been right about him all along.

'Tilly, a little sympathy wouldn't go astray,' Jess suggested.

Tilly reached around the bulky quilt and hugged Ellie. 'I'm sorry you're upset now but things will work out. I know they will.'

'How on earth am I going to work with him?' Ellie asked as she blew her nose again.

'You go to work with your head held high. You've done nothing wrong. *He* lied to you.'

CHAPTER ONE

ELLIE'S eyes were stinging and she could feel tears welling up, accompanied by an unexpected lump in her throat as the coffin slid soundlessly on the stainless-steel rollers and disappeared through the curtain. Behind the curtain, screened from the mourners in the chapel, her grandmother's body would be taken away and all that would remain would be able to be contained in a small urn. That urn would end up behind a small brass plaque, next to the ashes of Ellie's grandfather and parents.

'You okay?'

Jess was sitting to Ellie's left. She was holding out a pack of tissues.

Ellie took one and smiled. 'Yes, I'm okay.' Her grandmother had been eighty-eight years old and her death hadn't been unexpected but it did mean that Ellie was now truly alone, the sole remaining member of her family. She was an only child and her parents had been killed when she was eleven. Her maternal grandparents had been her guardians and now they were both gone too. Her tears were selfish ones.

Surrounding her, flanking her, protecting her, were her closest friends. Jessica and Ruby sat on her left, Tilly on her right. She and Jess had been friends for several years now since meeting at university where they'd studied nursing together. They'd gone through the highs and lows of good and bad results, good and bad relationships and good and bad times generally. Ruby and Tilly had become her friends more recently, since they'd all started sharing a house and working at Eastern Beaches Hospital. These three were like family to her but they *weren't* family.

As she waited for the funeral music to stop playing Ellie thought back over the past two months. In the space of nine weeks she'd lost her boyfriend—well, not so much lost as found out he was actually someone else's cheating husband—and now she'd lost her grandmother. True, she had her friends but they weren't what she longed for. Her friends were fabulous but they weren't enough. Ellie wanted to belong and she longed for a family to call her own. Stop being pathetic, she told herself. It was one thing to cry over the death of a loved one, that was allowed, expected even, but to sit here, at her grandmother's funeral, feeling sorry for herself was being a little too self-indulgent. She was twenty-three years old, she had friends, she would be fine.

But the empty spot in her heart refused to listen. Ever since her parents had died she'd been conscious of this space waiting to be filled. She knew it could only be filled by love but it was a spot for family and family alone. No matter how much she loved her friends that spot was still there, empty, waiting. What if she never found her soul mate, her one true love. What if she never had the family she dreamed of? What if that empty spot was never filled?

Ellie shook her head. She couldn't think like that. She had to be strong. She had to be positive. Somewhere her perfect partner waited for her, she had to believe that. Rob had been a mistake, it didn't mean her quest for love was over. At least she hoped not.

The curtain was closed, the music had stopped, the coffin was gone, and her grandmother too. There was nothing left to do here.

She stood and her friends stood with her. They moved en masse to the lounge for the afternoon tea and shadowed her as she spoke to the funeral director and some of her grandmother's friends, keeping a silent and protective eye on her until Ellie decided that she was able to leave without seeming rude.

'Stat Bar, anyone?' Tilly suggested as they made their way out of the funeral home. The Stat Bar was their favourite after-work haunt; a few hundred metres down the hill from the hospital where they all worked and only a few steps from the house they all called home, it was convenient and trendy.

'Would you rather go somewhere else?' Ruby asked Ellie. 'Somewhere you can be anonymous?'

Ellie knew the Stat Bar would be crowded with hospital staff and she knew her friends would understand if she wanted to avoid it today but she shook her head. 'No, that sounds good. I'm fine, really.' A few familiar faces weren't going to bother her.

The sun was still shining when they got back to Coogee Beach on Sydney's south-eastern shore. It was a glorious afternoon, something Ellie couldn't reconcile with a funeral. But, she decided as she sipped her drink, the sun did boost her spirits.

They'd managed to grab a coveted outside table overlooking the beach and the tangy smell of salt in the air, the crisp white sand framing the ocean and the sound of the waves breaking on the shore all conspired to make her feel better. Maybe the fact she was on her second vodka, lime and soda was also helping to improve her mood.

The Stat Bar was beginning to fill up with the after-work crowd. The allied health practitioners from the hospital were the first to file through the doors, followed by the junior doctors. As more people gathered in the bar Ellie decided it was time to freshen her make-up, she could only imagine the state of her foundation and mascara. She stood up, hauling her bag from under her chair.

Her high heels clicked on the tiled floor as she entered the ladies' room. She always wore heels when she wasn't at work as a way of compensating for only being five feet two inches tall. She dumped her bag on the counter and examined her face. Her eyes were a bit bloodshot but not too swollen, although the tip of her nose was still red from crying. She pulled a hairbrush and her make-up out from the depths of her handbag. Tipping her head back, she squeezed a couple of eye drops into the corner of each eye before sliding the Alice band from her shoulder-length blonde hair and running the brush through it. She repositioned the Alice band, using it to hold her hair off her face as she blended a little foundation over her nose. She leant forward, overbalancing slightly on her high heels as she checked her eyes. The drops were working, her blue eyes looked a little brighter now. She straightened up and applied a fresh coat of gloss to her lips. She removed a few long blonde hairs from her black dress, checking to see that she'd gotten rid of all the stray strands.

As she walked past the bar to return to her friends she saw Rob, her lying, adulterous ex, paying for his drinks. His distinctive appearance made him easy to pick out in a crowd. He was out of his theatre clothes and was wearing an immaculately pressed suit, a sharp contrast to the more casual clothes and various hospital uniforms that surrounded him. He had his back to the ocean and to the rest of the room and she could pass behind him unseen. She hurried past as Rob picked up his drink and turned from the bar.

'Rob's here,' Ruby pointed out when Ellie returned to their table.

'I saw him.'

'Are you happy to stay?'

Ellie nodded, 'Yes, I'm fine. Completely recovered.'

She'd had to recover quickly. She and Rob worked together on the orthopaedic ward so she saw him on an almost daily basis and she hadn't had the luxury of time to retreat to lick her wounds in privacy. She'd had to maintain a civil working relationship. Rob's personality was aloof and cool at the best of times, something Tilly had always delighted in reminding Ellie of, and since the breakdown of their relationship he certainly hadn't become any more amenable, but mostly they managed to work together harmoniously. Although she didn't want to socialise with him, she had no problem being in the same bar as him.

'I'm still embarrassed,' she admitted, 'but pleased the whole thing was such a secret that I don't have to live out my embarrassment in front of the entire hospital. I know I got caught up in all the possibilities of the relationship but I think I might have learnt my lesson, for a while at least. I'm going to take my time from now on, not dive in head first.'

Ellie's remark made Ruby grin and Tilly laughed.

'What's so funny?' Ellie demanded.

'Famous last words,' Tilly replied. 'I've never known anyone who falls in love as quickly as you.'

'I admit I'm a hopeless romantic,' Ellie replied to Tilly, 'and when you fell in love with Marcus, and Ruby and Cort sorted out their lives, I got a bit carried away, thinking I could be next, but I'm going to be patient.' She reminded herself that she was going to be strong. Positive. Her perfect partner was out there, she just had to bide her time.

She would find someone. 'There's someone out there for me and when the time is right he'll appear.'

'How about right now?' Jess interrupted. 'There's a hot guy at the bar.'

'I didn't mean today.' Ellie laughed.

'Check him out before you cross him off your list,' Jess advised. 'He looks okay to me.'

Ellie turned her head. It wasn't hard to see who Jess was talking about. Leaning on the bar, wearing faded jeans and a snug black T-shirt that hugged his sculpted arms and chest, was one definitely hot guy. He had one foot on the railing that ran around the base of the bar and his jeans were moulded to his very shapely backside. He was thin, not scrawny, but his waist was narrow. There was no sign of any spread around his middle and Ellie could see a slight ripple of abdominal muscles along his side. He looked naturally slim, not like he spent hours in the gym.

His face was in profile as he waited for his order. He had a square jaw darkened by a hint of stubble, full lips, one dark eyebrow that she could see and dark lashes. He got his order and turned away from them, unaware of their scrutiny as he moved through the crowd. Ellie straightened in her seat and followed his progress across the room. His walk was quite graceful, his long lean lines leant fluidity to his movement, and his steps were confident. He stopped to join the group of surgeons standing with Rob and Ellie watched, intrigued, as Rob introduced him to the others. How did Rob know him?

'Do you know who he is?' Jess asked. She'd shifted in her chair to get a better look.

'No idea,' Ellie replied.

She had a good view of him now. Standing beside Rob, she could see he was a few inches shorter, around six feet tall. Rob was getting thicker around his middle and the contrast between Hot Guy and Rob made Rob look older than his thirty-three years. Rob's hair was more grey than brown, although it was still thick. Hot Guy had thick, almost black hair, with a definite curl.

'If Ellie isn't interested, you should go and introduce yourself, Jess,' Ruby suggested.

Ellie couldn't remember saying she wasn't interested in the hot guy specifically but she bit her tongue because she had just said she was going to bide her time.

'No way. I'm not going to interrupt that group,' Jess said.

Ellie understood her sentiments. As very recent nursing graduates they still felt there was a pecking order among the medical staff and their social standing in the hospital certainly didn't allow them to fraternise with the surgeons uninvited out of hours. And if the group of surgeons included Rob, they'd definitely keep their distance.

But Ellie knew there was another reason why Jess wouldn't approach the hot guy. Jess had been quite genuine in pointing him out to Ellie and even if he hadn't been talking to Rob she wouldn't have gone over, because Jess was completely besotted with Adam.

Adam Carmichael; the token male in their house, their mostly absent landlord, Ruby's brother and their resident Casanova rolled into one. There was never a shortage of women traipsing through his door when he was in Sydney and the girls often joked that he should put a revolving door on his bedroom so he could move his conquests in and out more efficiently. And, even though he was completely wrong for her, Jess had a thing for Adam.

Ellie wished Jess would meet somebody who would take her mind off him, someone who was ready for a real relationship, someone who wouldn't break her heart. But despite Ellie's pleas Jess seemed quite determined to ignore any other possibilities, including the hot guy. And in that case, Ellie decided, *she* might as well enjoy the view.

She looked back into the bar. Hot Guy was still talking to Rob but he was looking at her. Their gazes locked and something flashed through her. A jolt, a strike, a shock to the heart, and the rest of the room receded as the spark of connection flared. She sat still, riveted to the spot as he looked her up and down without a hint of embarrassment. She should have been horrified but all she could do was wait for him to finish. Wait for his eyes to meet hers again. Without consciously acknowledging her actions, she was waiting to see if she could work out what had happened with that first glance. What was it?

His gaze returned to her face and there it was again. A flash of what? Recognition? Ellie wondered if he knew who she was. She mentally shook her head. No. Rob would never have talked about her.

She didn't move, she couldn't move. She knew she was staring but she couldn't stop. She felt a blush spread up her neck and into her cheeks but still she couldn't look away.

His smouldering good looks had a slight wildness about them, an edginess, which drew her to him. She imagined she could feel the heat radiating from him. Her fingers itched to touch him and if he'd been standing beside her she knew she would have reached out to feel him. She could imagine the heat of his hands burning her skin and that made her blush even more.

He held her gaze, a hint of mischief in his eyes, almost as though he could read her thoughts, and then he grinned at her. Ellie smiled back. She didn't mean to and she was surprised to find her face was capable of expression but her smile was an automatic response to the power of his.

She tore her eyes away from his, forcing herself to break the connection. She tried to focus on the conversation going on around her, tried to behave normally, tried to pretend she hadn't just shared a moment with a hot stranger.

She had no idea how successful she was being but thankfully the arrival of Ruby's fiancé, Cort, provided a welcome distraction.

Cort was a senior emergency registrar and Ellie wondered if he knew who the hot guy was. She didn't have to wonder for long.

'Do you know who the guy in the black T-shirt is over there? The one who's talking to Rob Coleman?' Ruby inclined her head in their direction as she asked Cort the question.

'That's James Leonardi,' he said as he took in the group. 'He's a new registrar.'

'In Emergency?' Ellie asked. Was the new reg working with Cort?

Cort shook his head. 'Orthopaedics.'

'Orthopaedics?' Ellie repeated. She didn't know whether to be nervous or delighted. The hot guy was an orthopod? She was going to have to work with him?

'He's transferred from Royal North Shore. I understand the director of orthopaedics poached him, and apparently there are high expectations of him.'

Ellie was vaguely aware that Cort was still talking but her mind had wandered off in the direction of the hot guy. James Leonardi. His name sounded Spanish or Italian. She should have known. That would explain where the heat was coming from, he would have passionate blood running through his veins, it was almost tangible. It was in his eyes too, in the look he had given her. Fire, heat and passion.

There was a silent humming in the air around her. She could feel it and she was convinced it was coming from him. How was it possible to feel such an instant connection with a complete stranger?

She shifted in her chair. She needed to change position. She needed something else to look at. She was going to be working with the man so she needed to picture him in a white coat, in a sterile environment. In theatre scrubs. No. That wasn't helping. He looked just as good in her imagination.

Maybe she should go home. Maybe it was a case of out of sight, out of mind.

CHAPTER TWO

ELLIE stepped into the shower and tried to let the water wash away thoughts of Dr James Leonardi. Out of sight, out of mind hadn't worked terribly well. He'd been in her dreams all night. Her subconscious had been infiltrated by a stranger.

But he didn't feel like a stranger.

She closed her eyes and his image burst into her head. She could instantly recall the line of his shoulder under his T-shirt, the slight curl in his black hair and the heat in his expression when he'd looked at her with his dark eyes. She let her memory linger on the curve of his butt and the long sinewy length of his back as she rinsed her hair before she opened her eyes, turned off the shower and attempted to banish all further thoughts of him from her mind. She needed to focus. She had to work with him. She couldn't let her fantasies rule her thoughts.

And a fantasy was all he could be. She wasn't going to date another doctor. She wasn't going to make that mistake again. It was too awkward when things went badly. She'd learnt that much from her experience with Rob. The orthopaedic ward was definitely off limits and, therefore, so was James Leonardi.

But putting him out of her mind was easier said than

done. Especially as he was all anyone wanted to talk about at handover that morning.

'Have you seen the new doctor?'

'Yep.'

'Isn't he superb?'

'Is he Italian? He looks Italian.'

'I was on yesterday when he started and he's as Australian as you and me.'

'Oh, you lucky thing. Is he as gorgeous as he looks?'

Listening to the nurses' gossip, it was as though the outside world had ceased to exist. This new world appeared to revolve entirely around Dr James Leonardi. Ellie kept quiet. She had nothing to contribute, she hadn't actually met or spoken to him, and her thoughts were not for sharing.

The CNC handed Ellie a stack of files. 'You can accompany Dr. Leonardi on his rounds this morning—you know the patients better than anyone. I've given you George, Mavis, Dylan and Jenny.'

Ellie wondered if she'd been given this job because of her silence rather than her nursing skills. Not that it mattered. She took the files and went to wait for the rest of the group.

Ward rounds in a teaching hospital tended to be rather large affairs. They would be accompanied by the ward physio, Charlotte, and however many physio students she'd have with her today. There were nursing students on the ward too and there would possibly be a medical student or two and an intern. It was rather daunting for the patients until they got used to it and daunting for the students also.

All the chatter from the other nurses still hadn't prepared Ellie for the jolt she got when she saw Dr Leonardi again. Her first official encounter with him was hardly going to be an intimate affair but that didn't stop her heart from racing with expectation. He watched her intently as she introduced herself.

'Dr. Leonardi, I'm Ellie Nicholson, I'll be doing your rounds with you this morning.' As she spoke she was aware of that strange connection again, that silent hum, that unexplained feeling that he knew more about her than he should, and she could see in his eyes that he remembered her.

'Hello again,' he said, and although his gaze didn't move from her face Ellie felt as though he was running his eyes over the length of her just as he'd done yesterday in the Stat Bar. His eyes were dark, dark brown and by the look in them she knew he was recalling yesterday too. She felt another blush creep up her neck as the corners of his eyes creased as he smiled and his eyes darkened further, reminding her of molten chocolate.

He extended his hand. It was warm, just as she'd expected, and now she could feel that silent hum pulsing up her arm. It was no longer just moving through the air, it was moving through her and it was definitely coming from him. She could feel herself wanting to close her eyes, wanting to lose herself in the force field that surrounded them. That was the only way to describe the sensation. She fought to keep her eyes open, fought not to succumb to his intensity.

She felt Charlotte watching her and knew she was wondering about Dr Leonardi's choice of words. *Hello again.*

She avoided the physio's gaze as she fought to keep a level head. She let go of Dr Leonardi's hand as she checked to see if the right people had assembled.

'Shall we get started?' she said, turning away from James Leonardi and forcing herself to concentrate as she led the group to the first patient on her list. Her job would be to make sure that all the medical staff was up to speed on the patient's condition and treatment regime. Charlotte would be responsible for ensuring that the physio angle was covered and together they would work out what else needed to be done or discuss discharge possibilities.

'Morning, George,' Ellie greeted their first patient, before introducing him to the group and handing his case notes to James. She took a step closer to the bed, putting some distance between her and James. She had to move away, it was impossible to stay focussed on her work when he stood so near. He smelt like limes, like a cool drink on a hot day, and she was finding him hugely distracting.

'This is George Poni,' she said, forcing herself to concentrate on the patient. 'He's a fifty-year-old who came off second best when his motorbike hit a guard rail six days ago. He sustained a fractured left ankle, left head of radius, clavicle and wrist. He underwent open reduction, internal fixation of his ankle and wrist and conservative, non-surgical treatment of his clavicle and elbow. He's had no complications and we're starting to consider discharge.'

'I can't go home,' George interrupted. 'My wife is going to kill me. Tell them, Ellie.'

'You'll be fine, George,' Ellie said in an attempt to placate him. 'I've spoken to Lilly and she's quite calm about the whole thing now as long as you promise to give up the motorbike and find some other safer hobby to pursue through your mid-life crisis. Her words, not mine!' she added at the end of her spiel. Out of the corner of her eye she could see James smiling. His smile was wide and it brought creases to the corners of his eyes. He had the smile of someone who smiled often and who was used to people smiling with him.

'Other than putting his life in danger, is there any other reason not to discharge George?' James asked. 'How mobile is he, Charlotte?'

'He's partial weight-bearing on his left leg and can manage short distances with one crutch, but we're planning on sending him home with a wheelchair as he can't use two crutches because of his upper-limb injuries. There's still a lot of swelling but nothing more than expected. Despite George's protestations, his wife is capable and willing to give support.'

James was checking the medication chart at the end of George's bed. 'He's still having four-hourly Panadeine Forte?' He directed his question at Ellie.

'For his elbow and ankle.' Ellie clarified George's pain relief requirements.

'Do we need this bed?'

'No.' Ellie shook her head. 'We're okay at the moment.'

'Okay, George. I'll do you a deal. Let's see how you go with painkillers every six hours but we'll start making arrangements for discharge and review your situation tomorrow.'

'Thanks, Doc.'

'Next?' James said. Ellie indicated the bed diagonally opposite George's, where a very thin, pale young man lay, and the group migrated to his bedside.

'Dylan Harris, twenty-four, also involved in a motorbike accident, six weeks ago. He sustained a fractured right femur and fractured pelvis. He's had a K-nail inserted into his femur and was in traction for his pelvis. He been a bit slow to get up and get moving.' In fact, if she was being totally honest, Ellie would say Dylan was being ridiculously pathetic. He regularly burst into dramatic tears whenever the physios came to do his treatment, even though his injuries were healing well and there was nothing to be concerned about from his recovery point of view.

'What seems to be the problem?'

'A lack of motivation and co-operation,' Charlotte contributed.

'I'm not using that walking frame, that's for old people,' Dylan sulked, indicating the gutter frame that was waiting beside his bed.

Charlotte sighed. 'How many times have we had this conversation, Dylan? The rate you're going you *will* be old before you get out of here. Once I'm confident that you're walking safely with the frame we can look at progressing to crutches.'

'I'll get up if Ellie walks with me.'

'You have to walk with the physios first,' Charlotte replied. 'It's hospital policy.'

'Why don't I come back with Charlotte after rounds and we'll get you out of bed together?' Ellie suggested. 'I'll be your second person assist,' she said to Charlotte.

'As long as you're sure,' Charlotte said.

Ellie didn't really have time to spend getting Dylan on his feet for the first time. She knew how long that process could take. Even just a few steps would be a massive task when he'd been lying in bed for so long. But there didn't seem to be any other way this was going to happen. She nodded.

'Any other issues?' James asked.

'None,' Ellie replied.

'All right. Dylan, if I come back tomorrow and find you haven't at least attempted to get out of bed I'll get you moved to another ward where you won't have Ellie *or* Charlotte looking after you,' James threatened, obviously figuring that was the way to get Dylan motivated. 'But if you start complying with treatment you can stay here.'

By the look on Dylan's face Ellie could tell he wasn't sure whether he'd just won the argument or been gazumped by Dr Leonardi. In Ellie's opinion it was Dr Leonardi 1, Dylan 0.

When James finished his rounds and left the ward Ellie

felt as though he'd taken some of her energy with him, although a hint of his fresh lime scent remained, tantalising her senses.

She threw herself into the morning's work, hoping that if she kept busy she wouldn't have time to think about Dr Leonardi. Wouldn't have time to think about his chocolate eyes and how they'd watched every move she'd made. Wouldn't have time to think about those full lips and how they'd curled into a smile when she'd said something that had amused him, and she wouldn't have time to think about the throbbing she felt in the air when she was near him or the way it pulsed through her body when he touched her.

In some ways she hoped his effect on her would wear off as he spent more time on the ward. Maybe it would fade away and she'd be able to work in peace. But a part of her enjoyed the buzz he gave her, the feeling of danger, as though he was forbidden fruit.

Maybe that was the attraction, the exact thing that had got people into trouble all through the ages—wanting something they *couldn't* have. After her disastrous fling with Rob she wasn't going to get involved with someone on the orthopaedic ward again. Not ever.

She'd just have to ignore those feelings, she told herself. That would be the sensible thing to do.

'Ellie? Are you awake?'

'Come in, Jess.'

The door opened. 'Good, you're up. Do you want to come for a walk with me?'

Ellie looked at her watch. Ten past eight.

'Now?' she said.

'Please,' Jess begged as she pulled Ellie's curtains back. 'Adam's home again and I don't want to be here when he gets up.'

Now the early morning walk made sense. Ellie knew

Jess wouldn't want to confront whoever it was who had kept Adam company last night. Their house belonged to Adam and the fifth bedroom was his to use whenever he was in Sydney. His work as a surgeon with Operation New Faces had him travelling around the world but when he was home there was always an endless stream of girls in and out of his bed, and Ellie knew Jess found that upsetting. Being reminded of Adam's casual attitude to relationships was almost more than Jess could handle and she hated having to play nice whenever her path crossed with one of his many women.

'Okay,' Ellie conceded, 'give me a minute to get dressed.' Her room was flooded with light. It was going to be a beautiful day and she may as well get up and enjoy it. She climbed out of bed and pulled on underwear, a sports singlet and shorts. She'd shower later. She went to the mirror to brush her hair and tied it back into a ponytail. She rubbed sunscreen over her skin and grabbed a hat and her sunglasses. She was ready.

A light northerly breeze was blowing along the foreshore as Ellie and Jess crossed Arden Street and headed for the path that hugged the beach. The morning sun was warm on Ellie's skin with enough heat in it to make the breeze feel pleasant instead of uncomfortable.

A low stone wall separated the beach from the path and Ellie and Jess had to dodge joggers and dog walkers as they headed north. At this early hour the only people who were up were people who had a reason to be—people who wanted to get their morning exercise in or who had young children. The lawn area was teeming with families and there were even some keen ones on the beach, building sandcastles and swimming.

Ellie kept her gaze averted from the young families. She didn't need a reminder of what she was missing. Since breaking up with Rob, she'd decided she would bide her time before starting another relationship. She'd had a few intense, short-lived relationships in the past year and she'd thought having a self-enforced break would be a good idea.

'Perhaps I should get a dog,' she said to Jess.

'What are you talking about?'

Ellie waved a hand in the general direction of the other pedestrians. 'Everyone here has either got kids or a dog. If I'm not going to have kids, maybe a dog is a good alternative. Lots of people do that.'

'Since when aren't you having kids?' Jess asked.

'Well, I won't be having any in the near future so a dog might be a good alternative,' she explained. 'Besides you know how, when you want something really badly, it seems to take for ever to happen and how, if you stop wanting it, it falls into your lap? Maybe, if I decide to get a dog, I'll meet the man who will be the father of my children just because I've replaced the idea of kids with the reality of a dog.'

'I don't get that logic at all,' Jess replied, and Ellie caught her sideways look, the one that said she thought her friend might be going mad. 'I think we need to walk a bit faster. We need to get to Bondi and see the backpackers—the young, single crowd who don't have kids *or* a dog. That's another reality, you know. Anyway, I thought you were taking a break from the dating scene.'

'I am,' Ellie replied, but even as she uttered the words she knew she could be tempted out of her self-imposed ban very quickly and it was all because of James Leonardi. Since he'd arrived at Eastern Beaches, on the orthopaedic ward, her hormones had gone into overdrive. She was overwhelmingly aware of him and his presence reminded her that she loved being in a relationship. Loved the idea of being in love. 'I think what I'm trying to say is that perhaps if I stop trying to find my ideal man, he might find me.'

Jess nodded. 'That makes a bit more sense but, you know what, I think you might just need to revise your definition of your perfect man. You might not want to hear this but I think you've been looking at the wrong type of men.'

'What do you mean?'

'You've always gone for the guys who appeared sensible and mature, older than you, ones who you think might be ready to settle down, without really worrying about what they're like. Maybe you should try dating someone your own age.'

'What's age got to do with it? Cort's older than Ruby and you're still lusting after Adam, who's older than you too, why do I have to date the young ones?' Ellie argued.

'Maybe not too young but maybe you should look for someone who's not so serious and staid, someone who knows how to have a good time, less of a father figure.'

Ellie frowned. 'Is that what you think I've been doing?'

'I think you're looking for someone to be the father of your children but I also think you want someone who will take care of you,' Jess explained. 'You don't need that, you can take care of yourself. I think you should choose a man because he's a good man, not because you think he'll make a good father. Look for someone who you can have a bit of fun with. You don't need to rush into the whole marriage and babies thing. You're still young. Relax.' Jess stopped talking as they walked up a steep stretch of path but as soon as they were on a downhill slope again she continued. 'If I told you your ideal man was waiting around the corner for you, tell me what you'd want to see.'

That was easy. 'Taller than me,' Ellie said, 'maybe a *bit* older, fit but not with weightlifter muscles, more of a run-ner's physique.' So what if her description was an identical match to James Leonardi? Surely there were plenty of other men who could be described in the same fashion!

'And what would he be like?'

'What do you mean?'

'Well, does he make you laugh or does he take life very seriously? Could he be divorced? Already have kids? Do you want a professional or someone who has a job where they get dirty? A dog person or a cat person? Tea or coffee drinker?'

They'd reached Gordon's Bay and turned for the trip home. As they walked down the hill around the northern end of Coogee Bay, past Rob's apartment building, Ellie quickened her pace, not slowing until they'd made it back to the stone wall that signalled the beginning of the beach. A few fishing boats were being taken out from the fishing club and there were a couple of games of beach volleyball under way. Ellie's attention was drawn to a game of two on two between four fit young guys. They were all wearing board shorts without shirts, their bodies tanned and firm in the morning sun. A few steps closer and Ellie's heart began to race in her chest. There was something familiar about one of them.

Olive skin, dark hair, a lithe frame. Her fictitious ideal man. James Leonardi.

He had his back to them and his calf muscles bulged as he propelled himself off the sand and into the air to block a ball at the net. His block was successful and Ellie watched as he high-fived his partner and waited for the ball to be returned. He scooped it up and prepared to serve. He tossed the ball high and raised his arms in the air as he hit it over the net. Ellie could see the muscles of his back ripple with the movement. She'd seen his face in profile as he'd served the ball over the net but, even without that glimpse, Ellie knew it was him, she could feel it. That humming in the air was back, getting louder as she got closer. Her senses were on high alert. The sun was a bit brighter, the tang of the sea a bit saltier, the air a bit warmer, but the sounds of the other people had faded a little. The humming was drowning the other sounds out.

'Well? What do you think?' Jess was still waiting for Ellie to answer her questions.

Without a trace of a doubt Ellie knew what she wanted. He was right there, in front of her.

As vaguely as she could, she answered Jess's last question. She tried not to watch James as she spoke but it was hard to keep her attention focussed elsewhere. 'He has a smile that could brighten any day. He should have a job he enjoys but he doesn't necessarily have to wear a suit and a tie to work. He needs to like being active, a physical kind of guy, but he'd have to smell nice. He needs a sense of humour and he needs to love his family. He doesn't need to have his life all mapped out but he would need to know how to treat a woman and he must be prepared to only date one woman at a time.'

Ellie wasn't sure if James qualified for any of those things, for all she knew he was already married with half a dozen children, but surely with that smouldering, Latin thing he had going on, not to mention the look he had in his eye, she was willing to bet he'd taken his fair share of women to bed, and she was willing, if he was available, to put her hand up to join that list. He could be her experiment, she decided. She could try choosing a man first and looking for a father for her future children second. She could live in the moment for a change. She didn't have to fall in love with him.

She managed to position herself between Jess and the beach so she was able to keep one eye on the volleyball, and on James, as they walked past. With her hair tied back and hidden underneath a cap she didn't think he'd recognise her so she thought she could check him out from behind her dark glasses. As they drew level he bent down to pick up the ball and Ellie felt safe enough to let her eyes run over him. His shorts pulled taut over his legs and butt as he squatted down to the sand and his biceps flexed as he retrieved the ball. As he straightened up he looked directly at her. Ellie had thought he wouldn't recognise her but he paused in mid-action and stood still, only for a second or two but Ellie knew that in that space of time he'd known it was her. She quickly averted her gaze and hurried past. She felt as though he could read her mind and she definitely did not want him to know what she was thinking.

She kept walking, resisting the urge to turn around as she and Jess continued on to the kiosk by the beach stairs where they stopped for coffee. While they waited for their orders to be filled she wondered whether she'd lost her mind. She was supposed to be getting her life into order and taking stock of her goals, not thinking about ripping the clothes of a virtual stranger.

She must be mad to think about James Leonardi at all. Dating was supposed to be off her list and dating another doctor from the same department would definitely be asking for trouble. But there was something irresistible about him. Not just his looks or the powerful, passionate vibe he exuded; it had something to do with that strange humming sensation, that magnetic pull that seemed to draw her to him. Even now, she knew she could turn around and instantly find him in a crowd. Somehow they were connected.

But she had to ignore these feelings. She kept her back turned to the beach as she waited for her coffee, resisting the urge to take just one more look. It didn't matter how much she fancied him, James Leonardi was not for her.

CHAPTER THREE

WHEN Ellie returned to work on Tuesday it was to one of the worst shifts she'd had in a long time and it was all thanks to Rob. Mostly they'd managed to work amicably together since the demise of their affair but occasionally she seemed to be in his firing line and today was an especially bad day. She was being blamed for every little thing that went wrong—a dressing that hadn't been changed, X-rays that had been misplaced and a blood test that had been ordered but hadn't been done fast enough to please Rob. None of these things were actually Ellie's tasks, she was up to her neck in admissions and discharge summaries, but Rob had decided to haul her over hot coals for the failings of the entire ward. And he wasn't finished yet. Ellie was completing paperwork at the nurses' station when she saw him marching towards her with a severe expression on his face. She froze, wondering what she was going to be blamed for now.

He stopped a few paces from her and snapped. 'I just saw George Poni and his wife getting into the lift. He tells me he's going home.'

'Yes, I'm filing his paperwork now,' she said, waving a hand towards the stack of papers on the desk.

'Who said he was ready for discharge? Mr Poni is my patient.'

'Yes, but you handed his care over to Dr. Leonardi.' Ellie tried to keep a neutral tone.

'I still expect the courtesy of being informed if my patients are leaving.'

First I've heard of it, Ellie thought, but she bit her tongue. 'I'm sorry, I didn't realise you wanted everything discussed with you. The physio said he was ready to leave, his mobility aids and equipment for home have been organised, I've made an outpatient appointment for George to see you in a fortnight and his discharge was discussed with Dr Leonardi,' she explained. She was tired of being made a scapegoat for Rob's bad mood today.

'Next time I would like to be kept in the loop,' Rob barked at her. 'I expect to have my orders followed. Is that understood?'

I was following orders, Ellie felt like saying. *You hadn't indicated that James wasn't to discharge your patients.* She knew the appropriate discharge procedures had been followed. 'Yes, Dr Coleman,' she replied, hoping he'd go away and leave her alone if she didn't argue. She couldn't believe he was treating her this way but she was powerless to prevent his verbal lashing and he knew it. Her meek and mild attitude had the desired effect. With one final glare in her direction Rob stormed from the ward.

'Boy, you're in his bad books today. I've never seen him that irritated.' Sarah, a first-year nursing graduate, who had been keeping her head down throughout Rob's tirade, spoke up the moment he left. 'What have you done to upset him?'

Ellie blinked back tears. She wasn't going to let him get to her. She knew exactly what she'd done to annoy him. She'd gone against his wishes and she knew Rob was annoyed over her refusal to continue their relationship but she couldn't believe he was choosing to take it out on her in this fashion. He had no cause to query her work performance; she was good at her job and she took pride in that. She knew what the problem was but there was nothing she could say, or do, that wouldn't put her in the spotlight. She couldn't tell anyone else why he was treating her this way. So she shrugged.

'Maybe he just got out of the wrong side of the bed,' she proposed.

'I see his mood hasn't improved at all.'

Ellie looked up from her paperwork at the sound of James's voice. How long had he been standing there, she wondered and what had he heard? She was only just feeling brave enough to face him after seeing him at the beach on the weekend and now he'd witnessed her latest embarrassing moment. She was ready to crawl under the desk at the thought that he'd heard that exchange with Rob.

'Any idea what that was all about?' he asked.

He was watching her with his chocolate gaze, seemingly oblivious to her discomfort.

'He was annoyed because George Poni has been discharged without his say-so,' Ellie told him.

James frowned, a crease marring his smooth olive forehead. 'I wonder why he didn't say anything to me about that.'

Ellie shrugged. 'Maybe I'm an easier target.' There was no reason for anyone to think that Rob's earlier behaviour was related to her in any way, shape or form, especially not if she appeared unfazed.

'He was biting people's heads off in Theatre too this morning so unless you did something to upset him before that I think you're off the hook,' James said.

And then he smiled at her, a wide smile that brought those lovely creases to the corners of his dark eyes. Instantly Ellie felt her confidence restored, just his presence helped to soothe her frazzled nerves and his smile almost completely eradicated all thoughts of Rob's tirade from her mind. That hum of electricity she could feel when he was present made everything else recede. Harsh words, colleagues, nothing else seemed to matter so much and once again Ellie had to force herself to concentrate on the tasks at hand.

She breathed a sigh of relief. 'So it's not just me, then.' She paused briefly and mentally crossed her fingers before asking, 'He didn't explain why he was so cross?'

'Are you kidding? He's an orthopaedic surgeon, he doesn't have to explain himself to anyone!'

Ellie closed the file she'd been working on and looked up at him. There were two bright spots of colour on her cheeks and her blue eyes were glistening but the panicked look he'd seen there a moment before had vanished. Her earlier nervous expression had been replaced by a smile as she laughed at his flippant comment.

'Are you here on a social call or is there someone you want to see?' she asked.

As she spoke her blonde hair bounced around her shoulders, catching the light and distracting him. Why had he come to the ward? He struggled to recall what he was doing there. 'I'm here to see Mavis Williams. I was paged, something about her temperature?'

Ellie nodded. 'Yep. Let me grab her file and I'll come with you.'

She collected the case notes and led the way and he trailed a couple of steps behind, enjoying the way her hips moved as she stepped out in front. She was a petite woman, several inches shorter than him but perfectly proportioned. Her waist was tiny, her hips narrow but they swayed enticingly.

She'd intrigued him since the first time he'd seen her

at the Stat Bar and he'd celebrated his good fortune when he'd discovered that not only did she work at the hospital but she worked on the orthopaedic ward. She'd be working with him.

When he'd seen her at the Stat Bar it was as though they had been the only two people in the room. She'd been surrounded by others but it was as if they had receded into the distance, leaving her standing alone, silhouetted by her own golden glow. It had been an odd sensation for James.

He'd felt her presence at the beach too. It had been more than just the feeling you got when you knew you were being watched. There had been something extra. Despite her cap and sunglasses, he'd known instantly it was her. He'd felt her and it wasn't until she'd walked away that he'd noticed she wasn't alone. She may have been walking with a friend but he'd only had eyes for Ellie.

She was the first woman to catch his attention in months, in almost seven months to be exact. Perhaps he was ready to move on.

'Morning, Mavis,' James greeted the old lady as they entered her room. 'You're running a temperature, I hear.'

Ellie retook Mavis's temperature as James checked her other symptoms. 'The nurses might be right, Mavis. It's possible you have a UTI. It's a common complaint in hospitals, I'm afraid. If you can stomach cranberry juice that's often a good natural combatant but I'll organise some tests and if necessary we can treat it with antibiotics.' He glanced at Ellie, who immediately picked up on his silent request.

'I'll go and organise the things for the urine culture,' she said.

James watched her go. She made him think of summer and sunshine and happy times. She was golden and if he believed in auras that would be how he would describe her. She had a golden aura and it seemed to envelop him whenever he was near her. It ensnared him and made it difficult to think past her and just being around her made him feel good.

'You're enjoying your new job, I see?' Mavis said with a smile.

'It certainly has some perks.' He wasn't embarrassed at being caught watching Ellie. Most of the males on staff did the same, he'd seen them. Almost everyone seemed captivated by her and he wondered if she was aware of the effect she had on men.

'You're not married, then?'

He hadn't been embarrassed until Mavis made that remark. Did she think he'd still be watching Ellie if he were married? He shook his head. 'No. I never quite made it down the aisle.'

'Why don't you ask Ellie out? She's single too,' Mavis the matchmaker replied.

'Is she?' His heart rate increased with the announcement. 'How do you know that?'

'You don't get to my age without learning a thing or two about people and, besides, I've been here so long I'm starting to feel like part of the furniture and when people get used to having you around they forget to watch their conversations. Trust me, she's single. You should ask her out.'

'I might take your advice. Thanks, Mavis,' he said with a wink as Ellie returned to the room. But even as he spoke he wondered if he would issue an invitation. What would be the sensible thing to do? Had anything changed in his life over the past few months? He was still committed to his job, still focussed on establishing his career. Did he have the time or emotional energy for the singles scene? No matter how enticing Ellie was, he wasn't sure if he was ready to date again.

* * *

There was a buzz of excitement in the room. The noise level had been high all evening, as was usually the case in a room full of women, but the level had increased noticeably in the last few minutes. Ellie checked her watch—ten-thirty. Her school leavers' reunion had been girls only until now and her old school friends were becoming distracted by the arrival of their boyfriends.

They had only been out of school for five years so there wasn't all that much to catch up on. They'd been doing one of three things—travelling overseas, studying or working or a combination of all of those. A few were married, a couple had babies but they were the exceptions.

Ellie watched as Carol, Amy and Fiona, in fact, most of the organising committee, went to greet their partners as they entered the function room. Two things were immediately obvious to Ellie. One, that three hours was the time limit allocated to catching up with friends before the girls needed to let their partners in on the evening and, two, the committee members were all in relationships, which was why the decision to include partners in the evening had been made. A third thing came to mind as Ellie watched the change in group dynamics—she wasn't in the mood to watch happy couples.

It had been three months since the disastrous dinner with Rob and her heart was well and truly mended. If she was honest, she'd admit her pride and her ego had suffered more than her heart. It was more about her dreams and what his lies had done to them. She was angry more than heartbroken and it wasn't difficult to be angry with a man who was a liar and a cheat. Her dreams might have been shattered but her heart was intact, though she still didn't feel like being surrounded by happy couples.

The reunion was being held in Sydney's infamous Kings Cross district in a private function room in a recently renovated and refurbished building. The building was typical of many in the Cross, with the businesses making the most of limited land by going upwards. There was a 'gentleman's club' in the basement, a traditional nightclub on the ground floor with function rooms on the first floor, and Ellie didn't want to know what was on the floor above that.

The reunion committee had booked out the function room until midnight and Ellie knew that gave them access to the nightclub afterwards. Normally she would be planning on partying until the small hours of the morning but tonight she was out of sorts. She was tired of the incessant noisy chatter going on about her but it was still too early to go home. To get some respite from the noise she slipped out of the room and onto the balcony that opened off it. Maybe watching people in the Cross, instead of her old school friends and their partners, would improve her mood.

She closed the balcony doors behind her and the change in atmosphere between inside and outside was incredible. Inside the air had smelt of perfume, hairspray and women and while initially that had been overpowering it was at least a clean smell. Outside the air smelt of petrol fumes, cigarettes, greasy takeaway food, alcohol and men. And the noise had changed from the high-pitched, excited chatter of women to car horns, music and deeper, loud voices.

If she had been down at street level she might have retreated inside but on a first-floor balcony she felt safe enough to watch from a distance. The balcony was divided in two by a low iron balustrade and a second function room opened onto the other half. From her vantage point Ellie could see people inside the other room but for the moment the adjoining balcony was empty.

She crossed the balcony and leant on the railing overlooking Darlinghurst Road. It was still early by Cross standards but the crowds were building. There were no queues outside the nightclubs yet; they were still advertising free entry and cheap drinks in an effort to entice patrons inside. There were the other enticements too and she could hear several men spruiking for customers as they promised visual, and other, delights. *'We have beautiful women, they will dance just for you!'*

Noise to her left caught her attention. A few guys had gathered on the adjacent balcony, beers in hand as they lit their cigarettes. They were all young—late twenties to early thirties at a guess and out of interest, and habit, she gave them a once-over. They weren't a bad-looking group, most of them looked reasonably fit, if you ignored the cigarettes, and neatly dressed. They were well groomed and looked educated and professional.

Through the open doors she now had a better view into the other function room and curiosity got the better of her. She looked more closely at the crowd—all men. She assumed it was a bucks' night, Kings Cross was a favourite site for bucks' parties, and Ellie thought it was just as well they didn't know about the reunion for St Barbara's Catholic School for Girls going on next door. That could have been a recipe for disaster.

As Ellie turned to go back inside she caught sight of a familiar face.

Dark crescent-shaped eyebrows above chocolate eyes, full lips and a square jaw darkened by a day's growth of beard. Long lean lines and firm muscles. Just the sight of him, ten paces away, was enough to start her pulse racing, and the sound of his voice when he said her name sent a shiver of longing through her.

'Ellie?'

Her voice was husky as she replied. 'Dr Leonardi.'

'Please,' he said as he came towards her, bringing that

strange humming sensation with him, 'my name is James. When you call me "Dr Leonardi" it makes me feel ancient.'

He'd closed the distance between them to a few inches, and they were separated only by the iron railing and surrounded by the humming bubble. She smiled up at him, her spirits buoyed by his presence. 'James.'

'What are you doing here?' he asked.

Ellie inclined her head towards the room behind her. 'A school reunion.'

'Are you having a good night?'

It just got ten times better, Ellie thought before she remembered her new list—no doctors allowed. She shrugged. 'It's been okay.'

James looked back over his shoulder. 'Co-ed school?'

'Catholic girls,' she said with a hint of a smile.

'Really?' He grinned at her and his chocolate eyes gleamed. 'I think you should go back inside and lock the doors before my lot find out who's in there.' He leant over the balcony for a better view into the function room and Ellie's face was almost nestled into the curve of his neck. He still smelt like limes.

Chocolate eyes and lime-scented skin—he was delicious.

He was leaning over her. She couldn't move. His scent had her mesmerised. She closed her eyes, blocking out the curve of his neck, the firm line of his jaw, the soft swell of his lips, but it didn't eliminate his smell. With her eyes closed her imagination kicked into overdrive. She could imagine how he would taste—like the rim of a tequila glass, lime with a dash of salt. She licked her lips, disappointed to find that the cheap champagne she'd been drinking tasted nothing like her imagination.

'Are you all right?' James' breath was warm on her cheek.

Her eyes snapped open. 'Yes, I'm fine,' she said as she

tried to remember the thread of their conversation. She looked across to James's side of the balcony. *My lot*, he'd said. 'You're on a bucks' night?'

He nodded. 'I'm the best man and it's only fair to warn you that not all of my friends can be trusted.' He was still smiling, the curve of his lips widening to reveal even, white teeth.

'Don't worry.' She smiled in return. It seemed his smile had the power to elicit a response from her every time. 'Most of the girls can handle themselves and, besides, the nuns have all left and the boyfriends have just arrived.'

'Nuns? Seriously?' he asked as he stepped casually over the railing and sat on it with his feet on her side of the balcony. He appeared completely at ease but his proximity was making her tremble. He was close enough to touch yet there was space between them. He wasn't crowding her but she was extremely conscious that he was *there*. That's all. She was just supremely aware of the fact he was there.

She needed to step back, to put some distance between them, before she could answer. She nodded. 'They still exist, you know. Not all the teachers were nuns but the girls were like family to them, especially the ones who boarded. We spent a lot of time with them.'

'You were a boarder?' he asked. When she nodded he asked a second question. 'Where is your family from?'

'Goulburn.' Ellie divulged the name of the country town where she'd spent the first thirteen years of her life.

'I've been to Goulburn a few times on the way to the snow. Do you ski?'

'Not any more.' As soon as the words were out of her mouth she wanted to take them back. She could see the quizzical expression on James's face and she willed him not to ask the question she could see waiting in his eyes. She kept her focus on the activity on Darlinghurst Road.

The Cross was starting to get busy now and it was easier to concentrate if she avoided looking into James's eyes. Somehow, the Cross, in all its seediness, was less dangerous. She chose to change the topic, hoping to distract him. 'So tell me, who's getting married?'

'One of my mates from uni.'

'Will you be next? Is that why you're the best man?' In her imagination, James was single and this was the perfect opportunity to find out if she was right.

'No.' He shook his head. 'We've been friends since for ever, that's why I got the gig. Marriage isn't for me.'

'Why not?'

'One in three marriages ends in divorce.'

Ellie shrugged. 'The odds are still in your favour of it lasting the distance, though.'

'I'm not sure I believe in people's ability to commit to something of that magnitude. "Forsaking all others till death do us part" seems to be more than most people can handle. The expectations are very high, aren't they?'

She frowned. 'Your view makes you a bit of a strange choice for best man, wouldn't you say?'

'People are still going to get married, no matter what I think,' he replied. 'And Pete and Karen have been together since we started uni. What else are they going to do?

'You don't sound that thrilled for them.'

'I think they're settling.'

'Settling?'

He nodded. 'I get the feeling they think this is as good as it gets. It's almost as if they can't be bothered to search for something better.'

'Maybe it *is* as good as it gets.'

He shrugged. 'Possibly, but I would want fireworks and passion.'

Yes, you would, Ellie thought. It emanated from every

pore in his body and he wouldn't be satisfied if that passion wasn't returned.

'Maybe they had that passion in the beginning,' she argued.

'Maybe they did but doesn't that make it worse, to think it's gone, that their best years are behind them? What's the point in getting married now, committing your life to one person, when you've had your best years?'

She wasn't convinced. 'Who's to say they've had their best years? They've got all that shared history and now they'll have a future too. If they've already been together for years I reckon they've got a pretty good chance.'

He was nodding his head. 'I guess they're one of those couples who reckon they'll make it,' he agreed.

Ellie smiled. 'I would say most couples who are planning on saying "I do" would tell you they thought they'd last the distance if you asked them. Otherwise why get married?'

'My point exactly.'

His smug tone made her laugh. 'I'm not agreeing with you,' she said. 'I'm saying that most people who get married believe their marriage will last.'

'Well, I hope you're right, for Pete and Karen's sake. You obviously have a less jaded view of marriage than I do. You believe in the whole happy-ever-after thing?'

She looked over the railing, turning her attention back to the action in the Cross, as she thought about her answer. Despite her many short-lived romances, including her most recent tumultuous break-up with a liar and a cheat, she did still believe in a happy ending. And for her, that included marriage. 'Yeah, I do. I'm still young and hopeful, not old and cynical like you.'

He laughed, a rich, deep laugh that drew Ellie's attention back to him. The tone of his laugh perfectly matched the dark intensity of his eyes. 'I'm not old and cynical,' he countered, 'I just want to keep my options open. Marriage doesn't allow for that.'

She was wondering if she could quiz him for more information when the sound of raised voices interrupted her train of thought. Two guys were being evicted from the pub across the road. They must have started a fight inside the pub and they showed no signs of giving up now they were outside. The two men, one in a leather jacket the other in a T-shirt, were throwing punches at each other and mostly missing. The guy in the jacket must have decided that tactic wasn't working and somehow he managed to get the other guy in a headlock.

Ellie watched horrified as the trapped man thrashed and kicked. 'Why doesn't someone do something?' There was nothing she and James could do from their first-floor vantage point and she wasn't about to try to break up a brawl between two men who, she assumed, had been drinking heavily. She didn't really expect any other passer-by to either but surely the security guards could do something? But the security guards had clearly abdicated responsibility now that they were off their premises.

'The police won't be far away.'

Ellie looked up and down Darlinghurst Road but couldn't see any sign of the blue uniforms. She wondered if she should phone 000 but then realised that James was right. This strip was usually heavily policed and they wouldn't be far away. If someone made a phone call every time there was a fight on Darlinghurst Road the phone lines would be permanently jammed. People were crossing the street, skirting the fight. No one wanted to get involved.

A girl came running out of the pub, yelling loudly, and Ellie's attention was pulled back to the action. The girl was very thin and dressed all in black, which accentuated her small frame. Ellie wondered what she was yelling about but without stopping to take a breath the girl leapt onto the back of the guy who was still trying to choke his opponent. Ellie couldn't believe what she was seeing. This girl, who couldn't weigh more than fifty kilograms, was pulling on the leather jacket of one man, trying to break up the fight. She had no chance as both men would easily weigh twice as much as her.

While keeping one arm around the throat of his opponent, the guy in the leather jacket reached behind him, grabbed the girl and flung her to the ground as easily as a cow swatted a fly with its tail. The girl tumbled through the air and her head collided with a metal street bench. Ellie's hand flew to her mouth. The girl was sprawled on the ground. She waited for someone to notice and go to her aid but people were still crossing the street to avoid the fracas and everyone seemed oblivious to the girl and her predicament. The fight was still in progress but the guy in the T-shirt had managed to get free of the headlock. Maybe the girl had provided just enough distraction to let him break free, but even he was more intent on attacking his opponent than helping the girl who had tried to help him. She still hadn't moved. Ellie waited for the girl to sit up. Nothing.

'She's not moving,' Ellie said to James, turning to look at him as she spoke.

But James was gone. He was running across the balcony to the opposite corner. Ellie frowned. Where was he going?

He reached the edge of the balcony and Ellie saw him stretch over the side. There was a metal ladder fixed to the wall beside the balcony. She recognised it as an old fire escape. James knocked the ladder loose and Ellie heard the screech of stiff metal as the ladder extended. Ten seconds later he was down at street level.

Ellie finally processed the scene and followed in James's wake. The metal of the ladder was cold and rusty under her hands and she was a little slower than he had been thanks to her high heels, but at least she was wearing trousers. By the time she reached ground level James was kneeling beside the girl.

Ellie ran across the street, feeling about as graceful as a newborn giraffe in her high heels. The police had finally arrived but they were busy with the brawlers. They had managed to stop the fight and the two men were being handcuffed. The guy in the T-shirt, which was now hanging together by a few threads, had a bloody nose but somehow he'd managed to give the guy in leather a cut above his eye. Both injuries were bleeding profusely.

Ellie knelt beside James. She couldn't be sure but she guessed less than a minute had passed since the girl had hit her head. The girl's face was covered in blood from the gash beside her temple, it had run down the side of her face and was dripping from the end of her nose. James' fingers were on the girl's neck, feeling for a pulse.

'Is she alive?' she asked.

James looked around and he seemed almost surprised to see her. 'I can feel a pulse but she's not breathing. Get the cops to call an ambulance,' he said as he used his shirt to wipe the blood from around the girl's nose and mouth. Ellie knew he was preparing to breathe for the girl. She quickly grabbed a tissue from her handbag, it was the only precaution she could provide him with, before he tilted the girl's head back and started breathing air into her lungs.

There was nothing else for Ellie to do so she went and confirmed that an ambulance had been called, and according to the police it was on its way and she hoped James hadn't been foolish by starting resuscitation yet she knew he had no other option. As a doctor he had sworn on oath to do no harm and that meant attempting to save a life if he could with no regard for his own. She returned to his side. 'The paramedics are on the way,' she said.

As she spoke she heard the girl breathe in on her own. James quickly sat back and turned the girl onto her side, narrowly escaping a stream of vomit that spilled from her.

'Don't move.' James had one hand on the girl's shoulder, keeping her in position. 'You've been in an accident, you hit your head and you need to be checked over.' The ambulance pulled alongside the kerb and the paramedics climbed out. Even though James was preventing the girl from sitting up, Ellie could see that her hands were moving so it didn't look as though she'd sustained any serious injury. She'd been lucky. Lucky too that James had been on the scene.

Ellie sat on the metal bench that had played a part in the drama and waited while James handed the girl over to the paramedics. She didn't know what else to do. She couldn't walk away but it felt strange waiting for James, as though they were in this together.

The two pugilists had been bundled into the back of two police vans. The cops were keeping them separated and under surveillance, obviously taking no chances, while the pub's security guards gave their version of the night's events. Next James had to give his details to the police and then he was free to go. Ellie stood and approached him when he'd finished. She put one hand on his arm and the warmth of his skin seeping into her fingers comforted her and unsettled her at the same time. She felt both safe and vulnerable. An odd sensation until she worked out that he affected her head and her body in different ways. Her head said he was a good person, honest and trustworthy. That was the safe part. It was her own body and her reaction to him that she couldn't trust.

'Are you okay?' she asked.

'Yeah.'

The bottom of his shirt was bloodstained from where he'd wiped the girl's face and there was a bloody handprint down the side where he must have wiped his own hand at some point. His forehead was wet with perspiration. Ellie could smell the faint metallic scent of blood but the smell of limes was still quite strong and there was now a definite saltiness to James's scent as well. Despite his dishevelled state, he still smelt fantastic.

'That was quite a performance, very James Bond, racing to the rescue down the fire escape,' she said.

'Oh God, James Bond?' He lifted his hands and rubbed his face, smearing his forehead with dirt and blood. 'I must have looked like a complete idiot.' Despite the grime he still looked striking. The dirt streaked his cheekbones, emphasising their sharp angles, and his teeth appeared even whiter in contrast to the dark smudges of grime.

Ellie shook her head. 'No. It was all rather impressive, to be honest. You saved that girl's life. She was lucky you were around.'

'I guess so,' he said modestly. 'I just hope she feels better tomorrow.' He'd been half turned away from her but now he turned to face her squarely, his chocolate eyes dark in his face. 'What shall we do now?'

'What do you mean?' Ellie asked.

'Are you going back to your party?'

Ellie looked up at the balcony. It was almost impossible to believe she'd started the night up there. She couldn't imagine going back now. She shook her head. 'I think I might head home. I've had enough excitement for one day.'

'Are you driving?'

'No,' she shook her head. 'I'll get a taxi.' There was no point in explaining she didn't have a car.

'I have my car, I needed to stay sober and responsible tonight. Let me take you home.'

'What about your friends?' she asked. As much as she would love a lift home, she didn't want him to feel obliged to help her.

James checked his watch. 'They'll be heading downstairs to the basement soon. I doubt they'll even notice I'm missing. Besides, I'm more than happy to skip that part.'

Ellie knew the basement housed a strip club, or, as the business owners phrased it, a 'gentlemen's club'. 'That's going to a lot of trouble for you. It's fine really, I'll catch a cab.' She gave him one last chance to change his mind.

'Please. I'd feel much happier if I drove you. I don't like the idea of you getting a cab on your own, not from the Cross. I'll drive you home and come back. Are you near the hospital?'

She nodded.

'That's settled, then. It'll be half an hour, easy.'

He took her hand and led her across the road. His touch startled her and set her pulse racing. She felt as though there was an invisible line running from her palm straight to her heart and the touch of James's hand had sent the silent hum that normally surrounded them directly through her veins. Her lips were dry and her heart was hammering in her chest yet he was behaving as if it was nothing unusual, as it if were something they did every day. But the familiarity, while not unpleasant, surprised her.

She expected him to let go of her hand once they reached the opposite footpath but he didn't. His hand felt warm and strong and gave her something to focus on instead of thinking about the drama she'd just witnessed. The drama he had single-handedly sorted.

He kept hold of her hand until they reached the parking garage and she concentrated on using his touch to make her feel safe as she tried to block out the other more primal sensations she was experiencing.

He only let go of her when he needed to dig his car keys out of his pocket, using them to unlock a black Jeep. His car wasn't old and neither was it new but, more importantly, there were no baby seats in the back or anything else to indicate that he might have a family stashed away somewhere. He'd said he wasn't going to get married but he didn't say he hadn't already been married, and either way he could still have children. Not that it should matter, she told herself. Even if smouldering, wild and dark hadn't been cut from her list, doctors had.

He saw her checking out the car. The back seat was strewn with clothes and, understandably, he misunderstood her interest. 'I've been living out of my car a bit for the past couple of weeks,' he explained.

'Why?'

'I live on the North Shore,' he explained. 'It's a bit of a trek in the traffic from the hospital across the harbour to my place depending on what shifts I pull so sometimes it's easier just to stay in one of the on-call rooms.'

No wife, no baby seats and happy not to go home every night—he was definitely single.

Not that it mattered, she reminded herself again, it was of no consequence to her. She wasn't ever going to date another doctor, even ones who smelt as delicious as he did and had chocolate eyes that could melt a girl's heart.

He held the door open for her before circling the car and climbing in to his seat. The small, enclosed confines of the car accentuated the tension in the air that constantly seemed to surround him. She could feel it throbbing around her and the air was filled with the aroma of limes. His smell.

Maybe getting a lift was a bad idea.

She shifted a little in her seat and crossed her arms over her chest, trying vainly to distance herself.

'Are you cold?' He reached for the controls for the heater.

'No.' She forced herself to relax. She couldn't very well tell him she needed to keep her arms folded to stop herself from reaching over to touch him. She couldn't tell him how his lime scent and the buzz she got just from being near him was enough to drive her crazy with desire. How she was tempted to reach over and taste him, to run her fingers through his hair and stretch one hand out to feel if his thighs were as strong as they looked under the denim of his jeans. She couldn't tell him any of that so she chatted about nothing as she directed him to the house on Hill Street.

'Did you want to come in and use the bathroom?' she asked as he pulled to a stop out the front. 'You've got dirt and blood all over you.'

He flipped the sun visor down and had a very brief glance at his face in the mirror on the reverse side. 'Might not be a bad idea, thanks.' He reached behind the seat and picked up a couple of T-shirts, choosing one and discarding the other. 'I should change my top too, I guess.'

He hopped out of the car and pulled his bloodied shirt over his head, not bothering to undo the buttons, and tossed it into the back seat. He was standing in the street, half-naked, and Ellie knew she should look away. She knew she was staring but her eyes were glued to the scene. It was a repeat of the beach volleyball episode, a shirtless James, tanned and muscled. But tonight was better because she was closer. His chest was smooth, brown and virtually hairless and she could see his abdominal muscles ripple as he ducked his head into the T-shirt and tugged it down.

His lean physique reminded her of a sleek cat, more black panther than lion, though, despite his name.

She was finding it hard to breathe. He had literally taken her breath away.

'One of the benefits of keeping my wardrobe in my car,' he said with a grin as his head emerged from his shirt.

She smiled back, hoping she wasn't grinning like a fool, before she led the way into her house. She found a clean towel and showed him to the bathroom.

'Can I get you something to drink before you go?' she asked when he emerged. She hoped she sounded like she was offering out of politeness and not as though she was propositioning him.

'Thanks, but I'd better get back to the bucks' night just to make sure everything is under control. Can I take a rain-check?' He stopped beside her and handed her the towel he'd used. 'Would you go out for a drink with me some other time? Somewhere a bit more civilised than the Cross?'

He was standing just inches from her. The faint metallic scent of blood had been washed from his skin and his fresh, lime scent filled her head once more. His offer was tempting, very tempting. She met his gaze. His dark eyes were watching her intently and she very nearly said yes before she remembered her list.

'I'm sorry, I can't.'

'Can't? Or won't?'

'Both.'

'Any particular reason?' he asked.

'I don't date people from work.'

A frown creased his forehead, his brown eyes puzzled. 'Why not?'

'It's complicated.'

'I promise I can keep it simple. You, me, a bar somewhere.' He smiled at her and replaced his frown with a wink.

It did sound simple. And tempting. What could be the harm in that?

But she'd been burned before. It really was too bad because he was truly divine.

'Let me know if you change your mind,' he said into her silence. His voice was just a breath in her ear and then he was gone. He moved easily, quietly and suddenly there was nothing except for a faint, lingering trace of lime to suggest he'd even been in her house.

But Ellie had the image of him in her head. How he'd run lightly across the balcony, his lithe frame moving quickly, dropping down the fire-escape ladder, kneeling over the girl on the pavement. How the touch of his hand had warmed her from the outside while his smile had warmed her from the inside.

James was hot. He made her insides melt and he smelt like her favourite things, but he wasn't for her. That was all there was to it. She'd have to look elsewhere.

She should go to bed and forget all about James Leonardi, but going to bed wasn't the answer. All she did was revisit all the things she knew about him. The way his hair curled at his temples, the creases that appeared at the corners of his eyes when he smiled and the warmth of his hand on her skin. The ripple of his abdominals when he'd changed his shirt and the beautiful golden tone of his skin.

Quite simply, he was gorgeous.

But, despite all that, he was still off-limits.

CHAPTER FOUR

For two days he thought she'd disappeared, like Cinderella after the ball, and he couldn't stop thinking about her. Was she rostered off or was she on nights? Why hadn't he thought to ask about her shifts?

Because he wasn't thinking straight, that's why.

And the more time that passed, the more he thought about her. About the golden glow that surrounded her and seemed to warm everything and everyone around her. It had wrapped itself around him and pulled him to her, drawing him in close. He'd had to drag himself away to go back to the bucks' party on Saturday night and it hadn't been easy. If he hadn't been Pete's best man he would probably have ditched his mates but duty had called.

He'd wanted to stay with Ellie and he'd wanted to kiss her. But he'd fought the urge. He couldn't take that liberty, especially not while she was refusing to go on a date with him. But he was sure that she'd been tempted to say yes. He was certain she'd been wavering. It wasn't possible that he was the only one who felt the chemistry between them. It was too strong to be one-sided.

He found it hard to believe that just two weeks earlier he'd talked himself out of asking her on a date. Despite Mavis's advice he'd gone with the sensible option, sticking to his bachelor ways, knowing he was busy concentrating on his career. Combining his career with a relationship hadn't worked out so well for him before but the minute he was alone with Ellie he'd forgotten all about being sensible. All he could think of was her and how she made him feel. He wanted to suffuse himself in her golden glow, he wanted to let it wrap itself around them both, cocooning them away from the world. She made him forget all his past failings. She made him believe anything was possible and he wouldn't rest until he worked out how to convince her to go out with him. But first he had to work out what shift she was on.

He finally remembered the nurses' roster that was pinned to the board on the orthopaedic ward. He checked it and was pleased to find that Ellie was on for an early shift the following day. He'd be in Theatre in the morning but he'd make sure he caught up with her at some stage.

The morning dragged, the cases on the operating list were routine, boring even, and James found himself, on more than one occasion, with one eye on the clock, waiting for the end of theatre. The only thing that helped to pass the time was quizzing people about Ellie. Did she date? What did she like to do? What could anyone tell him?

Rob didn't participate in the conversation and James could only assume it was because he had nothing to contribute. He seemed to be in another one of his moods, which James chose to ignore. Despite his infatuation with Ellie he was able to focus on the job while he was in Theatre so he knew Rob couldn't have any issue with him.

He changed out of his dirty scrubs as quickly as possible at the end of the list and headed for the canteen, hoping to run into Ellie. The canteen was busy and he scanned the room as he waited for his salad roll and coffee. She was there, sitting with Charlotte, the ward physio, and there was a spare table beside them. With luck that table would still be free once he had his order.

He paid for his lunch and weaved his way through the throng towards Ellie, grateful the canteen was bustling as it made it look quite natural that he would cross the room, searching for one of the few vacant spots. He was within a few metres of the empty table when two orderlies claimed it. He stopped, his plans thwarted. There was a third vacant chair at the table but it would be most unusual for him to sit with other hospital employees, particularly non-medical staff. The doctors tended to sit together, no one seemed to expect anything else, and to do otherwise would no doubt make everyone feel uncomfortable. He'd have to search for a different table.

As he stood there, pondering his options, Charlotte spotted him and came to his rescue.

'Hi, Dr Leonardi, you're welcome to sit with us.'

He gratefully accepted her offer. 'Thank you.' He closed the distance between them and put his coffee on the table. 'I haven't seen you on the ward for a few days, Ellie. Have you been off?' he asked as he sat down.

Ellie shook her head, her blonde hair shining in the light. 'I had yesterday day off, but I've been on nights.'

Nights. Of course. Movement to his left caught James's attention. Someone had stopped beside their table and was pulling out the last remaining chair.

Ellie made the introductions as this stranger, very confidently in James's opinion, took a seat.

'James, Damien Clark is a physio, he works in Outpatients. Damien, this is James Leonardi, the new orthopod.'

Damien extended his hand. 'I've seen your name on some case notes, it's nice to put a face to a name,' he said as he shook James's hand. 'Welcome to Eastern Beaches.' He didn't wait for a response from James. He sat on the other side of Ellie and James noticed that he moved his chair a fraction closer to hers as he sat down. Was he another one of Ellie's admirers?

'Are you thinking any more positively about the movie today, Ellie, or is it still not your favourite?' Damien was asking.

'It's nowhere near my favourite,' Ellie replied.

They'd been to a movie together?

James saw how Damien looked at Ellie, desperate for her approval, wanting to please her, and he experienced a sudden, unexpected flash of jealousy. Had Ellie been on a date with Damien? He knew it was none of his business except she'd told him she didn't date people from work.

'In that case, we'll have to try again,' Damien was saying.

James moved his leg, just a fraction, enough to bring his knee into contact with Ellie's. The slight touch had the desired effect. He could feel the energy pulsing between them and it moved Ellie's attention away from Damien and his proposal. Ellie looked at him and he knew she could feel the heat too, he could see it in her eyes. The feeling of jealousy that had surged through him was replaced with one of satisfaction.

James knew he was being juvenile but he couldn't help it, he wasn't going to sit here and compete with Damien for Ellie's attention. Not unless he was going to win. And he knew he held the trump card. He and Ellie had a connection, a strong connection, and he wasn't going to let go easily.

Ellie pushed her chair back from the table, her gaze still locked with his. 'I'd better be heading back.'

She leant down to pick her handbag up from underneath

the table and her hair brushed over his forearm. He quickly gathered up the remains of his lunch and stood too.

'I'll walk back with you,' he said. He wanted to walk away from this lunch victorious and the only way to do that was to make sure Ellie left with him and not Damien.

'I'll call you,' Damien said to Ellie. Whether Ellie noticed it or not, James knew that Damien recognised the competition and he was making sure James knew it too.

'You didn't enjoy the movie?' James asked as they walked together towards the lifts.

'Not particularly,' Ellie replied. 'It was supposed to be a romantic comedy but it wasn't very romantic nor was it particularly funny. The two lead characters had no spark.'

'You went with Damien?' He tried to keep his tone neutral but he wasn't sure how successful he was.

'And Charlotte and her fiancé,' Ellie replied as she pressed the button for the lift.

'And Damien works in Outpatients?'

'Yes.'

They stepped into the full lift and James saved his question, waiting until they got out again. He didn't want to have this conversation in front of a crowd.

'I thought you didn't date people from work?' he asked as the lift delivered them to the Orthopaedic ward.

'People from other departments don't count.'

'That's discrimination,' he said.

'Against who?'

'Me.'

Ellie laughed. 'Sorry, but that's my new rule.'

'Well, I'd like to go on record as saying that I think it's an extremely bad rule and I'd like to object to it.'

'You can object all you like but it makes no difference. Besides, I'd hardly call it a date.'

His response was a raised eyebrow.

'Going to the movies with a group of friends doesn't count,' she clarified.

'Does Damien know that?' he asked.

She shrugged. 'It wasn't ever a proper date.' Not in her mind anyway. Charlotte had bullied her into going to the movies. She'd been one of the few people who knew of her relationship with Rob and she'd been convinced it would do Ellie good to get out and meet someone new, someone who wasn't a doctor. Ellie had insisted that it should all be very casual and she'd only gone on the proviso that Charlotte and her fiancé came too. Charlotte thought she was helping to cheer Ellie up but Ellie had accepted for a different reason altogether, to distract her from her fantasies about James. Maybe Damien would suit her and maybe he'd get her mind off James, who was most unsuitable!

But of course it hadn't worked. There was no spark, no connection with Damien. She didn't get all warm and tingly when he looked at her. She didn't want to touch him, taste him, devour him the way she did James. No. The movie date hadn't done anything except show her that she could resist some men and remind her how she felt about James.

'So, by your admission, a date isn't a date if there are other people involved,' James said with a grin.

'Something like that.'

'So, a game of beach volleyball, two on two, wouldn't count?'

'Possibly not.'

'Good, because I need a partner on Sunday morning. Would you come and play with me?' He must have sensed her hesitation because he added clarification. 'It's not a date, we'll be in a public place with lots of other people.'

It wasn't the where or when that bothered her, it was the 'what'. 'Beach volleyball?' she queried. Ball sports were not her forte. 'Surely I'm too short?'

'You'll be fine. I'll cover for you.'

'Wouldn't you rather get someone else to partner you? Someone taller? Someone with better hand-eye co-ordination than me?'

James shook his head. 'I want you.'

She had no retort for that. *He wanted her!* A girl would have to be crazy to pass up the invitation now.

She'd sworn not to date another orthopod but if James was insisting this wasn't a date she could choose to believe him. Surely she could trust herself not to fall under his spell.

But she knew she wasn't immune to his charm when they were on the ward, she wasn't immune to his charm when they were in his car, and she didn't imagine she'd be immune on the beach, in broad daylight, surrounded by crowds. The more time she spent with him, the harder it was going to be to resist the attraction.

She shouldn't accept his invitation. It was madness. But she didn't have enough willpower to refuse.

'Okay, I just hope you know what you're doing 'cos I'll tell you now, I have no idea.' If James thought she was just talking about beach volleyball that was fine by her, but her comment covered a multitude of situations.

The morning sun was warm on her skin as she made her way down to the beach but it was nothing compared to the warmth that flooded through her when she saw James waiting for her. He crossed the beach, his movements effortless even through the soft, dry sand, and met her as she descended the steps. The air around them hummed as she was enveloped in his lime scent. He reached for her hands and the humming travelled through her body. She was convinced she could feel every individual nerve ending pulsing as it responded to his touch.

He leant forward and greeted her with a kiss on each cheek. His gesture took her by surprise. Unlike after the Kings Cross incident, when she'd half expected him to kiss her and he hadn't, this kiss was completely unforeseen and therefore all the more exciting. Her skin tingled where his lips met her cheeks but he was behaving as if his greeting was nothing unusual so she attempted to follow his lead.

'Good morning, I'm glad you could make it. Come.' He wrapped one arm around her shoulders and guided her to the courts marked in the sand. His arm was warm across her bare skin and she fought hard to concentrate on getting her feet to move forward. It was difficult to focus on anything else while he was touching her.

She'd spent ages choosing her outfit and now she wished she'd chosen something that covered her up a bit more. Despite there being a limited number of outfits that were suitable for a game of beach volleyball she'd managed to change her clothes half a dozen times before settling on a blue sports singlet and short white shorts. Bikinis were out, she wasn't prepared for the stress of worrying about which bits of her were spilling out of a pair of bathers, and she was too short to wear board shorts. Jogging clothes were the most flattering, she'd decided.

But slightly more protection might have been wise. It wasn't the sun she needed protection from, she'd applied plenty of sunscreen, but if James was going to keep touching her exposed skin there was no way she was going to be able to concentrate on a game of volleyball. She didn't have a clue how to play the game anyway and she knew James was going to be a huge distraction, albeit a very pleasant one.

Several people were already warming up, hitting the ball back and forth over the net. It didn't look too difficult. Normally, she would have declined the invitation, ball sports were not her thing, but it hadn't taken much for James to persuade her. Perhaps she could do this.

'Let me teach you some of the shots,' he said as he stripped off his shirt and tossed it onto a towel that was lying beside the beach wall. His skin was a smooth golden brown, his shoulders nicely square and his abdominal muscles rippled. A shirtless James was a sight she didn't think she could ever grow tired of. He took her beach bag from her as she stood admiring the view and put it with his things. If he noticed her fixation he didn't comment. 'It's a pretty easy game, there aren't too many things you need to know before you can make a decent go of it. You need to know a throw, a dig, a spike and a serve.'

'That's all?' That sounded like an awful lot!

'Here.' He picked up a ball that was lying on the sand and tossed it to her. To her relief, she caught it. 'First, the throw. Generally you try to use this when you receive a serve, it takes the pace off the ball and lets the next person set up a dig.'

Her expression must have been one of total confusion. 'Don't worry, it's not hard. Throw the ball to me, I'll show you.'

She threw him the ball, a flat pass aimed at his chest, just like she remembered learning in netball. James caught it.

'Good throw but in volleyball you do it like this.' He lofted the ball into the air and as it came down towards him he lifted his arms above his head pushing the ball back up into the air. 'There, that's all there is to it.'

Ellie had no idea what he was talking about. She hadn't seen what he'd done, her attention had been distracted by his arm movements and the flow-on effect it had had on the muscles of his back and shoulders. 'Can you show me again?'

He repeated the action and this time she forced herself to concentrate. She watched the ball, keeping her focus on the inanimate object.

'Your turn,' he said as he looped the ball to her.

Ellie reached up for it, squinting into the sun. The ball collided with her fingers but instead of flying back up into the air, as it had done for James, it stopped dead and fell to the ground.

'You need to keep your elbows bent and straighten them as you push the ball up,' James explained. He took a step to her side and held her elbows, lifting them up in line with her ears, with her hands above her head. 'Start here and when the ball lands on your fingers then straighten your elbows. You want to push the ball back to me. If you throw, I'll dig.'

'You know I'm not understanding a word you're saying, don't you?' Ellie laughed. *And I can't concentrate when you're touching me*, she wanted to add. She didn't give two hoots about volleyball, all she wanted was for James to run his hands back down her arms and from there to her waist. If she closed her eyes she could imagine exactly how it would feel. How he would feel.

'Trust me, it's not hard.'

'Are you sure you don't want to choose a different partner while you've still got time?'

'Positive. I'm going to teach you how to dig now.' He let go of her elbows and she could breathe again but her skin ached for his touch. 'You've got to use a different grip for this,' he said as he took hold of her hands. 'You have to interlock your fingers…' he threaded her fingers together '…palms facing each other…' he closed her hands '…and make a flat surface from your thumbs to your wrists…' He ran his fingers along her thumbs and up to her wrists.

'You want to hit the ball here,' he said as he circled a spot on her wrist.

Her skin was on fire, every nerve ending in her wrist, hand and fingers was quivering and she was surprised that she could see no visible shaking. 'Still no idea what you're saying.' She laughed. She knew she didn't have a hope in hell of getting the ball to do anything when her hands felt as though they didn't belong to her.

'Give it a shot.' James threw the ball to himself and used the 'throw' to pass it to her.

Somehow she managed to hit the ball but it went sailing backwards over her head. She collapsed in a fit of giggles. 'I'm guessing it wasn't supposed to go in that direction.'

'No.' He was laughing, with her she hoped, not at her, but at least he didn't look ready to trade her for someone else just yet.

'I thought you said this was an easy game.'

'It is. Let me show you.' He came and stood behind her this time. 'You need to keep your elbows straight for this shot.' He wrapped his arms around hers, laying them along the outside of hers as he straightened her elbows. His hips were pressing into her bottom and he used his legs to pull her down into a slight squat. 'Get yourself behind the ball and keep your elbows straight. Angle your arms down here…' he pulled her hands down to a forty-five-degree angle to the sand '…so that when the ball hits your wrists you're aiming it up and forward. Straighten your knees to get the power behind the ball.' He tightened his arms around her and pulled her up into a standing position. 'You need to master the "dig" because you're probably not tall enough for the "spike".'

She still had absolutely no idea what he was talking about, but she could feel his thigh muscles pushing against her buttocks, guiding her into position. Even through a couple of layers of clothing the sensation was highly charged. She didn't think she'd ever get the hang of the actual game but the lessons sure were enjoyable.

'Try again.' He let go of her arms and picked the ball up from the sand.

This time she managed to get the ball to travel forward. A huge achievement.

'Well done! Now a serve and that's it. Normally we aim for the back left corner of our opponent's court but anything over the net will be good.'

'Don't be rude! I'm sure I can manage that.' At least she knew what a serve was supposed to look like, that was fairly obvious from other games of beach volleyball that she'd walked past. She picked up the ball, went to stand behind the base line and popped the ball over the net just as James had told her to. 'I did it!'

'All right!' James grinned and high-fived her and Ellie felt invincible. 'Let's find someone to have a practice against.'

As she expected, a game situation was a little different. It was a lot faster and she didn't have James's hands around her to guide her. The ball went flying in all directions, occasionally making it over the net and landing in their opponents' court, but to his credit James just laughed and continued to encourage her, even when she served the ball straight into the back of his head.

'I'm so sorry. Are you okay?'

'Yes, I'm fine.' He laughed. 'I just wasn't expecting that one! I'll be ready next time.'

They persevered for an hour or so before James declared it was time to call it quits. 'I think we've lost by as much as we can. I reckon we should call it a day and go for a swim.'

Ellie hadn't worn bathers and despite the sunshine she knew the water would be cold. 'Too cold for me,' she said as she pulled her drink bottle out of her bag, 'but you go ahead.' She picked up their towels and carried them down to the water's edge.

James jogged into the water and dived through the waves. He swam several strokes out to sea before turning and swimming back to shore. He came out of the water, wet and glistening, and collapsed onto his towel beside her. The cool water had hardened his nipples and Ellie fought to keep her eyes fixed on the waves. She could feel the difference in their body heat now. He was sitting very close to her and the contrast between the coolness of his skin and the warmth of hers was palpable. She could smell him too, limes mingled with the salty tang of the ocean. A fresh, clean scent that would always make her think of him.

'Have you enjoyed our "non-date"?' he asked.

'I actually have,' she admitted. Despite the fact that she'd failed spectacularly at beach volleyball, she'd had one of the best mornings ever. 'Thank you.'

'My pleasure,' he said. He smiled at her and even though she hadn't thought the day could get any better, once again the power of his smile made everything seem just that little bit more special.

In James's opinion yesterday's 'non-date' had worked perfectly. He knew Ellie had enjoyed it and now it was time to up the ante. He was going to get her to agree to a proper date. He was going to get past her obstacles and over her objections. He picked up the phone in the doctors' lounge and dialled the extension for the nurses' station.

Ellie answered the ward phone, surprised to hear James's voice. Even from afar his voice sent her pulse racing.

'Ellie!' He sounded pleased she'd answered. 'I have a favour to ask. I've got a case study to present and I thought I might use Dylan Harris as he's got some interesting psychological aspects. Would you mind bringing me his case notes?'

If it had been any of the other doctors she would have told them she was too busy and they'd have to get the notes themself. But because it was James she was willing to do it. Did that make her a hypocrite? She knew it did but she didn't care. After their 'non-date' the attraction she felt was becoming harder to resist, the invisible link she could feel between them pulled her to him at every opportunity and it was getting stronger.

She found Dylan's file and carried it down the corridor to the doctors' lounge. James was waiting just inside the door and he held it open for her as she stepped into the room. She took a few steps forward, aware that James was close behind her. She stopped beside a small couch and turned and handed him the file. He dropped the notes onto the couch, making no pretence of looking at them.

Ellie looked around. Except for them the lounge was empty. It was a generously sized room but Ellie was only aware of how close James was standing. He hadn't stepped away from her and she hadn't moved. She didn't think she could. She was held motionless by their energy field, that invisible bubble. She waited for him to speak, somehow knowing he would, knowing he had something to say.

'The movie date you went on with Damien…'

'Mmm.' She heard his words but was grateful he hadn't formed a question because she didn't think she could articulate an answer while he was standing so close. She knew she should remind him that it hadn't been a proper date but her brain couldn't think beyond the basic senses. She could smell him, his now-familiar lime scent. She could hear him, his deep, warm, rich voice. She wanted to touch him, to feel his smooth olive skin and taste him. She could imagine how his lips would taste. It was as though all her functions had shut down except for the basics. She couldn't formulate anything sensible.

'Was it as much fun as our game of beach volleyball?'

She shook her head. 'It was nice.' Three words. That was all she could manage and even they were a struggle.

'Nice?' he queried. 'How about our non-date, how would you describe that?'

Now she was definitely lost for words. How did you tell someone your head was still spinning from the memory of the touch of his hand on her skin? How did you describe the way her heart raced when his arms wrapped around her as he taught her the game?

'Better than nice?' he suggested when no reply came from her.

She nodded.

'Would you go out on a proper date with Damien, do you think?'

This time she shook her head.

'How about with me? Has our non-date changed your mind about me at all?'

'Why would it have?' she asked, surprised to find she was able to tease him.

'Because of this.' He reached out and ran his hand along her arm. He started at her elbow, where her arm emerged from her short-sleeved shirt. His fingers burned over her skin until he reached her wrist. He turned her hand over and ran his thumb over her palm and a ripple of desire surged through her belly. The air around them buzzed. 'You feel it too, don't you?' She could feel a pulse in her throat throbbing, her heart was racing and her breaths were short and shallow. 'And I know you couldn't have felt that with Damien because there's no way on earth you could describe this as "nice". This is something else. This is chemistry. Pure and simple.'

She took a deep breath, inhaling his subtle lime scent, holding it in her chest.

'When he held your hand in the movies you didn't forget to breathe, did you?'

She couldn't remember Damien holding her hand but she knew James was right. It wouldn't have had the same effect. It wouldn't have come close. And he was right about her not breathing too. She couldn't breathe but she didn't feel as though she needed to. James's touch was all she needed.

Her legs felt like jelly. She didn't think she could support her own weight. James moved his hands to her hips, holding her up, supporting her. She looked up at him, into the depths of his chocolate eyes, as he moved towards her.

'And when his knee brushed against your thigh it didn't make you quiver with anticipation.' His voice was a whisper. His words a statement. He slid one hand down her thigh and the heat of it burned through the fabric of her trousers. She trembled, grateful she was pressed up against the back of the couch, sandwiched between the furniture and James's hips. She couldn't move. She didn't want to move. His face was mere inches from hers.

'And when he leant towards you, did you find yourself leaning in just a little bit closer?' He lifted one hand, pressing his fingertips to the pulse that was throbbing in her neck as his thumb brushed over her lips. Another ripple of desire ran through her. Automatically she parted her lips, her tongue darting out to lick them. She saw James's gaze follow the movement, she could see her own desire reflected in his eyes and heard him moan as he bent his head towards her, closing the gap. His chest pressed against hers as his head came down and she felt her nipples harden in response. His breath was warm on her mouth. And then his lips were on hers. Firm and warm, and this time it was her moaning.

CHAPTER FIVE

His lips tasted of salt, his mouth of coffee. His hand slid up her back, crushing her to him. His tongue was inside her mouth, exploring, as his hands moved over her body. His fingers brushed over one breast, sending a spark of desire through her, so intense it made her gasp. James stopped kissing her, pulling away, and she knew he was checking that she was okay. His eyes searched her face.

She was fine. She smiled and she could see passion flare in his eyes. There was fire in their dark depths. She'd thought his eyes were brown but now they looked black, as black as coal, and she knew how coal could burn.

'What are we doing?' She sounded out of breath. She was out of breath.

'Something I've wanted to do since the first day I saw you.' His hands were firm against her arms, holding her to him as if he were afraid she might leave. But there was nowhere she wanted to go.

Until she remembered where they were.

'What if someone walks in?' she said in a panic. She didn't think her heart could beat any faster but the idea that someone could walk into the doctors' lounge at any moment and find them there, together, scared her.

'I locked the door behind us.'

That surprised her. He must have thought this through

and it made her wonder how many times he'd been in this situation. Obviously more times than her! 'You were that confident I'd let you kiss me?'

'It pays to be prepared.' He grinned at her, not at all embarrassed. His eyes shone and desire flared in her again. 'But you're free to leave if you wish.' He stepped to one side. Ellie could easily step around him and make her escape but she made no such move. Instead she reached out to him, pulling him back to her. She had one hand on his back and she could feel the muscles flex under her fingers as he stepped towards her. She wound her other hand through his thick, dark hair and pulled his head down to her again. He didn't resist as she kissed him.

Ellie forgot about her list. About her pledge not to date another doctor. This wasn't a date. This was a chemistry lesson. Just as James had said.

But chemistry had never been this much fun at school.

Eventually she came to her senses and remembered she was in the middle of her shift. She couldn't believe she'd forgotten all about work. 'I'd better get back on the ward.'

She wouldn't have thought she was the type of girl who sneaked off at work but, then, she'd never felt this undeniable attraction before. She'd never been this powerless, never had her body betray her mind to such a degree.

'So I take it you'll have that drink with me now?'

So much for not getting involved with another orthopaedic surgeon! She didn't have enough willpower to stay away from him. She knew that if he wanted her, he would have her and she'd go willingly. She couldn't fight this feeling. She nodded.

'Tonight?' he asked.

She tried to recall what she was doing after work. Damn. She and Jess had a class to go to.

'I can't tonight.'

'You're not going out with Damien, are you?'

Ellie was tempted to say yes just to hear what he'd say, but he looked so anxious that she took pity on him. 'No, I'm doing a course with a girlfriend.' She was rewarded with a wide smile that made her add. 'And we'll probably go to the Stat Bar for a drink afterwards. Around nine.'

James smile grew even wider. 'Nine?'

Ellie nodded.

'I'll see you later, then,' he said, before he leant forward and kissed her on the mouth.

She knew she had to get back to the ward, she couldn't stay hidden away in the doctors' lounge with James all day, as much as she wanted to, but it was all she could do to get her feet moving one at a time when he opened the door for her. He stuck his head out into the corridor, making sure it was clear, and Ellie hurried back to the ward, hoping no one had noticed her absence. She ducked into the staff toilet to check her appearance. Her lips felt swollen and her eyes were a bright, sparkling blue but she didn't think anyone else would notice anything amiss. She ran her fingers through her hair, repositioning her Alice band, and straightened her shirt before returning to her duties.

She floated through the rest of her shift on a little bubble of happiness and even Rob's mid-afternoon visit to the ward didn't dampen her spirits.

Ellie kept her commitment to Jess, accompanying her to the wine appreciation class they'd enrolled in, but she spent the entire evening with one eye on the clock wishing she could leave and hurry to the Stat Bar. It didn't help matters that Jess had chosen the class thinking it might be a good place to meet men who weren't doctors but there certainly wasn't a lot in the way of potential. They both struggled through the class as Ellie regaled Jess with a slightly

edited version of the afternoon's events and after that it
didn't take much effort from her to persuade Jess to call in
to the Stat Bar to meet Ruby and Cort for a drink.

They'd only been at the bar a few minutes and were waiting for Ruby to arrive when Ellie felt the hair on the back
of her neck rise, as if a warm breeze has brushed over her.
She knew, before even seeing the look on Jess's face, that
James was behind her.

'Hello, gorgeous.' He leant over her shoulder and his
voice was soft in her ear as his breath warmed the nape of
her neck. To hear him use such a familiar greeting in public both surprised and excited her.

His fingers were resting lightly on her upper arm and
she was enveloped in his lime scent. She felt a rush of desire as the memory of the afternoon came flooding back
with his touch. She turned in her chair and greeted him
before introducing him to Jess.

'Can I buy you both a drink?' he asked.

'I'm fine, thanks,' Jess replied. 'Why don't you go with
James, Ellie?' she suggested.

'Are you sure?'

'Yes, go.' Jess waved them away. 'I can see Ruby heading over now,' she said as she dismissed them both, guessing correctly that Ellie didn't want to share James.

Ellie didn't need to be asked twice. She stood and left
with James.

Two steps into the bar she wished she'd stayed in her
seat because sitting at a table, right in their path, was Rob
with a woman Ellie didn't recognise. She was a brunette
and Ellie assumed she was Rob's wife but, with Rob's track
record, she wasn't about to jump to conclusions. But if she
was Rob's wife, she wasn't at all what Ellie had pictured—
she was tall and thin with long dark hair tied into a ponytail and a long face.

Rob stood to shake James's hand but ignored Ellie and made no attempt to introduce the woman he was with. James made the introductions himself as Rob sat down.

'I'm Penny, Rob's wife,' the woman responded to James's introduction.

Hearing her assumptions confirmed gave Ellie a moment of relief as she realised she'd been wondering what Rob's wife was like. She'd envisaged a glamorous English rose but the bitchy side of her was pleased to see that Penny was older and plainer than she'd imagined.

James was being far more gracious. 'I thought you must be,' he said. 'Welcome to Australia. How are you settling in?'

Ellie saw Penny glance at Rob as she answered, 'It will take a little bit of time to adjust but we're getting sorted.'

'We're just on our way to the bar—can I get you anything?' James offered.

'No, we're fine, don't let us hold you up,' Rob replied. His words were directed at James but he was looking at Ellie. His eyes were cold and hard, all traces of warmth gone from their green depths, and his stare made her feel uncomfortable. There was no invitation to join them, for which Ellie was grateful, but she was aware of the tension in the air and wondered whether James or Penny noticed it too.

James had. 'Well, that was awkward,' he said as they made their way to the bar.

'Mmm. Maybe they just wanted some alone time.' She almost mentioned their daughter but caught herself just in time. She didn't want to advertise the fact that she knew anything personal about Rob. Standing at the bar, she could feel someone's eyes boring into her back. She'd bet it was Rob and the thought increased her discomfort at the situation. 'Do you think anyone would miss us if we left?' she asked in what she hoped sounded like a casual tone. 'You're welcome to have a drink at my place.' She didn't care if he thought her forward, she didn't want to stay here under Rob's scrutiny any longer.

'Sure.'

They left the bar and walked across the road to the Hill Street house. James's Jeep was parked in front of her neighbour's place and he stopped beside it, unlocking the back. He flipped open the lid of an esky that was stashed in the boot and pulled two small bottles of beer from the ice.

'This wasn't quite what I had in mind when I asked you home for a drink,' Ellie said.

'Don't you drink beer?' he asked as he closed the ice box.

'I do but I have drinks inside.'

He smiled at her and Ellie delighted in the way his smile lit up his face. 'It was my buy, though, and this fridge was freshly stocked today,' he said as he flicked the tops off the bottles.

'Mmm.'

'What do you mean, "Mmm"?'

Ellie laughed. 'I'm just used to men trying a bit harder to impress me.'

'Hey, you invited me over and, remember, you're talking to a man who's living out of his car. But there's an additional benefit to that,' he said as he dived back into the esky. 'I can easily up the ante when required.' He emerged with a glass which he handed to Ellie. 'There you go, but I figured if you were prepared to go on a date with me, when you'd already been in my car, you're probably not into embellishments. There's not all that much about me that's impressive.'

'I wouldn't say that.' From where Ellie was standing there was plenty to be impressed with. At some point today he'd had changed out of the shirt and trousers he'd worn to work and was back in his faded jeans and black T-shirt. The same outfit he'd been wearing on the night she'd first seen him. The hot guy. She had no complaints.

The old, wooden, front gate squeaked on its rusty hinges as James pushed it open. He held it for Ellie. 'Do you want to sit outside for a bit?' he asked. Tucked against the side fence was a garden swing and he inclined his head towards it. 'It's such a beautiful night.'

It was too. The night was clear and still and the stars danced in the sky. To the north and west they competed with the glowing lights of the city but to the east, where they hung over the ocean, they were shiny and bright.

She kicked off her shoes and sat on the swing, her feet curled up beneath her.

James filled her glass and clinked his bottle against it. 'Here's to getting to know one another a little better.'

His smile was full of promise and it was enough to make Ellie tremble in anticipation of things to come. All in good time, she reminded herself. Even though the kiss they'd shared earlier in the day had been enough to make her change her mind about dating him, she still needed to try to take things slowly.

James joined her on the swing. He sat sideways and pushed off the ground, setting the swing moving gently. He pulled Ellie's legs out straight, settling her feet in his lap. He held his beer in one hand and rubbed the soles of her feet with his other.

It was heaven.

'What would you like to know?' she asked.

He took a sip of his beer before replying. 'What's your favourite colour?'

'That's what you want to know?' That wouldn't have been her first question.

He nodded.

'Blue,' she said. Or maybe chocolate brown now, she thought as she looked into the dark depths of James's eyes.

'Your favourite food?'

'Limes.'

'Limes are not a food.' He laughed. 'You're supposed to say smelly cheese or crayfish.'

'Well, I can't think when you're rubbing my feet like that,' she protested.

'Would you like me to stop?'

'No.'

He wiggled each of her toes in turn as he recited what he knew. 'I know you grew up in Goulburn, you were educated by Catholic nuns, you like blue, you think limes are a food.' He grinned at her. 'You work as a nurse and most of your male patients would love to be in the position I'm in right now. But I still need more.'

'How much more?'

'Like why you don't want to date a doctor.'

'I never said doctor, I said people from our department.'

'Either way, you've crossed me off your list.'

'Let's just say I've had a couple of bad experiences lately.'

'What happened?'

'Some false pretences and a lack of honesty.'

'Surely you can't attribute that to the fact they were from the orthopaedic ward?'

'No, it could have been coincidence but they were both doctors and I expected better, I guess.'

'So, no chance for me, then?'

'In your case I'm prepared to make an exception.'

James raised his eyebrows. 'Really? Why?'

'Because you certainly don't seem to be pretending

you're someone you're not. After all you're living out of your car and you have an esky for a fridge,' she teased.

'Hey, that's not fair, I only live out of my car sometimes. I have to be at the hospital at seven tomorrow morning and it's a hassle driving all the way across the city from Cremorne.'

'I'm not criticising you. You're one step ahead of me, I don't even have a car.'

'So my semi-nomadic lifestyle isn't putting you off?'

She shook her head. 'Honestly, after you kissed me this afternoon I'm prepared to overlook just about anything. I have never been kissed like that before in my life and I want more.'

'Why didn't you say so earlier?' He took her glass from her hand and put it on the ground with his bottle of beer. His hands cupped her hips and he pulled her forward, wrapping her legs around his waist, joining them together. His hands were warm and his body was firm between her thighs. Ellie imagined that this was what heaven would feel like. Warm and safe and perfect.

His lips were warm as he claimed her in a kiss.

His arms were around her, holding her, protecting her, keeping her safe.

The kiss was perfect.

She closed her eyes and surrendered to the sensation of being thoroughly kissed by someone who knew what they were doing. She parted her lips, her tongue tasted his, exploring his mouth. His hand was under her shirt, fingers splayed, warm across her back. She leant into him as he deepened the kiss.

It was heaven.

CHAPTER SIX

THE tell-tale squeak of the front gate interrupted the moment as someone else came home. Ellie froze and broke the kiss, her lips suddenly cold now they were no longer under James's caress.

'Wha—?'

'Shh,' she whispered, cutting off his question. She didn't want to draw anyone's attention. The front of the house was dark, casting no light on the garden swing. She watched as Tilly opened the front door and switched on the passage light. No one else was home yet.

'Who was that?' James asked as Tilly shut the door.

'Tilly. She lives here too.'

'Anyone else I need to know about?'

'Jess you met, we went to nursing school together. Tilly and Ruby, they're also nurses at the hospital, and sometimes Adam. It's his house.'

'Lucky Adam. Why is he only here sometimes?'

'He's a surgeon. He works with Operation New Faces so he's away a lot.'

'Adam Carmichael? This is his house?'

'You know him?'

'I've heard of him but I've never met him.'

'He's just headed off again otherwise I could introduce you.'

'I think I'd rather not meet him under these circumstances.'

Ellie frowned. 'What circumstances?'

'Kissing his tenant in the front garden of his property,' James explained. 'It's not quite the first impression I'd want to make.'

'Oh, and why is that?'

'You know what the medical fraternity is like. There's a definite hierarchy separating us junior surgeons from our more experienced and esteemed colleagues and it's important that I give the right impression.'

'And what would that be?'

'Being dedicated and responsible, and it's a bit hard to do that if the first thing they see is me kissing the nurses.'

'I know about the pecking order,' she interrupted before he could say anything else he might regret. At least she hoped he might regret his words. 'Are you embarrassed to be seen with me?' If she'd learnt one thing from Rob's betrayal it was never to accept a clandestine relationship again. She wasn't someone to be ashamed of.

'That's not what I meant. I've been bugging you to go out with me so of course I'm happy to be seen with you. I just meant that I would prefer to meet any senior surgeons when I'm in work mode, not in the middle of my recreation.'

Ellie realised she was being unfair. She shouldn't judge James by Rob's standards. She owed him an apology. 'Sorry, I didn't mean to jump down your throat.'

'Don't sweat it, I'd rather we didn't have any misunderstandings and I'm more than happy to continue this… conversation…' he smiled at her and the corners of his dark eyes creased with mischief as he ducked his head and kissed her softly on the lips '…another time but I probably should get going before the rest of your housemates come home.' He stood up and then took her hand, pulling her to her feet. 'Can I see you tomorrow? Are you going to the Stat Bar? The orthopaedic ward has organised drinks to welcome Penny Coleman to Australia.'

There was no way she was going to *that* gathering. She shook her head. 'I'm not going. I've volunteered to do a late shift.' That was at least partly true and she could hardly tell him the whole truth—*it would be extremely hypocritical on my part to welcome her to town when I had an affair with her husband.*

'Then I'll meet you at the hospital at the end of your shift and walk you home.' Now that he'd had a taste for her he knew he wouldn't be able to stay away. She was the type of girl who would get into his system. She seemed vulnerable. No, that wasn't the right word, fragile was perhaps more accurate. Not in a sense that she was delicate, just that she was the type of girl who needed someone to take care of her. She'd been to boarding school then nursing college and was now sharing a house with four others but he'd bet she wasn't the house mother. She would be the one that everyone looked out for.

He took a cool shower when he got to the hospital but then spent the night tossing and turning, thinking about Ellie. He knew he would probably have to take things slowly, but he needed some way of taking the edge off his desire, if he had to wait too long he'd go crazy.

The following evening he made sure he was back at the hospital before the change of shift as he didn't want to miss her.

'Did you go to the Stat Bar?' she asked him when he met her on the ward.

She smelt like sunshine; warm and happy, and that was how she made him feel too. How on earth could she smell so good at the end of a shift?

He nodded. 'Briefly,' he said as he took her hand, hoping she wouldn't resist. She didn't and he was surprised at how good it felt to leave the hospital hand in hand with her.

'Are you going back?'

'If I don't get a better offer I might,' he teased. 'What are your plans?'

'I'm going home for a shower and something to eat. How does that sound?' She raised one eyebrow and the corner of her mouth followed in a silent invitation.

'Too good to refuse,' he said, quickening his pace just a little as they walked down the hill.

His hand was warm and familiar as he led her away from the hospital. She barely knew him, how could it feel so natural?

The cool evening breeze carried his lime scent to her. He smelt so clean and pure after the chemical smell of the hospital. She breathed in deeply, letting his fragrance eradicate all the lingering traces of the orthopaedic ward.

She could feel the humming, their unique bubble enveloped her. She knew she should resist but, just as she'd feared, it was becoming harder and harder. The more time she spent in his company the harder it was to ignore the attraction. She was struggling to fight temptation. She was falling under his spell and she didn't think she could resist much longer.

Did it matter? she thought. Did she have to resist?

No, she just had to make sure she didn't fall in love.

He wasn't 'the one' for her. He'd already said he never planned on getting married. He definitely wasn't the one but that didn't mean she couldn't have some fun. She just couldn't take it seriously. He could be a distraction, some light-hearted relief. As long as she didn't make the mistake of falling in love, it could work.

By the time they neared the house she could barely concentrate on walking. All she could think about was James's touch. His grip was firm yet gentle, his hand was warm and she could already imagine how his hands would feel running over the rest of her body, running over her breasts, her stomach and her thighs.

They were two houses away and she felt her pace quickening. James's steps kept time with hers. They were both hurrying now, both eager to reach the house, and that's when she knew she was in trouble.

They barely made it inside.

As she pushed the front door closed James turned her around and pinned her against it. He had one thigh between hers and his hands were at her hips, holding her to him. He bent his head and Ellie closed her eyes as she breathed in his tangy lime scent and waited for his lips to meet hers. Her stomach did a slow somersault of desire.

She felt his breath on her cheek. It was warm and soft and disappeared as his lips brushed over hers. She opened her mouth to taste him and their tongues met and entwined, joining them together. Her hands wound around his back and his muscles were firm and sleek beneath her fingers as she leaned into him. She needed to use his strength to hold her upright and just when she thought her legs were going to give way her stomach rumbled and the noise echoed in the long hallway, loud in the quiet house.

James broke the kiss. He was laughing. 'Why don't you have a shower while I cook us something to eat? What do you have in the kitchen?'

'You're going to cook?' He was thinking about food? That was the last thing on her mind.

'If I want to keep you awake most of the night it sounds like I'd better feed you first or you won't make it,' he said with a smile.

That sounded better, much more in line with her own rampant thoughts.

'I have no idea what's in the fridge but you're welcome to see. The kitchen is through here,' she said as she ducked under his arm and led him to the bottom of the stairs and pointed towards the kitchen. 'You're welcome to use whatever is in the big fridge—the little one is Ruby's.'

'She has her own fridge?'

Ellie didn't have time for detailed explanations. Everyone else in the house was used to the dual fridge system, so she kept her reply brief. 'She's vegetarian,' she explained, as if it made perfect sense. She didn't elaborate any further, she was on a mission. She raced upstairs and stripped off her uniform, throwing it into the laundry hamper. She pinned her hair up to keep it dry as there wasn't time to wash it, and jumped into the shower.

Clean and refreshed, she rummaged through her underwear drawer. She had a bit of a thing for lingerie and only ever bought matching bras and knickers, as impractical as that often was. She found her favourite set and pulled it on. She sprayed her wrists and the backs of her knees with perfume and dabbed some on her throat before buttoning an old white shirt over her underwear. There wasn't much point in getting fully dressed, she hoped to be naked again very shortly.

She knew she shouldn't even be thinking about sleeping with James yet but she was finding him irresistible and perhaps the best way to get him out of her system was to take him to bed and then maybe the yearning would pass. She could do this. She could sleep with someone without falling in love and dreaming of babies. He wasn't planning on getting married so she could use him for sex with a clear conscience.

'Dinner smells good,' she said as she came downstairs. The smell of cooking had awakened her appetite for food and her hunger now almost outdid her sexual desire. Almost.

James was sliding omelettes onto plates and he looked up as she entered the kitchen. His eyes travelled from her face down along the buttons of her shirt to where the hem skimmed her bare legs and back again. He gave a low whistle. 'Wow, how quickly can you eat, do you think?'

'Let's start by putting the pan down,' Ellie said with a grin as she removed the frying pan from his hand. He was fixed to the spot and she recognised the fire in his eyes. She knew it was passion that made them burn like coal, turning them black.

James wolfed his omelette down in record time while Ellie sprinkled salt on her eggs and spread her toast with butter, teasing him as she ate her meal slowly and deliberately. She was desperate to feel his lips on hers, to feel his hands on her skin, but she knew it would be sweeter if she waited and she wanted him to want her just as badly.

But she hadn't counted on what he'd do while he waited for her to finish. What he'd do when he didn't have a knife and fork in his hands and food in front of him to keep him occupied.

He slid his chair closer to the corner of the table, closer to her. One hand disappeared under the table and she felt his fingers on her knee, just the lightest whisper of a touch but one that made her shiver with longing. His fingers brushed the inside of her thigh, inching higher and higher but, oh, so slowly. Ellie closed her eyes and breathed in, trying to control her senses, her meal forgotten.

The movement ceased. She opened her eyes, wanting to know why he'd stopped, wanting to tell him not to. His eyes met hers, even darker now, his irises and pupils all the same colour. He smiled, the corners of his mouth lifting very slightly before the smile broke open across his face. She knew then that he'd just been waiting for her to open her eyes, waiting to see his desire reflected in her. His hand moved again until it was merely inches from the top of her thigh. Ellie bit her lip and slid forward in her chair, pushing her hips towards his hand, urging him on.

James leant across the table, bending his head to hers, and his voice was soft in her ear. 'Are you ready for dessert?'

His lips nuzzled at her earlobe. Ellie nodded and tipped her head back, exposing her throat, and James pressed his lips to the soft spot under her jaw where her pulse throbbed to the beat of her desire. 'Sooner or later we're going to give in to this feeling,' he said as his fingers brushed across the fabric of her knickers. 'I think it might as well be sooner.'

Ellie couldn't argue. She couldn't even speak. She felt as though she was going to melt into the floor.

She pushed herself to her feet, taking her weight on the table as she wasn't certain her legs would hold her. James's hands moved to her waist and, for the second time in as many days, he supported her weight. She took his hand in hers and led him to the staircase. She gripped the banister as she concentrated on getting her feet to negotiate the steps. James followed behind her and she felt his hand on the inside of her thigh, connecting her to him as he trailed in her wake. She only just made it to the landing and into her bedroom.

James pushed the door shut and grabbed her hand, pulling her to him. His lips covered hers as his fingers popped the buttons on her shirt. She tugged his shirt out of his jeans and unzipped his pants, freeing him from the denim, before shrugging her shoulders out of her top. Her shirt fell to the floor and was joined by his shoes and jeans, and all the while their lips were locked as they feverishly touched and tasted.

He picked her up, as though she weighed nothing at all. She wrapped her legs around his waist and as he carried her to the bed she could feel his erection straining against his boxer shorts and she knew he wanted her as urgently as she wanted him.

She was wearing only her underwear; he still had too many clothes on. She reached out to him and slid her hands under his T-shirt, feeling the heat coming off his skin as she dragged his shirt up his back before pulling it over his head.

He bent towards her, kissing the hollow at the base of her neck where her collarbone ended. She tipped her head back and his lips moved down to the swell of her breast. She felt herself arch towards him, silently crying out for his touch. His hand reached behind her and with a flick of his fingers he undid the clasp on her bra and her breasts spilled free. He pushed her back, gently laying her down beneath him before he dipped his head and covered her nipple with his mouth. She closed her eyes as bolts of desire shot from her breasts to her groin. As James's tongue caressed her nipple Ellie could feel the moisture gathering between her legs as her body prepared to welcome him.

Her hands slipped under the waistband of his boxer shorts and she pushed them off his hips. His buttocks were round and hard under her palms.

James moved his attention to her other breast as she moved one hand between his legs and ran her hand along the length of his shaft. She heard him moan as her fingers rolled across his tip, using the moisture she found there to decrease the friction and smooth her movements.

She arched her hips towards him and he responded, removing her knickers and sliding his fingers inside her. She gasped as he circled her most sensitive spot with his thumb. He was hard and hot under her palm; she was warm and wet to his touch.

She was ready now. She didn't want to wait. She couldn't wait.

She opened her legs and guided him into her, welcoming the full length of him.

He pushed against her and she lifted her hips to meet his thrust. They moved together, matching their rhythms as if they'd been doing this for ever. She had her hands at his hips, controlling the pace, gradually increasing the momentum. James's breaths were short and she wasn't breathing at all. All her energy was focussed on making love to him. There was no room in her head for anything other than the sensation of his skin against hers, his skin inside hers.

James gathered her hands and held them above her head, stretching her out and exposing her breasts, and he bent his head to her nipple again as he continued his thrusts. The energy they created pierced through her, flowing from his mouth, through her breast and into her groin, where it gathered in a peak of pleasure building with intensity until she thought she would explode.

'Now, James, do it now,' she begged.

His pace increased a fraction more and as she felt him start to shudder she released her hold as well. Their timing was exquisite, controlled by the energy that bound them together, and they cried out in unison, climaxing simultaneously.

Never before had Ellie experienced the sensation of two people becoming one but there had been no way of separating the two of them, they had been unified by their lovemaking and it was an experience Ellie would treasure for ever. It had been everything she had expected and more. Their bodies had been made for each other.

Ellie woke at dawn as the first rays of sun hit her window. In their haste to tear off each other's clothes and get into bed last night she'd forgotten to close the curtains. James was lying beside her, still sleeping. He had his arm draped across her stomach but even without the contact she would have known he was there—she could feel the humming in the air and her room smelt of limes. It was almost as though even the particles in the air reacted to his presence. Nothing went unaffected, certainly not her.

She rolled onto her side to look at him. His face was relaxed and calm with just a hint of a smile tugging at the corner of his mouth. He stirred with her movement and opened his eyes.

'Good morning.' The smile that had been hovering at the edges of his lips burst across his face.

Ellie breathed out, relieved to see he was quite comfortable waking up in her bed and didn't appear to be looking for the nearest exit.

He rolled towards her and kissed her on the mouth. 'How did you sleep?'

'Short but sweet.'

'Sorry about that, I was enjoying our evening,' he said as his fingers found her breasts and started tracing circles around them, grazing her nipples.

'I'm not complaining,' she said.

She stretched her arms above her head, arching her back, and James groaned and ducked his head, taking her breast into his mouth and sucking on her nipple. His mouth was warm and moist and as his tongue flicked over her nipple Ellie felt it peak in response. She was ready for James to make love to her again. It would be the perfect way to start the day.

She brought her hands down to his back and ran them along the ridge of his spine. She felt the small indentations at the base of his spine and kept her hands moving further until she could cup his buttocks. She slipped one hand to his groin. His erection pulsed under her palm. He was ready too. She pulled him over on top of her until his weight pressed her into the bed. He covered her body with his and she opened her legs, allowing him to join the two of them together again.

'You're going to make me late for work,' he said once they had satisfied their desires. Again.

'You could have refused,' Ellie replied.

He grinned at her. 'I didn't want to appear ungrateful.'

Ellie thumped him on the arm. 'Hey, watch it.'

'I couldn't resist, does that sound better?' he asked as he kissed her on the mouth, before sitting up and swinging his legs over the edge of the bed, preparing to go to work.

In a frame on Ellie's bedside table, just inches from where he was sitting, was a family photograph.

He turned back to look at her as she lay on the bed. 'Are they your parents?'

She nodded.

'You've got your mother's eyes,' he said. 'Is it a recent photo?'

Ellie knew why he asked that. Despite the fact the photo had been taken twelve years ago her parents looked old enough to be the parents of a twenty-three-year-old. She shook her head. 'No. I was a late-in-life baby. They tried for ten years before they got pregnant with me. They were both thirty-nine when I was born and that was after several years of IVF treatment. They died in a car accident when I was eleven.' She picked up the photo in its frame. 'This was the last photo taken of them.'

'Oh, Ellie, I'm sorry.'

'It's okay, you didn't know.' She never normally volunteered the story of her parents' deaths, it was a part of her life she preferred not to revisit. Normally she would have only admitted that the photo wasn't recent and left it at that but around James things were anything but normal.

'What happened?'

This was her chance to say she didn't like to talk about it but instead she heard herself begin the story.

'We were coming back from the skifields—'

'We? You were with them?'

She nodded. 'We were coming down the mountain and we came around a corner and a grader was on the wrong side of the road. We ran into it and my parents were killed instantly.'

'And you? Were you hurt?' His eyes were roaming over her naked body, looking for scars and marks he might have missed while they'd been making love.

'Only minor injuries.'

'What about your siblings?'

'I'm an only child.'

It had been a long time since she'd revealed this much about herself in one conversation. Even Ruby, Jess and Tilly had only heard the story in bits and pieces. But she knew why she was confiding in James. It was partly because of the humming, that vibration that infused the air around them and made her feel as though they were encased in a private bubble, where time was suspended, and reality couldn't intrude. And it was partly because they'd had the most amazing sex of her life. If he could be that in tune with her physically she didn't think it could hurt to share some of her emotional self with him as well.

'That's why you don't ski any more,' he said. She nodded in response. 'So what happened to you then?' he asked.

'I went to live with Mum's parents.'

'And then to boarding school,' he filled in the gap. 'What about your grandparents, are they still alive?'

'My grandpa died a few years ago and my grandmother died recently. She was my last family member. I'm all that's left.'

'Just you? I had no idea.'

'Why should you? It's hardly a normal happy-families-type story. One day I'll have my own family, one day I'll belong to someone again, but in the meantime I have Jess, Ruby and Tilly. They're my surrogate family.' And meanwhile she could have some fun with James, she thought. 'What about you? What was your childhood like?' She'd talked enough about her story.

'Not quite as calamitous as yours, maybe a bit closer to normal and relatively happy. I have an older sister, she's married with three kids. We were brought up by my mum.'

'What about your father?'

'Not in the picture.'

James had said 'relatively happy' but Ellie found the idea of an absent father unbearably sad. In her opinion, not knowing your father was worse than having a father who'd died. At least she had her memories.

He stood up. 'I'd better get moving. I'll grab a shower at the hospital.' He started picking his clothes up from where they were scattered over the floor. The conversation was obviously over. Ellie lay in bed admiring the curve of his buttocks as he bent forward to pull his boxer shorts on. She could get used to this view. She just hoped she would get a chance to do it all again. What if he wasn't planning on revisiting last night?

He was buttoning his jeans now and he turned to see

her watching. He winked at her and her fears receded. He retrieved his shirt and pulled it over his head before he came back to the bed. He picked up a pen from beside the bed. 'Give me your number so I can call you later.' Ellie recited it and he wrote it on his hand before he kissed her goodbye.

She lay in bed, a smile playing around the corners of her mouth. It was okay. Everything was okay. He would call her, she knew he would. She'd see him again. He could be her transition man. She didn't have to fall for him.

'Doing the breakfast dishes already?' Tilly asked as she came into the kitchen to find Ellie with her hands in the washing-up water. 'Or are they last night's plates?' She looked from Ellie to Jess, who was sitting at the kitchen table. 'I know one of you got lucky, I saw someone sneaking out early this morning. Who has a confession to make?'

Ellie could feel herself blushing.

'Ah, Ms Nicholson, care to share? Who was he?' Tilly grinned and pulled out a chair, making herself comfortable beside Jess.

'James Leonardi,' Ellie admitted. She knew Tilly would get it out of her eventually.

'Who is he?'

'Do you remember the hot guy from the Stat Bar?' said Jess.

'I do!' Tilly's eyebrows shot up. 'The hot guy, wow. What's going on?'

Ellie shrugged. 'I'm not sure really, it's a bit soon to know, but I've never felt like this before.' Last night had been amazing but she wasn't ready to share the details yet.

Tilly raised an eyebrow and smiled. 'Really? You don't remember feeling like this with Rob and Nick and—?'

'I know what you're thinking.' Ellie knew that Tilly's

list could go on and on and it was true, she did throw herself into her relationships and she tended to fall hard and fast. 'But it's different with James. We have a connection.' She knew that didn't come close to explaining how she felt around him but how could she describe the feeling, how could she describe that invisible hum of electricity that surrounded them both, the one she knew only they could feel? How could she describe the sensation of knowing when he walked into a room even when her back was turned? She was sure they wouldn't understand. She was convinced no one else had ever felt like this.

'I thought you were having a break from dating?'

'I'm not sure you could call this dating and I'm not going to fall in love and start dreaming about babies. He's already told me he's a confirmed bachelor with no plans to settle down. I've been forewarned. This is just a bit of fun.'

'Are you sure you know what you're doing?'

'Not at all,' Ellie confessed as she emptied the dirty water from the sink and dried her hands. 'But I can't seem to help it.'

'Promise me you'll be careful,' Tilly said as she stood up. 'I don't want you to get hurt again.'

Ellie grinned. 'Is that today's motto—if you can't be good, be careful?'

'Something like that,' Tilly replied.

'I will be, I promise,' Ellie said as Tilly hugged her.

Ellie wasn't sure how good or how careful she was over the next few weeks but she had a lot of fun. James was delightful company, attentive and funny, not to mention gorgeous and sexy. She was happy.

CHAPTER SEVEN

ELLIE was happy until Rob put a pin into her bubble of joy and popped it.

She was enjoying work, her initial reservations about dating another orthopaedic surgeon had worn off as she and James settled into a very easy relationship. James had no problem with people knowing they were an item and after dating Rob, when she'd had to be so careful to keep their relationship very private, this was a welcome change. She and James had lunch together as often as possible, he would meet her after work and walk her home whenever their schedules allowed it and even on the ward, while there were no huge displays of affection, there was always a touch of his hand or a wink or a smile to let her know he was thinking of her. Even with the hours he worked and the stress of his job Ellie found James to be very composed and relaxed at work and his attitude in turn kept her relaxed. She was even finding it easier to keep a calm head around Rob, or at least she thought so.

Ellie had paged Rob to sign Dylan Harris's discharge papers. After the debacle around George Poni's discharge she had decided to ask Rob first when his patients were ready for discharge rather than assume James could organise it. That way, it was Rob's decision and it helped to keep her head off the chopping block. She did her best to be efficient and succinct in order to keep Rob on side. She'd completed the paperwork and was standing beside him, handing him the relevant pages to sign, when James reappeared at the nurses' station after visiting a patient. He winked at her as he approached the desk and Ellie beamed at him.

'What time is your lunch break?' he asked. 'I'll try to meet you in the cafeteria.'

Ellie glanced at the clock on the wall. 'Twelve, I hope,' she replied.

'Okay, I'll catch you later,' James said as he headed for the lift, leaving her alone with Rob. She watched James's back as he made his way along the corridor.

'You're still seeing Dr Leonardi, then?' Rob asked, interrupting her thoughts.

She was a little taken aback and wondered why it was any of his business but she had no reason to deny it. 'Yes.'

'You didn't waste any time.'

She knew she shouldn't get into a discussion about James with Rob at work or anywhere else but she thought his thinly veiled criticism was a bit out of line. 'What do you mean?' She couldn't stop herself from rising to the bait.

'Straight out of one bed into another.'

'How dare you?' Ellie fumed. 'I don't think you're entitled to comment, seeing as you had me in one bed and your *wife* in another at the same time!' They were alone at the nurses' station but Ellie was conscious of keeping her voice low regardless. She didn't want anyone to overhear this conversation.

'Not exactly. Penny wasn't in my bed, she wasn't even in the country.'

'She's still your wife and you were having an affair.'

'Information which I'm sure you would prefer to remain

between us. As would I. You're not planning on creating waves, are you? That could make things awkward.'

'Awkward how exactly?' Ellie said through gritted teeth.

'You're a good nurse, I'm sure the hospital wouldn't like to lose your services.'

'You'd get me fired?'

'I don't think that would be necessary but if people got wind of your indiscretion you might find it embarrassing to continue working here.'

'*My* indiscretion!'

'I know I'm not the first doctor on staff who's welcomed you into his bed and I'm obviously not the last.' He shrugged. 'Who do you think is going to look like the victim?'

Ellie wanted to slap him. How dare he threaten her? She clenched her fist and stiffened her arm, forcing it to stay by her side. Slapping Rob wouldn't help matters—he'd probably charge her with assault. 'Don't worry, no one's going to hear anything from me,' she seethed, before turning on her heel and storming off. She was furious, she needed her morning tea break, she needed a chance to get outside into the fresh air to clear her head.

She was amazed, again, at how badly she'd misjudged Rob's personality. What bothered her, though, was what her misjudgement said about her. Was she really such a bad judge of character or had he kept the real Rob very well hidden?

She was still upset about his comments at lunchtime and on several occasions she almost mentioned something to James before she caught herself. She wasn't confident that Rob's threats were empty ones and she didn't want to chance her luck. It would be just her misfortune that he'd meant every word he'd spoken.

But the following day Ellie still couldn't help but replay the conversation in her mind and it bothered her just as much. She and James both had the day off and he was making her lunch at his house. She was hugely excited because she was finally getting to see where he lived but Rob's threats were overshadowing the occasion and making it difficult for her to fully enjoy the moment.

'You're very quiet. Are you okay?' he said as drove her from the farmers' market, where they'd shopped for ingredients for lunch, to his house.

She was tempted to tell him about Rob. She wished she could discuss it with him, wished she could ask his opinion. She knew if someone else knew about Rob's threats then it would be that much harder for him to get rid of her if he ever felt like it. But she was more afraid that Rob would carry through with his threat regardless so she kept silent.

'Yes, yes, I'm fine. Just imagining what your house looks like,' she lied. She forced herself to smile and tried to push thoughts of Rob to the back of her mind. She didn't want unpleasant thoughts to spoil her day any longer.

'Imagine no more, this is it,' James said as he pushed a button and a garage door began to open.

The house was not at all what she had expected. It was a narrow, modern, two-storey building. The garage door and front door were polished wood but the house itself was rendered brick.

James parked his Jeep and lifted a large cardboard box out of the boot. Piled into the box were a selection of mushrooms, a huge loaf of bread, cheeses, pâté, olive oil, fresh pasta and a lime and coconut pie he'd selected at the market. Ellie had been amazed at the amount of produce he'd bought but he'd just told her she'd understand why when she saw the state of his fridge and pantry.

She carried her purchase, a bunch of irises, and followed him out of the garage to the front door. James put the box

down to open the door, letting Ellie enter the house first.
The hallway was narrow and a few paces inside a staircase,
with stainless-steel railings and steps in the same polished
wood as the front door, led to the floor above.

'Head up the stairs,' he told her. 'The living areas are
up there.'

Ellie followed his instructions and as she reached the top
of the stairs the narrow confines of the house gave way to
a magnificent open-plan living area with the most amazing harbour views. It was sensational.

'Wow.' The view led her to the front of the room where
glass bifold doors opened onto a balcony. Still carrying
the flowers, she went to stand by the doors. 'The view is
incredible.'

James had put the box onto the kitchen counter and was
standing beside her. 'I guess it is.'

'You guess! I can't believe you stay at the hospital instead of coming home to this. Don't you miss it?'

James shrugged. 'I leave home when it's dark and usually get back when it's dark too so I don't get to see the
view that often.'

'Can we eat lunch out here?' Ellie looked around, searching for a table. There was a barbecue and a small outdoor
setting on the balcony but although there was space inside
for a dining table there wasn't one. There was a leather
modular lounge, a flat-screen television, a bookcase and a
few stools at the kitchen counter but that was it for furniture. It looked like they'd have to eat outside unless James
planned on having them perch on the kitchen stools. Ellie
knew the minimalistic look was the latest trend but she always thought houses looked a bit better with a bit of clut-
ter. It gave them personality, made them looked loved.

Ellie then realised she was still carrying the flowers.
'Do you have a vase I can put these in?'

'You can check the kitchen cupboards while I pour us a glass of wine if you like.'

Ellie opened several cupboards, surprised to find most of them were only half-full. The cupboard above the fridge, which was where she would keep vases, was empty. The alcove for the fridge was huge and she had to stand on tip-toe to open the cupboard, although the fridge in place was only a small bar fridge. James opened the fridge as Ellie continued a fruitless search for a vase. He removed a bottle of wine and Ellie could see that, apart from wine and beer, there wasn't much else in there. If that was his only fridge, she could understand why he'd bought so much at the market.

She finally gave up looking for a vase when she found a jug. She filled it with water and decided it would do.

The lack of possessions made her wonder if James hadn't lived here long. Maybe he was still unpacking. 'Have you just moved in?' she asked as she put the jug of irises onto the bench and took the glass of wine he handed her.

'No, I've lived here for a few years but I'm thinking of selling.'

She wondered why he hadn't bothered buying furniture but she supposed he had his reasons. 'How can you bear to move away from the views?'

'There are plenty of views around Sydney if you can afford them. This was convenient when I worked at the Royal North Shore but driving across the harbour is a hassle, even with the tunnel. I want to be closer to Eastern Beaches.'

Ellie pulled out a kitchen stool and swivelled it so she could see both the view and James, where he stood beginning preparations for their lunch. 'But where's all your furniture?' Her gaze travelled around the room again. Everything was in neutral shades, stone, latte and white, and even the modern sofa was in neutral, stone leather, plain and simple without any decorative cushions to give it some added colour. Even some aqua- or maybe lime-coloured cushions on the sofa would give the room a lift, she thought.

The tiled floor was clean but cold; there was one small, white rug in front of the sofa but no coffee table. Several of the walls were blank, their clean expanses broken only by empty hooks, hooks that must have remained after the paintings had been removed. There were a few photos scattered around and some childish artworks in primary colours covered one section of the wall but even these were arranged haphazardly. 'Have you "decluttered" to put in on the market?' she asked.

'My ex took half of everything.'

'Ex? When?' Ellie wondered how long James had been living in this sterile atmosphere. She couldn't imagine living like this for more than a couple of weeks. Had he been in a relationship very recently?

'A few months ago,' he said as he put a platter of cheese, pâté and biscuits in front of her. 'When I called off the wedding she decided she deserved some compensation and she took it in the form of the furniture.'

Ellie nearly choked on her wine. 'You were engaged?' Hadn't he told her he was never getting married? An ex-girlfriend she'd expected but an ex-fiancée was a bit of a surprise.

'Is she going to get half the house too?' Was that why he was selling?

'No. I was lucky.' He shrugged. 'She could have argued that after being engaged for two years she was entitled to more. I was happy to give her the furniture in exchange for my independence.'

Forget the furniture, Ellie thought. What was the point of a two-year engagement? Surely the idea of an engagement was to get married. 'Two years! Who has a two-year engagement?' she asked.

'Not many people,' he admitted.

'What happened?' Ellie hoped he wouldn't mind talking about it. After all, he'd brought up the topic.

'I'm not sure. We were both really busy at work, she's a doctor too, and I guess I thought we had plenty of time. There was no hurry. But as our friends who got engaged after us started getting married before us she started to get into the whole wedding frenzy. And when she wanted to set a date I realised I just couldn't do it.'

'What do you mean, you couldn't do it?'

He shrugged. 'Our relationship had lost all the spark it'd ever had. And when we realised that, I realised I didn't want to fix it. I was concentrating on my career, expecting our relationship to take care of itself, and when that wasn't the case I realised I didn't really care enough to change. I didn't want to commit. I didn't want to make more of an effort. When I thought about it honestly I couldn't imagine spending the rest of my life with her. I realised I didn't love her and I knew that if we got married we'd end up divorced.'

'Why on earth did you get engaged in the first place, then?'

'I don't know.' He paused for a moment, as though trying to remember his reasons. 'She moved in and it seemed like the next step in our relationship.' He paused, as if trying to remember just what had gone wrong. 'I think all relationships go the same way. They start off as all consuming and you can't possibly expect that to last. That's why I'm not planning on getting married. I nearly made the mistake once and only a fool makes the same mistake twice. Marriage isn't for me.'

Ellie tried to put a positive spin on his revelation.

He was single, he was gorgeous and whether or not he thought he was marriage material was of no consequence to her. In fact, it was perfect. He was just what she needed to restore her confidence in herself and in men. He was honest and sexy and into her. He made her feel beautiful and, after Rob's deceptions had destroyed her confidence, James's attention was helping to restore it.

It didn't matter to her whether he intended to get married or not, he was only in her life temporarily. She was trying to live in the moment. She didn't need to waste time imagining a future with him. He'd made it perfectly clear where he stood on that issue, so all she needed to do was enjoy him. She knew the rules. She could handle this.

'How are things with you and James?' Jess asked as she and Ellie climbed into Adam's car. Adam was overseas again after a brief visit home and they were borrowing his car as it was the only one at their disposal and they needed to get to their wine-appreciation class. This was the fourth class in the programme but they'd missed the second because Jess had had a clash with her shifts and the third one as Ellie had gone out with James. 'I assume it's all going well seeing as I've hardly seen you for a few weeks.'

'It hasn't been that long, has it?' Ellie replied as Jess turned out of Hill Street and headed towards Bondi.

But Ellie knew Jess had a valid point. In the weeks since James had first kissed her, in the weeks since they'd first slept together, she knew she'd been swept up in the excitement of a new relationship. It was her way. It was all-consuming. When she was with James he was all she could think about and when she wasn't with him he was still all she was thinking about. It was only through sheer force of will and habit that she was able to stay focussed at work but when he was on the ward with her, when she was surrounded by their bubble, it was terribly difficult.

'Is he going to meet us at the Stat Bar later?'

Ellie shook her head. 'I don't think so. He's having dinner with his mother.'

Jess gave her a sidelong glance. 'Is that why you can make it to the class tonight?'

Between work and James she hadn't had a lot of time for her friends. She knew she'd been neglecting them but she wasn't strong enough to deny herself the pleasure that was James so whenever he was available she was with him.

'Yep, sorry.' Jess was right: if James had been free Ellie probably would have ditched the class in his favour.

'Don't apologise. I'm guessing the sex must be good: he's certainly keeping you occupied.'

Ellie laughed. 'The sex is fantastic but it's about more than that. I feel like we belong together. Like I belong with him.'

'And you didn't feel like that with Rob?' Jess asked as she flicked the car headlights on.

'Not really. I never really knew where I was with Rob. I never knew when I would see him and it was all very secretive. I thought it was just his reserved English nature and I thought it was sweet that he wanted to keep me to himself but there was always part of Rob that he kept locked up and now I know why. Obviously there was a lot of stuff he was hiding but with James everything just feels open and honest.'

'So he doesn't have a wife and kids stashed somewhere?'

'Not that I could see,' Ellie replied. The ex-fiancée didn't count, there was no need to mention her. 'We talk about everything.' They spent almost as much time talking as they did making love and she felt they had no secrets.

'So he knows you want to get married and have babies?'

'Okay, so there are a few things he doesn't know about me but they're irrelevant.'

'Irrelevant! For as long as I've known you, your primary goal has been to get married and have a family. Don't you think you might be setting yourself up for more heartache if ultimately he doesn't want the same things as you?' Jess asked.

'We're just having fun. Those things don't matter.'

'Since when?'

'Since I'm trying something different. Remember, I've taken your advice. I'm choosing a man because he's a good man, not because he'd make a good father.' How could she explain there was no reason to tell him about her plans when he'd made it perfectly clear he never intended to get married? 'He's my experiment. I don't expect that the chemistry we have can last, it's too fierce. It burns like a supernova. So there's no need to tell him about my future plans. I expect he'll be long gone by then.'

Jess turned the car around a corner and veered wide to get past a van that was parked very close to the intersection. 'Mmm,' she said as she glanced at Ellie, 'just make sure you don't fall in love with him before the attraction extinguishes itself, then.'

Ellie was pretty sure she had things under control. Knowing James didn't plan on getting married had immediately changed her perception of their relationship. Her heart was safe, she thought. She wasn't going to fall in love.

Out of the corner of her eye she saw a flash of movement. Someone was running. Running straight towards them. 'Look out!' she yelled, but her warning was too late. Too late for them and too late for the jogger.

She heard a thud as the jogger collided with the front left corner of the car before bouncing off the vehicle. Ellie was thrown forward against her seat belt as Jess slammed on the brakes. She saw the man fly backwards and land on the kerb in a tangle of bloodied limbs. Long, lean limbs. Long, lean limbs, olive skin and curly dark hair.

'Oh, my God. James.'

CHAPTER EIGHT

JESS pulled the car to a stop at the kerb. Out of habit Ellie made the sign of the cross with one hand while she undid her seat belt and threw open the car door with the other. 'Call an ambulance,' she said to Jess as she jumped out of the car and slammed the door behind her.

Her heart was in her throat as she darted to the sidewalk. 'James?'

She knelt down beside him.

The crumpled figure lying on the edge of the road was a boy, not a man.

It wasn't James. A surge of relief flooded through her even as she acknowledged that this person was still injured and still needed her help. His right leg was twisted at an awkward angle and he had a dazed expression on his face. He was looking at her but Ellie was certain he wasn't really seeing her.

She put one hand on his bare arm, making contact, trying to get him to focus. 'My name is Ellie. I'm a nurse. I think you've broken your leg but I need to know if you're hurt anywhere else.'

There was still no reply but neither was there silence. Ellie could hear music and she realised then that the boy had headphones in his ears and one had fallen out. It was his music she could hear playing.

Was that why he wasn't responding? Couldn't he hear her? She reached over and removed the other earphone, letting it hang, just as Jess arrived.

'Are you all right? I'm so sorry, I didn't see you until you were right in front of us.' Jess crouched down beside Ellie as she spoke to the still silent youth.

'Did you call the ambulance?' Ellie asked her.

Jess nodded. 'They're on their way.'

'Do you think there's a blanket in the car? We need to keep him warm.' He was wearing a thin singlet and shorts, running clothes, and Ellie knew his body temperature would drop quickly with the combination of the cool evening air and the shock. Jess returned to the car to see what she could find.

Maybe shock was the reason he wasn't talking. She kept trying to elicit a response. 'Can you tell me your name?'

'Harry.'

Finally she was getting somewhere. 'Okay, Harry, other than your leg, can you tell me if anything else hurts? Can you move your fingers for me?'

Harry opened and closed his fists.

Maybe simple questions were the way to go. 'What about moving your elbows?'

He turned his head to look at her and Ellie had another flash of recognition. There was definitely something about him that reminded her of James. They had similar colouring and the same lean frames but it was more than that. Maybe the angle of his jaw or the way he held his head was familiar but she couldn't immediately pinpoint it. Harry had straightened his right elbow but as he attempted to repeat this movement on his left side he gasped with pain and Ellie's attention was brought back to the matter at hand.

'Where does that hurt?' she asked.

'My shoulder.'

'Okay, we'll leave your arm for now.' Ellie touched his left leg, 'Try to move your foot on this side for me. Can you move it around in a circle?' She knew he'd done some damage to his right leg, her guess was a fractured tibia, but she wanted to know if his left side had escaped unscathed. Harry managed to complete that movement without significant discomfort just as Jess returned with a beach towel.

'This was all I could find,' she said as she draped it around his shoulders.

'That'll do,' Ellie said.

She could hear sirens approaching and she hoped that waiting for ambulances wasn't going to become a regular occurrence for her. It was only a few weeks ago that she and James had waited for the ambulance in Kings Cross and Ellie could scarcely believe how much had happened since then.

The ambulance turned into the street closely followed by a police car. As the paramedics emerged from their vehicle Ellie met them to hand over Harry's care and Jess approached the police to give them a statement. Ellie saw the police breathalysing Jess and she thought it was lucky they'd been on their way to the wine-appreciation class, not on their way home afterwards, although she knew the few sips they had while tasting wouldn't have caused problems. She knew they weren't going to make the class at all now, there would be no point by the time they'd finished up here.

The paramedics attended to Harry and took him off to hospital, where the police would get a statement from him later, but in the meantime they got a second statement from Ellie to confirm Jess' story.

'I saw him, but not in time to warn Jess. He just appeared from nowhere, well, from behind that van,' Ellie explained, pointing to the white van behind them. 'He ran straight out into the road, he didn't stop to look. He had headphones in his ears, and was listening to music.'

'How do you know that?'

'Because when I got out to help him I could hear the music coming through his headphones. It was pretty loud, I doubt he would have heard our car coming.'

The policeman jotted the details in his notebook before checking Jess's breathalyser results. He turned to her. 'Your blood-alcohol reading is 0.0. You're free to go but you'll both need to come into the station in a day or two to sign your statements when we've had a chance to type them up.'

Ellie and Jess did a quick inspection of Adam's car. There was a dent in the front passenger side panel but nothing that would stop them from driving home.

Jess pulled a face. 'Do you think he'll go spare?'

'No, it's just a car. He'd be more worried about the kid we hit,' Ellie replied.

'I wonder how much it'll cost to repair.'

'I wouldn't worry, his insurance should cover it. If we need to we can split the excess,' Ellie said as she opened the driver's door. 'Come on, I'll drive us home.'

James headed straight for the orthopaedic ward in the morning. He was worried about Ellie. When she'd phoned to tell him about the accident he'd offered to leave the dinner he was having with his mother to make sure she was okay, he knew his mum would understand, but Ellie had insisted that both she and Jess were fine and the boy they had hit would be okay too. But still he'd been worried. He knew it could be several hours before the reality of the episode sank in and he was worried about the girls going into shock.

Knowing Ellie and Jess had company in the form of Tilly and Ruby had eased his conscience slightly but he still wanted to see her this morning, just to make certain. It was Ellie's sense of fragility that bothered him. That feeling he had that she needed looking after. He thought he knew the reason behind it now—her family history would have contributed, he was certain—and even though she had her surrogate family, he wanted to be the one she turned to. He couldn't imagine what it would be like to be totally alone in the world and he wanted to be the one she could depend on.

He wondered when he'd made that decision. At work he was happy to have that responsibility, he'd been trained for it. He'd done years of study to equip him for those situations but he didn't want the same responsibility in his personal life. What if people depended on him and he let them down?

But it was different with Ellie. At least for the moment. He was prepared to be the one for her, for now. Short-term commitment was all he was thinking about. It was all he could offer.

He saw her the minute he stepped out of the lift. She appeared to be pacing the ward and the moment she sighted him she flew to his side.

'James!' She grabbed hold of his arm. 'Come with me.' She pulled him into the doorway of the doctors' lounge, out of the way of the main corridor and out of the way of the passing parade of people.

'What's the matter?'

'That boy we hit last night, he's been admitted to the ward.'

He knew the boy had sustained orthopaedic injuries and it was no surprise that he would be in this hospital, Eastern Beaches was the closest facility, but Ellie's brow was furrowed with concern and there was a small crease above the bridge of her nose. James wondered if the boy's injuries were more serious than they'd first thought. He wondered if that was going to cause a problem for Jess. 'Is there a problem?'

'I'm not sure. His name is Harry, Harry Leonardi. Do you know him?'

'Leonardi?' They had the same surname? James thought for a moment before shaking his head. Harry Leonardi wasn't a name he was familiar with. 'No, I don't think so.'

'Oh, I thought he might be related to you.'

'I've never heard of him. I'm sure there are plenty of Leonardis in Sydney.'

'But he looks just like you.'

'In what way?'

'He's got the same build as you, he's quite lean and his eyes are dark chocolate brown, like yours.'

'That could describe about a quarter of the males in Australia,' James said.

'I guess so,' she agreed.

'Was that all?' He should have bitten his tongue but it was too late, the words were out. He shouldn't have asked. He didn't want to know. But Ellie was telling him.

'It must be more than that 'cos he definitely reminds me of you. His smile is different but maybe the shape of his face...'

'Well, it doesn't really matter how similar we look, I've still never heard of him.'

'It's weird, though. He's almost the spitting image of how I imagine you would've looked at the same age.'

'What do you mean?'

'He could be a younger version of you.'

James could feel the blood drain from his face. 'How much younger?'

'He's fifteen.'

Fifteen years younger.

The hollow feeling in his gut was back. A feeling he'd first experienced eighteen years ago. As though someone had punched him hard enough to wind him and at the same time had ripped his heart out. He swallowed hard and forced himself to take a breath.

'Fifteen? What's he doing on our ward—shouldn't he be in Paediatrics?' He tried to concentrate. This 'Harry' wasn't an adult, he shouldn't be here.

'His growth plates are fused, and in Orthopaedics that means he's treated as an adult.'

James knew that was hospital policy but the shock had made him overlook the obvious explanation.

'Who is the admitting doctor?' he asked, mentally holding his breath while he waited for the answer, hoping it wasn't Rob Coleman. That could mean *he* could end up being responsible for this patient. Responsible for a fifteen-year-old boy with an identical surname.

'Bill Abbott,' Ellie answered.

Good. With any luck this Harry Leonardi would be a random stranger and nothing at all to do with him.

'Which room is he in?' he asked. There was no reason for him to cross paths with this patient or with any of his visitors but he'd make sure he kept well out of the way. Just in case.

'He's in Bed Twelve. Did you want to see him?' Ellie offered.

'No!' he replied as his pager buzzed on his hip. He'd heard enough about Harry Leonardi. He wanted nothing to do with him. 'I'd better answer this, I'm due in Theatre,' he said as he backed away quickly, leaving Ellie standing in the corridor with a slightly puzzled expression on her face. Perhaps she thought he was behaving strangely but he wasn't about to explain himself. 'I'll catch up with you later,' he said to her as he fled the ward in favour of

Theatre. If theatre was as far away from Harry Leonardi as he could get then that's where he'd go.

Hours later Ellie was still puzzled about James's strange reaction to her ponderings about Harry Leonardi. She couldn't understand what the big deal was. She shrugged. So she thought James looked a bit like the kid. It wasn't a major drama yet James had reacted as if she'd handed him a live grenade. She wondered if he would mention the incident again tonight.

She looked in the mirror as she dusted eye shadow over her eyelids. She could see James's reflection in her bedroom mirror as she applied her make-up. He was lying on her bed, watching her get ready. He was dressed in an immaculate dark suit, a brooding contrast to the white linen of her bed and the colourful array of her discarded clothes that surrounded him. She'd tried on half a dozen outfits before finally choosing a simple black dress, which was now hanging on her bedroom door. She was wearing a bra and matching knickers. James was fully dressed. She leant forward to brush mascara onto her lashes and she could feel his eyes on her backside.

She looked at his reflection again and her heart skipped a beat. His eyes had darkened, they were almost jet black now. Their colour intensified in direct proportion to an increase in his level of desire. He didn't look like he was thinking about Harry Leonardi.

She wished she had time to take advantage of the hunger she could see in his expression but they were already going to be late for dinner. Normally that wouldn't bother her but it was a work dinner and she didn't want to turn up looking as though they'd just climbed out of bed. And she knew that was how she'd look. Her eyes would be bright, shining with satisfaction, her cheeks would be flushed and her lips would be swollen from James's kisses.

He was perfect. He was smart, gorgeous and kind. He was funny, gentle and honest. He was delicious. He was everything she'd ever dreamed of except for one thing. His only flaw was that he was a committed bachelor. But that was only a flaw in *her* eyes.

She knew he was only going to be a temporary man in her life yet she couldn't imagine her life without him any more. That was when she knew he was going to break her heart when he left her. And he would leave. If he didn't, she would. She would have to. She still wanted to get married. But first she'd have to get over him. But she didn't need to get over him just yet.

She watched as he shifted his gaze from her backside to her face, meeting her eyes in the mirror. She forced herself to break eye contact. James seemed to be able to read her mind and they really didn't have time to fool around before dinner. She picked up her lipstick and applied the colour to her lips, capping the stick as James checked his watch. He got up from the bed and crossed the room. He kissed the back of her neck and his hands were unusually cool on her shoulders. 'You'd better get dressed—we don't want to be late.'

Ellie let him zip her into her cocktail dress before she slipped her shoes on and took his hand to walk the short distance to the Coogee Surf Lifesaving Club for dinner to say farewell to the retiring CNC from the orthopaedic ward.

After main course had been served and eaten, Ellie stepped out onto the balcony that overlooked the Pacific Ocean. The balcony was deserted save for one solitary figure. As her eyes adjusted to the gloom Ellie realised it was Rob. James was fetching their dessert and bringing it to her but she had no idea how long he'd be and she had no desire to be alone with Rob. He was the last person she wanted to be trapped on a balcony with.

'Sorry, I didn't realise anyone else was out here,' she said and turned to leave.

'You're welcome to stay. Don't feel you need to leave on my account,' Rob said.

'It's okay, I'm going to go and get my dessert.' Ellie made an excuse and turned around and almost collided with Penny Coleman as she tried to make her escape. She had just enough time to see Penny register her face before she looked at her husband and judging by Penny's expression she didn't look happy with the situation. Ellie had thought being on the balcony alone with Rob was bad but it seemed the only thing worse was being out there with Rob and his wife. She tried to step around Penny but she blocked her path. Ellie stepped to the other side but Penny blocked her a second time. Ellie stopped.

'What are you doing?' she asked.

'I have something to say to you,' Penny replied. 'Stay away from my husband.'

Ellie frowned. Being on the balcony with Rob had been perfectly innocent. 'What on earth are you talking about?'

'I'm warning you, I don't want you anywhere near him.'

'I—'

Penny cut her off. 'I didn't come halfway around the world to find my husband in bed with another woman, and if you think I'm going to ignore the fact that you were having an affair with him then you're sorely mistaken. I'm warning you—stay away from him.' Penny punctuated her words with a pointed finger, stabbing Ellie in the chest with her final few words.

Penny's grievance had nothing to do with tonight, Ellie realized, and she wondered how much Penny knew. She batted Penny's hand away. 'I think you should be having this conversation with Rob.'

'I have discussed this with Rob,' Penny said with a quick glare in her husband's direction. 'I've told him and now I'm telling you. Keep your hands off my husband.'

Ellie wasn't going to stand there and be bullied by Rob's wife. She bit back. 'I would never have got involved with him if I'd known he was someone's husband. Did he tell you he *forgot* to mention he was married?' Now it was her turn to glare at Rob. She couldn't believe he was standing there, mute. He'd obviously told Penny a version of events that suited him, though why he'd told her anything at all Ellie couldn't imagine. 'There was no sign that he was married, no wedding ring, and there was not one photo of you *or* your daughter in the apartment. I never heard him take a phone call from you and he never said a word until the end. Nothing. When he did remember to inform me I refused to see him again.' Over Penny's left shoulder she could see James walking towards the balcony doors. She had to get out of there. Quickly. 'I'm sorry that you two obviously have some issues and I'm very sorry that Rob has been unfaithful to you but I'm not the one to blame.'

She stepped around Penny and this time Penny let her go, turning to watch her leave. But before Ellie could escape from the balcony James appeared, carrying dessert. The air was thick with tension and James walked straight into the middle of it. This was worse than being trapped out here with Rob and Penny. *This* was now her worst nightmare.

James looked from Ellie's panic-stricken face to Penny's angry one. 'What's going on?'

'Nothing.' Ellie answered quickly, wanting to jump in before Penny had a chance to say anything. 'Can you just give us a minute?'

But Penny wasn't so easily deterred. She looked at James. 'They've been having an affair.'

'What?' James looked completely stunned. 'That's ridiculous. You can't accuse someone of such absurd behaviour. Ellie is my girlfriend.'

Oh, God, was he going to choose this moment to come to her rescue, to be her knight in shining armour? If the situation wasn't so disastrous she would have been thrilled at his announcement but under the circumstances she feared that the status quo was about to change. She couldn't bear to think that this was how James was going to find out about her affair. She'd thought it was probably inevitable but she didn't want it to happen like this, in a public showdown with the wronged wife.

'She might be your girlfriend now but who was she sleeping with before you? Ask her that! I don't want her anywhere near my husband.' Penny spat her reply at James before turning to Ellie. 'I'm going to get you transferred. You're going to be out on your tiny little backside.' And with those vindictive words ringing in Ellie's ears, Penny grabbed Rob's arm and dragged him away, leaving Ellie and James on the balcony.

Ellie was shaking. She couldn't bring herself to look at James. She didn't want to see the questions in his eyes.

'Is it true?' His voice was quiet but she could hear the hurt in his words. 'Did you have an affair?'

'Not exactly,' she said. She looked over the balcony at the ocean. The moon was reflecting on the water and she thought how beautiful it would all be if her day wasn't such a disaster.

'What does that mean?' James asked. 'Were you involved with him or weren't you? I would have thought it's a simple question with a yes or no answer.'

The truth was all she could give him. 'We did have a relationship but I didn't know he was married. No one did.'

'And how is it that no one has been gossiping about you? You work in the same department, people must have known.'

'Rob was adamant that his private life stayed private. He said he didn't want to be fodder for gossip. No one knew we were dating. It was only when I found out he was married that I realised why he was so insistent on that.'

'How *did* you find out?'

'He told me a week or so before Penny arrived.'

'What happened then?'

'I called him all sorts of names and told him I wanted nothing more to do with him.'

James smiled then and it wasn't until that moment that Ellie realised how terrified she'd been that he wouldn't believe her. That he'd think she'd willingly have an affair. 'Were you ever going to tell me about it?'

'No.'

'Why not?'

'I was embarrassed, ashamed.'

'All those times that Rob was coming down hard on you at work, was that why?' James was leaning on the balcony beside her, their dessert abandoned on a table, forgotten. He put his hand on her arm and the warmth of his fingers cheered her. 'You should have told me then. I could have spoken to him.'

'I could handle it.'

'But you shouldn't have to. That's harassment. I could have stopped it.'

'He said if I told anyone about the relationship it would cost me my job.'

'He'd fire you? He doesn't have that power.'

'You heard what Penny said,' Ellie replied. 'I think he

could make it happen or at the very least get me transferred to a different department. And I love my job, I wasn't
going to risk that. The relationship was over, there was
nothing to gain by telling you or anyone else about it.
Nothing to gain but a lot to lose so I kept quiet.'

'Do you want me to speak to him now?'

'No!' Ellie just wanted to pretend that none of this had
ever happened. 'That would just make matters worse.
Please just let it go. He means nothing to me. The thing
that bothered me most was not being able to talk to you
when Rob had a go at me at work. Because of his threats I
was too scared to say anything. I thought, if just one other
person knew, it would be harder for him to get me sacked.
And now you know. Now I can talk to you. That's all that
matters.'

She turned towards him, seeking comfort in his familiar
embrace. In her mind nothing would go wrong as long as
she was with James. In her eyes he was as close to perfect
as a man could be. She'd been so terrified of him finding
out about Rob, knowing that part of her history, but he'd
taken it all in his stride. He'd defended her. He'd believed
in her. And that's when she knew her heart was in serious
jeopardy.

She was falling for him. Despite all her resolutions, despite her bravado, she knew she was in danger of falling in
love.

She'd have to be careful. She couldn't fall in love. She
hadn't counted on that. And neither had James.

James was holding her against his chest. The top button of his shirt was undone. She stretched her hand up and
undid the next button, and the next, and ran her fingers
under the fabric and over the smooth, warm expanse of
his chest. She kissed his skin. He tasted of limes.

'Shall we sneak off early?' she suggested. 'No one is going to miss us.'

His answering smile was the only encouragement she needed. She took his hand and escaped down the outside stairs. She would take him home. He would distract her and she'd forget all about Rob Coleman and his wife. She would share her bed with James and she'd try not to fall in love.

CHAPTER NINE

ELLIE usually slept soundly when James shared her bed but last night had been an exception. She'd been worried about his reaction when he learned of her dalliance with Rob and his calm acceptance of the situation should have reassured her yet she'd slept fitfully. The confrontation with Penny had frightened her and despite James's company she'd woken feeling exhausted.

She still had an hour to go on her shift but she could feel her eyelids drooping. She needed some caffeine if she was going to last until three. She was about to grab a coffee when Harry Leonardi's bell rang. She had to check on him first.

When she got to his bedside she was struck again by how similar he was to James. Their colouring was almost identical, the same black hair, chocolate eyes and dark, perfectly shaped eyebrows. His jaw wasn't quite as strong and he was lacking the shadow of a beard but that was possibly just the difference that age made.

'Sorry to bother you,' he said as she stood beside him, 'but I need to go to the toilet.' He gave her a slightly embarrassed grin and that was when Ellie could see a difference. A smile always transformed a face and Harry's smile was different from James's. Smiling, they looked less alike.

Maybe she was being silly, she thought. Plenty of people had dark colouring.

She handed him a bottle and pulled the curtain around his bed to give him some privacy. 'I'll be back in a minute.'

Plenty of people had dark colouring but they weren't all called 'Leonardi', were they? And surely Leonardi wasn't a common name. She couldn't shake the feeling that there was a connection but James was adamant that he didn't know Harry.

She used the few minutes she'd allowed Harry to return to the nurses' station to check his notes. She flicked to his personal details, looking for his next of kin. Father's name, Antony Leonardi. Mother, Lucinda Parsons. She wasn't sure what she'd expected to see but that told her nothing.

She felt, rather than saw, James arrive on the ward. The now familiar humming enveloped her just moments before his scent surrounded her. She quickly turned Harry's case notes over so he wouldn't see what she'd been reading. Not that it mattered. She was allowed to read them but knowing why she was looking through them gave her a guilty conscience. Her perusal had nothing to do with patient care and everything to do with her own curiosity.

James leant over her shoulder and kissed her cheek. 'Hey, gorgeous. How's your day been? Have you seen Rob?'

'It's been a good day actually. Rob was here earlier but everything was fine. I think that situation has been diffused.' It had been a huge relief when Rob had behaved as though nothing had happened. Ellie was hopeful that his threats had been empty ones. 'I'm going to grab a coffee in a minute—have you got time to join me?'

James shook his head. 'I've got to go back to Theatre. We're running behind on our list, but I wanted to check on

Mrs Fisher and Julian Barnes and this gave me an excuse to check on you at the same time.'

'I'm fine, really,' she said as she pulled out the case notes he needed and handed them to him. 'Did you want me to come with you to check your patients? I just need to pop back to Harry Leonardi first.'

'No, no.' James took the case notes and stepped away from the nurses' station. 'I'm in a hurry, I'll be all right,' he said as he raced away.

Ellie shrugged. It wasn't like him to be hurried. The delays in theatre must have been worse than usual, she thought. She tidied up the nurses' station in preparation for handover before she went back to Harry to empty his bottle. As she approached his bed she could hear voices from behind the curtain. That was odd. She hadn't noticed anyone coming into this room.

'Harry, have you finished?' she asked, waiting for Harry's answer before she pulled back the curtain. The visitor was in profile to her and at first glance she thought it was James. But why would James have stopped here? Harry wasn't his patient.

The visitor turned to face her and she realised then he was a lot older than James but with similar build and colouring. This man must be Harry's father. He had the same lean figure and square jaw. Just as James's build was an older version of Harry's, this man's build was an older version of James's.

'Excuse me, is there an ice machine on this floor?' he asked.

Ellie pointed to her right. 'Down by the nurses' station,' she said. She should have offered to refill the jug for him but she was too surprised to think clearly. She frowned as Harry's father walked away. His gait was familiar.

Curiosity got the better of her and she grabbed the bottle

from Harry and took it to the sluice room to empty so she could watch for Harry's father to return. She needed another look at him. She spied a linen trolley that had been left by the sluice room and pushed it along the corridor, using it for some cover as she continued to refold towels that didn't need refolding, waiting.

He was coming back now.

She tried to keep her gaze focussed on the stack of towels as she didn't want him to realise she was checking him over but he wasn't interested in her. He was looking straight past her, down the corridor. She saw him frown.

'James?' she heard him ask.

Ellie turned to her left, following his line of sight. James had come out of Mrs Fisher's room and was walking towards her, walking towards them both. He looked up at the sound of his name and Ellie saw him freeze in his tracks, a look of panic on his face. His eyes darted left and right as though he was looking for an escape. The colour drained from his face, leaving his olive skin pale. There was nowhere to go so he turned around and began walking back in the direction from which he'd come.

'James, wait.' The man called out again and started hurrying after James.

Ellie knew James hadn't noticed her. She was stuck to the spot, she couldn't make herself move and she couldn't look away. It was obvious that Harry's father knew James. There was a connection and she knew she was about to find out the answer she'd been seeking.

The man caught up to James and reached out and grabbed his arm. Not roughly but enough to make James pause. 'Please. Wait.'

Ellie glanced around. The corridor was still empty, save for the three of them. She saw James shake free of the man's hand. Should she call Security? She knew hospital procedure would probably dictate that she should but she still couldn't make herself move.

'Can you give me a minute?' she heard the man ask.

'What for?'

'I just want to talk to you.'

'I have nothing to say to you.'

'Please, listen.'

James shook his head. 'You're eighteen years too late. I'm not interested in hearing anything you have to say. Not any more.'

James walked away again and Ellie waited to see what would happen next. Harry's father took one step in James's direction before he changed his mind and stopped. He turned around and went back to Harry's room, still carrying the jug of ice chips.

Ellie jumped as the fire door at the end of the corridor slammed shut. James had found his escape.

Eighteen years too late. Was that what James had said? What did he mean? Ellie stopped pretending to fold towels and abandoned the trolley, and followed James into the stairwell.

He hadn't gone far. She found him leaning over the railing, staring down to the bottom of the flight of stairs.

'James?' She put her hand on his back. 'Are you okay? What's going on?'

He didn't lift his head. His gaze remained fixed, staring down into the abyss. 'Nothing.'

'That man, Harry's father, do you know him?'

James looked at her now and his expression was one of grief. 'I knew him a long time ago.'

Eighteen years.

It all fell into place for Ellie. The physique, the walk, the name. 'He's your father too.' *That's* why James and Harry were so similar. They were brothers.

But how could James not have known that? 'Did you know who Harry was?' He must have known, she thought. The only explanation could be that he hadn't wanted to tell her.

James shook his head. 'No. I suspected but—'

'Why didn't you tell me?'

'Because it doesn't concern you.'

His words pierced her heart.

'But he's your brother.'

'He's my father's son. That's not the same thing as being my brother. I don't know Harry and I've spoken to my father about twice in the last eighteen years.'

'*Twice* in eighteen years?'

'He left when I was young.'

Ellie remembered James telling her that his father wasn't in the picture. 'I got the impression you didn't know your father.'

'I don't.'

'But—'

James held up a hand, effectively stopping her question. 'I know you think everyone else has an ideal family, I get that, and I know your childhood was far from perfect, but we didn't all grow up in a perfect world. My childhood certainly wasn't idyllic.'

'What happened?' Ellie wondered whether he would tell her or whether he'd tell her again that it didn't concern her. There was a long silence and just when she thought he wasn't going to break it he began to talk.

'Mum and Dad divorced when I was seven. Dad was moving to London with a lawyer he'd met at work, they were getting married. I found out when I was older that Mum had asked him to have marriage counselling, she'd wanted to try to save their marriage, but he wasn't prepared to do that. He walked out on her, on us, as quickly as he could and married Diane. But that marriage didn't last either. And then Dad met Lucinda. She was an Australian in London on a working visa. He divorced Diane to marry her and they came back here to live when I was about twelve. Dad hasn't been part of my life since I was seven.'

'But surely you saw him when he returned to Australia?'

'Once or twice,' James admitted.

Ellie frowned. 'Did he live interstate?' A shake of his head was the reply. 'Didn't he try to keep in touch with you?'

'For a while but I refused to spend weekends at his place. I refused to have anything to do with his new wife and eventually he stopped asking.'

'But why?' This made no sense to her. Why wouldn't James want to see his father? Why wouldn't his father insist they stayed close?

'I was angry.' James wasn't looking at her any more. He was staring into the distance, down the staircase, lost in the past. 'I thought he was moving back to Australia to be a father to my sister and me but it was because his new wife was pregnant and *she* wanted to come home. Dad wasn't coming back for us,' he explained. 'He'd replaced us. He didn't need us any more so I decided I didn't need him. I didn't want to have anything to do with him and his new family.'

'You knew about Harry?'

'I knew I had two half-brothers, Harry must be the younger one, but I've never met them.'

'Never?'

James shook his head.

'Aren't you curious about them at all?'

'No.' He looked at her then, just briefly. 'I don't want anything to do with my father and I don't want anything to do with his new family.' He took two steps down into the stairwell, obviously intending to have the final word. 'I need to get back to Theatre.'

And he was gone.

Ellie sank onto a concrete step as James disappeared down the stairs. The concrete was cold and hard but she barely noticed. She checked her watch. It felt as though hours had passed but it was actually only minutes. Her shift would be over soon and she needed to get back to the ward but she couldn't make herself move. She was stunned. She couldn't reconcile the conversation she'd just had with the person she thought she knew. Where had the considerate, thoughtful, generous James gone? The one who chose lime and coconut pie because he knew it was her favourite flavour, the one who massaged her aching feet at night, the one who brought chocolates to Hill Street for all the girls or spent the extra few pre-op minutes to calm an anxious patient. What had happened to him?

His reaction didn't gel with the man she thought she knew and if he thought he could avoid this topic by escaping to Theatre he was wrong. He couldn't pretend his family didn't exist. She couldn't let him. In her opinion there was nothing more important than family.

Ellie wandered aimlessly around the house. She couldn't relax, wound tight following the events of the afternoon. She grabbed a hat and left the house. Turning right, she headed for the beach. A walk would probably do her good, and the fresh air might clear her mind. She walked for over an hour, accompanied by her thoughts, but they didn't become any clearer. She was on the home stretch when she heard someone calling her name. James was coming towards her.

'I'm glad I found you.' He didn't give her a chance to say anything before he pulled her into his arms, hugging her tight. 'I'm sorry,' he said. His voice was muffled, his mouth was pressed against the top of her head, but she heard his words clearly enough. 'I handled things badly this afternoon.'

Ellie felt herself relax. The stress of the afternoon melted away under his touch, evaporating into the atmosphere, carried away on a breath of lime. He was back, the James she knew. Everything would be all right. She wrapped her arms around him as she let her head rest against his chest. His heart beat was loud in her ear. 'It's okay. I know it must have been a shock to see your father today. Eighteen years is a long time.'

'A shock is a bit of an understatement,' he said as he stepped back, taking her hand in his and leading her to a wooden bench that overlooked the ocean. He pulled her onto his lap.

'How are you feeling now?' He was holding onto her as if his life depended on it. He had obviously been quite thrown by the events of the day.

'I'm not sure. It's surreal really. I had an image in my head of how it would be if I ever ran into my father. What I would do. What I would say. But today was nothing like I'd imagined. Instead of behaving like a mature, thirty-year-old all I could think of, all I could feel, was the anger and hurt that I'd felt all those years ago.'

'Do you think you might want to see your father? Or Harry?'

James shook his head. 'No, that's not what I came to tell you. I have no intention of having a relationship of any sort with my father or his family.'

'You're going to ignore your own brothers, your own flesh and blood? How can you do that?' Ellie had been certain he would at least want to see Harry.

'My father left me. He walked out. As far as I'm concerned, he made his choice.'

Ellie was amazed. 'I would do anything to have someone to call mine, a parent, a sibling, a grandparent, a cousin even. Jess, Ruby and Tilly are the closest thing I've got to a family and they're fabulous and I'm very lucky but it's not the same. I can't believe you don't want to know them.'

'I have a family. I have my mother and my sister.'

'You also have two brothers. You have a sibling, right here, under your nose. Are you going to pretend he doesn't exist?'

'He's a half-brother. He's my sibling in name only.'

'I would always choose family,' she said.

'But I have two families to choose between. As did my father. He chose his new family and I'm choosing my old one.'

'But you're upset because your father *did* make a choice. Can't you see that by refusing to meet Harry you're repeating the pattern?' She tried to get him to see her point of view. Tried to get him to see that his reasoning didn't make sense.

'Just drop it, Ellie, this is not a decision you get to make. This has nothing to do with you. I don't know Harry and he doesn't know me.'

'Would you meet Harry if I asked you to?'

'I'm sorry, Ellie, I can't do it. Not for you, not for anyone. Surely you can understand. Can you imagine a father who would walk away from his family, leaving them without looking back? Off to start a brand-new life. Not once, but twice. What sort of a man would do that? That's not someone I want in my life.'

'But that doesn't stop you from getting to know Harry.'

'No, but Harry's a reminder that my father didn't want

us. I don't need my father. I don't need any of them. Can you respect that it's my decision?'

Ellie was watching him as he spoke. She could see the stubborn set of his jaw, the muscle bulging below his ear as he clenched his teeth. He meant every word. His mind was made up and he wasn't going to be swayed.

Had she misjudged his character too? She couldn't believe she was such a poor judge of human nature. Sure, she'd been fooled by Rob but she thought that had taught her a lesson. But now James was showing her a side of him that she hadn't expected. Or was he? Had there been glimpses of this independent streak and she just hadn't been paying attention? Had she not been listening?

He'd said all along he was a confirmed bachelor and he had one broken engagement to prove it. She wondered how much of it was due to his father's track record—three marriages was a lot by anyone's standards. But had she ignored all his words in the vain hope that he'd change his mind? She knew she had. She knew she'd been hoping they'd have a chance of a future. But if he wasn't going to open his heart to his brothers, how could she hope he'd open his heart to her.

He'd always been honest with her. Perhaps he meant it when he said he didn't need a family.

But she did.

Her desire for family overshadowed everything.

She couldn't believe he could pretend his family didn't exist. She couldn't love a man like that.

Love? Where had that idea come from?

Did she love him?

She was quiet for a moment. Thinking. Feeling. That empty spot in her heart, that spot waiting to be filled, wasn't empty any more. James had filled it. She loved him.

But her idea of a family was more important to her than anything.

Was it more important to her than James? She knew she couldn't have both but could she give him up? She didn't know.

Perhaps if he'd been willing to compromise, willing to meet Harry even, there would have been some hope. Hope that maybe one day he'd give up his bachelor life and choose a family of his own. But looking at him now he seemed so certain, so determined, and she couldn't afford to wait and see. It would only end in a broken heart. She needed to protect herself.

'You're right, it's your decision. I have to respect that but I don't agree. Family is more important to me than anything else.'

'Can we agree to disagree?'

She shook her head. 'I think I understand why you feel this way but I can't reconcile that with the man I thought I knew and it's at odds with everything I believe. I need some time to think.'

'What are you saying?'

'I don't think this relationship is going to work. I have to respect your decision but I can't abide by it. I can't see you any more, James.' Maybe she was being unreasonable but she couldn't open her heart to him any further. She couldn't take the chance. Only a fool would willingly give away her heart, knowing it would be crushed.

CHAPTER TEN

ELLIE was lying on her back on the garden swing. It was a beautiful day, not that she'd noticed. She had a hat covering her face, hiding her from the world like an ostrich with its head buried in the sand. She had one leg hanging over the side of the swing and every now and then she'd push off the ground with her toes, giving the swing a little momentum. She found the gentle rocking motion soothing.

She was supposed to be at work but she'd begged one of the other nurses to swap a shift with her. She'd had yesterday off but she needed another day. She couldn't face going back to the hospital.

Work had been horrendous and she'd spent most of her past two shifts fighting back tears. Working with James had been torturous and she'd struggled to get through the day. She had hoped he'd come after her. Had hoped he'd find her and tell her he loved her. Had hoped he'd tell her she was right and that he would get to know Harry. But, of course, he hadn't done any of those things.

Her heart couldn't cope with another day on the ward with him. Another day knowing he was no longer hers. She should have stuck to her plan of not dating orthopods. She should never have got involved.

She'd needed a 'mental health day'. A day to lie in the garden and wallow in her misfortune. Her heart ached.

She'd never understood that expression before but she did now. She could actually feel her heart in her chest and it ached, just like a torn and bruised muscle, and made it difficult to breathe. She wasn't actually sick, there wasn't anything wrong with her that a doctor could fix. Not a regular doctor anyway. Her illness could only be cured by Dr Leonardi and she didn't think he was going to be around any time soon.

She heard the telltale squeak of the front gate as someone entered the garden. Fixing the gate was still on Tilly's to-do list. Tilly had visions of herself as a handywoman and she had a list a mile long of all the things she was going to fix in her spare time. The trouble was she hardly ever had the time even though she had the inclination.

Ellie lifted the brim of her hat and turned her head to see who the intruder was. Disappointment surged through her when she saw Ruby and Tilly coming through the gate. Despite everything, part of her had hoped it would be James.

The movement of the swing caught the girls' attention and they changed course and headed across the garden. Ellie sat up, making room for them to sit beside her.

'Hi,' she said, as she sniffed and rubbed her nose.

Ruby was peering at her, trying to see behind her sunglasses. 'Are you all right?'

'Not really,' Ellie admitted.

'What's happened?'

'Remember when Jess and I had the car accident and we hit that boy, the one who was jogging?' She paused, waiting for the girls to nod. 'He's James's brother.'

'Really? Why haven't you told us?' Ruby asked.

'Because I didn't know.'

'James didn't tell you?' Tilly responded, obviously thinking that was what had upset Ellie.

'He didn't know either,' she admitted. 'Well,' she clarified, 'he wasn't sure.'

'What do you mean, "he wasn't sure"? That doesn't make any sense.'

'His parents are divorced and his father remarried and had a second family. James knew he had two half-brothers but he didn't know one was Harry,' Ellie explained.

'I don't understand why this has upset you,' Ruby said.

'Because James doesn't want to know about Harry, he doesn't want anything to do with him.'

'But why are you upset about that? James must have his reasons. Surely he can do what he likes,' Tilly commented.

'James doesn't want to have anything to do with his own family!' Didn't *anyone* get why this was such a big deal? 'How could I have fallen in love with someone who has no need for family?'

'You're in love with him?' Ruby and Tilly spoke in unison.

'I thought he was supposed to be your transition person,' Ruby continued, 'your experiment?'

'He was but it hasn't turned out quite how I expected. He's the one I've been searching for. He's the one who makes me feel complete.'

'Well, that's a pretty good reason to try to work out your differences. Are you going to try to figure this out or are you going to walk away over a disagreement over a half-brother who means nothing to you or James?' The no-nonsense, practical Tilly was in full flight.

Ellie looked at Tilly. 'I told him that having a family was the most important thing in the world and if he wouldn't make an effort to get to know Harry then I didn't want to be with him.'

'So what? Apologise. Tell him you made a mistake. Tell him you love him.'

Ellie shook her head. 'I *do* love him and I could say the right words but it doesn't change the fact that I think he should meet his brothers and unless he's going to at least consider the idea of opening himself up, he's not the man for me.'

'You realise you could be in a no-win situation, taking that stand.'

'He knows how important family is to me. If family doesn't matter to him, I can't ignore that.' Ellie wasn't letting go of the hope, of the relatively slim chance, that James would eventually see her point of view, and agree with her.

'Well, in that case I don't see much point in lying around here, moping,' said Ruby. 'I think this calls for a session at the Stat Bar.'

'I'm really not in the mood,' Ellie objected.

'Rubbish, you need a distraction. We'll all get changed and head over there now.'

Ellie knew there was no point arguing and lying on the swing hadn't solved her problems, maybe Ruby was right. She did as she'd been instructed and changed out of her shorts into a dress and slipped her feet into a pair of wedges. She brushed her hair and slid an Alice band into it to disguise her hat hair—it was hard to look glamorous after a day spent lying in a garden swing.

A dash of make-up and a couple of quick vodka, lime and sodas at the bar and she began to feel a little more sociable. There wasn't really much point in hiding. Sooner or later she was going to have to face facts—James and she had a difference of opinion and it was big enough to tear them apart. He was only supposed to be her transition man, she'd get over him. Eventually.

She was sitting at a small table with Ruby when the air around her began to vibrate. She knew without looking that James had walked into the bar.

'He's here, isn't he?' she whispered.

She saw Ruby glance over her left shoulder and then nod her head.

Ellie took a deep breath. She could do this. She could be in the same bar as him. As long as she didn't have to see him it would be fine.

But he didn't stay out of sight. He walked past them on his way to the bar and his fresh, lime scent washed over her. She closed her eyes as his familiar smell pervaded her senses. When she opened them he was in her direct line of sight. He was standing at the bar and she was looking right at him. At the lean line of his spine, the firm bulge of a biceps and the curve of his bum in his jeans. He was wearing blue jeans tonight, not black, and a red polo shirt. The colour suited him, a nice contrast to his olive skin and dark hair. She ran her eyes over him, committing every inch of him to her memory.

He ordered his drink and then turned in her direction. He looked straight at her. She didn't think it was an accidental glance. He must have known she was there, he must have seen her on the way in. Their gazes locked. Ellie couldn't turn away. Even now that strange connection was still working and it was too powerful for her to overcome. It held her transfixed. James gave her the slightest nod but he didn't approach her. He picked up his beer and headed for the opposite side of the bar and her heart ripped a little more as he walked away.

So that was how it was going to be.

'Go and talk to him,' Ruby said, giving her a nudge.

Ellie shook her head. 'He needs to make the first move.'

'Why?'

Because I have my pride. 'Because I'm not going to let him brush me off again and tell me his family is none of my business. And if I go to him, that's what will happen. I'm moving on.'

'O-kay,' Ruby said with a tiny shake of her head and a mini eyebrow rise.

But despite her claims Ellie couldn't ignore him completely. His red shirt was like a beacon, continually drawing her gaze, and she couldn't stop herself from glancing in his direction no matter how hard she tried. The constant pull of attraction was a strong as it had ever been and she couldn't resist it.

'Oh, for goodness' sake, if you're going to sit here and try to pretend he doesn't exist we might as well move the party to our house. At least then you won't be able to keep sneaking glances at him.'

Ellie opened her mouth to protest. She didn't want to leave. She wanted to stay near him but as those thoughts entered her mind she realised how ridiculous she was being. Ruby was right. What was the point of sitting here looking at him if she wasn't going to speak to him? She closed her mouth and stood up.

Ruby, Jess and Tilly gathered up a bunch of friends from the bar and invited them all back to Hill Street. Impromptu parties were one of Ruby's favourite things and people had learnt to accept her invitations because it was always fun.

But Ellie dragged her feet. She didn't want to leave the bar, not while James was there. Being in the same place as him was better than nothing. Despite their differences she hadn't reconciled herself with the fact that it was over. She knew it was probably only a matter of time before their relationship would have run its course anyway. On several occasions she'd thought their attraction, their chemistry, was too powerful to sustain. Sooner or later it would exhaust itself, and them, but she wasn't ready for the end just yet.

She escaped to the kitchen on the pretext of mixing a jug of drinks. She didn't need any more to drink but it gave her an excuse to get away from everybody else. It gave her an opportunity for solitude and a chance to think about James in peace and quiet.

She crushed some ice and measured the vodka into the jug before adding some lime cordial and soda water. She grabbed a lime from the fruit bowl, selected a sharp knife and began slicing the lime to add to the jug. The kitchen filled with the scent of limes, immediately reminding her of James. For a small fruit it was very fragrant.

'Hello, Ellie.'

The sound of his voice made her jump. She looked towards him, needing to make sure she wasn't imagining things, and as her attention was distracted the knife slipped off the side of the lime, slicing into her finger. 'Damn it.'

That was why the lime fragrance was so strong. He was here, in her kitchen, leaning casually on the doorframe as if nothing had changed.

She dropped the knife and lifted her hand to check the damage. The cut was shallow but bleeding freely.

He crossed the room, moving quickly to her side when he saw the blood. He took her hand in his and led her to the sink. He turned on the tap and held her hand under the running water, rinsing the blood away so he could see the cut.

'I didn't mean to startle you.'

She didn't answer. She was staring at his hand as it held hers. She watched as the water ran over her finger, turning pink as it ran off into the sink. James's fingers were resting over the pulse at the base of her thumb. She could feel the pulse beating under his touch, as he held her wrist and turned the tap off.

'Does it hurt?' he asked.

She shook her head. She couldn't actually feel her finger. All she was aware of was his touch. The skin around her wrist was on fire and she could feel every beat of her heart as it pushed her blood through her body and out of her finger. Suddenly the image of all her blood running down the drain made her feel dizzy. Her knees wobble. Almost instantly she felt James's arm hug her around her waist as he lifted her off her feet and seated her at the table.

'Put your head down,' he said as he pushed her head forward, tucking it into her lap, holding it there with one hand while he held her left arm in the air with his other hand.

Ellie took some deep breaths, forcing the air into her lungs, and gradually she felt her head clear. Her senses were returning. She could hear and smell and feel but she still couldn't talk.

She felt James change hands and then felt him wrap a cloth around her finger. She looked up and her eyes met bare skin. He was using his shirt to stem the bleeding. He must have taken it off when he changed hands. She would see the ridge of his abdominals, perfectly formed under his smooth, tanned skin and she felt herself hyperventilate again.

'The cut's not too deep,' he said, 'I should be able to hold it together with sticky plasters. Where do you keep them?'

Ellie pointed to a cupboard above the stove.

'Keep some pressure on here while I get them down.' His shirt smelt of limes. Ellie bent her head, immersing her face in his shirt and breathed in his scent, using the perfume to regain her focus. She lifted her head in time to see him stretching to retrieve the small first-aid box from the overhead cupboard. Her eyes were drawn to the curve of his back and the ripple of muscles around his shoulder blades. His beauty was breathtaking. She'd almost forgotten how graceful his movements were.

He came back to her, holding the box in his hands, and with every step closer her heart rate increased its pace.

He searched through the box, selecting a few sticky plasters of varying sizes before he unwound his t-shirt from her finger. The bleeding had stopped and he quickly taped the edges of the cut together before cleaning up the bloody knife and chopping board and throwing out the remnants of the lime.

Finally Ellie recovered the power of speech. 'What are you doing here?'

That was a good question. He hadn't really thought through what he was doing when he'd followed her home. He couldn't think of much at all once he'd seen her at the Stat Bar. Her presence had consumed his thoughts and he hadn't been able to keep his eyes off her. He had been conscious of her watching him too. Their eyes had kept meeting but neither one of them had been prepared to cross the room.

He'd thought he could distance himself from her, from her idea that all families were happy families, from her belief that he should get to know his brother. His half-brother. From her belief that he would *want* to know him.

But distance wasn't working. He missed her. The light had gone with her and his world was not as bright or as warm or as happy without her in it. He knew he should just let her go. He didn't need any complications. He didn't want to be in a serious relationship, one where they had discussions about their beliefs and desires and principles. He didn't want to get too involved with someone who'd made no secret of the fact she wanted a family of her own 'one day'. But he wasn't ready to give her up, not just yet. And that meant trying to find a compromise.

None of this was her fault. The situation between him and his father was not her doing and he shouldn't be blaming her for her perception of the circumstances. But that didn't mean he agreed with her. Not completely anyway. He didn't want anything to do with his father and he wasn't going to be persuaded otherwise. But he needed to make her understand. If he wanted her back in his life they needed to sort this out. He wasn't going to let his father ruin another relationship. His father had done enough damage to his own family and he wasn't going to let his father's actions interfere with any other part of his life.

He needed to talk to her but the Stat Bar was not the place for this conversation. He'd seen her leaving so he'd followed a few minutes behind, thinking maybe he'd have more luck getting a private conversation at her house.

He hadn't realised a crowd was going home with her and by the time he'd reached her house the garden and the lounge were filled with people. He'd used the crowd to his advantage, walking straight through the front door, unnoticed by everyone as he'd searched for Ellie. A brief glance around the garden and into the lounge and he'd known she wasn't there, he couldn't feel her. He'd continued on to the kitchen and he'd felt her presence getting stronger as he'd got nearer.

She was watching him, waiting for a reply. What had she asked? *Why was he there?*

'I needed to see you,' he replied. He pulled out a kitchen chair and sat at the table. 'I want a chance to explain.'

'Explain what?'

'That family *is* important to me. I need you to understand something before you judge me.'

'I wasn't judging you.'

'Yes, you were. You were expecting me to embrace a family that I have no connection with. I understand your

reasoning, but family to me is more than just blood rela-
tions. Family is the people who love you and support you
through the highs and lows of your life. They are the ones
you want to share things with and the ones you turn to
when you need encouragement. My family is important to
me but when I say family I mean my mother and my sister.
They are what matters.'

'And what about Harry?'

'Harry is not my family. Harry is a stranger.'

'But he doesn't have to be.'

'We have nothing in common—'

'Other than your father.'

'Who I haven't seen in almost eighteen years. I don't
need him and I'm sure he doesn't need me.' He ran his
hands through his hair and took a deep breath. He needed
to get this right. Ellie needed to understand his point of
view. 'Not wanting to meet Harry doesn't make me a bad
person. I have a family, my mum and my sister.'

She was shaking her head. 'I know your father's behaviour hurt you deeply but your father's behaviour isn't
Harry's responsibility or burden any more than it is yours.
You have a brother, two brothers, who you refuse to acknowledge, and I'd give anything to have just a little of
what you're prepared to throw away. That's what I don't
understand.'

'I can appreciate how hard it must have been for you to
lose your parents, especially as an only child, but having
a big family is not necessarily better than having a small
one.'

'I would be grateful to have one at all.'

'That's my point. I'm happy with the family I have. I
don't need more than that. My family is not my father or
his new wife or some half-siblings I've never met. I have
a family and I want you to meet them. Would you come

with me to my sister's house tomorrow? It's my nephew's birthday and we've been invited for afternoon tea.'

She was frowning. 'We? I've been invited? You want me to come with you?'

He nodded. 'I want you to meet my family, to see that I'm not a horrible, cold-hearted person. I want to show you that I do believe in family. I have a family that I love very much, a family who have loved and supported me my *entire* life. Please give me a chance to redeem myself.' He reached his hand across the table, imploring her to give him another chance. 'I've missed you, Ellie, please do this for me. For us.'

'You've missed me?' He was going to forgive her for their differences? Despite everything he still wanted her?

She remembered Tilly's words. *Are you going to try to figure this out or are you going to walk away over a disagreement over a half-brother who means nothing to you or James?*

Could she apologise? Could she say she'd made a mistake? Could she tell him she loved him?

She knew she could apologise. She could back down, relax her position on Harry, and perhaps, given time, he would see her point of view. She could hope for that and in the meantime it would give James back to her. But she couldn't admit she loved him. That wasn't going to happen.

'Come and meet my family and you'll see why I don't need more than them. Sometimes just one person is enough.'

He was leaning towards her and she could feel the heat radiating from him. She reached out with her right hand, wanting to touch him, needing to feel him. His skin was warm under her fingers. She could feel his heart beating and its rhythm travelled through her fingers, infusing her body with his pulse.

This was ridiculous. She could feel herself falling under his spell. She was letting him charm her with words. Letting his familiar scent persuade her to listen to him.

Maybe she should meet his family. If he was keen for her to see that side of him, what harm could it do?

Now *she* was being ridiculous. There was nothing to gain from letting him back into her life. He'd made his point of view perfectly clear.

But she knew she couldn't resist him, she knew she would give in.

One person, he'd said.

She knew he was right.

At the moment she only needed one person and he was sitting right in front of her.

Some would say she was young and foolish, naïve even, and they might be right, but she was also in love. She desperately wanted a second chance.

She ran her fingers down his arm, entwining their hands together. 'Let's talk about this upstairs,' she said as she stood, pulling him to his feet beside her. In the background she could hear Ruby singing, accompanied by Tilly on her guitar. She ignored all of that and she ignored the throbbing of her injured finger as she led James out of the kitchen and up the stairs. She ignored her conscience, which was asking if she'd given up her argument about Harry. She'd worry about him later. Right now the rest of the world and its problems could wait. With James beside her it was possible to ignore the outside world completely and she wasn't passing up this opportunity.

For the next month Ellie decided to take James's advice that sometimes one person was enough. She concentrated on him and ignored the fact that he was still reluctant to acknowledge his half-brothers. She still hoped he'd come around to the idea of meeting them but for now she kept quiet, choosing not to force the issue in exchange for spending more time with James.

One benefit of their debate over family was that she got to know James's mother and sister. By Ellie's judgement his mother was a confident, intelligent woman who had raised two caring and considerate adults. Because of James's attitude towards marriage Ellie had expected his mother to be scarred by her divorce but it was quite the opposite. He'd been brought up surrounded by strong women and Ellie realised his anti-marriage stance was really about his belief that people couldn't be relied on to make such a commitment. He had a good relationship with his mother and his older sister, Libby, and there was no doubt that his family was an important part of his life. He clearly loved his mum and his sister, as they loved him. He treated them with respect. He was protective and chivalrous without being condescending and he treated her the same way, making her feel safe and adored. It was a good feeling and he was a good man.

But today had been a difficult day. Not unpleasant, she'd spent it with James and his nieces and nephew at the beach, but she was feeling torn, knowing she should have been elsewhere. She'd enjoyed the afternoon and she had sunburnt shoulders to prove it. The only thing that had spoiled it was her own guilt.

They had swum, built sandcastles and played beach cricket. James's cricket was good, of course, but she'd been hopeless. Distracted by the picture of James in his board shorts and bare chest, she'd kept missing the ball. Even now, as she sat on the edge of her bed and tried to concentrate on rubbing moisturiser into her sunburnt shoulders, the sight of a semi-naked, still-shirtless James lying beside her was distracting.

But she was still feeling guilty. She'd always spent this day in Goulburn. For the last twelve years that's where she'd been, but today she'd changed her routine, she'd done what she'd wanted to do and now she was feeling guilty.

'Here, let me do that,' James said, reaching for the bottle of lotion. He took over the ministrations. 'Did you have a good afternoon?' he asked.

Her afternoon had been better than good, it had been almost perfect. She didn't regret choosing to spend it with him but she was starting to worry that she would regret some other sacrifices later on, for instance, sacrificing her dreams of having her own family in favour of James. He had almost convinced her that she only needed one person.

Yes, the afternoon had been wonderful but it came at a cost.

'It was almost perfect.'

'Almost?'

'I'm feeling guilty.'

'Guilty? About what?'

'Today is the anniversary of my parents' death. I should have been visiting their graves but instead I was at the beach with you.'

James stopped rubbing the moisturiser into her skin, pausing in mid-circle. 'Why didn't you say something to me earlier? I would have taken you to them.'

'To Goulburn?'

'Why not? Do you want to go now?' he asked, as if it made perfect sense.

Goulburn was more than two hours from Sydney. A round trip would take nearly five hours.

She shook her head. 'Thanks, I appreciate your offer

but it's already nearly six o'clock. After an afternoon in the sun I don't think we should tackle that drive.'

He kissed her shoulder. 'I'll take you another day, then. I'll make it up to you.'

'You don't need to do that. It was my decision, my choice. I love spending time with you and your nieces and nephews but today just reminded me of what's missing in my life.'

'What do you mean?'

Could she tell him how she felt? He looked so good lying on her bed, like he belonged there, and she liked the idea of him being there into the future, but her idea of the future might differ from his.

There was no 'might' about it. She knew they had differing views on that topic but it was time for her to be honest with him about some things.

'Do you remember telling me that sometimes one person is enough? That one person is all you need to feel complete?'

He nodded.

'I let myself believe you because I wanted to keep you in my life. You make me feel special and happy and positive but today I missed my family. I want what Libby has.'

'What's that?'

'Kids. A husband. A family of my own. I want to belong to someone who loves me, I want to be someone's wife but I want to be a mother even more.'

James had stopped nodding. He was frowning instead. She wondered if she should stop now, before it was too late.

'Have you some idea of when you might want to have this family?' he asked.

'I've dreamed of having a family of my own since I was about sixteen. Maybe because I lost my parents when I was so young or maybe because I had no siblings or maybe it's just in my genes, but each year that goes past I worry that my dream may be slipping away.'

'So you're not talking years down the track?'

She shook her head. 'I'd hope not.'

'But you're still young. You've got plenty of time.'

Why did everyone tell her that? One day she'd wake up and find that she was old and alone. She couldn't take that chance. 'It took my parents ten years to fall pregnant with me and I was eventually conceived through IVF. It could be the same for me.' That was her greatest fear—what if she couldn't have children?

'Your biological clock is ticking? Is that what you're telling me?'

Ellie nodded. 'I thought I could try living in the moment, I thought I'd see whether I could ignore that yearning, or even if it would pass, but it hasn't. I want a husband, kids, the happily-ever-after. The fairy-tale.'

James swung his legs over the edge of the bed, sitting up beside her. 'That's why it's called a fairy-tale,' he said. 'For the most part it doesn't exist.'

'What doesn't?'

'The whole happily-ever-after. Especially with marriages. My father is a perfect example of that. People aren't prepared for the commitment of marriage.'

'You're not prepared for that commitment, that's what you're saying, isn't it?' Ellie wondered how much of James's attitude stemmed from his father's three failed marriages. It wasn't a stretch of the imagination to see that he'd certainly been influenced by his family history. As had she.

He nodded. 'I'm not cut out for marriage. I've been honest with you all along about that.'

She couldn't argue with him. He was right. She'd known since the night in Kings Cross that he didn't plan to get married. He'd come close, something she hadn't known until later, but he obviously had no intention of getting that close again.

It was her turn to be truthful. 'And now I'm being honest with you. And with myself. I want my own family. I want the fairy-tale and I intend to have it.'

'And what is the rest of your plan? Where do you go from here?'

'I guess that depends on you.'

'I'm sorry, Ellie. You know that marriage isn't part of my future plan.' He wasn't telling her anything new but she wished it was different.

'No marriage? No kids?'

'You know it's not something I want. I don't *want* to have people depend on me, not in that sense. You have to admit, my family doesn't have a great track record of sticking things out for the long term.'

'You won't think about it?'

James shook his head. 'I have thought about it. A few months ago it was all I thought about and I made my decision then when I broke off my engagement. But I want you to have your dream. I can't help you but I won't stand in your way.' He kissed her softly on the lips before he got up from her bed. 'Go and find the man who will be the father of your children but make sure he treats you right, make sure he loves you. You deserve to be happy.'

He picked up his T-shirt and his car keys and left the room. Left her.

She could hear his footsteps on the stairs and the sound of the front door opening and closing as he walked away. She lay down on the bed, where he had lain, soaking up his warmth. She buried her face in her pillow and inhaled his scent and felt her heart breaking.

She disagreed with his idea that he wasn't cut out for

marriage. She was convinced that if he truly fell in love he'd change his mind.

Maybe that was the problem. He didn't love her.

She felt hollow. He had filled her heart with love and she'd felt complete with him.

Should that have been enough for her? Should *he* have been enough? Should she have settled?

No. She shook her head, talking to herself in her empty room. She needed to belong. Even if he'd been prepared to marry her she suspected that in a few years she'd regret not having a family of her own and end up resenting him even though she'd have known all along his feelings on the subject.

As hard as it seemed now, the best thing in the long term was to let him go. She would find someone who would love her back but now, more than ever, she needed her mum. She needed her mum to sit on her bed and stroke her hair. She needed her to kiss her forehead and tell her everything would be better in the morning, just as she'd done when she was ten years old.

She needed her mum and she needed James and she couldn't have either of them.

CHAPTER ELEVEN

SUNDAY was a dreadful day. The sun was shining but all James could see were dark clouds. His house felt dark and lonely. It was quiet, too quiet. The house felt as though it was mourning Ellie's absence. It needed to hear her laughter. *He* needed to hear her laughter.

Don't be ridiculous, he thought, the house couldn't possibly miss Ellie. But he could feel her absence.

He had drifted around the house all day. He needed to get out of here, away from these four walls and his memories. Everything he looked at reminded him of Ellie and if he closed his eyes he could picture her here. He needed to go for a run or a swim.

He went to change into his running clothes but Ellie's bikini was hanging in the shower and her toothbrush was on the basin. He went back upstairs but there were more reminders there. The photo they'd had taken at the surf-club dinner was on the fridge, held in place by an elephant magnet she'd bought for him. A vase of sunflowers took centre stage on the kitchen bench. Brightly coloured lime cushions were now scattered over the sofa and an old wooden coffee table she'd found at a recent trash and treasure market and had repainted in thick lime, white and latte stripes sat on the rug in front of the television. A bowl on the coffee table was filled with a collection of shells and pebbles that Ellie had collected with his nieces. She'd promised to help them decorate photo frames but, thanks to him, she wouldn't be doing that now. His family had adopted Ellie as one of them. How was he going to explain what had happened? How was he going to explain how it had all gone wrong?

He looked around the room. He didn't notice the missing furniture. He didn't notice the missing dining table or sideboard or pictures. All he noticed was that Ellie was missing.

She'd turned his house into a home again. But she'd wanted a family.

Should a home have a family? Could a house be a home *without* a family?

The two weren't mutually exclusive. One person could have a home, but that thought wasn't terribly convincing. Would it be better if more people lived there? People who loved each other?

The phone rang and he pounced on it.

But it wasn't Ellie. It was the real estate agent.

'Dr Leonardi, just wondering how you're going with plans for selling your house. Are you ready to sign the contract?'

He'd delayed putting his house on the market since Ellie had started to spend time there. With her there the house felt loved. When she was there he didn't notice the lack of furniture. When she was there he didn't feel like selling it. Having his house had given them somewhere of their own. The girls' house at Hill Street was filled with laughter but it was also filled with lots of other people and sometimes James had just wanted to have Ellie to himself. He'd loved being in the sanctuary of his own house with her. He didn't want to share her. And he didn't want to sell the house.

'No, it's not going on the market.' It was a link to Ellie. To their memories.

But what of their future? With Ellie in his life he'd been so positive about his future, about himself and the person he could be. But what now? What did his future hold if it wasn't with Ellie? Could he be the man she wanted? Could he give her the things she desired?

When he'd been engaged before he hadn't been able to imagine the future. He'd known the marriage wouldn't last that long. But with Ellie it was different. He couldn't imagine his future *without* her. Already he missed her. He missed hearing her laughter, he missed the feeling of warmth and sunshine she brought to his life. He missed the way she looked at him as if she couldn't wait to get him into her bed.

He wanted her in his life. He needed her in his life. She was his future.

He loved her.

The realisation struck him with full force.

He loved her.

He wanted her.

He needed her.

He picked up a handful of shells and pebbles from the bowl on the coffee table and let them run through his fingers and fall back into the bowl as he thought about Ellie.

He needed to talk to her. He needed to see her and apologise.

He needed to tell her he loved her.

But he had to do it properly. He'd only get one chance to explain. He would take his time and make sure he did it right.

He pulled his phone out of his pocket. Ellie's roster was on there. He knew she was working a late today, he'd already checked, but he wanted to know her movements for tomorrow.

She was on an early shift.

He knew what to do. He was in Theatre tomorrow but after work he'd pick up some supplies and a bottle of champagne, just in case, and invite Ellie to join him for a beach picnic.

Now he had to work out what he would say.

He'd been at work for less than twenty minutes but his plan was unravelling fast. He was doing a quick ward round and had expected to see Ellie but apparently she'd called in sick. He tried to reach her in the few minutes he had before his theatre list started but she didn't answer her phone.

Every chance he got between patients he called again. He didn't get an answer.

At the end of his day he went straight to the Hill Street house. He assumed if she wasn't well he'd have to reschedule the beach picnic but he needed to see her. He needed to know she was okay.

But there was no answer at Hill Street either. It was an odd situation—a house of four women and the occasional man and nobody home. If Ellie was sick, why wasn't she home? Where was she?

He ducked across the road to the Stat Bar, thinking someone must be there. Someone would be able to tell him what the hell was going on. But neither Tilly, Ruby, Jess nor Ellie were there.

He went home defeated but not deterred. Ellie was on another early tomorrow, he'd just delay his plans for twenty-four hours.

But the following morning she still wasn't at work. Charlotte, the ward physio, was doing the round with him. He pulled her aside at the end of the round. He needed to know what was going on, he was getting worried. 'Charlotte, do you know where Ellie is?'

'She isn't working today. She's off.'

James frowned. According to his phone she was on an early. Had he entered it incorrectly? 'Is she still sick?'

'No, I think she swapped shifts with Sarah. Why don't you ring her?'

He didn't bother explaining that he'd been trying to do that without success. Maybe he'd got her shifts wrong. At the end of rounds he quickly checked the nurses' roster. It showed the shifts for the next fortnight but Ellie's name had been crossed off. Completely. There was a big, thick, black line through her name. All her shifts had been allocated to other staff.

He was really concerned now. His first thought was for Rob Coleman. Had Penny Coleman got her way? Had Ellie been transferred to a different ward?

He checked his watch. His outpatient clinic was starting in five minutes. He'd have to solve this puzzle later.

Rob was also running a clinic. James told the receptionist he needed to speak to Rob and asked her to interrupt him the moment he was free.

'Can I have a word?' he asked as he stuck his head into Rob's office. Rob gestured for him to come in and James closed the door behind him. 'Do you know where Ellie is?'

'What do you mean?'

'Her name's been taken off the roster. Did you get her transferred?'

Rob frowned. 'Transferred? To where?' He looked completely confused.

'I don't know, that's what I'm trying to find out.'

'I have no idea what you're talking about. I haven't seen Ellie and I don't know where she is.' He gestured to the pile of notes on his desk. 'If you'll excuse me, I have a long list of patients to see, as I'm sure you do,' he said as he dismissed him.

James left Rob's office, none the wiser. He worked his way through his clinic list but instead of working on his research paper for the afternoon, as he'd planned, he took the rest of the day off. He couldn't concentrate until he'd solved the mystery of Ellie's disappearance. He wouldn't be able to concentrate until he knew she was alright.

The squeaky gate heralded his arrival at the Hill Street house and Tilly answered his knock at the door.

'Ellie isn't here,' she said the moment she saw him waiting there.

'Where is she?'

'Why do you need to know?'

Ellie must have spilled the beans about his reluctance to have a family. He certainly wasn't getting his usual warm welcome but he supposed he deserved nothing less. 'Because I owe her an apology.' *Because I love her.*

'About?'

Tilly was standing in the doorway with her arms crossed in front of her chest. James didn't want to have to explain himself to her, it was Ellie who needed to hear him, but he knew, by the expression on Tilly's face, that he wasn't going to get to Ellie without going through Tilly first. And she wasn't going to cave in without a very good reason.

'I said some things to her I didn't mean. I have things to tell her and I need to do it in person. I need to know where she is.'

'She's gone.'

'Gone?' His heart plummeted in his chest. 'Gone where? Why?'

Tilly shrugged. 'She wanted a break.'

'Please, Tilly,' he begged, 'I need to see her. Do you know where she is?'

'No,' she said with a shake of her head. 'She's taken her car and gone.'

'Car?' James frowned. 'She doesn't have a car.'

'She inherited some money from her grandmother and she used some of that to buy a car.'

'When?' He had no idea about an inheritance and he wondered how many other things he didn't know about Ellie.

'Yesterday,' Tilly sighed. 'Look, I'll try to get in touch with her and if she wants to see you I'll let you know.' She finally took pity on him.

'Thanks, I'd appreciate it.' He took a pen from his pocket and scribbled his mobile number on an old receipt he pulled out of his wallet. 'Please let me know what she says—even if she doesn't want to see me,' he said as he handed her the paper. He hoped she would pass on the message, he hoped Ellie would see him, but either way there was nothing else he could do here.

As he returned to his car he had a sudden flash of insight as to where Ellie might have gone. Was it worth a gamble?

If Tilly convinced Ellie to see him and his hunch was right, he'd be that much closer to her when the call came. It was less than a three-hour trip, he had time, he had nothing but time, and he had nothing to lose.

He jumped into his Jeep and headed south, convinced Ellie would have gone to Goulburn.

Three hours later he was driving aimlessly around Goulburn. What the hell was he going to do now? He hadn't expected to get to Goulburn without hearing from Ellie. Did this mean she didn't want to see him? Or hadn't Tilly been able to contact her?

Had he made a mistake? Another one?

He kept driving, willing his phone to ring, willing Ellie to materialise before him. But there was no guarantee she was even in Goulburn. That had been a whim, an impulse, on his part. Perhaps she wasn't anywhere near here. And if she was here he had no idea where to start looking. And he had no idea what car to look for either. He should have asked Tilly for that much information at least before he'd taken off on this crazy wild-goose chase.

Did he expect Ellie to be standing in the middle of the street, waiting for him?

What had made him so certain that this was where he'd find her? He was so tired now he couldn't even remember why he'd jumped to that conclusion.

What would he say to her? *He was sorry.*

He drove past the sign for St Patrick's Catholic Cemetery.

What would he say? *He needed her in his life.*

The Catholic cemetery. He hit the brakes and looked in the mirror at the sign at the cemetery gates. Suddenly everything made sense. Ellie had been taught by the nuns at a Catholic boarding school. She was a Catholic. He'd bet his last dollar her parents were buried here. This was where he'd find her. He turned off the road and drove through the gates. This was where he'd find her. With her family.

What would he say? *He loved her.*

A car passed him as he drove along the road past neatly tended graves. He glanced at the driver, hoping to see a familiar face, looking for Ellie. The driver had grey hair, a dark shirt and an old face. It was a priest behind the wheel.

He drove further, searching the grounds for Ellie's familiar figure. He could see a building at the top of a crest, a chapel of some sort. Perhaps he'd have a better view of the cemetery from up there.

Parked beside the chapel was a bright yellow Volkswagen beetle. James stopped his Jeep alongside the little convertible. He stepped out of his car. There wasn't another soul in sight. He tried the door handle at the chapel's entrance. It was locked. Had the priest locked it before he'd left? Was the cemetery deserted?

His gaze fell on the yellow Volkswagen. No, someone else was here. He just had to find them.

He walked around the building. The hill sloped gently away from him and he could see rows of headstones stretching into the distance as they guarded the gravesites.

And halfway down the hill sat a girl. She shimmered in the late afternoon sun as the light reflected off her golden hair. His breath caught in his throat. Ellie.

This was his chance. His only chance. He needed to get this right.

He walked down the hill towards her, his steps soft, muffled by the spongy grass. He watched her as he descended the slope. She looked so small and fragile sitting alone surrounded by the vast expanse of the cemetery. Surrounded by the headstones.

He made no sound yet when he was a few paces from her she turned around. He could feel their connection pulling him to her. Could she feel it too? Had she felt him approaching?

'James!'

Her blue eyes were glistening and the tip of her nose was red. She'd been crying.

His heart froze in his chest. She was here, alone and crying. Had he done this to her?

He took the last two steps to her side and squatted beside her. He gathered her in his arms, a reflex action, to provide comfort. As his arms encircled her he realised what he was doing and he tensed, hoping she wouldn't push him away. She didn't. She sank into his embrace.

He relaxed and hugged her tight. 'Ellie, my darling, what's wrong?'

She didn't answer but he thought he knew. She would be remembering her family, feeling their loss, feeling alone.

'It's going to be all right,' he whispered. 'I'm here, I've got you.' He was going to make sure she never felt alone again.

Her face was nestled into his shoulder and her voice was muffled when she asked. 'How did you find me?'

He smiled. 'Goulburn just felt right. I think I'm beginning to understand you but it took me a bit of time to track you down once I got to town. Is it okay that I'm here?'

She nodded. 'But why are you here?'

James changed position, unable to sustain the squat any longer. He sat on the grass behind Ellie and pulled her between his legs so her back was resting against his chest. 'Have you spoken to Tilly?'

'No.' She shook her head and her hair tickled his chin. 'My phone is switched off.'

Why was he here? Having her in his arms again had made him lose track of his thoughts.

What had he wanted to say? *I'm sorry. I need you. I love you.*

'I came to apologise. Seeing my father again brought back all the old feelings of betrayal and loss and fear of commitment. I got so caught up in the past that I let it interfere with us, with our future. You told me that my father's behaviour isn't my responsibility or burden but I've carried it with me for such a long time and it's still influencing my reactions. I was so angry at my father. I thought I'd gotten past all that but obviously I hadn't and I took it out on you. I didn't realise what I'd found in you until you'd gone and when I went looking for you you'd disappeared. You have to come back with me, Ellie, I need you.'

'I'm not sure I can go back.'

What? She had to come back with him. Where else would she go? What else would she do?

'I need a break,' she said. 'It was a mistake to get involved with you. I should have stuck to my rule about no doctors. I need to be away from the ortho ward for a while. I need some space.'

A mistake! No, this wasn't how it was supposed to be. She was supposed to want him as much as he wanted her. He needed her. He loved her.

He changed position again, moving around to kneel in front of her. He took her hands in his and begged her to talk to him. 'Tell me what's wrong. Tell me what I can do to fix this.'

'I don't know if you *can* fix this. We want different things. I'm here trying to sort out what I want. This is about me and what I need. And I need someone who wants the same things as me. This is about me and you but I'm not sure there can be an "us".'

'What do you mean?'

'I thought what we shared was enough for me. You made me feel special and safe and I thought that was sufficient. It didn't matter that we didn't want the same things. It didn't matter that you didn't want to get married or have children. It wasn't supposed to matter because what we had was only supposed to be temporary. But it does matter. It matters to me because I've fallen in love with you.'

'You love me?'

She nodded and his heart lightened with each movement of her head.

'But I wasn't meant to fall in love,' she said. 'You were supposed to be a distraction but somewhere, somehow, you've gotten inside my heart. You told me that sometimes one person is enough and I wished that were true for me. I wanted it to be true but it's not. I love you but I still need more. I wish that loving you was enough but all I see now are the things I won't have with you. I want a family with you but I can't have that. That's why I needed to get away. It was a mistake and I have to get over you. I will get over you.'

How could she think loving him was a mistake? Her words repeated in his head. Ellie wanted a family and he was here to offer her that. She stood up but he held onto her hand, he wasn't letting her go.

'No, don't.' He stood too and moved downhill so he could look her in the eye. 'This is not a mistake, we are not a mistake. I wanted to be the person you could rely on, the person who would support you and instead I let you down. My history, my past and my stubbornness stopped me from seeing what was important. I haven't been the man I wanted to be for you but I want to change that. I want to give you what you need. I *want* to share my life with you. I want to be yours. That's why I'm here. I want to be your family. My mum, Libby, even Harry if you want, we can all be your family.'

'Harry?'

'You were right about him too,' he admitted. 'None of this is his fault. I'm willing to meet Harry. I'll do it for you.'

'Don't do it for me. Do it because *you* want to.'

'No,' he said with a shake of his head. 'I will do it for you because I love you. I need you in my life and if you want me to get to know my brothers, I will. Please listen to me. This connection we have is a once-in-a-lifetime thing. You feel it too, don't you?' He searched her eyes, looking for confirmation, even though he knew what he said was true. 'I love you and I want you to have a family. I want *us* to be a family.'

He loved her? How she wished that was enough. How she wished it were that easy. She could feel James's heart beating as though it were her own. She could feel every breath he took as though it were her lungs breathing for them both. He was right, they were connected and her body responded to him in a way she'd never responded to anyone before. And she knew she would never love like this again. But it wasn't enough.

'A family means children. To me anyway.' She had to make it clear. She had to be sure he understood. 'I thought I could have a new dream but I can't. I need children.'

'I want you to have that. I want us to have that.'

He was holding onto her upper arms and his hands were warm and strong, making her feel safe and secure. She hoped this feeling wasn't just an illusion. 'You want children?' He nodded and she frowned. 'What made you change your mind?'

'You,' he said simply. 'Do you remember the photo of us that was taken at the ward dinner? It's on the fridge surrounded by all the paintings Libby's children have done for us? I was looking at those paintings and thinking, What if the pictures had been done by our children? And suddenly I could picture our future. I want a whole lot of blond-haired, blue-eyed children that look like their mother. I want to have a family with you.' He saw her smiling. 'What's so funny?'

'In my mind the children have curly, dark hair with eyes the colour of chocolate, just like their father.'

'Let's agree to have a mixture. As long as we have—'

'Four,' they said together.

'Definitely four,' he repeated. 'I want it all.'

'All?' Could she dare to hope that her dreams could come true?

He nodded. 'But only if I can have it with you. You make my life better. You make me a better person too. You make me think I can be the sort of man you want. The sort of man you deserve. You make me want to try. I want to be the best man I can be and I can only be that if you are in my life. I want to grow old with you. I want to build a life with you. We belong together. I want to watch our children grow, I want to watch our grandchildren grow. I want you to be able to depend on me and I won't let you down. I want you to marry me.'

'What?' Had she heard him right? 'You want to get married?'

'I want you to be the mother of my children but first you need to be my wife.'

'You want to marry *me*?'

'Yes. I'm not letting you go again. Ever.'

'I thought you didn't believe in people's ability to commit?'

'I know I said I wasn't going to get married but I never thought about the implications of that statement until I met you. Until I fell in love with you. When I was engaged before I could never imagine past the wedding, I'd barely been able to imagine that, and I certainly hadn't been able to imagine a long-term future. I'd known I would end up divorced, I thought it was because of my father, that I had too much of my father in me, but now I realise I had the wrong partner. *You* are the one I'm meant to be with and I can't imagine my future without you in it. I get it now. I can see how people believe and trust and hope that their love will last, that their marriage will be the one that makes it. I've found the person I want to spend the rest of my life with and I know we will make it. Together we can do this. I want to share the rest of my life with you. You can depend on me. I promise you that. You are my future.' He knelt on one knee and grinned at her, his chocolate eyes gleamed and her heart swelled with love. 'Now, do you have any more questions or are you going to let me propose properly?'

He really was serious. 'You're going to propose here?'

'I admit this isn't quite what I'd planned. We were supposed to be on the beach last night as the sun set, drinking champagne and toasting our future life together.'

'Last night?'

'I've been looking for you for two days,' he explained. He looked around. They were surrounded by lawns, rose bushes, headstones and silence. 'But it's quite beautiful here too and we are alone, with your family.'

She smiled, touched by his sentiment. 'You're right, this is perfect.'

He nodded and took her hand. Her heart was racing.

'Ellie, my love, I can't imagine my life without you. You bring the sunshine into my world, you bring balance and meaning, you are my centre. I love you, Ellie. Please, will you marry me?'

Tears, happy, emotional tears, were welling in her eyes and her heart was full. That empty spot wasn't empty any more. This was really happening.

She knelt down on the grass before him. 'Everything feels better when you are around,' she told him. 'I feel safe, content, loved and hopeful. Together we can have the life I've dreamed of. I love you.' She kissed him softly on the lips and warmth flooded through her. She loved him and he loved her. He wanted her and she belonged to him. 'And...' she kissed him again '...I will marry you.'

She was loved and she loved in return. She was going to marry the man she adored and have dark-haired babies with blue eyes who smelt like limes or maybe fair-haired babies with chocolate eyes who smelt like sunshine. Any combination was fine with her.

She hugged James to her. He was the love of her life. Her heart was full and her world was perfect.

* * * * *

WAKING UP WITH DR OFF-LIMITS

BY
AMY ANDREWS

First published in Great Britain 2011
by Mills & Boon, an imprint of Harlequin (UK) Limited.
Harlequin (UK) Limited, Eton House, 18-24 Paradise Road,
Richmond, Surrey TW9 1SR

© Amy Andrews 2011

ISBN: 978 0 263 88608 5

Harlequin (UK) policy is to use papers that are natural, renewable and recyclable products and made from wood grown in sustainable forests. The logging and manufacturing process conform to the legal environmental regulations of the country of origin.

Printed and bound in Spain
by Blackprint CPI, Barcelona

Amy Andrews has always loved writing, and still can't quite believe that she gets to do it for a living. Creating wonderful heroines and gorgeous heroes and telling their stories is an amazing way to pass the day. Sometimes they don't always act as she'd like them to—but then neither do her kids, so she's kind of used to it. Amy lives in the very beautiful Samford Valley, with her husband and afore-mentioned children, along with six brown chooks and two black dogs. She loves to hear from her readers. Drop her a line at www.amyandrews.com.au

Recent titles by the same author:

JUST ONE LAST NIGHT…
RESCUED BY THE DREAMY DOC
VALENTINO'S PREGNANCY BOMBSHELL
ALLESANDRO AND THE CHEERY NANNY

**Did you know these are also available as eBooks?
Visit www.millsandboon.co.uk**

Dedications

To three fabulous writers—Fiona, Carol and Emily—
it's been amazing working with you on this project.

And to über-cool surfie chick Jaiden Allan,
who answered every dumb surfing question I had
without rolling her eyes once—thank you.

CHAPTER ONE

THE last thing Jessica Donaldson expected to find in her bed on a stinking hot morning was a naked man. And certainly not this particular man—the source of every one of her feverish fantasies for the last three and a bit years.

Dr Adam Carmichael—occasional housemate, surgeon extraordinaire, playboy incarnate.

For a moment she wondered if her sleep-deprived brain had conjured him up. Was she *that* tired after her midnight call-in and subsequent eight hours of surgery she'd actually imagine a man in her bed?

And not just any man but Adam?

Wasn't he operating in some Third World country or schmoozing bigwigs at The Hague? She shut her eyes, shook her head to clear the fog of fatigue and opened them again. Nope. Still there. And still most definitely Adam.

Jess stood in the doorway, wrapped in nothing but a towel, droplets of water clinging to her undried skin. Suddenly she was very awake. A frigid blast of air from the wall-mounted cooling unit enveloped her, soothing a fiery blush.

The sheer perfection of his body momentarily distracted her from the fact that he was in her bed.

Asleep.

Naked. She'd never had a man in her bed, naked or otherwise, and her breath quickened that the first time it had happened fate had delivered her the man of her dreams.

Would it be wrong to look her fill?

Jess prided herself on having a strong moral code. There'd never been a cause to question it before.

But.

The morning sunlight poked insistent fingers into the darkened room from around the edges of the blackout blind, illuminating his deep golden tan to perfection.

And he was in *her* bed.

So…she looked her fill.

Adam lay on his stomach, his sandy blond head turned away from the window. Both arms were spread out, easily reaching the sides. His back was a tantalising palate of planes and angles, broad across the shoulders, tapering down to the dip of his back and the rise of his bottom.

The floral sheet had been pulled up to his hips. One leg was firmly entangled but the other had freed itself, causing the sheet to slip slightly and partially reveal a glimpse of naked buttock in all its tanned glory. It was firm, well defined, despite his slumber, and, she noted, the same nut brown as the rest of his body.

He obviously sunbaked naked as well.

Her gaze continued down his exposed leg. It was firmly muscled and deeply tanned. A covering of blond hairs added to its masculinity and Jess followed its length right down to the toes that stuck out over the end of the bed.

She drew in a ragged breath. How was it possible to look so masculine amidst floral sheets?

She knew for a fact he had navy satin sheets on his bed. She'd seen them hanging on the line once. Her dreams had featured an awful lot of satin ever since.

Adam chose that moment to move and Jess froze like a deer caught in headlights. What if he woke and caught her ogling him? But she just didn't seem able to stop. She watched in fascination as the previously dormant muscles in his back and arms tensed and rippled, assisting the move onto his back.

Jess held her breath.

Luckily, his subconscious chose to roll the way it did as his entangled leg dragged the sheet across his hips and legs, concealing his modesty from her gaze. But that still left a whole lot of male flesh on view.

One arm, bent at the elbow, was flung above his head, emphasising a taut bicep. His strong jaw sported a sprinkling of dark blond three-day growth as her gaze traced the fascinating contours of his full mouth.

A thatch of soft-looking underarm hair barely registered as the firmness of his beautifully tanned, smooth chest drew her gaze lower. It tapered down to a set of abs that would have been perfectly at home on a Rodin statue.

A trail of darker brown hair bisected his six pack. Jess's throat felt as dry as two-minute soup mix.

She didn't dare look any lower.

Not that she was any stranger to naked men. As a nurse, it was an occupational hazard. And as a country girl, nature, in all its forms, had infused her life.

But he wasn't one of her beloved patients. Or a prize-winning bull.

He was an entirely different proposition.

And this was voyeurism. Jess mentally shook herself. What the hell was she doing? The man was twelve years older than her and a total sex god. He was completely out of her league.

Not to mention Ruby's brother.

Oh, and her landlord!

But what the hell was she supposed to do now? He was in *her* bed.

Her bed. A bed that she would very much like to be in herself, getting some much-needed sleep.

A bed she'd been daydreaming about all the way home as each footstep down the hill from the hospital had brought her closer to home.

A bed she could almost feel beneath her as she'd pushed open the front door and headed straight for the shower, dunking herself quickly under the cool spray to remove all traces of hospital. *Why the hell was he in her bed?*

He had a perfectly good one of his own. She'd never seen it, never even peeked inside his bedroom, but it was there, opposite the kitchen door, always taunting her.

When he was away, which was often, the door was always shut. When he was home it opened and shut with monotonous regularity as a procession of women came and went.

He really should just install a revolving one and be done with it.

So, why was he camped out in hers?

She should wake him, demand to know what he was doing.

But...how? Call his name? Shake his shoulder?
Touch him?

Her breath caught in her throat as the thought shocked and tantalised in equal measure. Her pulse had doubled just scrutinising the man in her bed—what the hell would happen to her if she should actually touch him?

Touch a naked shoulder?

She recoiled from the very idea, her fingers curling into her palms. It was too much to even contemplate.

She sighed. There was nothing she could do. Ruby and Tilly had both finished night duty this morning and would be snoring their heads off in their beds. And Ellie was on afternoon shift and wouldn't be up yet.

It wasn't fair to disturb any of them.

She was going to have to go and sleep on the couch. In the non-air-conditioned lounge room. On a day that was tipped to reach forty degrees. And already felt like double that.

While Adam Carmichael slept in temperature-controlled comfort.

In her bed.

If she didn't have a massive crush on him and wasn't such a goody two shoes she'd have tossed him out on his ear. But he looked so peaceful. Not to mention sexy as hell. And at least she'd have *actual* fodder for her fantasies now instead of just a series of creative imaginings.

The image of him tangled in her sheets was going to stay with her for ever.

But she needed her clothes and they were in her room. Jess sighed. There was only one thing for it…

She dropped her bag quietly just inside the door and checked that her towel was firmly tucked. The last thing she wanted was to have a wardrobe malfunction—one naked person in this room was enough!

Jess tiptoed into the room, unable to drag her eyes from the steady rise and fall of Adam's chest.

That was her first mistake.

She promptly tripped over one of the numerous embroidered throw cushions that usually sat on her bed and which Adam had obviously tossed on the floor. She clutched at her cleavage where the towel end was firmly tucked as she stumbled perilously close to the edge of the bed before righting herself.

Her heart hammered wildly in her chest and she didn't move for a full minute in case just disturbing the air currents around the bed might cause him to waken. Finally, convinced he was sleeping soundly, she forced herself to watch her step instead of Adam as she continued towards her goal.

There were no built-in wardrobes in her room, just an old-fashioned art deco one that stood against the wall next to the bedside table. It belonged to her grandmother who'd insisted she bring it with her to the big smoke to remind her of home. It was beautifully crafted from dark wood with curved top edges and a full sized bevelled mirror between the two polished doors. Jess reached it without further incident and held her breath as she turned the key in the lock. The quiet scratch of metal on metal seemed amplified tenfold and when the door opened it creaked like a coffin lid in a horror movie.

Jess froze behind the door, waiting for Adam to stir, but a quick peek confirmed the noises hadn't disturbed him.

That was her second mistake.

As he slumbered blissfully on, his lips snagged her attention. They were full, parted slightly and looked, oh, so soft. The stubble that framed them looked deliciously scratchy and she wondered how the soft/rough combination would feel against her own mouth? Jess swallowed.

How would it feel to be the one allowed to kiss that mouth?

Adam shifted slightly and she ducked behind the wardrobe door again like a nervous Victorian maiden. But not before she noticed her pyjamas peaking out from the pillow beneath his head.

Great.

Cowering behind the door, her heart fluttered ten to the dozen as she actually considered, for one crazy second, trying to retrieve them.

But that would be a third mistake.

And there were plenty of things she could wear right here in her wardrobe. Her hand shook as she slowly pulled open a drawer and extracted a pair of white cotton knickers and a white cotton, knee-length nightie. Her mother had embroidered tiny yellow daises around the modest neckline.

From habit she sank her face into it. It smelled of sunshine and home and a fierce shaft of nostalgia pierced her right through the heart. For a moment she wished she was back there. Where things were simple.

Where Adam couldn't possibly be in her bed.

No matter how many times she'd fantasised about waking up with him, in her childhood bedroom, unchanged since she'd been seven years old, and her desires had been as innocent as *Black Beauty* wallpaper.

There was nothing innocent about her desires now.

She sighed inwardly as she shut the drawer carefully and then reached for her deodorant. Her still trembling fingers fumbled it and it thunked against the shelf. She made a grab for it as it rolled off the edge but it was already falling. It landed on the polished hardwood floor at her feet with a crash loud enough to wake the dead.

Or the devil anyway...

Adam sat bolt upright in bed, the sheet ruching around his waist. 'What the hell...?'

Jess opened her eyes and poked her head around the edge of the door. 'Sorry,' she apologised. 'I didn't mean to wake you.'

Oh, dear, oh, dear, oh, dear.

He was utterly magnificent.

His sandy blond hair, beyond messy, somehow cornered the market on sexy. His chest and six pack were beautifully delineated. He looked like he'd just come from riding waves in Hawaii instead of another humanitarian mission.

Jess hastily averted her eyes, chiding her lack of decorum. He was a brilliant surgeon doing vital work. Not a male centrefold.

Adam frowned, his brain heavily mired in the sticky web of jet lag. He really was getting too old for continually mixing up his time zones. Too old for running away.

'Jess?'

He blinked in case he was imagining her because this was not the Jess he remembered. Sweet Jess with the cute ponytail. Jess of the bare feet, jeans and T.

He'd never seen her with her hair all loose around her shoulders like this.

Or in nothing but a towel for that matter.

What the hell was she doing in his room? 'What are you doing here?'

Jess swallowed as he pinned her with his lapis lazuli gaze. It was too dark to see them but she knew from detailed memory that the blue was flecked with golden highlights. He rubbed at the tantalising stubble at his jawline. The delicious rasping noise sent Jess's stomach into freefall as the image of him scraping it against her belly took hold.

'Er...' Jess felt unaccountably nervous and hopelessly gauche in the face of his potent male virility. Which was utterly ridiculous. Adam was hardly leering at her. In fact, he was frowning at her like she was an annoying little insect that had dared to wake him up.

Instead of an almost naked, fully grown, nearly twenty-four-year-old woman.

She'd seen the way he looked at women. He was not looking at her like that. He'd never looked at her like that.

She doubted her chastity was under threat. Jess cleared her throat. 'Ah...this is my room.'

Adam's frown deepened as her response registered. He

looked around. Too-small bed, scatter cushions all over the floor, floral sheets. Romance novel on the bedside table.

Then it all came flooding back to him. The air-con in his room deciding to choose this sweltering day to break down. One on a list of many ailments suffered by his poor, neglected house.

The repairman not being able to get here until ten. His overwhelming weariness.

Adam ran a hand through his hair as the cogs slowly started to turn. 'I thought you were on an early today. That's what the fridge calendar says.'

Early on in their cohabitation the girls had devised a colour-coded system to keep track of each other. With four people coming and going on shift work, it made things much easier. Her roster was in yellow.

Jess frowned, wishing his logic was as easy to follow as the flex of his biceps, the path of his fingers. 'So you decided to…try out my bed?'

Her heart beat double-time at the illicitness of her suggestion.

Adam pressed the pads of his fingers into his eye sockets. 'So the calendar's wrong?'

'No. It's right. I was called in last night, though… I only clocked off half an hour ago.'

'Oh…' Adam felt his interest pique despite the heavy cloak of fatigue. 'Anything interesting?'

Jess couldn't believe she was having this conversation.

In her room. In a towel.

With Adam. In a sheet.

'Liver transplant.'

'Ah…'

Jess waited for something more forthcoming but Adam collapsed back against the mattress, his abs unfurling like flower petals, his eyes closed.

Oh, brother! He really did look centrefold material now, reclining in her bed as if he owned it.

'Adam!' she said, still not game enough to touch him.

Adam, already falling back into the blissful folds of sleep, prised his eye open. He raised himself slightly on bent elbows. 'What?' he demanded crankily.

It hadn't been her plan to wake him up but now he was he could damn well vacate her bed. 'Why are you in my bed?'

He watched her mouth move but it took a moment for the words to compute.

He hadn't noticed how pink Jess's mouth was before. Like fairy floss. Was it lipstick or natural? It was a little too dark to tell. 'Hmm?'

Jess noticed his heavy-lidded gaze on her mouth and almost lost her train of thought. She scrambled hard to get it back again. 'You're. In. My. Bed.'

He hadn't noticed how her hair flicked up at the ends like that when it was freed from its ponytail or even that it was so long. It brushed her shoulders and fell forward over well-defined collar bones.

Had it always been so blonde?

'Ah, but, Goldilocks,' he teased lightly, a smile spread across his full lips, 'your bed was just right.'

Jess felt her knees go weak as the smile warmed his face, taking it from sexy-but-tired to steal-your-breath sublime. She reached for the nearby wardrobe door and held on tight.

'Adam…'

He sighed. 'Sorry.'

His exhausted body protested as he curled into a sitting position again.

'The air-con in my room is on the blink. A fix-it guy is coming at ten.' He shrugged. 'Your room was empty. And air-conditioned. I checked the calendar. Sorry…I'm just exhausted, I guess.'

He rubbed his right eye with his hand. It felt gritty and unfocused. 'I think I've been in four different time zones in the last week.'

Jess felt everything solid inside her melt to liquid. He looked completely done in. She wanted to go to him, pull him down beside her, cradle his head against her breast, stroke his hair till he slept, hush him, tell him she was there for him.

Oh, God. She *still* had it bad.

'I thought you were in the wilds of Asia for three months? You've still got another few weeks left, haven't you?'

She couldn't help it. She always knew where he was. Would count down the days. His comings and goings were also marked on the calendar in black and she absorbed it like the big fat Adam sponge that she was.

Maybe *groupie* was closer to the mark.

'There was some unrest in the last province when we first arrived,' he said. 'The department of foreign affairs ordered us out. So I've spent the last week talking with international funding bodies, trying to organise for the patients to come to us.'

Jess felt ill at his casual reference to *unrest*. She certainly forgot all about the fact that they were both essentially naked and this was probably the longest conversation they'd ever had.

She knew he went to some remote places in his crusade to bring equality of healthcare to all but there'd never been any trouble before.

The mere thought of it had her heart palpitating wildly.

It was no secret she had the utmost respect for what he did. In fact, her housemates often teased her about her

hero-worship. But, hey, the man could be making squill-
lions of dollars as a plastic surgeon doing boob jobs and
lipo like his esteemed father. Instead he'd chosen to help
horrendously disfigured people that no one in the world
cared about, have a shot at a normal life.

He could easily have been a playboy.

But he wasn't.

Frankly, it got her hot just thinking about it.

'Unrest?' she squeaked.

Adam waved his arm dismissing the threat. 'Local warlord stuff. We were fine. Just the government being cau-
tious.'

Local warlord?

Dear God, was his work dangerous? What if…what if
he went away one time and didn't come back? What if she
never got the chance to…?

Adam studied Jess intently for an age. She was chewing
on that pink, pink mouth and he found himself suddenly
wondering what it might be like to run his tongue along
those lips and soothe them from her savaging.

The insidious thought that she was naked beneath her
towel hit him from out of the blue. He'd never thought
about Jess like that before. Not about her mouth. Or what
was under that towel. She was a friend of his little sister.

She was twenty-three, for crying out loud.

He was thirty-five.

And she read romance novels.

Time to leave. Way past time to leave.

Jess watched as he shifted, the muscles of his naked
arms and chest rippling as he began to pull the sheet aside.
'Stop,' she squeaked. 'What are you doing?'

Adam frowned. 'It's okay,' he assured her, consulting
his watch, 'I've had a couple of hours. I'll be fine now till

the air-con guy gets here.' Even though he felt like his eye-balls had been rolled in shell grit.

'Adam…' She shook her head. 'You haven't got a stitch on under that sheet.'

It was on the tip of Adam's tongue to tell her she didn't have a stitch on under her towel either but then another thought struck him.

'Well, now,' he drawled as he leaned back on his splayed palms. 'And you would know that how, Jessica Donaldson?'

Realising her gaffe, Jess blushed furiously. A more so-phisticated woman may have been able to come up with some witty reply but Jess was mortified.

'You were peeking at me,' Adam stated and seeing her cheeks grow an even more fetching shade of pink—*as pink as her mouth*—he laughed.

The rich, deep sound filled the room and Jess felt her skin break out in goose-bumps.

She really must turn the air-con down.

'Don't be ridiculous!' she blustered. Her heated denial only seemed to deepen his mirth and she glared at him im-patiently, waiting for his laughter to subside.

'You were covered by the sheet,' she blurted out. *Mostly.*

Adam laughed again, enjoying the way she blushed and looked like she wanted aliens to swoop in and abduct her.

'Well, as I walked naked from my room to your room I don't have anything to cover me.'

Of course he had.

Any normal person would have taken the time to throw on some undies or sling a towel around themselves but Mr Centrefold had preferred his birthday suit.

'Tell you what, why don't you throw me that towel you're wearing? That ought to do it.'

Jess felt her cheeks grow even hotter. Her heart drummed a heavy beat in her ears. She swallowed hard.

Her nipples tightened and she was pleased for the thickness of the towelling as she imagined standing before him with nothing on.

Naked in front of a man.

In front of Adam.

'Would you like a hand?' he teased as Jess's fingers clutched ever tighter at the fastening of the towel. Jess frowned as a heavy fog of confusion muddled her brain. He was smiling, his voice was light and teasing. She risked a brief glance at his face—there was a glint in his eyes.

Was he flirting with her?

But why?

He never flirted with her. Hell, he barely contained himself from ruffling her hair and patting her on the head on those rare occasions he was home and graced the rest of the house with his presence. Instead of being holed up behind closed doors, going for gold in the sexual Olympics.

He must be jet-lagged. And she was obviously delirious!

It would be foolish to read too much into any of these crazy last minutes.

Although dropping the towel just to wipe the smug smile off his face was exceedingly tempting.

She dropped her gaze instead. To the floor. Desperate to gain some composure.

Who knew she'd actually find her salvation?

She smiled and then squatted down, picking up two of her throw cushions and lobbing them at him. 'These should do the trick.'

Adam caught them automatically as they hit him square in the chest. They'd been an irritation a couple of hours ago when he'd been trying to offload them so he could get horizontal as quickly as possible. Like an insurmountable mountain.

SAVE OVER £41

Subscribe to Medical today to get 6 stories
a month delivered to your door for 12 months,
saving a fantastic £41.70.
Alternatively, subscribe for 6 months and save
£16.68, that's still an impressive 20% off!

FULL PRICE	YOUR PRICE	SAVINGS	MONTH
£166.80	£125.10	25%	12
£83.40	£66.72	20%	6

As a welcome gift we will also
send you a FREE L'Occitane
gift set worth £10

**PLUS, by becoming a member you
will also receive these additional benefits:**

- 🌹 FREE P&P Your books delivered to your
  door every month at no extra charge

- 🌹 Be the first to receive new titles two
  months ahead of the shops

- 🌹 Exclusive monthly newsletter

- 🌹 Excellent Special offers

- 🌹 Membership to our Special Rewards programme

No Obligation- You can cancel your subscription at any time by writing
to us at Mills & Boon Book Club, PO Box 676, Richmond. TW9 1WU.

To subscribe, visit
www.millsandboon.co.uk/subscriptions

MILLS
BOON

'Look at that,' he murmured, his gaze locking with hers. 'They do serve a purpose.'

And then, his eyes never leaving her face, he rose in one fluid moment, one cushion clutched to his front, the other to his back.

Jess took a step back as his superior height overwhelmed her. At five-six in her bare feet she wasn't exactly short— but she felt positively diminutive in the presence of his all-encompassing maleness.

'Sweet dreams.' He winked and turned on his heel, sauntering out.

Jess followed his retreat, amazed that somehow he still managed to look one hundred per cent male even with a purple cushion covering what she knew to be one hell of a swagger.

Not even her door shutting quietly, blocking her view, was going to be enough to erase that image from her brain. Groaning, her heart tripping, her hands trembling, Jess collapsed on her back on the bed.

She picked up her pillow and plonked it over her head. Adam's edgy masculine scent filled her nostrils and she sucked in big, deep lungfuls of him. She threw it aside in disgust, rolling onto her stomach.

The same tantalising aroma wafted up from the sheet wrapping her in Adam.

She couldn't decide if it was heaven or if it was hell.

She did know she was never going to wash these sheets. Ever again.

CHAPTER TWO

THE next morning Adam sat on his board out to sea with a line of other eager early morning surfers, waiting for the next wave to come in.

It was probably going to be a while.

The surf was non-existent. The ocean was flat and glassy, with just an occasional gentle swell bobbing him in the water.

But for Adam, surfing was about more than the waves. Sure, he liked the exhilaration of riding a monster wave as much as the next guy, but what he enjoyed most was this. The sense of stillness, of the world waking up, of being connected to the planet, in tune with its pulse.

The sun was rising rapidly in the sky behind him, spreading golden fingers over a still sleepy Coogee. It was already warm on his shoulders, shaping up to be another scorcher no doubt.

The light murmur of his fellow surfers melded perfectly with the distant sounds of the sea lapping against the beach.

Everything was as it should be.

Except for that damn image of Jess in nothing but a towel, with water droplets clinging to her skin, that had lodged itself stubbornly into his grey matter.

Prior to yesterday Adam had probably never given Jessica Donaldson a second thought. Sure, she was a nice enough kid but he doubted they'd ever said more than a handful of things to each other in the last three years.

Jess was just a friend of his sister's who, along with Ellie and Tilly, had helped Ruby with the rent in his Hill St house.

Why had he never noticed her incredible bone structure before? Or how hot that little pink mouth was?

Because.

Adam gave himself a shake.

Because she was barely out of her teens, that's why! Twenty-three, for crying out loud.

The only other time he'd dated a woman in her early twenties, Francine, it had been an unmitigated disaster— one that he had no intention of repeating.

Once bitten, twice smart.

Younger women were complicated. They had romantic stars in their eyes. They wanted things. Like declarations of love.

They were needy. He didn't do needy.

He did sophisticated. Worldly. Independent.

Women. Not girls.

And he wasn't about to start just because he'd dreamed about Jess and that mouth all through his marathon eighteen-hour sleep.

He felt things begin to stir beneath his boardies as they had earlier, prodding him from his slumber, and he looked up at the headlands either side of Coogee bay, determined to distract himself. To focus on something—anything— other than Jess.

He could see a couple at the monument to the Bali bombing victims and further back towards the front a lone jogger pounded the footpath, the majestic Norfolk pines forming a dramatic backdrop. His gaze lifted higher, to the hilly suburban sprawl behind and the Eastern Beaches Hospital perched atop, dominating it all. He could even see his house from here, his eyes easily locating the double-storey monstrosity badly in need of some TLC.

His gaze fell on Jess's window and he found himself wondering if she was still asleep.

Did she sleep nude, like he did?

Had it been her plan yesterday to shimmy the towel off her body and just drop straight into bed?

He closed his eyes as a vision of him brushing his mouth across a bare shoulder blade assailed him. Her skin would be cool from the kiss of the air-con and he could almost feel the tiny hairs feathering her skin brush his mouth as they stood to attention beneath his lips.

His groin stirred again and he almost groaned out loud. *This was madness!*

What he really needed was a date. Obviously it had been too long if he was lusting after a woman—a *young* woman—*twelve years his junior.*

And it'd been a long time since he'd had any female company.

His time away with Saving Face was always frantic and there was never time for socialising. Long days of operating, often well into the night, followed by travelling on to the next place and repeating it all over again wasn't conducive to sexual liaisons.

Frankly, even if he didn't have a strict no-sleeping-with-colleagues rule, he was too exhausted for anything other than snatching vital hours of sleep whenever he could.

But when he came home between missions, that was a different story. That was his down time. Time to surf, top up his tan, spend time with Ruby, see his mother, tolerate his father and date pretty women.

Time for liaisons.

'Wave!'

Adam looked over his shoulder as the excited cry worked its way down the line. He felt his adrenaline kick in as the mediocre wave emerged from the ocean behind him and he flattened his belly against the board in anticipation.

He welcomed it. Riding a wave was an all-consuming pastime and he welcomed the break from his internal dialogue. No time for thoughts of Jess and her cute pink mouth.

Just him and the ocean.

He felt the drag, could feel the kick in his chest as his pulse picked up a notch. His board started to lift at the back and he paddled frantically to position himself perfectly for when the wave crested.

He leapt to his feet at just the right moment, bending his legs, cutting across the face as if he'd been born with fins. The wind ruffled his hair and he could taste salt on his tongue.

It was just him and the wave.

He whooped out of sheer exhilaration as he conquered the wall of water. He was unstoppable.

Until the second he wondered if Jess could surf.

And then he promptly lost his balance and tumbled off his board head first into the ocean.

'Good morning,' Jess chirped as she flipped over some frying bacon.

'How on earth can you be so damn happy at this ungodly hour of the morning?' Ruby bitched as she shuffled into the kitchen and headed straight for the coffee pot she knew Jess would have brewing.

Jess laughed. She didn't have to tell her friend that back home she would have been up two hours ago. 'This is the best part of the day.'

Ruby shook her head. 'You country chicks are mad.' But she smiled as she took her first fortifying sip.

Jess loaded up her plate with the bacon and waited for the eggs to cook. 'What are you doing up this early anyway?'

'Cort got called in at four. I haven't been able to get back to sleep since.'

Jess frowned. 'Everything okay?'

''Course,' Ruby dismissed. 'Just can't sleep without him.'

'Oh,' Jess murmured. 'That's so sweet.'

She envied Ruby. And Tilly and Ellie. They'd all found love this past year. Oh, she was thrilled for them too but it was a little hard to be the single one in a house full of couples.

And she wanted what they had. What her parents had. What her grandparents had.

The fairy-tale.

Was that so wrong?

No.

But who she wanted it with was just plain, never-going-to-happen crazy.

Jess turned back to the pan. 'Do you want some bacon?' she asked as she lifted her eggs onto the plate. 'I've cooked too much.'

Ruby shook her head. 'I don't know how you have a greasy cooked breakfast every morning and manage to stay so skinny.'

Jess grinned. 'Good metabolism.'

The door that led from the side of the house into the kitchen was pushed open and Jess swung around in time to see all her happily-ever-after fantasies in all his six-foot-two glory entering the house.

His wet boardies, riding low on his belly, barely hung

onto his hips as they clung to meaty quads. Great slabs of muscular flesh—shoulders, pectorals, abs—were exposed to her view as they had been yesterday.

A tantalising trail of hair drew her eyes down from his belly button.

Down, down, down.

'That smells amazing,' Adam said. 'Don't suppose there's any extra?'

Jess dragged her gaze up, up up and nodded dumbly. 'Bacon.'

'Great.' Adam smiled. 'I'll have a quick shower and throw on some eggs.' He ruffled Ruby's hair as he went past and earned a grumpy glare.

Jess stood in the middle of the kitchen, staring after his straight tanned back as it disappeared from view.

Tilly passed Adam and entered the kitchen dressed in a strappy little beach-dress thrown over her bikini, ready for her regular morning dip in the bay. She shook her head. 'It should be illegal for your brother to go shirtless, Ruby.'

Jess couldn't have agreed more.

She plonked her plate on the bench and went to the fridge for eggs.

'What are you doing?' Ruby frowned.

'I might as well do his eggs,' Jess said. 'It won't take a jiffy.'

Ruby rolled her eyes. 'He's a thirty-five-year-old man whose skill with a scalpel has given countless people all around the world a better life. I'm pretty sure he can handle an egg flip. Sit and eat before your breakfast gets cold.'

'But—'

'No buts,' Ruby said crankily, thinking how their mother had waited on their father hand and foot all their married life and how he'd let her.

She and Adam hated him for it. And they hated how

their mother had allowed herself to be completely absorbed by him, totally losing herself in the process.

He doubted Adam would thank Jess for her ministrations.

'Sit,' Ruby said when it looked like Jess was about to object again.

Jess raised an eyebrow at Tilly, who turned to Ruby. 'More coffee,' she suggested, sweeping Ruby's cup up as Jess placed her meal on the table and sat. A few minutes later they were chatting about their rare day off together when Adam swaggered back into the kitchen. He was wearing dry boardies and a snug T-shirt and Jess's throat suddenly felt as dry as the toast she was eating.

'These are yours, I believe,' he said, handing Jess her two cushions as he passed her by.

Jess, aware of the speculative gaze of her friends, blushed furiously. The thought of just where those cushions had been deepened the colour to scarlet as she dropped her gaze to her plate.

'Thank you,' she murmured.

'So,' Ruby, said looking from Adam to Jess then back to Adam again, 'what're you up to today?'

Adam smiled to himself as he opened the fridge door and reached for the eggs. Jess's blush was so damn cute it made him want to tease her more.

A lot more.

'I have an appointment with Gordon Meriwether later today about organising some visiting surgeon rights.'

All three of them sat up a little straighter. Jess almost inhaled a piece of bacon. Was he coming to work at Eastern Beaches? In the operating theatres?

Her operating theatres?

'Dr Meriwether from up the hill?' she clarified.

Adam nodded as he sauntered to the fry pan and turned

up the heat. 'As I was saying yesterday, we had to abort this last mission due to some unrest. There were quite a few cases that we'd reviewed a few months ago that were scheduled to be done. Some bad burns contractures from a horrific fire that wiped out a couple of villages and one really major reconstruction case. We had to leave them.' He shrugged. 'That's not ideal.' Jess ignored more speculative glances between Tilly and Ruby at Adam's referral to *yesterday*. The plight of the people that Adam spoke about turned her already soft heart to complete mush. 'Oh, how awful,' she murmured.

'So...you're going to do them at Eastern Beaches?' Ruby asked.

Adam nodded as he cracked his eggs into the pan. 'That's the plan. We've negotiated with some international charities to bring the patients to Australia, I just need to tee it up with Gordon to use his theatres.'

'Can't see that will be a problem,' Tilly said with a wry smile. 'Gordon does like publicity.'

Adam smiled back. 'That's what I figured. Plenty of photo ops make Gordon a happy boy.'

Jess head was spinning. So...the man she'd fallen head over heels for ever since Ruby had introduced her brother three years ago, the man who had been naked in her bed just yesterday, was going to be walking the same sterile corridors as her?

Maybe the universe was trying to tell her something? *Seize the day?* Maybe it was her turn to find happiness?

'So you'll be working at the hospital soon?' Jess was pretty sure she managed to keep the squeak out of her voice.

Adam flipped his eggs. He knew Jess had been in the operating theatres for the last few months. He tried to picture her in blue theatre scrubs and failed.

All he could see was that damn towel.

'If all goes ahead it'll be a PR exercise so there'll be a couple of weeks of settling in and fanfare with the obligatory interviews in women's magazines and for current-affairs television. And the usual press conferences for both the charities and the hospital.'

'That's fair,' Ruby said.

Adam, used to schmoozing and pandering to whatever interests could fund Operation New Faces, simply nodded. He knew full well how this game was played and was prepared to do whatever was required to see that the organisation he'd dedicated the last six years of his life to thrived.

He slipped his cooked eggs onto the plate and joined the women at the table. Jess was studiously mopping up every last scrap of yolk with a piece of toast.

He had a sudden urge to know her. To know Jess, the nurse. Not Jess, his sister's friend, or Jess, the farm girl, or Jess, the blushing housemate.

Jess, the competent professional.

He didn't understand why.

Had someone put a gun to his head he wouldn't have been able to explain it. But suddenly he seemed to want to know *everything* about her.

Not least of all what was beneath that towel.

And how the hell she cleared her bed so quickly of all those damn cushions when the occasion arose. As she must most assuredly on a reasonably regular basis.

Unless all male staff at Eastern Beaches were completely blind. Or stupid.

'It'll be a few days' worth of surgery—there's nine major operations all up. I'll need a team. Are you interested?'

Jess looked up sharply from her plate. Interested? She'd give up her claim to the family farm to work with him. Just to be in the same operating theatre as him as he unleashed his magic would be a supreme honour.

'I've only been in Theatre for a few months. I doubt I'm experienced enough for you.'

As soon as the prophetic words were out, Jess wished she could take them back. On *so* many levels, she just wasn't up to his skill set.

Adam stilled. He could see pink tinging her high cheek-bones again and he suddenly wasn't thinking about the job. Suddenly he was thinking about all the things he could teach her.

Her teeth sank into the lushness of her bottom lip and his brain temporarily short circuited.

After a moment he blinked and forced himself to shrug casually. 'Eastern Beaches is a teaching hospital. It doesn't have any facio-maxillary specialists so it's not something you'll probably ever see if you choose to stay at the hospital. It'll be good experience. Are you up for it?'

Jess forgot all about her plan, which *did not* involve staying at Eastern Beaches at all. The outback was her first love—red dust ran in her veins—and once she'd completed a year each in the OR, Emergency and ICU she was going home to the chronically understaffed bush.

All she heard was his *Are you up for it?*

She was up for anything he was offering. Three years of barely even recognising her and suddenly he was offering her a place on his surgical team?

It wasn't anything romantic, she knew that. But after existing on crumbs for the last few years this was her chance to prove herself worthy. To finally be noticed.

Maybe even as a woman too?

'I'm up for it.'

Adam had to remind himself as Jess looked at him like

he'd created the moon and the stars that she was young and impressionable and very, *very* off-limits.

Remember Francine.

Remember Ruby.

He inclined his head. 'I'll see if I can swing it.' Jess smiled at him and for a moment he forgot what he'd agreed to do as he smiled back.

Ruby and Tilly exchanged looks. 'Hot date tonight?' Ruby asked.

Adam glanced at his sister. Normally a hot date was the only thing on his mind after he'd caught up on some sleep. And sometimes even before that. There'd been more than one occasion he'd pulled up in a taxi outside his Coogee residence not so fresh from the international airport, dragging a woman through the perennially squeaky front gate.

But with Jess smiling at him across the table in her sweet, innocent way, suddenly the names in his little black book didn't seem as appealing.

And that was stupid with a capital S.

'You know me.' He shrugged, thankful for Ruby reminding him of who he was. 'Work hard. Play harder.'

Jess felt his words slam into her heart as if they'd been delivered by a sledgehammer.

Adam Carmichael was a player.

Not the handsome prince!

The following week Jess hurried along to the staffroom. She was late. The orthopaedic list she'd been scrubbing for had run a little over time. James Leonardi, Ellie's orthopaedic surgeon fiancé, usually ran a tight ship but sometimes these things happened.

The soft, well-washed cotton of her baggy blue scrubs shifted against her body as she moved, the clip-clop of her clogs reverberated down the corridor.

All the occupants of the room looked up as she entered but she only had eyes for one. 'Sorry,' she apologised to Adam, smoothing her theatre cap self-consciously.

'No worries.' Adam smiled. 'We haven't started yet.'

Jess smiled shyly back at him and Adam felt a strange kick in the centre of his chest. Her theatre cap obscured her hair and exposed her face in a way he'd not seen before. Her eyes, the exact shade of her scrubs, practically glowed beneath the fringe of mocha lashes, and her flawless skin flowed over high cheekbones and dipped into interesting hollows near her mouth.

And that mouth. *Man, that mouth!* All wide and pink with full soft lips that pulled at him like a homing beacon. She didn't wear any make-up and her gaze was open and honest with absolutely no artifice.

She was just plain...lovely.

Lovely?

'Shall we begin?' prompted Martha Cosgrove, the NUM of the operating theatres.

It took a moment for Adam's brain to realise the room had fallen silent and people were looking at him expectantly. 'Of course,' he said.

He turned and headed for the whiteboard attached to the far wall, castigating himself as he went.

Since when did he do *lovely*?

Hot, sexy, bodacious. These were things he did. *Lovely? Definitely not.* He turned to face the room, his gaze somehow automatically finding Jess. She was now sitting on one of the low chairs that lined the walls. Her legs were crossed and she was looking at him with interest. And suddenly, sitting amidst her nursing colleagues, dressed in her scrubs and cap, she didn't look so young any more. Gone were the jeans and Ts and the ever-present ponytail that made her look like she was still stuck in her teens.

She looked like a professional. Capable. Confident.

She looked all grown up.

'I'd like to thank you for joining me today,' he said dragging his gaze from her and getting back on task. 'Congratulations, you're all part of a team that's going to make a huge difference to the lives of nine human beings who would otherwise be outcasts amongst their own people.'

A feeling that she was doing something worthwhile consumed Jess and she started to clap. Others followed and she took the opportunity to look around her at Adam's team. An anaesthetist, five nurses—three senior, two junior—a surgical registrar and a surgical resident.

She flicked her gaze back to Adam. It was the first time she'd ever seen him in his theatre garb and his magnificence was breathtaking. She'd thought nothing could top the floral sheets but the scrubs definitely made the man.

He looked like every charismatic screen doctor she'd ever watched on television rolled into one. He oozed sexiness and virility and that special brand of confidence that highly skilled surgeons exuded so effortlessly.

In some doctors it would be described as arrogance.

In Adam it was pure self-belief.

'We're hoping to begin the three days of surgery in a fortnight,' Adam continued. 'There's a lot of stuff going on behind the scenes—dotting all the Is and crossing all the Ts with the different charities involved and from a humanitarian visa point of view and certainly for Lai Ling, our most complicated case, there needs to be further imaging and bio-modelling to be done before it can go ahead.'

As he spoke Jess was distracted by wisps of his sandy blond hair that had escaped the theatre cap. She was reminded of how it had looked lying against her pillow. All shaggy and badly in need of a cut and crying out to be ruffled.

Gesturing intermittently, his arms also drew her gaze. The blue scrubs were a stark contrast to the deep brown tan that only seemed to accentuate the flex of muscles in his forearms, the dusting of blond hairs unmistakeably masculine.

How was it possible to look so poised and comfortable talking about cutting-edge surgery and yet look like he'd just come in from the beach?

Adam spoke for half an hour, covering all the logistics, and he had his team's full attention. There were occasional interruptions for questions when pertinent, but otherwise they listened intently. Jess listened too. And not just for the information he conveyed. But the way he conveyed it. The deep sexy timbre of his voice, the effortless way he used wit and humour, the unconscious movement of his body as he gestured with his hands and leaned in towards his team as if gathering them closer.

He wasn't just a sight to behold. He was exceedingly easy on the ear as well.

The briefing broke up when a journalist and photographer from a weekly women's magazine arrived at the door. Jess watched Adam stride across the room and greet them, his movie-star smile radiating confidence and charisma.

'This is Brad Hennegan from *Week About*,' he said, introducing each of his team to the reporter, who was looking a little out of place and very overawed in his scrubs, cap and the blue paper booties he wore over his shoes.

'Brad's here to do some publicity shots and will be in and out during the next few weeks as his magazine is doing some feature articles on the project.'

Brad nodded to the assembled staff. 'I'm looking forward to following the story.'

Adam gestured for Brad and the photographer to precede him out into the corridor. 'I've teed up Theatre Eight with Martha Cosgrove, our nurse manager,' he said.

Brad nodded. 'Can I have one of the nursing staff too, perhaps?' he asked. 'We want the readers to see it's a team effort. Get a real feel for how dynamic the operating theatre really is.'

'Ah, sure,' Adam said, turning back to the staffroom door just as Jess stepped out.

'She'll do,' Brad said.

Great... 'Jess?'

Jess felt her pulse kick up a notch as she approached Adam. He had this amazing magnetic pull that was hard to resist. She probably would have gravitated towards him even if she hadn't been called.

'What's up?' she asked as she drew to a standstill.

'I was wondering if you'd mind being in a couple of photos with Dr Carmichael?' Brad asked. 'Our readers want to know about the nurses involved as well.'

'Sure.' She nodded. Her parents, her grandmother and all the folks back home would be tickled pink to see her in the glossy pages of a national magazine.

And if it meant she got to spend more time with Adam then that suited her fine as well. Between her shifts and his social calendar she'd barely seen him since he'd been home.

They all trooped down to theatre eight and Brad chatted with them about the project while the photographer scoped the room out. When Adam divulged that he and Jess were actually housemates as well, Brad became very excited, talking about how it would make another great angle for the photos.

Half an hour later, Jess was thoroughly sick of smiling. They'd had their pictures taken in every place and pose imaginable. Near the operating table, in the anaesthetic room, with trays of instruments and in front of imaging equipment, with their masks on and their masks hanging half off, scrubbing up at the sinks and drying off.

'Just a couple more,' Brad said, consulting with the photographer over their cache. 'How about more casual shots this time? More like two friends, two colleagues having a laugh together after a hard day's work in the OR?'

Jess thought that Brad watched too much television but if it meant that her facial muscles could soon cop a break then she was game.

'How's this?' Adam asked, slinging an arm casually around Jess's shoulders.

'Good, good,' Brad enthused as the photographer clicked away.

Jess wasn't so sure about that as her whole body went on alert. Her nipples tightened in her bra and she thanked goodness for the bagginess of her scrubs. All she had to do was a lean a little and her whole side would be pressed against his.

She could smell his clean male aroma, warm and vital in the cool, sterile surroundings, and the urge to turn her face and burrow it into his neck was surprisingly urgent.

'Now look up at each other,' Brad instructed to the clicking of the lens. 'Like it's been a good day and you're going home to veg out in front of the tele with a nice cold beer.'

Adam laughed. 'I usually hit the surf when I get home.'

'Okay, that's good.' Brad nodded. 'What about you, Jess? What do you like to do when you get home?'

Wait for Adam to come home from the surf in his wet boardies.

Jess swallowed. 'This time of the day I usually head to the Stat Bar, meet the girls for a drink.'

Adam laughed. 'You mean perv at the guys that jog by with no shirts on.'

Jess gasped and looked up at Adam. 'We do not.' Well, she didn't anyway. And the other three didn't any more either.

'Ruby reckons that's exactly what you all do.' He grinned.

The teasing light in his eyes twinkled at her and his smile was so sincere she found herself smiling back. 'Well, maybe occasionally,' she admitted.

He laughed and she laughed back, his hand light on her shoulder.

'Perfect.' Brad beamed as the photographer nodded at him. 'Perfect.'

Fifteen minutes later Jess was stepping out of the front door of the hospital in the jeans and T-shirt she'd worn to work, her hair in its regulation ponytail. She sucked in a deep, satisfying breath.

Working in a windowless environment after growing up in the wide open spaces of the outback was something she just couldn't get used to and she never took that first breath of fresh air for granted.

'Hey, Jess, wait up.'

Jess didn't have to look around to know it was Adam calling her. But she did anyway, powerless to resist his lure. He was also in jeans but wore a business shirt to dress them up—untucked, of course. It seemed to strike the perfect balance between casual and professional.

'You heading home? I'll walk with you.'

Jess nodded and they fell into step. Home was an easy ten-minute walk down the hill.

'You heading to the Stat Bar now?'

'Yep,' she confirmed. 'You going for a surf?'

Adam smiled. 'How'd you guess?' They walked in silence for a few moments. 'Did I notice on the calendar that it's your birthday in a couple of days?'

Jess nodded. 'Sure is.'

'Are you having a shindig?'

Jess shook her head. 'Nah. I'm going home for the weekend so no doubt Mum and Gran will throw a little party for me.'

'Oh, come on,' Adam cajoled. 'I didn't think you girls needed an excuse to throw a party. It's your birthday. You can't just do nothing. Besides, I feel like a party.'

Jess looked at him. 'Really?' She wondered if she'd be so bold as to ask him for a birthday kiss? 'Well, I guess…'

'Good. That does it then.' He grinned. 'Get the girls to spread the word.'

Jess rolled her eyes. 'Yes, sir.'

Adam chuckled. 'So how old are you going to be?'

Jess took an internal breath. 'Twenty-four,' she murmured.

He slapped his forehead theatrically to cover the internal groan as she gave voice to the paltry number. 'Still a baby,' he teased.

Jess opened her mouth to object at the unfairness of his statement. To say, no, not a baby. A woman. A fully fledged woman with a woman's desires. But a car beeped as they waited for the lights to change at an intersection and people crowded all around them, also waiting for the green flashing man.

It was hardly the kind of thing you said to someone surrounded by a bunch of strangers.

She wished she didn't look so young. That she could add ten years. Hell, she wished she could add one or two. She didn't want to be twelve years younger than him. She didn't want him to think of her as some young girl with a silly crush.

As a baby.

Maybe it was time she showed him she was all grown up?

CHAPTER THREE

Jess eyed Adam's bedroom door from the kitchen as she mixed a dash of melted chocolate into the already decadent icing mix. He hadn't come home last night. Not that she'd seen anyway and she'd stayed up very late, feigning interest in some rubbish movie.

He'd gone on a date with some ward nurse from the hospital so she figured he was still *playing hard.*

The radio, which she'd tuned to the country music station, serenaded her as she took her frustrations out on the icing, beating it into lumpless submission.

The oven timer rang, interrupting her activity, for which her arm muscles were exceedingly grateful.

Jess turned and opened the oven door. A wave of heat rolled over her as the aroma of perfectly cooked Anzac biscuits permeated the entire room. Jess inhaled deeply as she took them out and upended them onto a cooling rack.

The kitchen smelled like baking day back home and she felt suddenly homesick. Her forthcoming trip home couldn't get here fast enough.

Jess pushed the biscuits aside and dragged the chocolate cake she'd cooked that morning closer. She'd just spooned a dollop of icing onto the cake when Adam sauntered into the kitchen.

'Mmm. Something smells amazing,' he said.

Jess looked up. He was lounging in the archway, one shoulder shoved against the jamb, a suit jacket hooked via his index finger over the other. His tie had been pulled askew. A hand buried deep in a trouser pocket pulled the fabric interestingly against a firm bulky quadriceps.

'I'm baking,' she said unnecessarily as her heart lifted a little. He hadn't gone out last night in a suit so maybe he had come home after all?

She marvelled at the many faces of Adam—boardies, scrubs, birthday suit and now a business suit. They were all so tantalising she couldn't decide which one she preferred.

'So I see,' he remarked, pushing off the jamb and prowling into the kitchen. His stomach rumbled and he realised his meeting had run over and he hadn't eaten any lunch. He slung his jacket around the back of a chair and reached for a cooling biscuit.

'Be careful,' Jess said, blowing out of her eye a piece of fringe that had loosened from her ponytail. 'They're hot.'

Adam's mouth watered. They weren't the only things that were hot. Jess bouncing around the kitchen in a ponytail and an apron was pretty damn hot too.

He gave himself a mental shake as he picked up the closest biscuit. Since when had he ever thought domesticated women were hot? *Where had it ever got his mother?*

He bit into the biscuit gingerly to hide his confusion.

'Wow!' he said as golden syrup and melted brown sugar infused his taste buds with glorious sensation. 'This is a damn good biscuit.'

Jess felt her heart fill with joy at his enthusiastic compliment. His look of bliss as he'd savoured that first bite would be duly categorised in her memory banks as one of her best Adam moments. 'You wait till you taste the birthday cake.'

'You're making your own birthday cake?'

Jess laughed. 'Of course. You can't have a birthday party without cake.'

'We could have bought you a cake. You shouldn't have had to make your own.'

Jess waved her hand at him, dismissing his suggestion outright. 'Why buy one when I can make something much better?'

Adam eyed the cake. 'It's *that* good, huh?'

Jess pulled the spoon out of the icing and they both watched as its glossy texture slid off the back like treacle. For good measure she licked the back of the spoon and sighed. 'Hell, yeah.'

Adam, who had followed every single second of Jess's pink tongue gliding across the metal surface, temporarily lost his train of thought as a bolt of desire ignited his loins. In any other woman he would have said it was a deliberate come-on but Jess just looked at him with the same openness she always did.

No hint of coyness or agenda.

'I didn't know you baked,' he said, changing the subject.

Jess nodded. 'Always. I love to bake. Which is just as well seeing as how I have a terrible sweet tooth.'

With the image of Jess licking the spoon fresh in his mind, Adam had to admit there was something about a woman who loved to eat. Too many of the women he dated barely ate a thing. It was a revelation to see one embrace the whole process with such enthusiasm.

'Well, these biscuits are winners.'

'They most definitely are,' Jess said with pride. 'They're my grandmother's recipe. She's known throughout the district for them. They've won her the blue ribbon at the Edwinburra Show for the last thirty-eight years.'

Adam chuckled. He took in the whole scene. A country

song played in the background. The kitchen smelled like an old-fashioned bakehouse. Jess was dressed in a gingham apron with *'Bless This House'* embroidered across the yoke.

He eyed her speculatively. 'You really are a country girl, aren't you?'

Jess wasn't sure if admitting it was a good thing or a bad thing. But she refused to pretend to be something she wasn't. Even for Adam. 'Through and through.'

A look of contentment infused her features into a mask of pure serenity and kicked him hard in the chest. Had he ever felt the way she looked?

The urge to know more surprised him.

'Tell me about home,' he said, pulling up a kitchen chair.

Jess looked at him uncertainly. 'The farm?'

'Is that where you grew up?' She nodded. 'Tell me about the farm.'

Jess paused for a moment as a hundred images crowded her mind. She shrugged. 'It's…beautiful out there. The sky is so…blue…not like it is here. Like this giant glass dome that seems to stretch on for ever, and the smells…they're so different to the city. Dirt and eucalypt, campfires and horses. And at nighttime the stars…they take your breath away.'

Adam stilled as the far-away look in her eyes seemed to reach deep inside him and squeeze. 'The sunsets are stunning—ochres and reds and then…scarlet skies full of cockatoos. The billabongs are surrounded by gum trees and in the late afternoon hundreds of pink galahs feed on the banks…'

Jess felt her earlier sense of homesickness return with a vengeance and she became aware of Adam watching her intently. She blushed as she realised she'd been prattling on and on.

She looked down into the depths of warm, sludgy icing. 'Sorry,' she murmured as she absently stirred it again. 'I get a little carried away.'

Adam dismissed her apology with a wave of his hand. He'd liked hearing her voice soften and watch her eyes follow invisible flocks of cockatoos as she'd painted her outback picture for him.

'It must have been hard to leave.'

Jess nodded, feeling the wrench of leaving all over again. 'It felt like I'd lost my best friend.' She'd cried for the entire seven-hour bus trip. 'But…' Jess shrugged and looked at him '…it's a means to an end.'

'Oh?'

'Once I've got city experience under my belt I can go back home to where I'm really needed. There's a chronic nursing shortage in the bush—too many people have to go to the city, leave all that's dear to them, to get medical care. It's not right.'

Adam felt relief flood his system, knowing Jess was planning on heading back out west. That alone should be enough to kill any ridiculous notions that had filled his head since she'd cluelessly licked that spoon and put his body on high alert.

'Is that why you became a nurse?'

She nodded. 'My grandfather died when I was twelve in a Sydney hospital. He'd wanted to come home to Edwinburra but there were no beds at the hospital because there were no nurses to staff them. So he died far away from the house he'd helped his father build and the land he'd worked his entire life.'

Jess felt the old feelings of injustice resurface and well in her chest. It was amazing how raw it still felt from time to time and she dropped her gaze back to the bowl of icing.

'I grew up in that house, the only kid in a houseful of

adults. I saw him every day of my life until he got sick and I didn't get to say goodbye.'

Adam felt the ache in her voice right down to his bones. 'I'm sorry,' he murmured after a moment.

Jess sucked in a breath and blinked hard. 'Thanks.' She gave him a small smile. 'Anyway,' she said briskly, suddenly feeling foolish for confiding in him, 'this isn't getting the cake iced.' She touched the biscuits, satisfied that they'd cooled enough, and stacked them in a nearby container.

Adam guessed that the abrupt changing of topic and sudden flurry of activity was his signal to drop it. And if he wasn't mistaken, her cheeks looked pink. He hadn't wanted to embarrass her. So he stood and followed her lead.

'Are these for tonight?' he asked, reaching his hand into the container to snag another biscuit.

'No, and just as well,' Jess said pointedly as she removed them from his reach, pleased to be back on solid ground. 'Anzacs are not party food. But the oven was on and they're Cort's favourites.'

'So what are we eating tonight?' Adam asked as he took a step towards her, angling to get closer to the biscuits.

Jess nearly rolled her eyes. Typical man—suggested the party then left it up to everyone else to organise. She shifted the biscuits again as he closed in on them.

'We're getting in some of those Lebanese-style pizzas,' she said.

Coogee had some truly magnificent ethnic eateries and Jess adored the Lebanese take-away. The closest thing to ethnic in Edwinburra was imported olives at the local deli.

Adam reached across her but Jess tugged the container out of his reach. They looked at each other for a solid moment. He, demanding to be allowed another. She, daring him to try again.

But suddenly he realised how close they were and she smelled like chocolate and treacle and his appetite turned... carnal.

His body moved from high alert to defcom four.

He sighed. 'That's it. You leave me no choice.' And he dipped his finger in the nearby icing bowl.

She automatically slapped his hand but it was too late. He was bringing the icing-dipped finger back to his lips and slipping it inside his mouth.

Jess watched as if it was playing in slow motion. The way his lips parted, the glide of his chocolate-lubricated finger as it slid inside his mouth, the soft clamp of his lips, the slow passage of a stray drip as it trekked down his chin, the way his cheeks hollowed as they created enough suction to strip the icing off, his finger reappearing a few moments later clean and moist from the ministrations of his tongue.

'Mmm, mmm.' Adam shut his eyes as layers of sweetness coated the inside of his mouth. 'This,' he said, opening his eyes, 'is very, very good.' He licked his finger again, hoping for any residual flavour.

Jess didn't know what to say. Or do. All she could think about was the smudge of chocolate icing on his chin. So very, very near his mouth.

'You have chocolate on your chin,' she said, hating the suddenly breathy quality of her voice.

Adam looked down at her, at her gaze fixed just south of his mouth. The sadness that had lurked in her eyes before was well and truly gone. There was heat now—lots of heat. His body tensed even further.

'I do?' he asked.

Jess nodded and handed him the washcloth she had handy. 'Here.'

Adam regarded it. Any other woman, with this much

sexual tension filling the air, would have offered to lick it off. God knew, he'd lost his mind enough to let her. But that obviously wasn't her style.

And that should have been a turn-off.

But there was something so sweet about her primness, especially with all that heat in her gaze, it only intrigued him further.

'Thanks,' he said, taking the proffered cloth.

He cleaned his chin and passed it back to her. There was another moment when she just looked up at him and he gave serious thought to kissing her. Her mouth was pink and parted slightly and he knew she'd taste like chocolate icing.

'Any time,' she murmured.

Adam stared at her lips as they moved. 'Happy birthday, Jess.'

Jess smiled. 'Another year older.'

Adam nodded, dragging his gaze from her mouth and stepping away.

Still the same age as Ruby.

He unhooked his jacket from the chair. 'I have a couple of meetings to go to so I'm going to be late to the party. Start without me.'

And then he was gone.

Jess blinked. She could have sworn he was going to kiss her. And then she'd gone and spoilt it by reminding him of her age.

Stupid.

Stupid, stupid, stupid.

'I need a dress. A sexy dress. A very sexy dress.'

Tilly looked up from blindly trying to find the hole in her ear with the hook of her dangly earrings.

'Okay...I thought you were just wearing jeans.' She

looked down at her own casual attire. 'I thought we weren't getting dressed up.'

'It doesn't have to be dressy. Just...'

'Sexy.'

Jess nodded. 'Very sexy.'

Tilly nodded towards her wardrobe. 'Help yourself.'

Jess clapped her hands, entering Tilly's purple room and scooting over to what she knew to be a veritable treasure trove of girly dresses.

'Is there a man you're hoping to impress tonight?' Tilly asked hopefully.

Jess refused to even think of Adam as she flicked through the multitude of coat hangers. 'Nope, just tired of being the jeans and T girl.'

'Right...'

Jess looked at her friend. 'It's my party,' she said defensively. 'I want to look like the party girl.'

'Of course.' Tilly nodded.

Jess narrowed her eyes. 'What?' she demanded.

Tilly bit her lip, choosing her words carefully. 'Well...it's just that...you're not really the party-girl type...are you?'

'I am tonight.' She held up a red dress with no back and a plunging neckline.

Tilly shook her head. 'What about this baby-doll dress with the—?'

'No,' Jess interrupted, shaking her head vigorously. 'No *baby* anything.'

'Okay...let's see.' Tilly hunted a bit more. 'What about this one?'

She held up the chocolate-brown short cotton sundress against Jess. It had a funky fringed hem and the colour suited Jess's blonde hair and emphasised the amazing blue of her eyes. The V-neckline wasn't too risqué and given that Jess was a couple of inches shorter than Tilly, it would probably fall to mid thigh.

'It's an amazing colour on you,' Tilly said.

Jess inspected herself in the mirror on the inside of the wardrobe door. 'Is Marcus around?'

Marcus was an obstetrician at Eastern Beaches. He and Tilly had met when Marcus had tried to shut down Tilly's beloved birth centre.

He'd seen the error of his ways.

Tilly shook her head. 'He doesn't finish for another hour.'

'Good.'

Jess whipped off her T-shirt and threw the dress over her head. It did suit her but the neckline gaped because Jess didn't have enough cleavage to do it justice. She plucked glumly at the sagging material.

'Here.' Tilly reached into a drawer behind them and pulled out a shopping bag. 'Use this. It'll work a treat.'

Jess looked at the fancy push-up bra that seemed more padding than anything else. How it would ever fit Tilly she had no idea.

Tilly seemed to read her mind. 'I bought it in a hurry on sale without trying it on. I never did get round to taking it back. Consider it a birthday gift.'

Jess held the bra against her. 'Really?'

Tilly nodded. 'It's yours.'

Jess gave her friend a quick hug. 'Thanks. You're a lifesaver.'

The party had been in full swing for two hours when Adam finally showed. Jess was aware of him the second he entered, even though the lights had been dimmed right down and music blared out from the sound system.

She was determined to stick to her strategy, though. Look damn good and completely ignore him.

Tilly's bra helped the first part of her plan immensely. It managed what nature and genetics had not—cleavage—and several appreciative looks from men had boosted her self-confidence significantly.

Even Cort, Marcus and James, three of the most seriously in love, monogamous men, she knew, had stared at her like she'd got full body ink done instead of thrown on a dress and a push-up bra.

'Wow.' Marcus had whistled. 'Little Jess is all grown up.'

It had earned him a swift elbow to the ribs from Tilly who, after this afternoon, was particularly aware of Jess's sensitivity about how old she looked.

Jess had laughed. She really didn't mind it coming from Marcus. Or anyone else, for that matter.

Just not Adam.

She knew she'd been cursed with youthful looks. She was constantly carded at night clubs and bottle shops and patients sometimes looked at her like she was still a uni student 'practising' on them.

It was inconvenient at times, for sure. But she'd never seen it as a real issue until she'd fallen for a man twelve years older than her.

Her confidence in the new improved *party-girl* Jess lasted until she came back from the downstairs bathroom where she'd snagged her third beer for the night. The bathtub had been filled with ice and was being used as a makeshift esky.

The first person she saw was Adam. He hadn't bothered to change out of his suit from earlier. Just pulled off his tie and undone the top button. He was smiling down at three women who were all gazing up at him adoringly.

She recognised them from Eastern Beaches and was dismayed to see how confidently they flirted. How they swayed their bodies, laughed, touched his arm, pushed their hair behind their ears, played with their necklaces, tipped their heads to the side as they chatted.

And to add insult to injury not one of them looked like their cleavages needed enhancement.

Suddenly she felt young and gangly again.

'Hey, Jess.'

Jess smiled at Nicholas, one of the orderlies from Theatre, as he approached. She took a deep swig of her beer. This was her party and she *would not* feel sorry for herself or mope around over a man who had no idea she existed.

It was her birthday and she planned to have a damn good time. When Nicholas kissed her on the cheek and wished her happy birthday, she plastered a smile on her face and leaned in close to hear what else he had to say.

Adam worked the room for the next couple of hours, watching Jess surreptitiously as men flocked to kiss the birthday girl. Not that anyone would describe Jess as a *girl* tonight. Hell, the country girl he'd left in the kitchen a few hours ago surrounded by pots and pans and smelling like chocolate and treacle had morphed into some gorgeous, sophisticated city chick.

With cleavage.

Her heavily kohled eyes drew attention to the startling blue of her irises and her lips shimmered with something glittery. It reminded him of jelly crystals and he wondered if she tasted as good. Her blonde hair, freed from its regulation ponytail, hung loosely around her face and shoulders, kicking up at the ends. Dangly chandelier earrings brushed the side of her neck.

And then there was *that* cleavage, constantly drawing his gaze south.

She looked a good two or three inches taller and he recognised Ellie's red retro shoes with the ridiculously high cork platforms she'd worn out the other night. They made Jess's slender legs seem even longer and the dress, its fringed hem swinging enticingly around her upper thighs, even shorter.

Yep—there was nothing *girly* about her.

As the clock struck eleven Jess wondered how much longer she had to endure the pretence. Everyone, it seemed, was having a good time. Except her.

Oh, sure, anyone looking in from out on the street would say it was a pretty rocking party. People were dancing and laughing and chatting and enjoying themselves. Hell, she'd even cracked a laugh or two.

But deep down it just wasn't enough.

She spied Cort and Ruby plastered together on the makeshift dance floor and Marcus laughing at Tilly as she strummed her guitar in a dark corner. She looked a little further afield and noticed Ellie sneaking up the stairs with James in tow.

Her three best friends were blissfully happy and she was miserable. On her birthday. Not that she wasn't happy for them, she was. She just wanted a little of what they had for herself.

Was that too much to ask?

She'd hoped that Adam might at least actually acknowledge her but he hadn't said a word to her all night. And it wasn't like he wasn't in the mood. Oh, no, he'd been very *chatty* to plenty of women!

As one more busty female approached Adam, she guessed maybe it *was* too much to ask.

Snagging another bottle of beer from the bathroom, she escaped to the kitchen. She unscrewed the top and drained half of it in one long swallow. She may look like a sip of champagne would knock her flat but she'd grown up with farm boys—she'd been drinking beer since before it was legal.

A pleasant buzz already bubbled in her veins and she was hoping she could kick it up to *don't-care-what-Adam-does-with-whom* level. She leant her hips against the table and looked over at the sink and the surrounding benches overflowing with the detritus of a well-attended party. Her cake sat in the centre of the draining board and she wandered over, picking up a fork and shovelling some of it into her mouth.

Which was how Adam found her moments later. She was bent slightly at the waist, her elbows on the bench, her bottom sticking out slightly and swaying to the music. The fringed hem of her dress swung in time and brushed the backs of her upper thighs.

If it had been any other woman, he might have moved in close, stroked a finger down her spine. Whispered something flirty in her ear.

But it wasn't any other woman. It was Jess.

She rocked her left foot from side to side, testing the flexibility of both her ankle and the cork heel.

'Careful,' he said from the archway. 'You might break your ankle in those things.'

Jess almost choked on her beer as she spun around to face him, licking cake crumbs from her mouth. 'Adam.'

Adam couldn't decide which was more tantalising, the dress fringe still in motion swaying against her thighs or a pink tongue swiping at errant crumbs. 'You seem deep in thought,' he murmured.

Jess took another swallow of her beer and Adam watched

as her head tipped back, exposing the length of her throat. Her earrings brushed the side of her neck and the way that cute pink mouth pressed against the opening of the bottle should have been illegal.

'I'm contemplating cleaning up,' she said.

Her words dragged his brain back to the conversation as he held up some empty beer bottles. 'Great minds.'

He moved towards her and plonked them down amongst the mess. 'Let's leave it,' he said. 'We'll all attack it tomorrow and it'll be cleaned in a jiffy.'

Jess gave a half-laugh. 'You know we're going to regret that in morning, right?'

Adam grinned back and turned so he too was lounging against the bench, facing the door. 'Probably.'

Jess rolled the beer bottle between her palms. 'You seemed to be enjoying yourself,' she said, watching the gold flecks in the label catch the light just like the ones in his eyes. 'I thought that ward clerk from female surgical was going to swoon.'

Adam chuckled. 'You ought to talk. I think every man at this party kissed you at least twice.'

Not *every* man. Jess shrugged. 'It's my birthday. It's customary.'

'Once is customary. Twice is just plain old greedy.' As far as he was concerned, she'd been way too indulgent in the kissing department.

'And you've not even scored one.'

The foolish words were out before she could stop them. *Yep.* The beer buzz had most definitely kicked in.

'Exactly.' He chuckled. 'Terribly remiss of me.' he said. 'I'm usually first in line to kiss a birthday girl.'

Jess's heart thumped loudly in her head as Adam leaned in. But his *girl* comment needled and she was gripped with the urgent desire to show him she was all *woman*.

She turned her face just as his lips were about to connect with her cheek. 'Woman,' she whispered as she pressed her mouth against his.

For a moment Adam was too stunned to react. But then her lips parted and moved against his and a rush of high octane lust slammed into his gut. He pulled back, shocked by the intensity.

Jess sucked in a breath as his wild-looking eyes searched hers. 'I'm a woman, Adam,' she murmured, dropping her gaze to his mouth. 'Not a girl.'

Thanks to Ellie's shoes, the distance between their mouths was less of a handicap and this time she didn't wait for him to make the first move. She kissed his un-protesting lips once, twice, three times. Brief butterfly presses. The fourth time she opened her mouth more and murmured, 'Adam.'

Adam heard the half sigh, half plea and was powerless to resist. He opened his mouth on a groan and swallowed her answering whimper.

He sucked in a breath as his senses infused with the essence of her, shoving his hand into her hair, tilting her head back, demanding more of her mouth. She tasted like beer and chocolate cake and he wanted more.

He wanted all she could give.

A shrill bubble of laughter burst in through the arch-way and they sprang apart. But not before Ruby and Tilly had witnessed at least some of the kiss. Breathing hard, Adam couldn't even look at Jess. *What on earth had just happened?*

Recovering first, Ruby looked at Adam. 'All right… what the hell's going on here?' she demanded.

Adam shook his head. 'Nothing. Just a birthday kiss.'

Jess tried not to let his denial hurt as she struggled to regain her breath. After all, it had probably meant nothing.

To him.

Ruby eyed them both then looked at Tilly. 'I'll take him. You take her.' She looked at her brother with disgust. 'We need to talk.'

Adam, his body in revolt, was too dazed to tell his little sister to mind her own business. And frankly he was pleased for the easy getaway. He followed Ruby out of the room without argument, without looking back.

Jess and Tilly watched them go. 'You want to tell me what just happened?' Tilly asked after a beat or two.

Jess shook her head. Partly to deny any wrongdoing. Partly to clear the fireworks that were popping and fizzing behind her eyes. 'Nothing,' she denied, turning to the bench and absently clearing the debris. 'It was like Adam said. Just a birthday kiss. That's all.'

Tilly snorted. 'It bloody was not.'

Jess stopped what she was doing. Tilly was a dear friend but with a swag of younger siblings she missed terribly she did tend to mother them all. Her in particular.

'He keeps referring to me like I'm a child. A…bloody teenager…or something. I just wanted to prove I was a woman.' She turned to her friend. 'I'm a woman, for crying out loud. I have…needs.'

Tilly nodded. So that's what the dress was about. 'I know, I know. Of course you are. Of course you do. But, Jess, you're playing with fire there. Adam likes to flirt. And he's…well, he's, you know…experienced. *Really* experienced. And you know I adore him…'

Tilly broke off, choosing her words carefully. She didn't want to ruin the birthday of one of her best friends. 'I know you've had a crush on him for ever but, sweetie, you're just not his type. I'd hate to see you get your hopes up.'

Jess knew every word Tilly said was the absolute truth.

And she knew her friend was just worried about her. She was lucky to have such good friends.

'I know, Tilly,' she said, squeezing her friend's hand. 'It's okay, I do know that. It was just a little birthday kiss that got out of hand. I'm not stupid enough to think it'll mean anything more to him than that.'

Tilly put an arm around her shoulder. 'He doesn't mean to be that way, Jess. He's just been hurt in the past.'

'I know,' Jess murmured.

And she did know. She knew all about Adam's long-ago fiancé who'd broken his heart. But right now all she wanted was to escape to her bedroom and relive that kiss over and over and she knew Tilly wasn't going to let her go until she was satisfied she was okay.

'I promise I won't get my hopes up,' she said, squeezing Tilly's hand.

'Are you sure?' Tilly asked.

Jess nodded. 'Cross my heart.'

'Are you freaking insane?' Ruby hissed as she slammed her brother's bedroom door.

'Don't be melodramatic,' Adam said. He could still taste Jess on his lips and his pulse rate was marching to a strange tattoo.

'I mean it, Adam, don't play with her. She's not like your other women. She's not your type.'

Adam looked up. 'I have a type?'

Ruby glared at him. 'Yes, fast and loose.'

'Your opinion of me is flattering,' he said, his voice heavy with derision.

'You know what I mean, Adam. She's not some thirty-something go-getter who knows the score and is happy for a couple of quick nights in your bed.'

'Maybe I don't want that any more?' Ruby, who had

taken up pacing, stopped abruptly and stared at him like he'd grown a second head. He couldn't blame her—where the hell that thought had come from he had no idea.

Except being home this time felt different.

It didn't feel like prison any more. He didn't feel the urge to run.

Ruby snorted. 'Since when?'

Adam shrugged. 'I don't know. I'm just…' he pressed the heels of his palms into his eye sockets '…tired these days.'

'Well, lie down and have a nice long sleep,' Ruby snapped, resuming her pacing. 'Just leave Jess the hell alone. For crying out loud, she wants to move back to outer whoop-whoop, get married and have babies. She comes from generations of men and women who mate for life. She thinks that love cures everything and that there's one special person for everyone.'

'Ruby,' Adam said firmly. 'It was just some harmless flirting. Jess is a grown woman. I think she knows that.'

Ruby stopped in front of her brother. 'She has a crush on you, you idiot!'

Adam looked up alarmed. *She did? 'She does?'*

Ruby shook her head, annoyed that she'd let Jess's secret slip. But, honestly, her clever brother could be exceedingly dim-witted sometimes.

'Yes,' she sighed. 'She does. A big one. Do you remember what happened with Francine? How crazy that got?'

'Jess is hardly like to turn into some nutty stalker, Ruby. I think we both know that.'

That had been a harrowing time in his life. Francine, a hairdresser, had been twenty-two. He'd been an intern. After three dates she'd been totally obsessed and had not taken well to being blown off.

He'd gone on his first humanitarian mission overseas

just to get away from her. The only silver lining from the whole nasty incident. 'She's my friend, Adam. And one of the nicest people that I know. And as much as I love you, I'm not going to sit by and watch you destroy all that lovely Pollyanna sunshine when you break her heart.'

'Ruby.' Adam shot his sister an exasperated look. 'I have no intention of getting involved with Jess. I'm twelve years older than her, for crying out loud.'

And if he said it enough, it might just help him remember it next time Jess looked at his mouth like she wanted to own it.

Jess, who had a crush on him. *A big one.* 'It was just a birthday kiss.'

'To you,' she yelled, thankful for the music still blaring outside.

'I think you're overreacting.'

Even though the news of Jess's crush did complicate things.

Damn.

'Well, I hope you're right, big brother. I really do. I hope, for Jess's sake, this isn't something you regret come morning.'

Adam shot his sister a grim look. Unlike the dishes, he doubted he was going to have to wait till the morning.

CHAPTER FOUR

THE next morning Jess sat on the second bottom stair of the main public steps that led down to Coogee beach, absently staring out to sea. She wiggled her bare feet in the sand, the dry, cool grains sifting easily through her toes.

She adored this time of morning and she filled her lungs, trying to inhale the loveliness of it all.

The salt air, the sun winking over the horizon, gilding marshmallow clouds, the occasional cry of a seagull circling lazily overhead, the swish and suck of the waves as they lapped against the beach to a rhythm as old as time.

It was about as different from the outback as it was possible to be. She missed home dreadfully and, as far as she was concerned, there was nothing like a country sunrise, but the scene before her was pretty good too.

She dropped her chin onto her bent knees, feeling a pang. She'd miss this when she finally moved back to Edwinburra. Which had been a revelation. She hadn't expected to miss anything about the city.

She'd been prepared to *endure* her time away from home only. Suffer quietly through it with her eye firmly on the ball.

But to her complete surprise she loved it here and she *would* miss it when she finally went back home. And it wouldn't just be the panorama before her she'd miss. There were a lot of other things.

Her friends.

Eastern Beaches Hospital, which somehow felt like home.

The house on Hill St.

The Stat Bar.

And Adam.

She'd lain awake most of the night, reliving their kiss, and unfortunately it had lost none of its impact in the cold light of day. It was still setting her heart aflutter.

Finally. After dreaming about it for the last few years it had actually happened.

And it *had not* disappointed.

She hugged her knees and rocked. Not even the hardness of the gritty concrete beneath her butt or Tilly's well-intentioned warning could stop the swell of possibility blooming in her chest.

Yes. It was foolish. But what Tilly hadn't seen had been the way Adam had looked at her. Like he saw her, really saw her, for the first time. Saw her as a woman. Not as a girl. Or even as someone out of bounds.

She'd seen desire flash as brightly as those irresistible golden flecks in his lapis lazuli gaze. Heard the suck of his breath and the deep groan that had seemed torn from his chest. Felt the tremble of his hand as it had burrowed into her hair.

Adam Carmichael had been…shaken.

And shaken she could work with.

Maybe it was time to seize the moment?

Adam paused at the top of the stairs and looked down at the lone figure sitting hunched at the bottom. Her blonde ponytail brushed her shoulder blades as she rocked slightly and memories of their hot birthday kiss taunted him again as they had through the endless night.

The softness of her lips, the husky timbre of her whisper, the heady satisfaction of that little whimper.

Not even Ruby's stern disapproval had been able to obliterate the whimper. But his sister was right.

It was an attraction he couldn't explore. For numerous reasons.

They had to talk. About the kiss. About the crush. About their total unsuitability for each other.

He hadn't planned to do it now but it seemed fate had intervened.

A light ocean breeze ruffled his hair as he adjusted his board under his arm and descended the stairs.

'Hi,' he said as he passed by, stepping onto the soft sand and turning to face her as he dropped his board at his feet.

Jess started as Adam and his mouth appeared before her. His mouth, however, promptly lost its fascination as she realised he was practically naked before her. A brief pair of swimming trunks was the only thing that stood between him and total nudity.

She'd never known a man to wear so little so consistently! She swallowed, refusing to look any further south than his chest.

'Hi.'

He looked at her for a moment, his gaze drawn to her pink mouth. 'I didn't realise you were a walker,' he said, indicating her gym clothes.

Jess shrugged. 'I'm not. Not really. Just…couldn't sleep.'

He nodded. Now, *that* he could relate to. He'd never been more relieved to see strips of daylight illuminating the sky through the blinds of his bedroom window.

'We need to talk.'

Her heart thumped like a rotor in her chest. 'Okay.'

Adam cleared his throat. 'About the kiss.'

Jess held her breath. 'Yes?'

'I shouldn't have…let things get out of hand like that. It was…wrong of me.'

Jess didn't want to hear *wrong*. It had been a good kiss—a great kiss—and they were both adult and single. There had been nothing *wrong* about it.

And maybe he wanted this too? Deep down. Maybe he just needed a push?

'Did you enjoy it?' she asked, cutting to what was, in her opinion, the crux of the matter.

Hell, yeah was his most immediate thought. But he was smart enough to know he was damned, no matter how he answered. 'Of course I enjoyed it, Jess.'

Jess felt a little kick of triumph deep in her belly. 'Well, isn't that all that matters?'

Adam sighed. If only it was *that* simple. 'No, it isn't. You're quite a bit younger than me and you're Ruby's friend and you live in my house. We shouldn't be kissing…at all… and especially not like that.'

Because it was going to lead to more. Hell, he already wanted more.

How could that be?

How could he want to yank her into his arms and kiss her again? Kiss her better. Wetter, deeper, harder.

It was insane.

Jess regarded him seriously. She knew she probably wasn't going to get another opportunity to make her case so, despite her heart thudding so loudly she could barely hear herself, she pushed a little more. 'Even though we enjoyed it?'

Adam nodded. 'Especially because we enjoyed it.'

Jess watched as the light ocean breeze ruffled his shaggy hair. The sun rising higher over the horizon behind him highlighted the tips and it seemed to glow like a golden halo.

'Look…Ruby told me…about your…about the crush.'

Jess stilled as a bloom of colour whooshed over her from the roots of her hair to the tips on her sand-buried toes. She dropped her gaze.

Ruby? *How could she?*

She wanted to die. She wanted to dig a big hole in the sand and bury herself in it. She wanted to cough and splutter and deny it and pretend that Ruby had lost her mind.

She wanted to stamp her foot. Giggle. Cry.

Anything to get through this excruciating moment.

Running away was another option.

But, staring at her toes buried in the sand, she knew she couldn't. This was the ultimate test of her adulthood. A child, a girl would run away and hide. Adults didn't. They talked about their issues. No matter how difficult or embarrassing. They faced things head on.

Just like Adam.

Adam couldn't bear it as the silence stretched, broken only by the cry of a seagull. He'd embarrassed her—that much was obvious—but surely she didn't think this conversation was any easier for him.

'Jess?'

Jess took a steadying breath and looked up. Time to prove to him, in a less overt way than last night, how mature she could be.

'I'm twenty-four years old, Adam. Crushes are for teenagers.'

She took a breath to gather herself to lay it all out. To speak up for a change instead of keeping it all to herself.

'I think you're sexy. Hot. Delicious.' She could feel her face getting warmer but she plunged on. She couldn't back out now.

'But more than that, you're amazing. You're smart and kind and what you do for a living is sexy. And it makes me proud to know you. Proud to be part of the human race. You're noble and that's sexy. So sexy it makes me hot all over. And even if you were ugly, which...' she couldn't help herself, she looked him up and down and sighed '...God help me, you're not, you'd still make me hot all over.'

There, she'd said it.

Every part of her wanted to drop her gaze from his stunned face, to hide the embarrassed flush, to sink into the ground. But if she did, if she blinked, all the things she'd said would lose their impact.

So she kept her chin firmly up.

He needed to know that this was more than just some silly girly crush. He needed to know that what she felt for him was very, very adult. And that it was about more than the external package.

Adam was speechless. Stunned. Too stunned to even move. Well, most of him anyway. One part of him was having no problems in that quarter. Her *so sexy it makes me hot all over* was having an alarming effect and he wasn't exactly dressed to conceal involuntary reactions.

'Can I have a moment to process that?' he asked as he hastily lowered himself to the same step that Jess was sitting on but as close to the opposite end as was possible without falling off.

Jess, pleased to break the intense eye contact, nodded. 'Sure. It's a lot to take in,' she said, returning her gaze to the ocean, feeling as light as the gull still riding the air currents above.

Finally, she'd got it off her chest.

Adam stared out at it too, feeling decidedly burdened as his brain grappled with Jess's words. Quite a few women had called him sexy. And hot. Usually they were between sheets at the time but the point was, he was used to being flattered by women. Compliments about his body weren't exactly a new thing.

Surfing kept him in good shape and he certainly worked it to his advantage. He enjoyed the way women looked at him. He liked their candid appreciation. That look in their eyes that told him they'd already undressed him.

But Jess's impassioned little speech wasn't like that. There wasn't that frank look in her eyes when she called him sexy. No sexual overtones when she'd told him she was hot for him. Her eyes didn't do that flirty thing that let him know she'd put him next on her bucket list.

There was just honesty. And appreciation. Of him as a human being. Not just as a man with a good body.

And something else. Adoration. For what he did. For his skills. His brain. His humanity.

Somehow it was sexier than any amount of being mentally undressed.

Frankly it was…well…hot.

Finally he understood why his old man, *the chief*, got such a kick out of it. Why hundreds of fawning patients and colleagues and myriad accolades despite his terrible arrogance and unprofessional conduct puffed out his chest. Why his mother's total adoration, unwavering even after forty years and several affairs, was such a huge ego trip.

The thought of his parents' screwed-up relationship put the brakes on his own burgeoning ego. He wasn't his father and he didn't want that kind of relationship with anyone, especially not a woman.

Blind adoration may be flattering but he'd rather be involved with someone who had her own agenda, was her own woman. That's what he'd loved so much about Caroline—as a kindy teacher and having not grown up in a medical family, she hadn't given a toss about his medical pedigree or whose son he was.

She hadn't even cared that his father disapproved of her—*not malleable enough, son*—in the beginning, anyway.

She'd just taken each day as it came and asked nothing of him other than letting her be her own woman. She'd been the complete opposite of his mother. And he'd adored her for it.

He hadn't wanted to fall into the same pattern his parents' marriage had taken. His mother eclipsed and happy to be so. Ready and willing to drop everything to do her husband's bidding.

And he'd desperately wanted to stick it to his father. Show *the chief* what a real relationship was about. One that involved *mutual* respect.

But in the end, having escaped an overbearing father when her mother had divorced him in her teens, Caroline hadn't wanted anything to do with the great Gregory Carmichael—including his son.

She hadn't been convinced that Adam wouldn't turn into his father one day.

That had been gutting.

And he'd spent every day since proving her wrong.

He dragged his gaze from the ocean and found Jess looking at him with that open, honest gaze. 'Jess…I'm flattered. Really, I am.'

Jess could hear the *but* coming from a mile off.

'But you and I just aren't going to happen.'

She felt the inevitability of the rejection but refused to be dissuaded. If he thought she was going to take it meekly then he was wrong.

She was a country girl and they spoke their minds.

And she'd already laid herself bare. What did she have to lose?

'Because your twelve years older than me?'

Adam groaned inwardly as she said the age difference out loud. It sounded obscene and instead of young and virile he felt old and dirty.

'No. Not just because of that, although, God knows, that's bad enough.'

He rubbed his hand through his hair as he searched for the right words to let her down gently.

'It's just… Jess, we want two different things from relationships. I'm not the settling-down type and, as Ruby so rightly pointed out last night, *you are*. I can't in all honesty kiss you and know that while I'm thinking about how quickly I can get you into bed, you're thinking about what colour to paint the nursery. That wouldn't be right, Jess.'

'See,' she joked lightly, her heart expanding even more at his innate sense of fairness. 'I told you you were noble.'

'Jess…'

She sighed at the warning in his voice. 'How do you know you're not the settling-down type when you've never even tried, Adam? I know you came close once but that was a long time ago.'

So Jess knew about Caroline. Ruby must have told her. But did she have any idea how devastated he'd been?

'Jess, I'm only here for a handful of weeks before I go off on my next mission. And I can't get into something with you that could have repercussions for your relationship with Ruby and with the important surgeries we've got coming up. If you were ten years older, ten years wiser, if you didn't live in my house and I wasn't about to become your boss, I'd totally be up for a fling. But that's all I could offer you. I don't do anything serious.'

Jess contemplated the temptation for a moment. A fling

with a man she'd lusted after for three years. The same man who sat not two metres from her with practically every muscle, every inch of skin he had exposed to her gaze.

It was so very tempting. 'Maybe I'm totally up for a fling too?'

Adam narrowed his gaze at the bravado he heard trembling in her voice. 'Really?' He cocked an eyebrow, his heart pounding in rhythm with the surf. 'You wouldn't want more?'

Of course she would. Even before their kiss she'd wanted more. And her grandmother always told her to be true to herself and others.

She looked back towards the horizon. 'I'd want everything.'

Even though her words were barely more than a whisper Adam heard them loud and clear. They slipped under his skin as he also turned his gaze to the rising sun. 'I only give everything to my job.'

Jess nodded. In her heart of hearts she knew that. It was, after all, one of the things she admired about him. But he suddenly sounded utterly miserable and she realised she'd done that. She'd brought the man down when all he'd no doubt been hoping for when he'd come to the beach this morning had been to catch a wave or two.

To be exhilarated, not aggravated.

It's not like he'd ever given her crush any encouragement. Until last night, and the naked-in-her-bed thing, he'd been absolutely above board with her.

It wasn't his fault she was besotted with him.

And she didn't want him to feel awkward or like this was somehow his fault. She looked back at him. 'Guess we're just going to have to stay friends, then, huh?'

Adam looked at her sharply. 'You think we can do that?

Ignore this whole…awkward conversation and go on like before?'

No. She didn't want it to go back to what it had been. But Jess felt a responsibility to fix what she'd broken with her seize-the-moment attitude.

'No. I don't want it to be like it was before. We were just acquaintances, passing each other like ships in the night. You barely spoke to me, for crying out loud, which is crazy because your sister is one of my closest friends and we're going to be working together. Our paths are kind of inter-twined—whether you like it or not. I'd like to think we could be friends.'

Adam couldn't think of a single woman friend he'd had whose pants he hadn't wanted to get into. And usually did.

But this wasn't any woman. It was Jess. Ruby's friend. And it was a very sensible suggestion.

He smiled. 'Now, that sounds like something I could live with.'

Jess responded to his smile despite herself. He was in-credible in this early morning light as the soft morning sun stroked gentle fingers over all his golden glory. He looked fit and healthy and very, very male.

'Go surf,' she ordered. *Before I push you down right here in the sand.*

Adam grinned. 'Yes, ma'am.'

All the serious talk had put paid to his erection so he leapt to his feet, bending to pick up his board. He was grateful for the familiar weight against his body and for the invisible pull of the waves.

But a sudden pang of conscience tugged at him and he looked over his shoulder. 'If you want off the team, you know I'd understand.'

Jess recoiled from the suggestion as an immediate rebuff hovered on her lips. 'Do you want me off?' she asked, holding her breath.

'No.' He shook his head emphatically. 'Absolutely not. Just…you know… Thought it might be easier…'

Nothing was easy where her feelings for him were concerned. So what difference did it make? 'Wild horses couldn't drag me from the team.'

Adam smiled again, buoyed by her emphatic reply. He'd been looking forward to working with her. 'Good.'

Jess sat and watched the swagger of his butt until it disappeared into the ocean.

A week later Jess somehow found herself sitting in the middle of a press conference, the Eastern Beaches Hospital logo behind her and flashes strobing in front of her. She was a most reluctant participant but as the other nurses in Adam's team were all in surgery, she hadn't been given a choice.

'Just fake it,' her boss had advised. 'They're not interested in you anyway. You're just a prop.'

'Gee, thanks,' Jess had murmured.

Martha laughed. 'Sorry. What I mean is…this is all just a publicity exercise for the hospital and the charities involved so we put on our scrubs and we play along.'

'Scrubs? But nobody wears their scrubs outside the operating theatres.'

'Yes, you know that and I know that but the general public, who've had a steady diet of medical shows for the last thirty years, don't. Gordon Meriwether wants us in scrubs. We wear scrubs. He's the boss.'

So here she sat in her scrubs, hair tucked into her theatre cap, in what felt like the middle of a circus as her fellow performers were introduced by Gordon.

Adam, of course, followed by Rajiv, the anaesthetist, Paula, the surgical registrar, and the two charity CEOs.

And next to her sat Lai Ling, the *star* case.

Beside her, an interpreter.

At nineteen and obviously embarrassed by her condition, Lai Ling seemed very overawed by all the noise and attention. She barely lifted her gaze and when she did she looked shyly through her fringe.

All the patients had arrived on a flight yesterday morning and the surgical team had met them in the afternoon. And in three days' time, on Monday morning, the first case would be operated on. Lai Ling was scheduled for Wednesday.

'Dr Carmichael,' someone yelled from the back of the room once the floor had been thrown open to questions. 'Can you tell us about Lai Ling's condition?'

Adam, also resplendent in scrubs, smiled and Jess's heart did a silly flutter in her chest. She'd not seen a lot of him this last week but had been pleased that any awkwardness had passed quickly and they could chat and laugh like they'd never kissed at all.

'Lai Ling has a congenital facial deformity known as a Tessier cleft. They are very rare and caused by the failure of the face to fuse properly in utero. They involve both soft tissue and the bony elements of the face.'

Jess felt Lai Ling move closer to her as all eyes swivelled her way. She grabbed for the young woman's hand under the table and gave it a squeeze. She knew that Lai Ling had lived a solitary life, unable to make friends or be included in village life, because of her condition.

Looking at the defect, Jess felt incredibly protective of her. The young woman's face was 'separated' in the middle where the bones beneath hadn't fused properly. This had the unfortunate result of displacing both of her eyes laterally and the formation of a bifid nose—two complete half-noses separated by a smooth expanse of skin.

It was a complex condition that required complex surgery.

Despite this, though, she had smiled shyly at Jess as she'd taken the seat next to her. More questions followed that required no input from her. Rajiv answered questions about the difficulty of anaesthetising cranio-facial patients and the charity heads spoke about Operation New Faces and praised Eastern Beaches and Dr Meriwether for their generosity.

'Dr Carmichael, I'm curious as to why you chose this line of work when you could have gone into plastic surgery like your father, the great Gregory Carmichael, and made more of a name for yourself.'

Jess watched Adam tense and she flicked her gaze towards the assembled press pack, identifying the journo who had asked the question. Where had he said he was from? Some gossip rag or other.

Adam forced his shoulders and jaw to relax lest he say something like *Because I didn't want to turn into a rude arrogant bully who cares more about prestige than patients.* 'I didn't become a surgeon to make a name for myself,' he said tersely.

Jess watched as the journalist's gaze narrowed, sensing a story behind Adam's clipped reply. 'And you think your father did?' the journalist persisted.

Gordon, who granted Gregory Carmichael operating rights from time to time and earned quite a bit of money for the hospital in the process, leapt into the conversation.

'Dr Gregory Carmichael is a consummate professional. As is his son. Next,' he announced.

But the journo was not easily put off. 'Is your father proud of the work you're doing?' he persisted.

Adam knew for damn sure he wasn't. His mother was inordinately proud but his father had always thought what Adam did was a waste of time and that his son would go to his grave poor and unrecognised.

Gregory Carmichael just didn't realise neither of those things mattered to Adam.

'Well, I guess you'd have to ask him that.' Adam fobbed the question off.

He was damned if he was going to make the chief look good by lying.

'Next!' Gordon called again, more insistently.

'Lai Ling, how are you feeling?' a female journo called.

Jess dragged her gaze away from Adam's stony face as she felt the young woman tense. She squeezed her hand again as the interpreter, a greying man, murmured quietly to her.

'She says she's feeling good. Nervous but good.'

'What are you hoping to look like after the surgery, Lai Ling,' another voice called out.

Everyone waited while there was more conferring with the interpreter. 'Lai Ling wants to look beautiful. Just like Jess.'

The interpreter indicated Jess and Lai Ling smiled shyly at her as general laughter followed. Jess blushed and smiled back as she squeezed the young woman's hand again.

'What do you say to that, Jess?' a deep voice called from the back.

Jess looked at Lai Ling as she spoke, ignoring the media pack. 'I say that I can already see through Lai Ling's gorgeous eyes the beauty that lies beneath.' She paused for the interpreter. 'And that's the only beauty that matters.'

Lai Ling shot her another shy smile as the interpreter conveyed Jess's reply. The cameras snapped wildly.

Another couple of questions followed for Jess about the

nursing role and working in a multi-disciplinary team. And then the journalist from earlier piped up again.

'I notice from the article in *Week About* that you live with Dr Carmichael.'

Jess could feel Adam's concerned gaze on her and the animosity flowing off him in thick, angry waves. 'I live in a house owned by him with his sister who is a friend of mine and two other friends.'

'So there's no intimate relationship between the two of you?'

Adam thumped the table. 'I hardly see that that's relevant,' he snapped.

'Our readership likes to know the intimate details of celebrities' lives.'

'We're doctors and nurses, doing our jobs,' Adam said icily. 'Not celebrities.'

'But your father is,' the man persisted.

'My father's not here,' Adam said stonily.

'Okay,' Gordon intervened. 'I think we've got a bit off track... Last questions? Somebody other than our friend from *Behind Closed Doors*.'

A few more questions were thrown to the charity directors then someone asked if everyone wouldn't mind saying what they'd take away from the experience. 'You first, Jess,' the journo prompted.

Jess took the opportunity to refocus the press conference on the reason they were all there. After the comparisons to his father and speculation about their relationship outside work, Jess felt that Adam and what he was trying to achieve had been belittled.

'The opportunity to work on this project with all these incredible professionals is truly amazing. It's easy to forget with all this hoopla that nine lives will be changed as a result of what we're doing.'

Jess turned and smiled at Lai Ling before seeking Adam's lapis lazuli gaze and locking tight.

'This is all down to the vision and drive of Dr Carmichael. The work he does is truly inspirational. The opportunity to work with him, to be part of his team, is beyond what I've ever hoped for. He may not be a fancy celebrity plastic surgeon but the world has enough of them. What the world doesn't have enough of are dedicated surgeons who strive to make the world a better place.'

There was a moment of utter stillness as, for the first time in half an hour, every person in the room fell silent.

Then someone clapped and soon the room rang with applause. Jess flushed bright pink and dropped her gaze.

Adam breathed out slowly.

He'd never been more turned on in his life.

CHAPTER FIVE

THE Stat Bar was jumping on Sunday afternoon as the Norfolk pine shadows lengthened over the beach and the ocean darkened beneath a scarlet sky.

'That was some press conference I saw on the news the other night,' Cort said, lifting his beer and taking a swig.

Jess blushed and glanced over her beer bottle at Adam, sitting opposite. The subsequent flutter in the press over her impassioned dialogue had practically gone viral.

'Mmm, I see *Behind Closed Doors* did a very interesting story on the... What was it, darling?' James asked Ellie, who was sipping her vodka lime and soda.

'The seething sexual tension between the son of famed ex chief of staff at Sydney Central, Gregory Carmichael, and his nurse,' Cort supplied.

'Bloody gutter journalism,' Jess spluttered as she noticed Tilly and Ruby exchange glances. 'I'm not anybody's bloody nurse.'

Adam, who still felt a fire in his loins at the things Jess had said, could see the conversation was making Jess squirm. Interesting, though, that she hadn't disputed the seething-sexual-tension bit.

'Is that my tie you're wearing?' he asked Cort, deftly changing the subject.

Cort and he went way back to a time when Cort had

been married to another woman and even now Adam found it difficult to wrap his head around Ruby being with his friend. But if anyone deserved to be happy again it was Cort, and his sister obviously adored him.

They adored each other.

But it didn't change the facts—that was most definitely his tie because he'd been looking for it yesterday and hadn't been able to find it. He'd also noticed Marcus wearing one of his favourite business shirts the other day—one he'd had specially made in Singapore.

Cort looked down. 'Oh, yes.' He fingered it. 'I'd forgotten a tie one morning and Ruby grabbed one from your cupboard. Sorry, must have forgotten to give it back.'

Adam looked at Ruby. 'You loaned him my tie?'

Ruby shrugged. 'Sure. You're never here and the guys are sometimes caught short.'

Adam looked at the three couples sitting around the table. 'Oh, really? So you just…go to my cupboard and help yourselves?'

Ruby nodded. 'Pretty much.'

Adam shook his head at Cort's chuckle. 'Does this apparent sharing around of my stuff also extend to my car? 'Cos I noticed a little ding in the front left yesterday when I drove it into the city.'

'Ah,' Ellie said. 'Sorry. Jess and I were going out to this wine appreciation thing—'

'To meet men,' James butted in, winking at Ellie.

'And,' Ellie continued, ignoring her fiancé, 'Ruby said we should use your car while you were away… So, anyway, we hit somebody—'

'I'm sorry?' Adam almost choked on his beer. 'You *hit* somebody?'

'Just winged him really,' Ellie dismissed with a wave of her hand. 'Anyway, it ended up being Harry, James's half-brother—you know, you met him at Jess's party last week?'

Adam nodded. 'He didn't seem particularly maimed.'

Ellie laughed. 'No. He's fine. He's been coming around a bit, which is great.'

'Probably because the poor kid has a crush on Jess,' Marcus teased.

Jess blushed and Adam felt a quick jab of something hot in the middle of his chest. It stood to reason. Jess was very pretty and Harry, from what he'd ascertained when they'd met, was sure as hell closer in age to Jess than he was.

It was an unaccountably depressing thought.

'Anyway,' Ellie continued, 'we have all the insurance quotes and so on. I was just waiting for your return.'

'Okay, fine, thanks,' he muttered. 'What about you?' he asked Jess. 'Have you loaned some guy anything of mine? Is there some random man I'm going to bump into on the streets of Coogee or at the hospital, wearing my socks or a jacket?'

Jess blinked. Was that his way of checking how many men she'd had stay over? If only he knew that no man had ever stayed over. That, thanks to her three-year infatuation with him, no man had made it past second base. That she was still a virgin at twenty-four.

'Absolutely not,' she said primly.

Adam was unaccountably pleased with the answer.

'So, big day tomorrow,' Tilly said sensing Jess's discomfort and changing the subject.

The conversation turned to the next few days of surgery and Jess was happy to watch Adam as he talked about the culmination of what had been many weeks of behind-the-scenes negotiations.

He was obviously used to this sort of bureaucracy but just listening to the thread of anticipation in his voice it was even more obvious he preferred to be at the actual coal face, where he made the most difference.

'So it's a morning list tomorrow?' Ruby asked Adam as he drained his beer.

'Afternoon. We had to fit the project ops in around the already scheduled lists. Tuesday we have a morning list and then Wednesday we have Theatre Four all day for Lai Ling's op.'

There was more discussion about the intricacies of the Tessier cleft repair before Tilly and Marcus stood to go. 'Gotta dash,' Tilly announced. 'Our table's booked for seven.'

Ellie and James departed with them. Jess watched them leave hand in hand, stifling a sigh. Cort and Ruby stayed another five minutes and they also left.

Before Jess knew it, she was alone with Adam. Something she hadn't been since the press conference.

'So are you ready for this?'

Jess raised her long-necked beer to her mouth and swallowed a decent slug to hide her sudden nervousness. *Ready for what?*

She licked her lips. 'For…tomorrow?'

Adam's gaze was drawn to her mouth as he followed the dart of her tongue. 'Uh-huh,' he murmured.

'Of course.' She shrugged. 'It's going to be an amazing experience. I can't wait.' She took another mouthful of beer.

Adam watched. He really, really shouldn't be staring at her mouth. But he didn't seem to be able to stop either… He remembered how she'd tasted like beer and chocolate cake at her party and how that little whimper had gone straight to his groin.

'I'm a little nervous,' she admitted, because she had to say something other than *Kiss me* as he stared at her mouth.

Adam dragged his eyes upwards to look into hers. 'Oh?'

'I'm the most junior member of the team. I want to be as efficient as everyone else. I've worked with some surgeons who don't tolerate any…hesitation. I don't want to let y—the team down.'

He could see a glimmer of self-doubt lurking in her blue gaze. 'You'll be fine,' he said, reaching for her hand that lay on the table and giving it a squeeze, the way she'd comforted Lai Ling at the press conference.

Except the touch of her skin on his didn't feel comforting as they both stilled. In fact, it felt very, very unsettling. Before he could stop himself he'd turned her hand over and swept his thumb over the pulse point at her wrist. Her lips parted and something primal glittered in her eyes that tightened his gut.

Jess stared at her wrist as his finger created havoc. *Everywhere.*

'So…' she swallowed, mesmerised by the slow graze of his finger pad '…you're not the kind of surgeon who throws instruments around the operating theatre?'

Adam's finger stilled. 'No.' He withdrew his hand. 'That's more my old man's forte.'

Jess, desire curling delicious fingers deep down inside, almost whimpered at the abrupt withdrawal. Her mind cleared of the sticky tendrils of lust instantly. 'Oh, sorry, I didn't mean… I wasn't thinking.'

How could she think with him touching her like that?

She knew that both Adam and Ruby were embarrassed by their father's prima-donna rep. Gregory Carmichael was, apparently, a right bastard to work for, regularly hurling instruments across the operating theatre in mid-surgery and either pompously lecturing or bawling out theatre staff when the whim took him.

Adam took a swig of beer. 'Thanks for leaping to my defence in the press conference. It was…sweet.'

God, she didn't want him to think of her as sweet! Her thoughts certainly hadn't been running to sweet just now and she certainly hadn't been thinking sweet nothings when she'd let loose in front of the media.

She shrugged. 'I couldn't bear for that horrible man to make this whole thing out to be something sordid instead of honourable. About your father instead of you. Some journalist he is!'

Adam chuckled. 'Well, thank you but I'm old enough to look after myself.'

Jess hesitated. Had he emphasised the *old?* Was it another hint for her benefit? 'It seemed to bother you.'

'A little. Usually it just flows off my back but… I don't know…' He drummed his fingers on the table. 'It was unexpected, he caught me off guard.'

A well of empathy rose in her chest. It didn't matter that he was twelve years older than her, he suddenly looked vulnerable, and before she could caution herself to stop, she'd reached for his hand and covered it with her own.

'It doesn't matter how old you are—family issues can still get to you like that,' she said.

Adam looked down at their hands as the earlier unsettled feeling returned. He looked up at Jess. The heat of desire that he'd seen in her eyes after their kiss lurked in her steady gaze. But the feeling that she understood him, that she could see beneath his skin, was perhaps the most unsettling.

He shifted his hand and interlinked his fingers with hers. 'I'm nothing like him,' Adam said, his gaze fixed on their hands.

'Of course you're not,' she murmured, also mesmerised by the sight of their joined hands and the warmth that was creeping velvet fingers of desire up her arm. The surroundings seemed to fade until the world shrank to just him and her.

She raised her eyes to his face. 'You're Adam.'

Adam looked up too and their gazes meshed. She was looking at him in her inimitable way—with complete candour—and he had the most absurd urge to let go and fall into all that openness.

'Why don't you get on?' she asked.

And then held her breath.

She hoped she hadn't damaged the fragile walls of the warm cocoon they seemed to be enveloped in. But the notion of not being close to your father was utterly foreign to her.

She missed her father every day. Missed his dry country humour, his rough, calloused hands that belied his gentlemanly manner and his tough, can-do countenance.

Adam shut his eyes for a moment. He didn't talk about this stuff to anyone but sitting here with her, in this strange bubble, their fingers linked, lulled by the crashing of the waves on one side and the low murmur of voices all around them, a strange compulsion to unburden took hold.

When he opened them again his mind crowded with reasons.

'Because he disrespects my mother, who adores him. Because he considers people in a lower socio-economic bracket than him to be unimportant and inferior.

'Because he's the worst kind of surgeon. A prima donna who overcharges, cuts corners, throws tantrums in the operating theatre and has absolutely no respect for his patients or the people who work side by side with him.'

'But he's supposed to be the darling of the celebrity set,' Jess murmured.

Adam snorted. 'If only they knew.'

Jess's heart went out to Adam. He'd been angry at the press conference. Now he just seemed disappointed.

'There must have been a time when you were closer to him. When you were little?'

He looked at her. 'Oh, yeah, I hero-worshipped him. Wanted to be a famous surgeon. Just. Like. My. Daddy.'

Adam's mouth twisted into a bitter smile.

'And then I worked with him. Saw how arrogant he was. How atrociously he treated people. How he philandered. And I was determined to be the opposite of him. Determined to never even be associated with him. To not let his reputation taint mine. To get away and do something the complete opposite.'

The light slowly dawned on Jess. 'So you joined Operation New Faces.'

Adam nodded. 'I did my first humanitarian mission abroad just to annoy him.' He gave her a crooked half-smile before obscuring it with his beer bottle and taking a long swallow. 'But then I got hooked.'

Jess was beginning to understand his nomadic lifestyle a bit more. H*e was running away.* Not sticking around long enough for the toxic tentacles of his father's fame to taint him.

'And the fact that you spend most of your time out of the country is obviously attractive.'

He shrugged. 'I don't want to ever get stagnant or lazy. Corrupted by fame and money, like him. And not being known in and around Sydney, not having people connect the family dots, is a big attraction.'

Jess nodded, despair welling inside her. How could she ever hope to have a shot with Adam when he was too terrified to stay still?

A woman walked nearby and laughed. It tinkled all

round them and broke the trance-like state they seemed to have entered. Adam withdrew his hand.

Jess glanced up and noticed the woman look over her shoulder and smile at Adam. She was gorgeous. About his age with chestnut curls loose around her face and shoulders and a dress that swung around shapely calves and clung to an amazing cleavage.

Jess felt hopelessly gauche in her ponytail and A cup.

Even more so when she saw Adam noticing her too.

She looked down to where their hands had been joined only moments ago. 'Are you coming home?' she asked. 'I'm going to make grilled cheese sandwiches and watch a movie.'

Adam looked at Jess. Her idea of a Sunday night wasn't his usual style but with her looking at him like that—free of artifice or agenda, unlike the woman with curly hair and come-on eyes—it sounded like bliss.

But at the same time he recoiled from it. From her. From the compassion in her eyes. He'd never told anyone the things he'd told her just now. He wasn't used to opening up, to being vulnerable.

He could feel tension coiling in his body and knew she was the cause. He suddenly felt embarrassed by his admissions, by the empathy shining in her eyes. He didn't want her pity.

Going anywhere with her right now would be a bad idea. He was either going to fight with her or have sex with her.

Neither were good choices.

He shook his head and took a measured drink. 'Think I'll stay here.'

No. No. No. Jess felt his rejection right down to her toes. They'd shared something tonight.

She'd felt it deep inside.

Still, she dredged up a smile and forced it to her lips.

Just because they'd held hands and he'd opened up about his father did not afford her any say over what he did. Or… she glanced again at the woman hovering nearby…who he did it with.

'Sure,' she said, rising to her feet. 'I'll see you later.

'Night.' He nodded.

Jess departed, her shoulders stiff, her composure crumbling.

Jess didn't see Adam again until just before the afternoon list commenced. He hadn't come in by the time the movie had finished and she'd climbed the stairs to bed irritable in the extreme. She'd tossed and turned all night, straining to hear the front door, torturing herself with images of him and the woman from the bar.

Still, her silly heart went into a wild flutter when he strode into the operating theatre to check if everything was ready. Decked out in his scrubs, his shaggy surfie hair constrained in the blue paper cap, he looked every inch the surgeon extraordinaire.

She just wished she didn't know how he looked in nothing but two cushions.

'All set?' he asked Donna, who was scrubbed and conducting the count of swabs and instruments with Jess, who was down to be the scout nurse with Lynne for today's cases.

'Patient is being anaesthetised as we speak. Paula is scrubbing. Just waiting for you.'

Adam chuckled and winked at Jess. 'Guess I better hop to it, then.'

He made his way out through the swing doors, where his surgical registrar was meticulously attacking her nails with a sterile scrubbing brush. He donned a mask and they made polite conversation but his mind was on Jess.

He'd stayed out till way past midnight last night, trying to wrest control over a restless kind of feeling that he didn't understand and sure as hell didn't trust. He'd chatted with Danielle, the woman with the curls, for a little while but despite the invitation in every eyelash flutter and not-so-subtle touch, he hadn't been able to bring himself to follow through.

Hell! *He always followed through.*

And then here she was this afternoon—Jess—a mask obscuring all except her eyes but still meeting his gaze in that steadfast way of hers. The touch of her hand was still vivid in his memory and he fought against the hum in his blood purring like a motor, urging him to follow through with her.

But he couldn't. Not with Jess. Not after last night. He'd already let her too close.

And anyway she was out of bounds. He'd be leaving again soon enough and she wasn't the type of girl who *played*. She was a self-admitted *everything* kind of a girl. An all-or-nothing girl.

Yes, she was hot for him but it was more than sexual.

And Ruby would never forgive him.

The taps' automatic shut-off device activated and he realised he'd been scrubbing for more than the required three minutes. He held his arms up for a moment so the water could sluice down and off his elbows. When only the odd drip remained he held them up in front of him and headed into the theatre.

He turned at the swing doors, using his shoulders and back to nudge them open, and then strode across to Donna, who handed him a green sterile towel to dry his hands.

Adam concentrated hard on drying thoroughly from his fingertips down to his elbow on each arm and not Jess watching him in the periphery of his vision. He discarded the cloth in a nearby linen bin.

Next he was passed a folded green, long-sleeved gown with white cuffs, which he held out in front of him. He gripped an edge of fabric and let the rest of it drop and fall open, careful to hold it high enough so that it wouldn't touch the floor.

He thrust his arms into the sleeves, keeping his hands inside the cuffs, and waited for his gown to be tied at the neck.

He knew it was Jess, even though he hadn't seen who had ducked behind him to do the honours. Her fingers brushed against his nape as she gingerly found the neck ties and, touching only the very ends, fastened them. He felt her feather-light touch right down to his groin and had to stop himself from leaning into it.

'Size nine is right, Adam?' Donna asked, indicating the gloves she'd opened on a trolley for him.

Adam's attention snapped back to the job at hand. 'Yes, thanks,' he murmured, turning to the trolley and snapping his gloves on over his cuffs, pulling on the sleeves of his gown to advance his hands all the way into the gloves, the cuffs moving up until they sat snugly against his wrists.

When he looked up Jess's gaze clashed with his and for a moment it was as if no one else in the operating theatre existed. Deprived of seeing her other facial features, her eyes seemed even more remarkable and although he couldn't be certain, he was sure she was smiling at him.

'Ready to drape?' Paula asked, as the orderlies lifted the first patient onto the operating table.

Adam dragged his eyes from Jess. 'Sure,' he said, taking a green drape he was handed. They'd draped the patient in a minute and prepped the area with an antiseptic solution.

'Okay to start, Rajiv?' Adam asked the anaesthetist.

Rajiv nodded. 'Ready when you are.'

Out of the corner of his eye he could see Jess standing near the wall and he felt a moment of unaccountable nervousness. Forget the press interest, his professional standing and his father's opinions—how would she rank him after this?

Suddenly, her opinion mattered more than all the other factors combined. The thought was startling and he focused on what was in front of him to quell it.

'Scalpel.'

Two incredible days followed and Jess cherished every moment. Not just Adam, although he'd been breathtaking, even when things hadn't gone exactly to plan with one case, which had added two hours to the operation. But the feeling of being part of a dynamic team, that they were doing something amazing, was an absolute buzz.

By the time Wednesday morning came around Jess felt as high as a kite. When Donna told her she could scrub in for Lai Ling's op it was the absolute icing on the cake.

She'd already been into the anaesthetic room and spoken with the nervous but excited nineteen-year-old. Lai Ling had held her hand tight and Jess had told her she'd be right there, beside Adam, helping him. Lai Ling had smiled at her and Jess had felt her exhilaration crank up another notch.

'Joining us today?' Adam said as he accepted the towel from her, his wet arms held up in front of him.

Jess wasn't sure if he was pleased or not—masks made reading expressions very difficult—but she held his gaze and said, 'Yep. Is that a problem?'

Adam shook his head. 'Not at all,' he murmured accepting the gown her gloved hands thrust towards him.

Even if the thought of standing next to her for the next

eight-ish hours did seem a particularly heinous form of torture.

Working with her over the last two days had been a pleasure. She was a quick and efficient scout nurse but, as such, they hadn't really been too close. Today she'd be right there, opposite or maybe beside him. And that would be a distraction he probably didn't need.

An intubated Lai Ling was wheeled into the theatre and transferred to the narrow operating table. Her facial deformity looked even more out of place in the high-tech environment and for a moment everyone contemplated the sort of life Lai Ling had been forced to endure.

'Okay,' Adam said. 'Let's help this young woman come out of hiding.'

Jess blinked back a sudden well of moisture in her eyes and her skin broke out in gooseflesh beneath the thickness of the green gown.

She was about to be part of a miracle.

Adam made the first incision to the thundering sound of his own heartbeat in his ears. He knew that the complexity of the surgery and the degree of difficulty were almost secondary to the expectations that were riding on what he did today.

Which was fine. No one could put higher expectations on him than he already put on himself.

But he'd have to be completely ignorant to the external factors. The national interest since the press had become involved had been pretty intense, and then there was his relationship with Lai Ling itself.

Normally he didn't meet the patients he operated on. It was nothing to operate on dozens of patients day after day with no time to meet any of them. They were all screened, prepped and ready to go when he came into first contact with them—such was the nature of the work they did.

But Lai Ling, and the others from the last two days, were different. He'd met them and their families, talked with them about their lives and witnessed the impact of their conditions. He'd made a personal promise to each of them. Had looked Lai Ling's father in the eye and promised him she'd be all right, that she was in good hands.

He'd never reneged on a promise in his life—he wasn't about to start.

And then there was Jess. It was suddenly terribly important to succeed in her eyes too.

The first step was to reflect Lai Ling's scalp and Adam made the necessary incisions before going on to remove the frontal bone and then separating her face from her skull.

He worked methodically through the procedure, focused on the steps and his team around him as they all worked in unison to keep the surgery running smoothly. Paula and Shamus, the surgical resident, were opposite, Rajiv was at the head and Jess was at his right elbow, literally his right-hand *woman*.

He was acutely aware of her every move. Every contact of their arms, every touch of their fingers as she passed him instruments, every word as she counted sponges with Paula, every brush of her shoulder or hand or arm against him as she reached in front of him to suction or to remove equipment.

It was like they had a current pulsing between them, humming gently at times, glowing and arcing at others as their bodies came into contact.

It, this thing between them, seemed to have grown more intense since he'd opened up to her the other night.

It should have been distracting but it was strangely invigorating. He felt alive. Potent. Focused.

'You want the biomodel now?' Paula asked.

Adam nodded and it appeared before he even had a

chance to ask. 'Thanks,' he murmured looking down at Jess.

Jess felt a little kick in the region of her heart but didn't say anything. She just turned back to her trolley and checked if she needed to ask for any more clamps or sponges, while the surgeons consulted about the next phase. It was her *job* to predict what he wanted. It would be dangerous to feel flattered by his thanks.

Especially standing this close to him with every cell in her body buzzing.

Adam observed the sterilised soft plastic bio-model that had been constructed from Lai Ling's MRI and CT scan images. He'd been practising this stage—removal of tissue from the central portion of her face—for the last few days.

Use of such models as a guide in complex surgeries cut theatre time down and reduced the risk of blood loss. They were expensive but had revolutionised this type of surgery. Adam had been thrilled when the Australian company that made the model had donated its time and product to the cause.

Using the model as a reference, he set about removing a portion of tissue that allowed the two halves of her face, including her orbits, to be centrally rotated and fixed together with wires. He then fixed the joined face back to the skull with wires.

The last stage was the reconstruction of Lai Ling's nose. Adam used bone from her skull and the leftover nose skin flaps to make one central nose.

Jess stared mesmerised as Adam closed the incision with fine sutures, completing his handiwork. Lai Ling's face was a little swollen and would continue to swell over the next couple of days, but there was no mistaking the complete transformation.

'Oh, my God,' she breathed. 'It's amazing, Adam. You did it. You really did it.'

Adam looked down at Jess, the expression of awe in her eyes and her heartfelt compliment going straight to his head.

And other parts of his anatomy.

He shook his head and smiled down at her. 'We did it,' he said, then looked around at his team. 'We *all* did it.'

Jess's breath caught in her throat. A ball of emotion that had swelled low in her belly at the miracle before her bloomed like a mushroom cloud into her chest as the flecks in his lapis lazuli eyes flashed all golden and inviting.

'Bravo,' Rajiv added.

'The media are going to go crazy when they see this result,' Paula agreed.

Adam shook his head. 'As long as Lai Ling and her family are pleased, that's all that matters.'

Jess's heart flopped in her chest at Adam's sincerity and she felt a rush of blood to her pelvis. She was suddenly hotter for him than she'd ever been. She felt like they'd split the atom or mapped the human genome and she wanted, more than anything, to show him how incredible she thought he was.

With her body.

'Well, I think that deserves a round of applause,' Donna said, peering through the gap between Shamus's and Paula's bodies. And she started to clap. Everyone followed suit.

Adam chuckled. 'Okay, okay. We're not done yet, let's get her cleaned up.'

And then Jess was passing him gauze to remove blood smears and material for a nose plaster and some dressings to cover the wounds and getting involved in the general clean-up. And Rajiv was organising the transport to ICU.

It was an hour later before Jess and Adam spoke again.

He'd been to ICU and on to a brief press conference to let the media know that the operation had been a complete success. When he entered the staffroom he was given another round of applause.

Jess grinned at him as he looked embarrassed at the praise. She was tired—her feet ached from almost eight solid hours of standing in the one spot and her eyes were strained from such intense focus—but she felt strangely exhilarated.

'Let's have a party!' she said as she approached him.

She didn't wait for his reply. They had a lot to celebrate tonight and despite her weariness she felt like she could groove all night.

'Hey, everyone,' she called over the general din. 'Party at our place.'

Judging by the cheers, it was a popular decision.

CHAPTER SIX

ADAM smiled as Jess flitted by, laughing with Rajiv, chatting about miracles and teamwork. She'd been floating around a foot off the floor for the last two hours, obviously high on success.

He didn't mind admitting it was damn infectious.

'She's happy,' Tilly murmured, sidling up to Adam. 'Anyone would think she'd done the operation.'

He chuckled. 'We all did our part.'

Tilly glanced at Adam as his gaze followed the playful swish of Jess's ponytail. 'It's hard to believe she'll be heading back out west in a few short years. We're all going to miss her so much.' Tilly shook her head. 'God, she's going to be dynamite out in the bush, isn't she?'

Adam, his back propped against the wall, one leg bent at the knee, his foot flat against the wall, raised a beer to his mouth and took a measured swig, letting Tilly's comment hang in the air before he pierced her with a knowing look. 'Did my sister send you?'

Tilly feigned innocence. 'She's gone to work.'

'Hmm,' he said, knowing full well that Ruby had probably urged her friend to wait until after she'd left for the hospital before having this not-so-subtle talk.

Tilly shrugged. 'We worry about her.'

Adam wanted to object but the way the four friends

stuck together was touching. He'd been living the life of a nomad for so long that he'd forgotten how it was to be part of a community.

He felt strangely envious.

Which irritated him. *He loved his life.*

Adam drained his beer. 'She's a grown woman, Tilly.'

She did her job like a grown-up. She moved all grown up. And she sure as hell kissed all grown up.

'Doesn't stop us worrying.'

Adam dropped his foot to the floor. 'Tell Ruby not to worry,' he said, pushing off the wall. 'I keep my promises.'And he would. But as he went in search of another beer he couldn't deny that a little of the night's sparkle had faded.

'Ah, here he is, the man of the moment.' Jess grinned as Adam entered the kitchen.

He'd dressed down in scruffy jeans and a *Hang Ten* T-shirt that left nothing to the imagination, and Jess fought the urge to run her hand down his abs.

'Another beer?' she asked, bumping the fridge open with her hip and pulling out a frosty bottle.

'Thanks,' he said, acknowledging Rajiv and three others all chatting in the kitchen. He joined them, laughing and joking as they recounted some of the hairier moments of the last few days.

Jess wasn't sad when the others drifted away, leaving the two of them. She'd really wanted to tell Adam how privileged she felt to be included in the project, how much she'd grown just being a part of it all.

But then the opening notes of 'Sweet Home Alabama' blared from the stereo system and she felt an insane urge to move. 'My favourite! Let's dance.' She grinned, her shoulders already moving to the beat, the toes of her bare feet tapping against the lino floor.

Adam forced a laugh out past the spike in his pulse as her shimmying did strange things to his equilibrium. 'Thanks, I'll pass.'

'Not a dancer?' She laughed at him over her shoulder, arms raised above her head, snapping her fingers to the beat as she boogied around the kitchen table.

'I'm okay.'

Jess grinned. 'Don't believe you. I've seen you on a board and you're pretty damn light on your feet.' She shimmied towards him, wiggling her bottom and thrusting her hips. 'I bet you're an awesome dancer.' She swirled her hands through the air and reached for him.

He took a step back. 'It's not my kind of music.'

Still on a high, Jess continued undeterred. 'Let me guess. You into the Beach Boys, old man?'

This time when she reached for him, her hands connected with his abdomen and she slid her hands up his shirt until her palms were flat against his pecs. Adam's hands automatically found her hips pressing gently against her forward momentum as she tried to dance closer. Her sweet scent enveloped him and a thrum of something primal stirred his blood.

He looked at her pink mouth as it pouted up at him.

Do not go there.

'How much have you had to drink?' he teased.

'Not even a full beer. I'm just...high on life, Adam. On what we did.'

He looked at the awe and wonder etched into her lovely face and felt like a god. Operations such as Lai Ling's weren't such a big deal for him or for the teams he worked with because they saw tragic cases every day, made a difference every day.

It was fascinating to see it through her eyes.

Adam grinned. 'You're like a kid on Christmas Eve, aren't you?'

'I love Christmas Eve,' she sighed, stroking her fingers along meaty muscles hidden beneath a thin layer of fabric.

Adam chuckled. 'I just bet you do.'

'At least then I'd have mistletoe as an excuse to do this.'

As Adam had her hips firmly in his grasp and firmly at a distance she leant forward from the waist, rising on tiptoe and capturing his mouth in a brief, hard kiss.

She pulled back before he could, his harsh inward breath a satisfying sound in the vacuum they suddenly seemed to be sucked into.

Adam's fingers dug into her hips as he fought for control of his breathing. Of his head.

'You shouldn't do that.'

'And what if I want to do it again?'

Adam swallowed at her husky question. His gaze dropped to her mouth, still moist from their kiss.

He'd promised Ruby.

He pulled her hands off his chest and stepped away from her. 'Denial is good for the soul,' he said, before resolutely turning away from her and leaving the kitchen.

Jess almost whimpered as she watched him go, a wellspring of frustration beating a rapid pulse through her head. She watched his tall head weave through the throng, navigating his way to his bedroom. She could just make out his door open and then close.

Damn it!

Her fingers curled into her palms.

How could he just walk away? She'd seen the flash of desire in those golden flecks, felt the tension in his arms as he had held her away, the dig of his fingers into the flesh of her hip.

Yes, she wanted everything and he didn't do everything

but that could change and right now she just needed to be with him. She'd never been intimate with a man but she knew enough about Adam, about her feelings for him, to know that he was the one.

She'd known for three years.

And even if she didn't end up being the one for him, if he pushed her out his revolving door tomorrow, at least she would have lost her virginity to an incredible man she felt deeply for.

Her grandmother had always told her there was no shame in waiting. To hold out for an honourable man. For someone who was worthy of such a gift.

And right now she was so pleased she had. Because she couldn't think of a man more worthy than Adam.

And she didn't want to wait another moment.

She set off after Adam, determination in every step. Tonight had had a preternatural feel about it from the beginning—their gazes meeting constantly across the room, both aware of something building. Like an invisible string was connecting them—a silvery strand of spider web, fragile yet amazingly tensile—and slowly, inexorably drawing tighter, drawing them closer.

Fate had extended its hand and Jess knew that the moment was now.

She was tired of watching everyone around her all loved up when she was missing out. Didn't she deserve that too?

Adam *was* interested, no matter how much he tried to deny it. He'd flirted with her that first day when she'd found him naked in her bed, he'd kissed her thoroughly for her birthday and opened up to her the other night.

There was definitely something between them.

And she was tired of being a country bumpkin in his eyes.

It was time to speak up.

* * *

Adam was lying on the end of his bed, his feet flat on the floor, staring at the ceiling, praying for strength, when his door opened abruptly. He curled up instantly, his eyes narrowing as a shaft of light spilled into his darkened room and Jess stepped inside, shutting the door after her.

He collapsed back against the mattress, wondering how much more temptation a man could take before it killed him. 'Go away,' he half growled, half groaned.

Moonlight streamed in through the slats of his window blinds, throwing the bed and him into a milky spotlight. Even reclined he looked big and male and potent.

Undeterred, Jess took a step towards him. 'I want to talk to you.'

Adam ran a hand through his hair and took a deep, steadying breath. He sat again and held out his hand, motioning her to stop. 'Jess…no. We're not talking in my bedroom.'

Jess halted. Her heart banged loudly behind her rib cage, coursed like a raging river through her ears as she sought to hold onto her courage.

'Okay.'

She swallowed, her mouth dry, her throat as arid as the drought stricken ground of the outback. She advanced another step.

'So let's not talk.'

He stood. 'Jess. Stop.'

She faltered, the note of warning in his voice unmistakeable. But it was the tinge of desperation in it that gave her hope. 'I don't think you want me to stop.'

Adam clenched his fists. Of course he didn't want her to stop. He wanted to grab her, roll her on the bed and feel her under him, around him.

He'd never had to deny his natural sexual urges before and he was holding on by a thread.

'Jess, you have to leave,' he said, striding past her to the door.

Jess spun to face him as he reached for the doorhandle. 'Not before I tell you what I came to tell you.'

Adam placed his forehead, his palms on the back of the door. Muffled sounds of the party continuing on the other side were encouraging—they were hardly likely to get into anything with dozens of people in their house.

He turned, leaning against the hard wood. 'Is this about me being hot again? Because I think you pretty well covered that already.'

Jess shook her head, feeling the heat rise to her cheeks, and was pleased that her face was hidden now by night shadows. 'No. This is a thank you. For including me in the team. I'm honoured to have been a part of such an amazing project. You are a truly gifted human being.'

Adam felt his resistance to her crumbling. She was so lovely and he wanted to sweep her up and inhale her, devour her. 'Jess…it's my job.'

'No.' She took two steps towards him. 'Don't say that. You could be doing anything else, you could be in private practice, raking in the money. You could be like your father.' She saw him flinch but carried on anyway. 'But you chose this instead. It shows your honour. It tells me you're a good, good man.'

'Don't.' He shook his head. 'I'm not a good man.'

If she knew what he was thinking right now, she'd know that for sure. How much he wanted to touch her, to whip the T-shirt over her head—tear it if he had to—to get her out of her jeans.

She took another step closer. 'Yes.'

She was close now. So close he could smell her perfume and the thud of his heart was outdoing the thump of the music outside.

'No, if I was a good man I'd be turning you away. I'd have opened this door and insisted you leave the second you came in. I would have taken this conversation outside. Don't paint me as some kind of saint, Jess, because I *am* just a man. Let's leave the good out of it.'

It was darker by the door, his face was in shadow and his eyes were impossible to read, but Jess could hear the strain in his voice, the husky timbre betraying every *keep-away* vibe he'd been trying to project.

She may be a virgin but she was familiar with desire. With lust. How you could tremble with it. How it could colour your voice. Hijack your bodily functions.

She could sense Adam was balanced on a knife edge and heat pooled down low in her belly. Her nipples tightened. Her thighs trembled.

The next step had to come from her.

'Make love to me,' she murmured, taking the last step towards him, bringing their bodies a hair's-breadth from touching. The words sounded odd, unfamiliar. Victorian almost.

But for Jess, it was exactly what the act was about.

Adam's breath hissed out as desire slammed into him. He was hard in an instant. And she was so close. It would be so easy. His nostrils flared as her scent curled seductive fingers around his gut.

But still he fought against it. Hadn't he told her that denial was good for you?

He shook his head slowly. 'Look, you have a little crush, I understand that—'

Jess saw red. 'Don't do that. Don't talk to me like I'm some sort of sixteen-year-old kid, damn it! You confided in me about your father the other night. You know I'm quite old enough.'

Adam swallowed. God help him, he did. 'I promised Ruby.'

Jess dug her teeth into her bottom lip. 'I won't tell her.'

Adam shut his eyes against a surge of desire. 'I can't...'

Jess could easily have raised herself on her tippy toes and kissed him. But it was suddenly very important that it was Adam who kissed her. She'd initiated the previous two and she needed him to declare himself.

In the cold light of day she wanted to be certain that he had wanted it as much as her. She wanted him to be certain too.

But. He was grimly resolute, his arms firmly folded across his chest, his jaw set into a line of steely determination.

He was going to need a push.

Jess did the first thing that came to her mind. A little manoeuvre she'd seen on a telemovie the other night. It was scary, far from virginal, and her heart fluttered madly at the mere thought of it. If he still rejected her, there would be no way her dignity would ever recover.

But it was going to be scarier if she left this room with her virginity intact.

She grasped the edges of her T-shirt and pulled it over her head, tossing it on the ground. 'Make love to me,' she insisted.

Adam felt every cell in his body grind to a halt as those seductive fingers grabbed a handful of intestine and squeezed hard. He licked his lips.

'Oh, man. You shouldn't have done that,' he said, looking at her lacy bra and the sweet, gentle slope of her breasts. 'You really shouldn't have done that.'

Jess was suddenly embarrassed and moved to cover herself. It wasn't like she had some amazing cleavage to show off. Not like the woman on the TV. Not like Adam's usual type at all.

'Don't,' he said, stopping her, pulling her arms to her side.

She lowered her gaze to the floor. 'They're not much.'

'They're beautiful,' he breathed, placing a finger under her chin, raising her face. 'You're beautiful.'

Her sweetness, her uncertainty was his undoing.

'Oh, God, Jess,' he groaned, and reached for her waistband, dragging her hips forward and furrowing his fingers into her hair. She barely had time to blink as he swept her against his body and slammed his mouth against hers. Her head spun and her belly went into freefall. Her hands connected with his shoulders and her fingers curled into his T-shirt, bunching the fabric as she clung to him.

His mouth opened over hers, demanding entrance, and she ceded eagerly to his questing tongue on a primal moan. Then he was pulling her hairband out, freeing it from the ponytail to fall around her shoulders. His fingers fisted at her nape, grasping a handful, tugging gently to angle her head back further.

He spun around, pivoting her with him, pushing her against the door. Jess registered the hardness of wood at her back on a peripheral level as the hardness of solid male at her front consumed her on every other level.

'I want to kiss every inch of you,' Adam panted against her mouth. 'Taste every inch of you.'

His mouth blazed a fiery trail down her neck and Jess could do nothing but hang on. To him. To the door. Fireworks exploded behind her closed eyes and she gasped, 'Adam,' as his tongue flicked over the pulse thrumming in the hollow at the base of her throat.

Then his hands were pushing down the straps of her bra as his mouth continued its southward assault. And then somehow he had it off and his hands were cupping both breasts, his gaze feasting on them, muttering, 'Beautiful,' as he lowered his mouth to first one rosy-tipped peak then the other.

Jess's head thudded back against the door at the first touch of his tongue. She cried out and grasped his shoulders as he sucked her puckered nipples deep into the wet, warm cavern of his mouth one by one.

'So perfect,' Adam groaned, his hands sweeping down her ribs, across her belly to her back, sliding down to cup and squeeze her bottom, grind his arousal into the sweet spot at the junction of her thighs.

'Take off your jeans,' he whispered roughly in her ear as his hands worked their way behind her waistband to the round warm flesh of her buttocks and he laved the side of her neck with his tongue.

Adam's husky request ricocheted around what little part of her brain hadn't been turned to mush.

This was happening. It was really happening.

Her head spun at the all-consuming urgency of it. The totally desperate way she wanted it. She hadn't expected it to be like this in all those hazy fantasies. She'd always imagined a slow, revealing loving for her first time. Something languorous and decadent.

Not this crazy, seething, roaring imperative.

This primal need turning her insides liquid and even the most insignificant, asexual parts of her body into seething erogenous zones.

Part of her wanted to slow down. To confess her total lack of experience. To demand the fantasy.

But her body craved this passionate oblivion even more. Wanting, needing him to kiss every inch, taste every inch. Wanting it with shocking certainty.

And she only needed one functioning brain cell to know

that while confession was good for the soul it would be very, very bad for what was happening right now.

This fever.

Like a bucket of ice water.

She'd come this far and she didn't want to give him any reason to not finish what she'd started.

'Jess,' he growled.

Jess, her thoughts scattering all around her like debris swirling in the funnel of a tornado, desperately clutched for the order of proceedings.

What had he said? *Jeans?*

Jeans.

Her fingers fumbled the button and shook hard as she pulled the zipper down. His hands took over pushing them down over her hips and somehow she shimmied them down her legs and kicked out of them.

She clutched at his torso for balance, her fingers coming into contact with bare, warm, male flesh.

He'd taken off his shirt.

She gasped at the sheer masculinity of him, flattening her palms against his pecs, gliding up and over his shoulders to the other side. Down his back, sliding around to the flat of his belly and the ridged perfection of his ribs.

She dropped a string of kisses across a pec, flicking her tongue over his nipple as he had done to her. The harsh suck of his breath was dizzying and she did it again. And again.

'Hold on.'

Jess had barely registered the low growl that rumbled through his chest when Adam grasped her buttocks and boosted her up the door. Her legs locked automatically around his waist and her hands tangled in his hair as he feasted on first one breast than the other.

She moaned out loud as the sweet eroticism went on and

on. Her head lolled back against the door and her breath panted in and out as she wantonly arched her back and held his head firmly to her. 'Yes,' she whimpered. 'Yes.'

Adam lifted his head from her chest. 'I need to be in you,' he muttered.

He claimed her mouth in a deep, rough kiss and Jess welcomed it, meeting it, matching it with a greedy intensity as Adam fumbled between their bodies.

Then he was pulling her knickers aside and she felt the big, blunt girth of him prodding against her most intimate place.

She tensed, she couldn't help herself. She wanted him inside her more than her next breath. But he felt big and solid and she was suddenly excruciatingly aware that she hadn't done this before.

Would it hurt? Would he fit?

He felt so big. Too big.

She didn't want to disappoint him. Or give herself away.

But then in one brief, searing thrust it was over. He was inside her. She cried out, a deep guttural bellow, throwing her head back, digging her finger nails into his shoulders. Her whole body tensed and clamped around him.

She bit down on her lip as he stretched her beyond all possibility. She felt heat and fullness and an unbearable tension that burned and tingled somewhere between pleasure and pain.

Adam stilled instantly. He shifted slightly for better balance as he looked up at her. 'Jess?'

The movement jarred through the very centre of her, spiralling heat and pressure into an unbearable sensation. 'Stop!' she panted, gripping his shoulders hard, her eyes shut tight. 'Just wait. Don't move for a moment.'

Adam looked at her incredulously as realisation dawned. 'Oh, my God—you're a *virgin*?'

The heat started to dissolve and a wonderful tingling started to soothe stretched nerve endings and infuse bubbles of pleasure through her bloodstream. Her muscles started to relax.

She lifted her head from the door. 'Well, technically not any more.'

A sensation, like an itch that couldn't be scratched, built at the point of their joining and she moved against him slightly, hoping to ease it.

It didn't.

Adam gripped her hips as all her tightness undulated along the length of him. He squeezed his eyes shut as he placed his forehead against her chest and swore under his breath.

What had he done?

Guilt suffused him. He'd let her flattery sweep him along. Let her sweetness seduce him. This should have been special for her—candlelight and roses—and he'd come on all Neanderthal, all *I need to be in you.*

And then taken her up against a door.

No, no, no.

The muffled party music entered the edges of his awareness.

Taken her up against a door as a party raged less than a metre away.

Shame nipped at his conscience and he started to withdraw.

'No!' Jess tightened her thighs around him. 'Don't stop, please don't stop.'

Adam stilled again. 'Jess…'

'No,' she murmured, pulling his head off her chest. She kissed his eyes, his nose, his jaw, his mouth. 'Show me,' she whispered against his mouth. 'Show me how to be with a man.'

He groaned against her mouth, claiming it in a deep, wet kiss, his erection surging inside her. 'This isn't right,' he murmured, tearing his mouth from hers. 'This isn't how your first time should be…rushed and hurried, against a door.'

She furrowed both hands into his hair. 'So take me to the bed.'

Adam grimaced. 'That's not what I meant. It should be special…with someone special.'

Jess stroked her finger down his cheek, 'It is. You are.'

Adam felt a weight slam into his heart. 'Jess…I…'

Jess smiled at his confusion. 'Are you telling me that me giving you my virginity isn't special to you too? That you don't feel honoured?'

Adam searched her gaze. Even in the darkened environment he could see her earnestness. He wanted to deny it, to stymie any fanciful notions immediately. But he couldn't. Because it did mean something to him. He did feel honoured.

'Jess…'

She pressed a finger to his lips. 'Adam, it's done now. Please don't leave me hanging like this. I wanted you inside me. And I need you to finish what you started.'

She replaced her fingers with her mouth, putting every ounce of desperation and longing into a truly devastating kiss.

When she pulled away they were both breathing hard.

'Hold on,' he panted.

Adam slid his hands up her back, lifting her away from the door, turning and carrying her over to the bed, still intimately joined. He lowered them down to the mattress, watching the moonlight spill over hair, her breasts. Still hard inside her, he pushed himself up on his arms to withdraw.

'No, no, no,' Jess murmured, clamping his buttocks to her.

Adam shut his eyes at the delicious torture. 'Condom,' he muttered, his breathing ragged.

How could he have forgotten about condoms?

'Pill,' she countered.

He opened his mouth to remind her that it wasn't just about pregnancy but she raised her head up and captured his lips and he lost all rational thought.

The kiss went on and on. And when Jess locked her legs around his waist Adam wasn't sure how long he could last. And, damn it all, he owed her a good time. He pushed himself up again to withdraw.

'No,' Jess objected, keeping her arms linked firmly around his neck.

He looked down at her. Her blonde hair spread out on the mattress around her like a halo in the moonlight. The milky beams made her pink nipples look like strawberries and cream.

'I want to kiss you all over. *Everywhere.*'

Jess felt a strange contraction around all his thick maleness inside her and she shifted against it slightly. There was time for exploration later. For now, she needed this.

Connection.

'No.' She clamped down around him. Her arms left his neck to grasp his buttocks. 'Stay. I want you to stay inside me.'

Adam found it hard to deny her demand as her hot tightness contracted all round him and her urgent hands streaked fire straight to his loins. He looked down at her for a moment. She was looking up at him with frankness and honesty.

Who was he to deny a request from a lady?

He tried to withdraw again and her hands tightened further.

He smiled down at her. 'Jess…I need to be able to… move a little.'

'Oh.' Her cheeks flamed. 'Sorry.'

Adam chuckled until he felt her ease up the pressure on his buttocks and then he did what his body had been screaming at him to do ever since he'd first thrust into her.

He eased out and did it again.

'Ah,' Jess said, her back arching as she felt his delicious slow withdrawal and his slow pulse back into her again.

Adam watched as her breasts thrust upwards and rocked slightly. 'Okay?' he asked.

Jess bit her lip as he took her closer to the stars. 'Oh, God, yes, don't stop. Please don't stop.'

Adam lowered his mouth to a strawberry and cream tip as he thrust again. Her guttural moan and wild, desperate clutch at his shoulder took him closer to the edge.

'You're so beautiful,' he panted as he released her nipple and watched the rock of her alabaster body, the jiggle of her pert little breasts as he pulsed inside her again.

Jess opened her eyes and their gazes locked. 'Mmm,' she moaned as he pulled back and surged forward again.

Adam couldn't tear his gaze from her face, couldn't break their eye contact as they stared into each other's eyes. He didn't do this, look into a woman's eyes when he was buried deep inside her. But with Jess, he couldn't stop.

Jess felt the slow delicious build-up as Adam eased in and out of her, supporting himself on his arms, looming over her as he rocked in and out in agonising slow motion. It spread hot ripples of pleasure to her breasts, her thighs, her very centre.

He grabbed her thigh and bent her knee up and she gasped as something tightened inside with an almost violent pleasure. She arched her back, a whimper escaping unchecked from her lips.

Adam felt the inexorable march towards his orgasm hit warp speed as she clamped around him tighter. 'It's okay,' he murmured, dropping his head to nuzzle her neck, her collar bone, her nipples. 'I'm here, Jess. Let it go.'

Jess shook her head as everything started to tighten. For a moment she was frightened. Frightened that this torrent of pleasure might actually kill her. Or that she might actually lose her mind.

It was too, too much.

She whimpered, louder this time, as her body began to tremble, to spin out of control. She tried to cling to sanity, to Adam, to the bed, to the here and now, but the sensation was building, spinning her round, lifting her.

'Jess,' Adam groaned as she stiffened in his arms.

He lifted his head from her neck to look at her again. Her eyes were wide open and he could see the fevered pleasure burning bright amidst the milky light surrounding her. The awe, the passion he saw there was a potent aphrodisiac.

'Yes, Jess, yes,' he muttered, thrusting a little harder, a little less controlled as he started to lose it, as the primal man took over.

'Adam,' she gasped.

'I know,' he murmured, their gazes still locked. 'I know.'

Jess stared at him in amazement. 'Oh, I…I…' She was beyond words. There were no words for this incredible experience. For looking into Adam's eyes as he woke her body to a treasure trove of erotic secrets.

And then there weren't any words as something broke inside and wave after wave of pleasure popped and zipped and ricocheted like an out-of-control firecracker through every cell of her body.

Adam kept thrusting, holding off his own climax as she

rode hers. Watching her eyes as she came was the sexiest thing he'd ever seen—full of wonder, like she'd been shot into outer space and was floating amongst a million stars.

Jess felt a tear trickle out of an eye. 'Adam!' she gasped as the orgasm rocked her to the core.

The tear was Adam's undoing, pushing him beyond control as he stopped trying to hold back and let his climax rush up to meet hers.

CHAPTER SEVEN

JESS had no idea how much time passed before she became aware of her surroundings again. The moonlight spilling across her face. The feel of the mattress against her back. The weight of Adam against her front.

The settling of two frenetic heartbeats. The mellowing of two rapid breaths.

A delicious warmth radiated from her centre, soothing the slight ache where his hardness still nestled deep inside her.

'Wow,' she murmured, her lips brushing a warm shoulder.

Adam, his face buried in her neck, chuckled. He couldn't have put it better himself. 'Indeed.'

When was the last time sex had been this...sweet? This special?

Jess pressed a kiss against the solid roundness of his shoulder. It was round enough to bite, smelled and tasted good enough to eat and despite an all-consuming lassitude she found herself wanting more.

'Again,' she murmured, turning her head to press a kiss against his throat.

Adam laughed. 'I might need a minute or two.'

Jess smiled against his throat as the rumble of his words

tickled her lips. She moved against him. 'Doesn't feel like it.'

Adam sucked in a breath. Every cell urged him to pull out and plunge back in again.

Out, in. Out, in. Out, in.

But.

They needed to talk first.

With a monumental effort he silenced the mantra thrumming through his blood, roaring through his ears, and gently withdrew.

Jess gasped as he left her body. The glide of him against sensitive skin was delicious. The ache left in his wake illicit.

But still she mewed a protest as he shifted off her and said, 'We need to talk.'

'I don't think I'm capable.'

Adam laughed as he settled onto his back. He could most certainly relate. 'That makes two of us.'

Jess rolled on her side, resting her head on his shoulder and sliding a palm across Adam's chest until it was tucked down his opposite side. His arm curled up around her back and his hand came to rest on her shoulder. Jess sighed contentedly.

She'd always known it could be like this.

Adam lay in silence, appreciating the feel of her pressed against him and the aromas of sweet, sweet woman.

'Why didn't you tell me?' he asked eventually, to ward off the tug of post-coital lethargy.

Jess fluttered her eyes open. There was no use pretending she didn't know what he was talking about. 'Would you have gone through with this if you'd known?'

Adam stroked the skin beneath his fingers with long, languorous strokes as he stared at the ceiling. 'No.'

'That's why I didn't tell you.'

Adam shut his eyes as guilt began to rear its ugly head. 'It would have been nice to know, Jess…'

'What difference would it have made other than you running a mile?'

He opened his eyes. 'I certainly wouldn't have taken you against a door.'

Jess pushed herself up on her elbow and looked down at him. 'Why not?'

He looked into her earnest face. 'It's hardly sexual intercourse 101, Jess. There are…easier ways.'

Jess could hear the guilt rampant in his voice. 'No. Don't do that, Adam. It was…amazing. I wouldn't change a thing.'

Adam shook his head. 'I'm sorry. I figured you probably hadn't had a lot of experience, I didn't realise you'd had none.' He pushed a lock of hair that had fallen forward back over her shoulder. His gaze fell to her mouth. 'You don't kiss like a virgin.'

Jess smiled. 'Oh, and how do virgins kiss?'

'I have absolutely no idea. But not like you. Not all hot and heavy and…just the right amount of hard and soft and…not with tongue or that little whimper at the back of your throat.'

Even thinking about that whimper got him hard all over again.

Jess grinned at his detailed recall of their passionate kisses. 'I have been kissed, you know. Quite a bit, actually. I've had boyfriends. Dates.'

'So why didn't you…?'

'Go all the way?'

'Yes.'

Adam dropped his gaze as a knot of emotion tightened his gut. Now it was over, the thought of anyone else introducing her to the intimacies they'd shared did *not* sit well.

Jess waited until he looked at her again. She wanted him to see the honesty of her answer when she replied.

'I hadn't planned on being a virgin at twenty-four, Adam. It was just the way it worked out.' She shrugged. 'I'm an old-fashioned girl. I was brought up to think that my virginity was something special. That it should be saved for someone special.'

Adam shut his eyes and groaned. What had he done? Taken something that he didn't deserve? 'For a husband?' he asked, opening his eyes.

Jess shook her head. 'Not necessarily. My grandmother always says I'll know who when the time comes. And I did. You're that person.'

No. He wasn't. He loved and left. His next mission was only weeks away and he had every intention of being on that flight.

He'd taken her against a door, for crying out loud.

He wasn't who she thought he was. 'Jess.'

She could see the denial forming in his lapis lazuli eyes and couldn't bear to hear it. 'Shh,' she murmured, dropping a kiss on his mouth. 'Don't talk,' she whispered. 'Just kiss me.'

He groaned against her mouth as he devoured it like it was his last-ever chance to kiss her.

When they pulled apart they were both breathing hard again. Jess looked down his body. His breath wasn't the only thing that was hard. She looked back at him as her hand slid down his belly and her fingers connected with the thick bulk of him.

He sucked in a breath as she closed her palm around him. 'You like that? Tell me what you like.' Adam shut his eyes as she squeezed him. A bolt of desire jolted through his belly, his thighs, his loins. 'Jess.' His breath hissed out her name.

'Show me,' she murmured against his mouth.

Adam opened his eyes. The desire to do just that, to take her hand, to push her down, to flip her over, to show her where he liked to be touched and how was so, so tempting.

It was like a thousand male fantasies rolled into one.

Initiating a virgin.

But it felt wrong.

Jess was a novice and it should be about her. Not about his own selfish needs and fantasies. He'd yet to love her properly. To run his tongue over every inch of her. To taste her everywhere but especially where he knew she'd taste the sweetest.

To make her come while he did it.

The extent of his desire for her was frightening.

And somehow with her hand locked around him and her eyes innocently begging him for sexual tutelage it made him excruciatingly aware of their age difference, of the yawning gap in their experience.

It reminded him of his broken promise to Ruby.

She moved her hand up the length of him and his hips bucked involuntarily. He quickly covered her hand with his, stilling any further action.

'No,' he murmured as he moved swiftly, flipping her onto her back, covering her with his body.

'But—'

Jess didn't get another word out as he smothered her protest with a kiss that left her clinging and gasping when he finally broke away.

'This time,' he said, kissing her neck, 'I'm going to taste you all over.' He moved his kisses further south, trekking across her throat and along a collar bone. 'Lie back,' he murmured against the swell of a breast. 'Enjoy.'

'Wait,' she protested, raising her head off the pillow. She

didn't want to just lie there and be serviced, she wanted to participate.

But then he swiped his hot tongue across a rapidly tightening nipple and she fell back against the bed as all her bones melted in a scorching-hot blaze. She cried out as bolts of desire pinned her to the bed.

And when his mouth trekked lower she could no more have stopped him than flown to the moon.

Jess woke as the bed shifted beside her. A beam of soft sunlight filtered through the blinds and she squinted. Adam was rising from the bed, his back to her. She reached out her hand but he was too quick and her arm fell uselessly against the mattress.

'Come back to bed,' she murmured.

He spun around. 'Sorry.' He grimaced, his voice low. 'I didn't mean to wake you.'

Jess sucked in a breath at the perfection of his naked body. The sunlight painted tawny stripes across his chest and abs and he looked every inch a virile male animal. She hadn't seen him fully naked in daylight and the sight of him was truly magnificent.

She dragged her gaze upwards. 'Did we even get to sleep?'

Adam smiled. 'Briefly.'

He hadn't slept at all actually, watching her as she slept a deep, deep sleep of absolute exhaustion. He'd lost track of how many times he'd taken her body last night. How many times he'd kissed her. How many times she'd cried out, begged him for more, begged him to stop.

Begged him to *never* stop.

He'd been curiously calm about something that should be making him very nervous. And even now, looking at her exposed to the waist, legs tangled in the sheets, a thoroughly sated look on her face, he still felt at peace.

He should have known when he'd opened up to her about his father that she was different from the rest.'

'It's five am.' She dropped her gaze again tracking downwards to admire him. 'Come back to bed.'

Adam felt himself twitch and then begin to harden before her gaze. Her hand was resting on her belly where the sheet sat low on her hips and all she had to do was push her fingers underneath and she'd…

He swallowed. *Don't go there.*

Jess wasn't a woman who had any experience of sexual games. He doubted she knew the first thing about the multitude of ways to turn a man on besides ogling his naked body. He was damn certain she didn't know how to tease, how to suggest.

Or how watching a woman touch herself could be even more alluring than doing it yourself.

God knew, he was finding it hard enough staying out of his bed just looking at her looking at him with eyes that still seemed innocent despite the things he'd done to her body last night. If she ever got sexually confident enough to tease him, he'd be a goner.

'Oh, no, you don't,' he said, turning away, striding to his wardrobe and reaching for his boardies. 'I need to recharge my batteries.' He stepped into them and tied them before turning back to her. 'I'm going hit the ocean.'

She'd rolled on her side, her head propped up by her hand. Her hair fell forward over her shoulder and her small high breasts, the nipples erect, lay bare and proud before his eyes. The sheet had dipped lower and he could just see a hint of dark shadow.

He wanted her again. *Bad.*

But he was afraid he'd break her with the weight of his desire. The extent of his need.

Overwhelm her.

Overwhelm himself.

'Come with me,' he said, the thought of not being near her suddenly unthinkable. 'Let me teach you how to surf.'

Jess had absolutely zero desire to learn how to surf. In fact, she wasn't even that enamoured with the ocean. Sure, she loved to look at it, to hear it, to sit on the beach and feel the sand between her toes, but going in it had never been her favourite pastime.

Conquering its waves even less so.

But at this moment Jess knew she'd do anything to prolong being with Adam. So she opened her mouth and said, 'Yes.'

With one arm occupied by the board, he didn't hold her hand on the walk down the hill to the beach. She hadn't expected him to. And she didn't reach for his either, keeping both her hands firmly buried beneath their towels. Instead she fretted that he was trying to pull away already and it nagged at her all the way to the beach.

But when he picked her up near the water's edge and strode with her into the surf, laughing and kicking, her worries melted away. He dumped her in the sea and then kissed her hard when she came up for air.

He also dropped a kiss on her shoulder as she practised on the beached board. His hands strayed frequently over her bottom and low on her hips and belly as he helped with the transition from lying to standing.

And when his tongue trailed a hot path up the back of her thigh as they paddled the board together on their stomachs, she barely suppressed a whimper.

By the time the lesson was over Jess was so turned on

she could barely see straight let alone remember any of the things he'd taught her.

Was it any wonder she couldn't stay on the damn thing?

Jess beached the board after her seventh failed attempt at the baby waves close to shore.

'You'll do better tomorrow,' Adam said as she joined him in the shallows where he was watching one of his fellow early morning surfers glide across the surface of a good-sized wave further out.

'Well, I can't do any worse.'

If he'd been any other man she would have politely declined any further lessons. But while he wanted to be with her, she was going to take all opportunities presented to her.

She watched his profile as he tracked the path of the surfer. 'Are your batteries recharged?' she asked.

Adam grinned as he admired a beautifully executed cutback. 'Fully.'

'Well, then, let's go back to bed.'

Adam felt an instant streak of lust slam into him at the forthright words coming from her sweet mouth. He turned to stare at her, the surfer forgotten as his wet, clinging boardies suddenly became tighter.

Thank God for his surfboard.

'I've created a monster, haven't I?'

'Yup.' She grinned and turned to walk back up the beach.

She could feel his gaze on her butt and added an extra swagger to her hips and deliberately bent over with as much provocation as she muster to pick up the towels.

'Jess,' he growled.

She grinned over her shoulder, throwing him his towel and taking off ahead of him.

Jess was pleased to find the house still quiet when she

arrived home a minute ahead of Adam. Tilly was probably out indulging in her regular morning dip. Ellie was working the afternoon shift and no doubt hadn't roused yet. And Ruby's night shift hadn't yet finished. She crossed to Adam's bedroom and was sitting naked on the side of his bed when he opened the door a minute later.

Adam hissed out a breath. 'Jess.'

He'd gratefully wrapped the towel around his hips for the walk back to the house but now, feasting his eyes on the gloriously naked sight of her, it seemed as insubstantial as a postage stamp.

He crossed over to her and stood before her. Her hair hung in wet strips to her shoulders, there was a dusting of sand on her belly and he could smell the salt on her skin.

But she glowed and she was looking at him like he was the only man in existence.

Like the original Adam.

She smiled at him and he reached out and stroked the back of his forefinger down her cheek.

'You're beautiful.' Jess felt her heart expand in her chest. The revelation that she loved him pushed painfully at her ribs.

It shouldn't have been a revelation at all.

She'd been obsessed with him for ever. But she'd never let herself think in terms of the L word before.

Besotted. Infatuated. Smitten.

Yes.

All of them.

But never love. It had seemed too unattainable and she just hadn't ever allowed her head to go there.

But the revelation was easy this morning.

Of course she loved him. She'd loved him from the beginning.

The desire to tell him, to blurt it out pushed the words to the tip of her tongue. But self-preservation won out.

Telling him now would be suicide.

Jess smiled at him, covering his hand with hers. She brought it to her mouth, dropping a kiss against his knuckles.

I love you.

'You're beautiful too.'

The innocent gesture touched Adam somewhere deep inside. A warmth flowed through him, circling around his body and nestling under his skin. He dropped his hand. 'Lie back,' he murmured huskily.

Jess looked up into his eyes, the golden flecks making the blue even more remarkable. She shook her head and reached for the towel at his waist.

She didn't want to be passive any more. She wanted to explore his body. To know more about what made him crazy, what rolled his eyes back, what brought him to his knees.

She wanted to be active.

She wanted to lead.

She wanted to love him.

Adam was only vaguely aware of the towel falling away as her gaze locked on his crotch. He got harder. And he hadn't even thought that possible. When she reached for the tie he cleared his throat. 'No.'

Jess looked at the bulge straining against the wet boardies. She stroked a finger along it and was curiously pleased when it pushed against her. 'It says yes.'

Adam shut his eyes against the urge to thrust his hips. 'I hate to break it to you but it always says yes.'

Jess would have laughed if there hadn't been so much strain in Adam's voice. She dropped her hand. 'Lucky me.'

'Jess…I don't think—'

She looked up at him. 'I want to taste you.'

Adam swallowed to moisten his suddenly parched throat. 'You don't have to do that.'

Even though he wanted to feel her mouth around him more than he'd ever wanted anything. Wanted to look down at her as she performed an act so intimate the mere thought almost buckled his knees.

She pulled the ties. 'I want to. Just like you tasted me.'

A loud rip echoed around the room as Jess separated the Velcro opening and Adam's erection nudged through the fabric.

'Jess.' Adam reached for the slender hold he had on his libido. 'Some women don't…like it.'

Adam liked oral sex. Giving it. And receiving it. Hell, he was certainly no stranger to receiving it. But that was from women who were experienced in sexual matters. Who knew what they wanted and what they didn't. What they liked and what they didn't. Adam knew those kind of intimate preferences came from experience.

And Jess had none.

Jess parted his fly, pushing the wet fabric back, allowing Adam's erection free rein. It was big and thick and hard and she could smell salt and sand and something else quintessentially male.

He was so beautiful her mouth watered.

She looked up at him. 'Do *you* like it?'

Adam almost groaned. 'Of course… I don't think I've ever met a man who doesn't.'

She smiled at him. 'Well, that's all I need to know.'

And then she returned her attention to his erection, grasping it firmly before tentatively flicking her tongue across the engorged head. She felt Adam tremble and just heard the low guttural expletive that left his lips.

She repeated the manoeuvre and then flattened her

tongue against him, circling the spongy sensitive tip. When she took him fully in her mouth his groan seemed to come from somewhere primal and she felt a surge of power shoot through her system like a tequila shot on an empty stomach.

He was at her mercy.

And it felt incredible. She held his pleasure in her palm. It was dizzying.

For the first time in her life she actually understood why sex and love and lust could make people crazy. Why empires fell and wars were waged over it.

She couldn't remember ever feeling this powerful.

This…adult.

This…female.

Adam was gone from the first tentative flick of her tongue. Every movement of her mouth against him was a revelation as she experimented with stroke and rhythm. It was almost as if it was his first time all over again.

And just when he thought it couldn't possibly get sweeter her hands moved down his shaft, moved lower to cup him. Squeeze him.

He moaned out loud and grabbed for her shoulders as his knees threatened to buckle again.

Jess looked up at him, pulling her mouth away. 'You like that?' she whispered.

Adam nodded, unable to form words. He hadn't seen anything more erotic in his life. Her big blue eyes looking shyly up at him, like she'd just discovered the world's most amazing secret.

And it was her.

Her pink mouth was moist, her lips slightly swollen from their ministrations. She looked incredible. Then she took him back into her mouth running her tongue up and down his shaft and he had to suppress the wild impulse to grab her head, to rock his hips to the wild rhythm that was coursing through his blood demanding that she take him deeper, suck harder.

His body trembled with the urge to take over. To seek his pleasure quick and hard and fast. He dug his fingers into his thighs, cried out with the frustrating mix of pleasure and impatience and the unnatural curtailing of the dictates of his body.

Even through the haze of feminine power and hormones Jess could hear the strangled note in his voice. 'What?' she asked looking up at him. 'Tell me what you like.'

Adam sliced a hand into her hair. She was so beautiful and it was exquisite. It wasn't her fault his body wanted to take over, that lust cared only about end result, not technique or experimentation. 'You're doing fine,' he murmured.

'No.' He looked like a man who had an itch he couldn't quite reach. 'Damn it, Adam, tell me.' He sucked in a breath at the fierce glitter in her eyes.

'Harder,' he whispered.

Jess didn't need to be told twice recapturing his swollen girth and turning up the suction. When the hand buried in her hair clutched convulsively and a deeply satisfied groan tore from his mouth, she intensified it some more.

Adam felt the first stirrings of orgasm tighten his groins like purse strings. 'Oh God, yes. Yes.'

He looked down at her as her mouth devoured him. It was such an erotic picture and the strings pulled tighter. It was hard to believe the mouth that had so innocently kissed his knuckles not ten minutes ago was now engaged in such a carnal activity.

Ripples of pleasure darted from where she cupped and squeezed him. They streaked to his thighs, his belly, his groin.

'Yes,' he gasped.

Jess heard the note of desperation. Could feel his whole body trembling and knew he was close. She took him deeper, sucked a little stronger, squeezed a little harder.

The ripples turned to waves, then an avalanche. 'Jess!' he cried out, his knees locking, his hand curling into her hair as his orgasm rushed out.

She kept up the pressure, milking him as he rocked into her mouth, welcoming his release.

The completeness of his surrender and the salty taste of him was a powerful aphrodisiac.

It was a while before the ringing in Adam's ears subsided, before he could open his eyes and unlock his knees and trust that he wasn't going to fall in a heap.

He looked down at her. His hand was buried in her hair at the back of her head and he couldn't for the life of him remember how it had got there. His fingers automatically started to caress her scalp as she smiled up at him.

There was something different about her now. She looked at him with knowing eyes, with an awareness that hadn't been there before.

'I think you can put me down in the *like* column,' she murmured.

Adam smiled back before leaning down and claiming her mouth.

CHAPTER EIGHT

'WHERE are you going?' Jess murmured as Adam eased away from her sleepy form an hour later.

Adam looked over his shoulder. 'I'm going to check on Lai Ling and my other patients. We don't all have a couple days off, little Miss Sleepyhead.' He smiled.

He rose from the bed before her pretty pink pout, tousled hair and wandering gaze convinced him to stay a bit longer.

Jess yawned and stretched. 'I can't help it if you're insatiable.'

Adam watched as her nude body rippled with the stretch like a contented feline. Her shoulder blades came together, arching her back, undulating her breasts and belly. Her legs and toes elongated before curling back towards her body.

His loins stirred and his nostrils flared as she stared at him with eyes that told him she knew exactly what she'd done and what effect it had on him.

He chuckled. 'Well, isn't that pot calling the kettle black.'

Yesterday Jess would have blushed. This morning, after being thoroughly loved by Adam and loving him back, she proudly owned her part in their sleepless night.

She sighed and shut her eyes, snuggling into the pillow. 'I'm going to be waiting for you when you get back.'

She kept it deliberately light, playing on her sleepiness but inside she was a tangle of nerves as she awaited his reply. Would he say no? Tell her to leave? She held her breath, waiting for the rejection, for the excuses.

For him to point to the revolving door.

Adam swept his gaze down her naked body, knowing he should tell her to go but knowing he wanted more. Knowing he was far from done.

Strangely enough, it didn't even terrify him.

And what the hell, he'd already crossed the line. 'You'd better be,' he growled, reaching down for the sheet and throwing it over her to quell the impact her nudity and that sexy little stretch had on his body. 'Or I'm going to come and hunt you down.'

Jess kept her eyes shut but inside her chest her heart bloomed and a trill of excitement lit her insides. She fluttered her eyelashes open as the cool sheet fell lightly against her heated flesh.

'I won't move a muscle,' she murmured.

Jake clenched his fists as her gaze wandered over his body, lingering at the juncture of his thighs. He felt himself twitch beneath her sleepy appraisal.

'Jess.'

'Hmm?' she asked innocently, suppressing a grin at the note of warning apparent in his husky voice.

Adam took a step towards the bed. How could he want her again so soon?

His gaze fanned over her, taking in the bedside table behind her and his alarm clock. He pulled himself up short, cursing under his breath.

'God, is that the time?' He shook his head to clear it of the fog of lust that was clouding more than just his vision. 'I have to have a shower and get going. My round is supposed to start in half an hour.'

Jess watched him stalk off to the en suite and smiled. She hugged herself under the sheet. He found it hard to leave her. And he wanted her in his bed when he got back.

It wasn't a wedding ring but it was more than she'd dared hope for.

She heard the water turn on and images of a wet and slippery Adam filled her head. An insidious voice that Adam had woken last night whispered, *Shower sex*. She'd seen it in movies and read it in books but never experienced it.

It took less than five seconds to kick off the sheet. And in ten she was sliding the shower door open.

'I thought you weren't moving a muscle,' Adam said as she fused herself against his unprotesting body and kissed him deep and wet and hungry.

'Shower sex,' she murmured against his mouth.

It took Adam no time to boost her up the tiles. And no time for her legs to automatically circle his waist and lock tight.

'I'm going to be so late,' he groaned as his gaze zeroed in on a rosy nipple and his head descended.

Ruby was in the kitchen when Adam strode out of his bedroom twenty minutes later. He faltered slightly at the sight of her, his broken promise suddenly weighing heavily on his conscience.

'There's no coffee,' Ruby grumbled, staring at the empty coffee pot in her hand.

'Good morning to you too,' Adam murmured.

Like his sister, he needed a coffee before heading to work as well but this morning he was running on sex.

'There's always coffee,' Ruby continued. 'Tilly or Jess always have one going by now.'

Adam ignored his sister. She wasn't a morning person at the best of times and night duty did not bring out her sunny side. He didn't think explaining to her that Jess hadn't started the coffee this morning because she was sleeping very soundly and very, very naked in his bed would improve her mood.

'Why don't you just go straight to bed?' he asked as he quickly popped two slices of bread into the toaster. He was already running late—he didn't have time for his sister's mood.

Ruby shook her head. 'Not without a coffee.'

Adam sighed as Ruby looked at the pot like she didn't know what to do with it. She was so *not* a night-duty person. He took the pot off her and busied himself with the percolator.

'Won't it keep you awake?'

Ruby snorted. 'A brass band playing at the end of my bed wouldn't keep me awake.'

He pressed the on button. 'Coffee in two minutes,' he announced.

Ruby sat at the kitchen table. 'Thanks,' she said as she flipped through the mail that someone had left on the table. There was one addressed to both Adam and herself and even as she opened it she knew it was from their parents.

'Oh, hell,' she grumbled as she opened and scanned the elegant, thick card. 'Dad's holding another one of his dreadful dinner parties.' She passed it to Adam.

Adam looked at it with distaste. The very last thing he wanted was to spend an evening listening to his father being pompous and self-important in their pretentious house at Whale Beach while his mother ran herself ragged, trying to be the perfect hostess.

Something which his father never appreciated and only ever noticed when she was too busy with some stupid finicky detail to be by his side, stroking his ego.

Little wonder he chose to spend as much of his time out of the country as possible.

'We'll have to go, of course,' Ruby sighed.

Adam tossed the card on the table. 'Of course.'

He and Ruby couldn't leave their poor mother to face something like that alone. She was a wonderful, warm, giving human being who deserved a medal for putting up with his father's rubbish over the years.

She sure as hell didn't deserve her husband.

But even after all these years she was still besotted with him.

'Cort's invited, I see,' he said as he poured two cups of coffee.

'Yes.' Ruby stared morosely at the table. 'Just as well he loves me.'

Adam plonked a coffee in front of Ruby and sat down opposite her in a gesture of silent solidarity.

What the hell, he was already late.

Ruby took a couple of sips of her coffee, inspecting the invitation again. 'You're a plus one, I see.'

'Not going to happen.' Adam's thoughts slid to Jess curled up in his bed. The last time he'd brought a girl home it had been Caroline and his father had been an over-bearing brute. The mere thought of subjecting Jess to *the chief,* to his parents' screwed-up dynamic sent an itch up his spine.

Ruby rolled her eyes. She let the invitation slip from her fingers. 'So how was the party last night? What time did it wind down?'

Adam looked into his coffee, avoiding his sister's gaze. 'I don't know,' he said evasively. 'Pretty late. It was still going when I…went to bed.'

'Jess was pretty high. I bet she lasted until the end. It might also explain why she's not up yet. Normally she would have been up flitting around happy as a lark a couple of hours ago.'

Adam kept his gaze firmly fixed on his coffee as he toyed with being noncommittal. Saying something vague and getting the hell out of the house. But the truth was going to come out soon enough.

Especially as he intended spending more time in bed with Jess.

And this was his house. He wasn't going to sneak around in it like a teenager.

He was thirty-five years old, for crying out loud.

Telling Ruby the truth in her current tired and grumpy state probably wasn't the best timing but he had an opening.

Adam placed his mug on the table and looked at his sister. 'She's not up yet because she spent the night with me.'

Ruby blinked. 'What?'

Adam stood, picking up his coffee. 'You heard me,' he said as he walked to the sink.

'Adam! You promised,' Ruby spluttered, also standing.

He kept his back to her as he took a couple of mouthfuls of his coffee. 'I don't have time for this now.'

'You promised,' Ruby repeated.

Adam turned, feeling guilt and exasperation in equal measure. 'I don't have to account for my actions to you, Ruby, and I'm not seeking your approval. I'm just letting you know because Jess and I are going to be spending a lot of time together.'

Ruby frowned. 'What? But…you don't do that.'

Adam understood her confusion. It was rare for him to spend more than a couple of nights with one woman. But there was something about Jess that made him want more.

'Maybe I've changed.'

Ruby quirked an eyebrow. 'Are you still leaving for God knows where in a matter of weeks?'

'Of course.'

She shook her head. 'You're going to break her heart.'

'She knows.'

'Yes, but does she? *Really*?' Ruby demanded.

Adam opened his mouth to tell his sister to stop being so damn theatrical and to mind her own business. That he and Jess were adults and that he'd talk to her about expectations. But his pager beeped.

He knew what it was about without having to pull it off his belt and look at the message. 'I'm running late,' he said impatiently, turning back to the sink and tipping the dregs of his coffee down the drain. 'I'll see you later.'

He didn't give her a chance to reply, heading straight for the door and banging out of the house.

Adam flipped open his mobile as his long stride ate up the incline between the house and the hospital. He dialled the number on his pager and let his team know he was going to be another fifteen minutes.

Ruby's accusation taunted him all the way up the hill.

You promised.

Does she? Really?

Guilt revisited. But, hell, it wasn't like he'd deliberately planned it. Or that he hadn't had every intention of keeping his promise.

It was just…life.

Sometimes the best-laid plans went awry.

For God's sake, it wasn't as if they were kids and they'd pinkie-promised or made some kind of blood oath. This was the real world. And in the real world promises got broken.

He was still mulling over it when he strode through the

front entrance of Eastern Beaches to find his team waiting for him in a huddle.

'Here he is,' Paula teased. 'Getting too old to party?'

Adam, who had no intention of explaining why he was late, chuckled. 'I see you all pulled up okay. What time did it finish?'

'I was one of the last ones to leave about two,' Shamus said. 'But you'd know that if you hadn't piked.'

Adam smiled. 'Too late for me.' Even though he'd been awake, wide awake, long past that. 'So,' he said, taking the top chart from Shamus's arms. 'How are our patients this morning?'

With the subject smoothly changed, Adam shut everything from his mind—Ruby's censure and Jess's comeback-to-bed eyes—and got down to business.

Their first stops were the two surgical wards, male and female, where the eight surgical cases they'd done on Monday and Tuesday were recovering. Eight faces beamed at him and his team and despite the language barrier Adam felt their emotional gratitude right down to his toes.

He was pleased with all eight's progress and was happy for them all to be discharged to their host families later today.

Host families had been arranged by one of the charities as a friendly, restful environment for the patients to recover in for a couple of days before flying back home. Big, modern hospitals were far from ideal places to convalesce for people who came from comparatively primitive circumstances.

Adam would see them all just prior to them flying home and again at the end of next month when his scheduled mission took him near their homes.

Next they made their way to the ICU to see Lai Ling. Adam had chosen to visit her last because he knew that the

ICU round would be finished and he could consult with the on-coming intensivists.

Lai Ling was asleep when he approached her bed after talking to Dr Diane Cleary, the ICU consultant.

'How's our champion?' Adam asked the bedside nurse, who happened to be someone he'd spent a night or two with a couple of years back.

She smiled at him and said, 'Good morning, Doctor.'

Adam nodded, noting the fluttering eyelashes, the *well, hello there* look in her gaze, the flirty smile on her heavily painted mouth.

It did absolutely nothing for him.

'Lorraine,' he acknowledged. 'Any issues?'

'A slight fever overnight otherwise everything stable.'

Was it his imagination or had Lorraine put slight emphasis on the word *fever*? 'We'll keep an eye on the temperature,' he said briskly. 'She's on triple antibiotics so she has pretty broad cover.'

He walked over to the bedside. Lai Ling was wired to a monitor and looked like a little girl instead of a nineteen-year-old woman amidst all the medical equipment.

'Minimal ooze,' he noted as he inspected the dressings.

Lai Ling's eyes fluttered open. He smiled at her and, after a couple of seconds where she seemed momentarily confused, she smiled back.

'Okay?' Adam asked, aware that Lai Ling had only rudimentary English and there was no interpreter currently around.

Lai Ling smiled and nodded. She looked around at all the people surrounding her bed then looked back at Adam. 'Jess?'

Adam felt that one soft enquiry sucker punch him unexpectedly as images from last night assailed him. He'd managed to put Jess from his mind for a little while but she was back—front and centre.

Sweet, sweet Jess. Home, waiting for him in his bed.

Naked.

Then Ruby's *Does she, really?* rudely pushed its thorny finger into the lovely little bubble.

'You'll see her in a couple of days,' Adam said, holding up two fingers.

Lai Ling smiled and nodded and promptly fell asleep again. Adam chuckled then looked up at his team. 'Okay, so the ICU team is happy for her to be discharged to the ward some time today.'

'How much longer do you think she'll need to be an in-patient?' Shamus asked.

''Bout five to seven days, I guess, depending on her progress,' Adam confirmed. 'Then she'll go to a host family for a few more weeks, where we can do some regular follow-up. She should be able to fly home after that if all goes well.'

The round ended and his team scattered to deal with their regular patient loads. Adam went to his temporary office to review all the notes and jot down his own observations. He made some phone calls and attended a meeting with Gordon Meriwether to keep him up to date.

Two hours later he'd done all that had to be done. And it was time to go home. To Jess.

But.

Ruby's voice hadn't let up. It was on continual loop in the back of his head. He knew he was going to have to talk to Jess. To establish the boundaries of whatever the hell they were doing. To make sure she knew that he was out of here in a handful of weeks and would be gone for a couple of months.

He'd never had to do that with women like Lorraine.

Women who played the game as hard as he did and knew the score. It was just unspoken.

But Jess was different.

It wasn't a conversation he relished. Hell, it wasn't a conversation he'd even had to have since Francine all those years ago.

He'd made sure of that.

No one was around when Adam opened the front door, for which he was grateful. He'd been practising his spiel all the way down the hill and he just wanted to get it over with. Not even the sound of gulls or the ocean roaring in the distance had been enough to distract him.

He crossed to his bedroom and quietly turned the doorknob. He felt a brief confusing moment of panic that she might not be there, which was quickly dispelled as his gaze connected with her slumbering perfection.

She had her back to the door and her legs curled up. The sheet was anchored under her arms, covering her front and her legs, but had slipped low on her back, just revealing a tantalising glimpse of the rise of her bottom and the slope of one sweet cheek.

Shafts of strong midday sun bathed her body in a golden spotlight. Her blonde hair shone like a halo. It was as if she'd been delivered by the gods, laid out for his pleasure.

Half-unwrapped.

He wanted nothing more than to shuck off his clothes and join her. Slide his legs in behind hers, glide a hand up her ribs and down her belly.

He gripped the doorknob hard. This *was not* helping. He shut the door and strode towards the bed, sitting down gently beside her. Her eyelashes fanned her cheeks and he could smell soap and shampoo. And sex.

She was close. So close.

The temptation factor increased tenfold.

'Jess,' he whispered. She didn't stir. He reached out a hand to shake her shoulder but withdrew it—once his fingers hit her skin he doubted he'd have any kind of control over them.

He leaned forward instead and dropped a light kiss on her shoulder. It was logistically easier to control his mouth than the long reach of his arms near all that tempting naked flesh.

'Jess,' he murmured against her skin. 'Wake up.'

Jess stirred. Her eyelids fluttered open and Adam came into focus. Her heart did a crazy tap dance in her chest. 'You're here.' She smiled.

Adam returned the smile. 'I am.'

Jess shifted slightly so she was on her back, the sheet pulling across her body. 'How's Lai Ling?'

'Asking about you.'

Her smile widened. 'Really?'

Adam chuckled. 'Yes really.'

His laughter reached deep inside her and oozed into all those places that had harboured doubt as she'd drifted off to sleep.

He was wearing the same clothes he'd left the room in. Dark grey trousers, an aubergine business shirt and a diamond-patterned dark green tie. He was incredibly sexy.

But way too clothed. She raised a hand to his face and stroked her fingers across his mouth. 'I missed you.'

Adam's breath hitched as his gaze searched her face. The sheet covering her slipped a little, exposing the slopes of her breasts. Her fingers toyed with his mouth and he pressed his lips against them before pulling back slightly.

'We need to talk,' he murmured.

Jess felt her heart skip a beat at the sudden seriousness clouding the golden flecks in his lapis lazuli gaze.

No. No, no, no.

Not yet. Not so soon.

Okay, so this was vintage Adam. After years of watching women come and go, she knew his pattern. Love them and leave them. But it was too soon. She wanted another night.

Hell, she'd settle for one more time in his arms.

She sat, letting the sheet fall to her waist, sliding her arms around his neck and leaning forward to press a kiss to his mouth. 'Later,' she whispered against his mouth.

Adam inhaled, his nostrils filling with her scent as her lips teased his. 'Jess…'

'Shh,' she murmured, moving forward, rising to her knees, their lips still locked, throwing one leg over his lap until she was straddling him.

She swayed against him and Adam grabbed her hips to steady her.

Big mistake.

Because now his hands were full of her sweet, soft flesh and she was anchoring her arms around his shoulders, her breasts crushed to his chest, pressing kisses all over his face.

He could feel himself harden as he ran his hands up her naked back then back down to cup two glorious cheeks. There was something exceedingly erotic about having a completely naked woman plastered against his fully clothed body.

'The things you do to me,' he whispered.

Jess, balanced on Adam's lap, pulled back slightly and smiled, dropping a kiss against his temple. She felt his grip on her bottom intensify, holding her fast. 'I think we can get rid of this,' she said, loosening the knot of his tie and pulling it off him with a satisfying slither of fabric.

Then she kissed him. Deep and hard. 'And this,' she said, pulling away again as her hands grabbed at his shirt and pulled it free of his waistband. Then she kissed down his neck as her fingers went to work on the buttons.

When she'd undone the last one she pushed the shirt off his shoulders, exposing his chest and abdomen. He slammed his mouth against hers and she revelled in the harsh suck of his breath as he dragged air in and out of flared nostrils. She felt a hand slide to the small of her back and haul her closer.

Her hands trekked down his bare sides, feeling the dip of his ribs then the contraction of his flanks. When she reached his waistband she followed it around to the zipper and then down to the bulge in his trousers.

Her hips, almost of their own volition, ground down against it. The rough fabric of his trousers abraded in all the right places and she gasped out loud as the pads of his fingers dug into her back and his groan thundered through her ears.

She pulled back, her lungs desperately sucking in more air. 'You like that?'

'God, yes,' Adam whispered against her mouth.

And when she did it again he plundered her mouth, pushing a hand up into her hair and forcing her mouth nearer, wider, deeper.

Jess fumbled for the zip, found it, yanked it down, felt his hardness straining to be free, reached for it, liberated it.

'Ahh,' Adam groaned as Jess's hand enveloped him.

'You're so hard,' she whispered, palming his wonderfully naked length—one stroke, two. But it wasn't enough. She needed more. Needed to feel him against her. In her.

She released his girth and rocked her pelvis along all his meaty hardness. It was hot and slick down there and a delicious friction built, stoking an even greater ache.

Adam nostrils filled with the scent of them and he dug

his fingers into the flesh of her bottom as his pelvis thrust against hers. 'Now, Jess, now.'

Jess gasped as she felt him press urgently against her. She rose on her knees to accommodate him. His hands held her hips steady as she reached for him, guiding him to her entrance. She felt his girth nudge her and then she sank down on to him in one slick, sure movement.

'Ahh,' she cried out as she gripped his shoulder hard. He filled her so completely it was as if he was made for her.

'Jess?' Adam breathed hard, fighting the wild call of his body to pull out and plunge in again as all her sweet, wet heat gripped him in a tight velvet glove. 'Are you okay?'

Jess nodded as a ferocious tingling infused her pelvis. It prickled and burned, spreading ripples of heat and pleasure to every cell in her body. A shockwave of lust.

'I'm fine,' she murmured against his temple as she flexed her hips and undulated internal muscles, feeling every inch of him rammed to the hilt inside her. 'Perfect,' she sighed as she lifted a little then sank down a little.

Adam sucked in a breath. 'Yes, yes.'

Jess lifted a little higher and sank down a little further. 'Oh, God, yes.'

Jess lifted all the way until she could feel him at her opening again then sank back down until he was snug to the hilt.

Adam stifled a groan, plundering her mouth. His hands slid up her back, his fingers hooking over her shoulders and anchoring there. Her body lifted again and their kiss broke. He shut his eyes as her internal muscles grabbed him hard and pulsed around him like a thousand massaging fingers.

His forehead fell against her chest as she set a rhythm that took him closer and closer to the edge. Her breasts bounced in his face and he nuzzled one, sucking a rosy nipple deep into his mouth.

When she cried out he sucked the other one.

Harder.

Jess's head lolled back as the pleasure intensity spiked to a new high. Her nipples pebbled tight and the sensation arrowed straight to her core. She clutched his head to her chest, keening her pleasure as he lavished her breasts with attention.

When his teeth grazed a sensitive tip her orgasm hit warp speed, rushing forward, hurtling from her centre, twisting and swirling, burning and tingling, destroying everything in its path.

'Adam,' she cried out, clenching down hard as every muscle tightened to an unbearable tension. 'Oh, I… It's…'

Adam clamped her against him hard, gripping her shoulders tight, bucking his pelvis, taking over the rhythm from her, feeling his own climax begin to spiral out from his loins as she milked his length with her tight velvet walls.

He whispered, 'Yes, yes,' against a breast as his climax trembled through him, shaking him like a leaf, shaking him right down to his core.

He threw back his head in a primal roar as everything imploded and a mighty orgasm engulfed him. It fanned the dying embers of hers and he held her as she cried out again.

Held her like he never wanted to let her go.

Adam collapsed back on the bed a minute later, dragging her down with him. Their breathing was loud, laboured in the silence, and neither spoke as they struggled for control of their breath.

Adam's hand sat firmly in the middle of her back as he heaved air in and out of his lungs. Her skin was covered in a fine sheen of sweat and she was warm against his chest.

He grimaced. They must look a sight. She, stark naked sprawled over his chest. He, clothes askew, partially undressed. Just barely on the bed, his feet on the floor. Puffing and panting like they'd just run a marathon.

Another minute later, his pulse and breathing near normal, Adam said, 'Can we talk now you've finished ravaging me?'

Jess smiled as his voice rumbled up through his rib cage, connecting with the ear she had pressed to his chest. Even knowing what he was about to say, she was too spent to stop him. Or her brain cells were still too post-coital to give a damn.

At least she'd had her one last time.

She eased off him, her insides giving a delicious shudder, rolling onto her back, her legs also hanging over the edge of the bed although not quite reaching the floor. She followed Adam's example and stared at the ceiling. 'I can't promise I'm too coherent,' she said.

Adam chuckled. With his own brain currently oozing out his ears, he could relate. He sobered again, fixing his clothing. Somehow it didn't seem right to have this conversation with his trousers half pushed down, his underwear askew.

Even if she was stark naked.

'Ruby knows.'

Jess lifted her head off the bed and stared at him. 'What?'

'She was in the kitchen this morning, moaning about the coffee not being ready and speculating what was keeping you in bed past your usual early hour. And…I told her.'

Jess fell back against the mattress. 'How did you tell her?'

'I said you'd spent the night with me.'

Jess blew out a breath, disturbing a strip of fringe that

had half fallen across her eye. 'It might have been better coming from me.'

Adam rolled his head to face her. 'She'd have still been angry with me. I promised her I'd stay away from you.'

Jess rolled her head to face him. 'You did?'

He nodded. 'And I had every intention of doing just that.'

Jess grinned. 'That didn't really work out, did it?'

Adam smiled back. It faded quickly though as he scanned her lovely face. He hadn't expected to be so totally blind-sided by someone he'd known for three years and had never thought of as anything other than his little sister's friend.

'How was I supposed to know your chocolate-cake kisses were so hard to resist?'

There was humour in his voice but his blue, blue gaze was serious. The last thing Jess had wanted was to become a bone of contention between two people she loved. 'I'll talk to her.'

Adam shook his head. He didn't need a champion. But he did need to establish some boundaries. For the first time in a very long time he wanted more than a quick roll in the hay with a woman. But it couldn't last.

His lifestyle just wasn't conducive to relationships. And he didn't let anything distract him for his work.

'She thinks you don't know that I'm only in town for a matter of weeks and that whatever we have going on has a very short shelf life.'

And there it was. The crux of the matter. Jess kept her face completely neutral, masking the hammer blow to her stomach as all the delicious post-coital glow fizzed.

She swallowed. 'I know that.'

'Do you?' he asked, repeating Ruby's question. 'Because this is my life, Jess. I'm a gypsy. I travel around the world. I go where I'm needed.'

Jess felt an absurd urge to cry. What if she needed him to be here? She quelled it. She didn't do teary and emotional—that wasn't her style. But neither was she going to meekly accept his narrow life parameters.

Keeping her voice non-confrontational, she said, 'So you're going to do that for ever?'

Adam opened his mouth to confirm it but suddenly for ever stretched out bleakly in front of him and he recoiled from it. Thinking about how jet-lagged he'd been this time around, the prospect of putting his body through that at sixty was very unappealing.

He shrugged. 'It's who I am.'

Jess lifted a hand to his face and traced her fingers along his mouth. 'No, Adam, it's what you do.'

She wanted to say so much more. That he was living only half a life if he defined himself only in relation to his occupation. That family and friends and the hobbies you indulged in and the sports that you played, the books that you read, the movies you saw and the place you called home were the things that defined you.

But she'd spent less than twenty-four hours in his bed and just because she loved him it didn't qualify her to dish out home truths. She certainly didn't want to annoy him with her opinions. That was relationship territory and she didn't want to scare him away.

Adam considered her statement. As far as he was concerned his job was his life—one didn't exist without the other. But it was novel to realise that for some people it was just part of who they were. One component.

How could he want her so badly when she was practically his polar opposite? His lips tingled where her fingers had trailed moments before.

'Is this about her?' Jess asked into the growing silence. 'The woman who broke your heart?'

Adam frowned. 'Caroline?'

Caroline. The woman who had ruined him for all others.

'This is nothing to do with Caroline.'

'Except she's the only woman you've ever committed to and since she broke your engagement you haven't had a significant relationship with anyone.'

Adam shook his head. *Ruby was too damn chatty.* 'I loved her, yes, and I'll admit that her leaving did screw with me for a while.' He'd been mad as hell at his father for three years. 'But, Jess, that was a decade ago. I'm totally over her.'

'So you're not still in love with her?'

'No,' he denied. God, no. He hadn't thought about Caroline in years even if their break-up had subconsciously coloured every relationship since. He'd heard that she'd got married a few years back and he'd felt nothing other than happy for her.

'Definitely not.' He looked up at the ceiling. 'I'm not still pining for her deep, deep down, Jess. Trust me, my reasons for not forming significant relationships with women have nothing to do with a long-forgotten fiancée. I just don't have the time for relationships. My work is totally consuming. That would just be selfish of me.'

Jess looked at the ceiling too as relief coursed through her body. His voice was full of conviction and she believed him. 'Okay.' It was good to know she wasn't competing with a ghost. That her love just might stand a chance.

But.

How could she hope to reach a man whose one true emotional connection was with something as functional as his job?

Adam turned his head back to face her. 'You and I are very different. We want different things.'

Jess nodded. They most definitely were. But that didn't have to be bad. Opposites were supposed to attract, were they not? He was looking at her like she was a puzzle he could figure out if he just looked at her long enough. But there was no puzzle with her—she knew what she wanted.

He was the one hiding from life.

'What do you want, Adam. Right here, right now, what do you want?'

Adam blinked. He hadn't known what her comeback would be but it wasn't this. It had been many years since he'd had a proper conversation like this with a woman in his bed. He doubted any of his bed partners since Caroline had cared about what he wanted unless it had a sexual connotation.

It was so startling he didn't even think about ducking the question

'I want to keep doing this, you and me. Until I head overseas again.'

Jess could see sincerity blazing from the golden flecks in his eyes and hear it in the steady timbre of his voice. It never occurred to her to deny him. 'Well, all right, then.'

Adam shut his eyes briefly. 'No, Jess, it's not all right. You told me on the beach that morning that you'd want everything. But I can't offer you that. I'm going to be gone for a couple of months. I'm always going to be gone somewhere for a couple of months. All I can offer you is these next few weeks.'

Yes, she had said that. Yes, she did want everything. She loved him. She wanted his ring and his name and his children. She wanted to grow old with him.

She wanted the fairy-tale.

And he didn't.

But something told her he might. If she just persevered.

If she showed him what he was missing. If she gave without expectation, if she loved him in silence.

And even if he never did want the things she wanted she knew in her bones she was willing to sacrifice the fairy-tale, what she wanted, to be with him here and now.

Until this moment she never would have believed it.

But she knew with utter certainty that she'd take whatever he was willing to give for as long as he would have her.

Because she loved him.

'I can't make you give me everything, Adam. But I can make the most of what you're willing to offer.'

Yes, she was going to get her heart broken but her grandmother had always said it took courage to love. 'I'll take these next few weeks and cherish them for the rest of my life.'

Adam rolled on his side, supporting his head on his palm. She was gloriously naked stretched out before him.

He already wanted her again.

He looked down into her face, inspecting it for signs of artifice. Her answer had quickened his pulse. He wanted so much to believe it but it was a big ask to go from *everything* to just a few weeks. 'Why?'

Because I love you.

Because I want to love you so thoroughly you'll want the fairy-tale as well.

'Because you only live once. Because I'm twenty-four and when I'm old and grey I want to be able to scandalise my grandkids with stories about the surfing surgeon I had a wild, passionate fling with.'

He gave a throaty chuckle and her heart swelled with its resonance. 'And because you asked me.'

Their gazes locked and neither of them said anything for a moment or two.

'Don't go falling in love,' Adam said.

He wasn't entirely sure whether he was talking to her or himself.

Jess nodded. 'Roger.'

If only it wasn't too late.

CHAPTER NINE

THE next week was one of the happiest of Jess's life. Long nights spent in bed with Adam. Early morning surfing lessons. Hanging out at the Stat Bar like a real couple with the gang. Not feeling like a fifth wheel for a change.

Being able to reach out and touch him, hold his hand, cook for him, smile at him with come-hither eyes, see lust and frank sexual appreciation reflected in the golden flecks of his hey-baby gaze.

Jess revelled in the envious looks from women everywhere. On the beach, at work—where rumours about their liaison had circulated like wildfire—at the Stat Bar.

Unless she pulled off a miracle she had a very short amount of time to bask in their against-all-odds relationship.

So bask she did.

And everyone had been supportive. Even Ruby. After her initial *keep hold of your heart* warning she'd been true to her word and not said another thing. Tilly and Ellie had also been fabulous, although she could see her friends were concerned about her.

About what happened after Adam left.

But for now Jess refused to think about that. She was living in the moment. In a bubble.

A wonderful, joyous, love-filled bubble.

* * *

The bubble burst a few days later when Adam announced, in bed that morning just prior to getting up for another surfing lesson, that he and Ruby and Cort were going to a dinner party at his parents' house that night and not to wait up.

The blow was surprising in its intensity.

For the first time since the party, Jess actually felt… temporary.

It had been easy these last amazing days to think of them as a couple but this was a resounding slap in the face. They were *not* a couple.

They were a fleeting hook-up for a few weeks that involved sex and fun and laughter.

It definitely did *not* involve meeting the parents.

'Okay,' she said, trying not to betray in her voice the blinding disappointment she felt in every cell of her body.

Adam heard the catch in her voice and rolled onto his side, dropping a kiss on her bare shoulder. 'It's going to be stuffy and unbearable and my father will be his usual egotistical self, regaling everyone with stories about him, him, him. We're only going for Mum's sake. Trust me, I'm saving you from being bored to death.'

Jess plastered a smile on her face as she nodded. 'Of course,' she said. 'I've got a late shift anyway.'

But she could have swapped it.

If he'd asked.

If he'd wanted her to be there with him.

Her smile was bright but it didn't quite reach her eyes and deep inside he knew she was upset at not being invited. 'Jess,' he murmured. 'It's nothing.'

Jess broadened her smile. 'I know.'

But she knew she had to get up and get out of the bed because she felt absurdly close to tears.

And she did *not* cry.

She was not a crier.

She kicked the sheets aside and slipped out of bed, her body already missing the heat of his. She headed for the bathroom, her heart beat drumming in her chest, needing to get away.

Adam heard the shower turn on and frowned. *Damn it.* He'd upset her. He hadn't meant to but he had absolutely no intention of exposing all her loveliness to the chief.

Not after Caroline.

He'd vowed never to expose another woman to his father ever again.

It was bad enough that he had to go. Adam rolled out of bed and headed for the en suite. He lounged in the doorway for a moment, watching her distorted figure through the frosted glass of the shower screen. The urge to open the door, watch the water course over her curves, to join her, tingled through his feet and he gripped the architrave hard to stop himself.

He doubted his presence in the shower would be appreciated right now.

Although he'd bet his last cent he could persuade her to forget what had just happened in under one minute.

'Aren't you coming down to the beach?' he asked instead.

Jess froze beneath the spray as his voice carried to her. She opened her eyes and saw him lounging against the doorframe, all naked and lethal. She shut her eyes again and pushed her face into the hard spray to arrest the still threatening tears.

'Think I'll give it a miss this morning,' she said. 'I'll have the coffee on when you get back.'

Adam debated about whether to push further but she'd turned her back on him and maybe she just needed a little space. 'See you in a bit, then?'

Jess nodded as a huge lump lodged in her throat. 'Sure,' she choked out.

He turned and left and she finally let the tears flow and mingle with the warm spray.

Jess got home from work at nine-thirty. Her feet throbbed and she had a headache. The shift had dragged and she hadn't been able to concentrate on even the simplest of requests from the eye surgeon working his way through seven intra-ocular lens implants.

The house was quiet and it took less than a minute to establish that Adam and Ruby were still not home. With Tilly on nights and Ellie and James out to dinner she was alone. And the house had never felt so empty.

Jess prowled around, not able to settle to anything. She had a shower. Took a couple of painkillers for her headache. Washed them down with a glass of wine and a huge bowl of ice cream with caramel topping and chocolate sprinkles.

Watched a bit of television.

Watched the clock.

But he'd told her not to wait up.

So, with the time now nudging eleven, she decided to go to bed.

But which bed?

It somehow didn't feel right going to his bed without him being there. Why, she wasn't sure—too presumptuous maybe? But, then, her bedroom felt kind of alien too. She hadn't slept in it for nearly two weeks, just visiting it to grab clothes, and in a crazy way she felt she'd outgrown the floral sheets and embroidered cushions.

And what kind of message would that send to him if she went to her bedroom? That she was in some kind of a snit?

Or worse.

That she was into childish acts of retribution when things didn't go her way? Testing him in some way?

Because she didn't believe in those kind of games.

And she wasn't mad at him. She was mad at herself. For building castles in the sky when he'd expressly told her not to. For hoping, even subconsciously, that he'd have a change of heart. That he'd fall for her too.

For letting awkwardness build between them this morning.

But, still, as she stood in his bedroom doorway she just couldn't bring herself to lie down on the bed without him. It seemed something that a girlfriend would do, a partner, a wife.

And at the moment she didn't know where she stood.

She was pretty damn certain she was neither of the first two and finally absolutely certain she'd never be the third.

Lying down on his bed seemed like she was trying to make a statement about her importance to him. And after not inviting her to his parents' dinner party, it seemed stupid to presume again.

She turned away, shut the door and climbed the stairs to her room where, with the help of the wine, the headache tablets and a good book, she fell into a troubled sleep.

It was nearly one when Adam returned home. Ruby had gone to stay the night at Cort's and all he'd been able to think about on the drive home was sinking into Jess's sweet body.

Getting lost in her eyes and her sighs and her kisses.

It was only thoughts of Jess that had kept his anger at bay. Gregory Carmichael had been his typical self and Adam had had become more and more tense as each minute had passed.

His father's audacity was breathtaking. After years of

ridiculing what Adam did as a low-paying waste of time, he'd greeted Adam like the prodigal son. It seemed if you got yourself on television and in glossy magazines then you could be forgiven for refusing to follow in Daddy's footsteps.

Totally ignoring Ruby and Cort, he'd squired Adam around the room, introducing him to all his plastic-surgeon colleagues as his son, the humanitarian surgeon, who did vital work in Third World countries.

Any of the chief's esteemed guests would be forgiven in thinking that Gregory Carmichael was a man immensely proud of his son but Adam knew different. Adam had felt his disdain and disapproval for many years and wasn't fooled by this sudden father-of-the-year performance.

He felt like one of the many ridiculous trophies on his father's mantelpiece and it was only the silent plea in his mother's eyes and Ruby's murmured 'Think of Mum' that kept him from walking away.

Adam endured his father's sexist jokes about female doctors and the ridiculing of his patients' vanity all through dinner. His father seemed totally oblivious to Ruby's silent outrage and the obvious embarrassment of his wife and some of the other women present.

Gregory had alternated between obsequiously sweet and patronising to his mother, even having the nerve to gossip about a colleague whose wife had just caught him in flagrante delicto with his secretary. Considering his affairs were common and painful knowledge, his lack of insight into his own behaviour and its effects was astonishing.

How his mother stayed, Adam would never know.

And if that was the power of love, he wanted nothing of it.

But none if it was at the forefront of Adam's mind as

he strode through the house, stripping off his tie heading straight for his bedroom.

Jess was all he could think of.

Her sweet smile. Her tinkly laugh. The sparkle in her open, honest gaze.

Her warm, willing body.

His shirt was half-undone when he threw the door open and stopped abruptly at the threshold as his empty bed greeted him.

What the hell?

Where was she?

A primal grunt of pure frustration tore at his throat, begging for release. The tempo of his pulse picked up as it bounded in his chest and washed through his ears. He thumped his fist against the door.

Goddamn it!

There had to be an explanation as to why she wasn't in his bed. Maybe an emergency surgical case had come in before and she was working overtime? Maybe she'd gone out with some friends after work and was still at the Stat Bar.

Maybe she'd joined Ellie and James?

Or.

His heart beat harder as worse possibilities entered his head.

Maybe she'd been knocked down by a car as she was walking home from work.

Or been mugged.

Or abducted.

Damn it, he'd told her to not walk home from the hospital at night!

Panic took hold as fear beat like a jungle drum in his head. He whirled away from the door and headed for the lounge room, looking for evidence she'd come home from work.

No bag on the coffee table. No shoes on the floor. Television off.

Nothing.

He headed for the kitchen. The sink held a wine glass and a bowl with the remnants of what appeared to be ice cream and chocolate sprinkles.

Adam sagged against the sink as a flood of relief swelled through his chest. The bowl hadn't been there when he'd left with Ruby, and Jess did have a penchant for sprinkles on her ice cream.

He felt a wave of nausea sweep through him and for a moment he actually thought he might vomit in the sink. His arms trembled with the effort to keep it at bay.

She was here. She was safe.

It took a minute to pull himself together and start to think analytically again.

So, where was she?

He turned and rested his butt against the sink. His gaze fell on the staircase and he wondered...

Was she in her own room? Sleeping in her own bed?

She'd certainly been upset with him this morning. Maybe she still was? Maybe she was telling him in no un-certain terms that he couldn't have it both ways. That the last thing she wanted to do tonight was sleep with him. Maybe this was her way of saying it was over?

No.

If there was one thing he knew about Jess it was that she was too honest and open to play stupid passive-aggressive games. She didn't have a vengeful bone in her body.

It just wasn't her.

He pushed away from the sink and headed for the stairs, taking them two at a time. Despite her reasons for not being in his bed he wanted to know where she was, assure himself that she was okay.

Damn it, he wanted to talk to her.

He enjoyed talking to her just as much as rolling around with her on his sheets. Although, God knew, he wanted to feel her under him pretty damn fiercely as well.

He could see by the slim crack in her doorway as he approached that it wasn't completely shut and he pushed the door open quietly when he reached it.

And there she lay in soft yellow lamp light. Sound asleep on her side, the floral sheets twisted around her legs, her blonde hair fanned out on the pillow behind her, a romance novel discarded beside her on the bed.

He lounged in the doorway, drinking in the sight of her. She was wearing some kind of nightdress—not naked, like she'd been in his bed every night—and between it and the sheet she was pretty obscured from view. Thankfully one leg was exposed and the nightdress had ridden up high on her thigh and he could see lots of lovely skin.

It reminded him of the first day he'd come back and he'd woken in her bed to find her ogling him.

A surge of desire swamped him.

He wanted her. Wanted to get lost in her. To forget this whole horrible night. The audacity of his father. His king-sized ego. His lack of insight.

The farce of it all.

Adam felt…sullied. And he desperately wanted not to. He wanted to feel fresh and shiny and new. He wanted to affirm life. To know that there were people out there that were good and decent and selfless.

People like Jess.

Without any further thought he took two paces into the room, shutting the door quietly as he passed by. He ditched his half-undone shirt and quickly divested himself of the rest of his clothes.

He was as hard as a rock when he slipped into bed behind her and nuzzled her neck.

'Jess?' he murmured, his hand running up from the flat of her belly to cup her breast. Even though the thin cotton fabric was an annoying barrier, he could still feel the puckering of her nipple.

Jess stirred as the delicious scrape of Adam's whiskers brushed shivers of delight over her skin. Her nipples beaded, her skin goosed. His hand at her breast sent a bolt of pleasure to her core and her eyes fluttered open.

She turned her head to say hi but he claimed her mouth before she could say a thing and the rampant power of his kiss had her turning, wrapping her arms around his neck, mashing her body hard against his.

She could feel his erection pushing against her belly as his mouth left hers to ravage her throat and his hands stroked boldly down her body.

'I missed you,' he muttered against her neck as he pulled up the fabric of her night attire. 'I need you. Now.'

Jess had no intention of denying him, wouldn't even have been capable as he unleashed a maelstrom of lust upon her. His mouth was savaging all the sensitive places of her neck, plundering her mouth. His hands, rough and urgent against her. Kneading her breasts, pushing her pants down, slipping between her legs, his fingers probing, seeking entry, his thumb pressing hard against the spot he knew so well.

And when he moved over her, her thighs spread to accommodate him, her pelvis eagerly cradled his, her legs locked around his waist.

She cried out when he entered her in one swift movement, raking her fingers down his back as she hovered on a knife edge between pleasure and pain. He slammed his mouth against hers and the pain dissolved in a starburst of pleasure as a delicious heat bloomed from her core.

Adam grabbed her leg, bending it at the knee, needing more. He couldn't get close enough, deep enough, as he pounded into her. He didn't want to just be joined to her. He wanted to get inside her skin, dissolve into her, be part of her.

He wanted to consume her. Devour her.

Be cleansed by her.

She moaned into his mouth and grabbed both of his butt cheeks and it stoked his need even higher. Three more thrusts and he could feel the turbulent power of his climax tightening deep inside, twisting through his groin and tearing at the backs of his thighs.

He pounded more. Rode it. Built it higher. Felt it ripple out in excruciating waves like rivulets of hot lava spewing over his abdominals.

And then it broke and he cried out into her neck, clutching at her convulsively as every cell seized and then fibrillated to the motion of his orgasm, rocking, trembling, sighing.

Jess held him tight until the last of his climax subsided and he collapsed against her.

It was several minutes before either of them had sufficient breath to speak.

Jess, shifting under his steadily increasing weight, spoke first. 'Do you want to tell me what that was about?'

Adam, his face buried in her neck, slowly came back to reality at the sound of her voice. His head spun as he eased up and off her, rolling onto his back. He felt drained, sapped of energy, the movement a monumental effort.

He ran a hand through his hair. 'I'm sorry,' he said, turning his head to look at her. Her nightdress was ruched up around her neck, there were whisker burns on her throat and her mouth was swollen.

'I don't know what came over me... I was...an animal... Did I hurt you?'

Jess pulled her nightie down and rolled up onto her side. 'Of course not.' She smiled at him, lifting her hand to his face, running her thumb over his mouth. 'There's something enormously sexy about a man who's that desperate to make love to you.'

Adam shied from her choice of words. That hadn't been love. It had been lust—pure and terrifying.

It certainly wasn't something she'd find in one of her romance novels.

'I take it the dinner party wasn't a barrel of laughs.'

Adam rolled his head back to face the ceiling. His sigh was loud in the stillness of the night. 'My father is an utter bastard.'

Jess's heart went out to him as he stared gloomily at the ceiling. She had no idea what had transpired but Adam had been really keyed up when he'd climbed into her bed. Tense. Angry even.

'He's had several affairs, you know,' Adam murmured, looking back at her. 'They've devastated my mother.'

Jess wasn't sure if this was leading anywhere or why he'd brought it up but it was obviously one of the many things that weighed on his conscience where his father was concerned.

And part of her couldn't help but think the longer they were together, the more he was opening up. Surely that meant something?

'Why doesn't she leave him?'

'Because all she ever wanted to be was the great Gregory Carmichael's wife. She gave up everything she wanted, including a nursing career she absolutely loved, to be just that. To dedicate her time to doting on him. Her whole world revolves around him.' Adam's lips twisted. 'She won't hear a bad word about him.'

Jess frowned. 'You sound angry with her.'

Adam felt the cut as Jess zeroed in on the gaping wound. 'I guess I am…in a way.' He hated to admit it. Felt disloyal. He loved his mother.

But…

'She's the nicest, sweetest, gentlest person you could ever hope to meet. She's too good for him. She's certainly the only reason why we tolerate him. But she won't say no to him. She's let him dominate her until she's this…sad kind of…non-entity.'

Jess could hear the anguish in his voice. It must hurt him to see someone he obviously loved not getting the respect she deserved. But maybe she had what she wanted in life. Maybe being a wife was all she wanted? 'Is she happy, do you think?'

Adam shook his head slowly and searched her face. 'Honestly? Apart from the humiliation of the affairs, I think she is…'

Jess could understand the confusion in his voice. It didn't sound like any relationship she wanted to be in. She lifted her hand and traced his lips with her finger. 'Well, then, maybe that's all that counts?' she suggested softly.

The thought had crossed Adam's mind constantly. His mother *was* happy. So maybe it was none of his damn business. Maybe he should just grit his teeth and be happy for her too. Adam grabbed her hand and pulled it down to his chest, tucking it securely into his. 'You know I would never do that,' he said capturing her gaze. 'Right?'

Jess didn't dare breathe at the intensity of his gaze. Something had really affected him tonight. This conver-

sation was a far cry from the light and flirty Adam she'd
known these last weeks.

Sincerity blazed from the gold flecks in his eyes. 'I
know.' And she did know.

Adam held her gaze. 'I know I have a reputation for
playing the field but I'm not like that. I'm *not* like him.'

Jess didn't blink. 'I know.'

He waited a beat. Shifted his gaze to their joined hands.
'Caroline thought I was.'

Jess felt her heart leap in her chest. Adam's voice was
ominously quiet and his heart thundered beneath her palm.
'Caroline thought you were like your father?'

Adam shifted restlessly against the mattress. 'Her father
was very similar to mine. Except, of course, *her* mother
had the good sense to divorce him when Caroline was fourteen. She was scared that nature and nurture would win in
the end. She didn't want to risk it.'

Jess didn't know what to say.

Stupid cow didn't seem appropriate right at the moment.

She took a breath, trying to see it from Caroline's point
of view. Not everybody was blessed with two parents who
loved and respected each other, like she was. So maybe
through the lens of an angst-ridden childhood Caroline's
logic made sense.

But.

Her ingrained fears had obviously hurt him.

And it was clear to Jess that his ex-fiancée just hadn't
known him at all.

'She was a fool.' If she had his love, his ring, his declaration of intent, she would never squander it.

Adam gave a half-smile. 'You've never met him.'

Jess felt the jab right in the softest part of her heart. She
knew he hadn't meant it to mean anything but she felt his
lack of the dinner invitation all over again.

She took a breath and pushed it aside. He needed her tonight. This wasn't about her. 'I know,' she said, freeing her hand and tapping her chest. 'I know in here.'

He smiled at her gorgeous, earnest, open face. Why? Why did she, who'd been with him for a matter of weeks, know and Caroline, who had been with him for nearly two years, hadn't?

'He didn't like her…Caroline. He always felt I could do better than a teacher. He was…polite but distant with her.' His lips twisted. 'Not so reserved with me.'

Adam felt like he'd spent the entire eighteen months they had been together being a buffer between his fiancée and his father. Defending her. Championing their love. Caroline had liked his mother so they'd persevered for her sake but it hadn't been easy.

Jess couldn't imagine Adam being with someone who wasn't gorgeous and witty and wise, no matter what she did, and as jealous as she was of the only woman who had ever claimed his heart, she also felt strangely protective. Reading between the lines, it sounded as if Adam's father hadn't exactly kept his dislike of his future daughter-in-law to himself.

'Well, I guess that was his loss, wasn't it?'

Her hair had fallen forward over her shoulder and he pushed it back. How had she known the perfect thing to say?

'Sorry,' he murmured, his palm gliding over the rounded ball of her shoulder. 'I don't know what's got into me tonight.'

Jess shivered at his touch. 'It's fine.'

'This is why I didn't want you to come. He makes me crazy. I always leave so wound up. I'm sorry for…' he waved his hand in the air '…everything. Particularly for pouncing on you like some horny teenager.'

Jess smiled at him, forcing a light, flirty note into her voice. No matter what had happened before he'd entered her bedroom she had the man she loved back by her side and another intriguing layer had been peeled away. 'You *were* a little wound up,' she said, running an index finger along his lower lip. 'Maybe if I'd been there I could have helped you with that a lot sooner,' she said, dropping a kiss on his nose and his cheek and his chin. 'Like in the car...' Her finger trailed down his belly. 'On the way home.'

Adam chuckled as the tension from his shoulders started to ease. 'Well, I didn't think of that.'

'Obviously,' she murmured against his mouth.

Adam claimed it in a soft kiss as he dragged her on top of him and tunnelled his fingers into her hair, which had formed a wispy curtain around his head.

His chest filled with an emotion he didn't want to analyse as she opened her mouth to him.

But this time, when he rolled her over and pressed her into the mattress, he loved her with the tenderness that was her due.

CHAPTER TEN

A WEEK later Adam was standing in the shallows as the sun poked golden fingers over the horizon, watching Jess leap to her feet on the board and ride a baby wave. Her tongue poked between her teeth in concentration. She was becoming quite competent at standing and had even extended the amount of time she managed to stay on the board.

She looked up at him, smiled and waved then shrieked as she lost her balance and plunged into the ocean. Adam laughed.

He loved these early mornings with Jess. Most of the women he'd seen in the past didn't tend to be early risers and he'd lost count of the number of times he'd left a sleeping naked woman in his bed while he'd hit the waves.

Of course this had also given him a great opportunity to not be in the bed when they had woken, sending a potent message about the fleeting nature of their liaison to the few who'd thought they were different.

But with Jess it was almost as if he'd found a kindred spirit.

She paddled towards him and rose out of the ocean. Water streamed from her hair and sluiced down the very sensible one-piece that somehow seemed sexier than a micro, string bikini.

'Okay, that's it,' Jess said, handing the board to him as

she collapsed in the shallows next to his feet and flopped backwards. The water gently lapping at the beach cradled her weight. 'I'm exhausted.'

Adam turned and pushed the board high on to the sand well away from the tide mark and sat in the shallows beside her. 'You're getting better,' he murmured.

Jess snorted. 'Liar.'

Adam chuckled. 'You are. You've got a good technique going.'

Jess shut her eyes, tuning into the smell of salt and sand and the feel of the water washing in and out of her ears as it ebbed and flowed around her. It wasn't the vast dryness of the outback but sitting next to the man she loved, it was pretty blissful.

'I've got a good teacher,' she murmured.

God knew, she was only doing this because of him. No way would she ever have got on a board if it hadn't been at his urging. If it hadn't seemed so important to him.

Adam looked down at her. Her blonde hair floated around her head in the current. Moisture beaded on her face, on her pink mouth. The water lapped at her sides, making an island out of her torso. The wet one-piece outlined the contours of her breasts and the hard points of her nipples to perfection.

Her legs, in slightly deeper water, were submerged and it wasn't such a stretch to imagine that beneath the surface a tail swished lazily in the current.

She sure as hell looked like a mermaid.

His mermaid.

A feeling so foreign he didn't even know what to call it filled him. Swept like the tide from his toes to his head. Its intensity was confusing and for a moment he didn't even dare breathe.

Then it came to him.

Contentment.

It was a very odd revelation. He doubted he'd ever felt it with a woman, not even Caroline. He'd been too busy trying to make it all perfect, to constantly shore up the foundations so he could prove something to his father, to feel content.

The only thing in his life that roused similar sentiments was his job. And now that seemed kind of insignificant compared to this amazing surge of rightness.

Looking down at her, he knew he wanted to come back to this after his next mission overseas.

To her.

To her laughter and her smile.

To their conversations—on the beach and in bed.

To this feeling that all was right with the world. That she understood him. Accepted him for who he was. Didn't want him to be someone else.

Like his old man.

Didn't want anything from him.

He wanted to be able to look forward to coming back for a change. Coming back to something other than a crumbling house and the surf. To spend every day of the two months he was away anticipating his return.

Anticipating their reunion.

To know that while he was away, somebody, other than Ruby and his mother, was looking forward to him coming home.

Jess opened her eyes to find him looking down at her intently. She smiled at him. 'What?'

Adam smiled back, his gaze drifting lower to her breasts.

Jess felt his gaze as potently as if he'd yanked her one-piece down and flicked his hot tongue over her nipples.

They pebbled even tighter as the wet fabric abraded them painfully.

'I'm cold,' she said defensively.

Adam chuckled. 'I can see that.'

Jess shut her eyes again. 'If you're going to look at me like that, you'd better be prepared to follow through,' she murmured.

Adam's breath hitched in his chest. He loved how she'd grown sexually confident. How she looked at him with sex in her eyes. How he caught her watching him sometimes and would know, without a doubt, she was mentally undressing him.

Jess shivered as she felt the soft weight of his hand on her belly. She smiled as it inched slowly north. His warm lips pressed a kiss on her shoulder and she sighed.

'Jess.'

She opened her eyes to find him lying on his stomach beside her, the water lapping his elbows as he supported himself and looked down into her face. His shaggy hair blew lightly in the early morning breeze and his lapis lazuli eyes stared at her with breathtaking intensity.

He looked very, very serious.

Her smile faltered. 'What?'

Adam's heart was beating so hard against the sand he was afraid the tremors might set off an underwater earthquake far out to sea. 'What would you say if I asked you to be waiting for me when I get back from my next mission?'

Jess saw the words come out of his mouth, she even heard each one with a startling clarity despite the noise of the ocean in her ears.

It did, however, take a long moment to compute their meaning.

An eerie silence descended around them as everything seemed to stop. Time and motion. Even the gentle rocking of the ocean. Her silly heart bounced around in her chest like an out-of-control firecracker but her ever-present practical side urged caution.

After all, it wasn't a declaration of love. It wasn't a marriage proposal. And he had been most specific when setting up the boundaries of their affair that he could only give her a few weeks.

She bent her knees and lifted herself up on her elbows, displacing his hand. The sand washed away beneath her soles and her elbows sank her down deeper. It brought their heads closer and she looked him square in the eye. 'I'd ask why.'

'Because I really like you and I'm going to miss you. And that's not something I've said to any woman other than Caroline. Because I think we've got something good going on and it feels…right. To me. It feels easy. Because I want to know that while I'm slaving away in the developing world somewhere, you're here thinking of me, waiting for me.'

Jess was stunned by his admission. By what he was offering. She smiled to hide the maelstrom of thoughts and feelings all competing for equal billing in her brain. 'You think I'm easy?'

Adam gave a half-smile at her attempt at a joke. 'I'm serious, Jess.'

She could see that. 'I'm…confused,' she said slowly. 'I thought there was a clock ticking on this?'

He shrugged. 'So did I. But…I don't want this to end yet. I don't think you do either.'

Well, that was the understatement of the year. She loved him.

But.

'So…you want me to wait for you while you're off overseas, sleeping with any nurse or pretty little intern who bats her eyelashes at you for two months, and then just pick up where we left off?'

Adam frowned. 'No. Absolutely not. Even if there was time, even if I didn't collapse into bed every night utterly exhausted from twelve- and fourteen-hour days, as I told you the other night, I'm not like that. That's my father's speciality.'

Jess bit down on her bottom lip. The possibilities glimmered like stars, twinkling tantalisingly close.

Maybe she *could* wait?

She wasn't going anywhere just yet. She had a year in Emergency and a year in ICU before she planned on returning home.

She did have time.

Maybe this was the next step? These last weeks had been the first. Maybe this was the next?

Adam was a man who'd spent a lot of time avoiding commitments such as the one he was proposing now. Running from his father and therefore everything else that staying put offered. It made sense that he wasn't going to rush headlong into something that smacked of permanency.

Maybe this was one step closer to him falling in love with her?

Maybe she could bend her perfect fairy-tale to suit a skittish prince? And if this was all he could offer her, maybe she could rewrite the fairy-tale altogether?

Maybe this princess couldn't have it all?

Maybe that's what happened after the happily-ever-after. *Compromise*. Maybe she was all right with that.

She looked into his earnest face, making her decision without hesitation. 'Good,' she said. 'Because I'm only interested if this is an exclusive arrangement.'

Adam nodded. 'I give you my word.'

Jess sat up, suddenly overwhelmed by the situation. By

her decision. She hugged her knees as she looked out to sea. The ocean stretched before her, rising and falling to an invisible rhythm. Her heart beat in unison with it.

Daring to hope.

She felt Adam turn and vault forward to join her in her inspection of the horizon.

After a minute she said, 'Okay, then.'

Adam only just heard it. He turned his head and grinned at her, nudging his shoulder into hers. 'Okay, then.'

Then he made a grab for her, wrestling her back as she shrieked and laughed. But when he kissed her there was relief and gratitude and a promise of all the good times to come.

A fortnight later Jess sat in her scrubs in the middle of a press conference where Lai Ling was the undisputed star. The media had gone crazy when they'd seen the spectacular results of her surgery.

She was grinning madly, her new face a testament to Adam's skills and the commitment of Operation New Faces, Eastern Beaches and several charities. Her facial sutures had been removed for a while now and her slight scars glistened with a special ointment to keep them supple and reduce their pinkness.

Eventually they'd turn white and be barely noticeable.

The whole team was there, sitting in the same positions as last time. Jess sat next to a beaming Lai Ling, holding her hand again under the table. The interpreter sat on the other side.

Adam sat opposite her, looking every inch the debonair surgeon in his scrubs and cap, and winked when the non-stop flashing of cameras caused her to squint. Her heart filled with the joy of them despite the blight of his imminent departure the next day.

But she was trying not to think about that. They had this press conference to get through and then tonight he was taking her to his parents' house. His mother wanted to see him before he went and had invited him to tea.

Jess had just about melted into a puddle when he had asked her to accompany him. She knew it was a big step for Adam—huge—and it had come with dire warnings about his father's insufferable arrogance but she had leapt at the chance.

Gregory Carmichael did not scare her.

And then after dinner they had a whole night in each other's arms. Jess smiled to herself—she doubted either of them would be getting much sleep.

'Dr Carmichael?' A journalist at the back made himself heard above the din. 'I understand you've been with Operation New Faces for about six years now. It strikes me as a rather high-stress job and one that takes you away from loved ones for long stretches of time. How much longer do you think you can keep that up for?'

Adam grinned at the camera. 'As long as there are people who need me, as long as Operation New Faces is around, I'll be doing it,' he confirmed with a broad grin at the camera.

Jess felt her smile fade a little as her heart slowed right down in her chest.

As long as there are people who need me? That seemed like a very long time.

'You must have a very understanding girlfriend,' the journalist joked.

Adam slid a glance towards Jess. 'I do.'

Jess rekindled the smile as the cameras clicked away. But her future suddenly lost a bit of its glow.

Was she willing to wait for him *for ever*?

Put her life on hold *for ever*?

* * *

The sky was a brilliant shade of crimson as Adam drove along the clifftop road to Whale Beach. They'd put the top down on the retro sports car he'd owned since he'd been an intern and the wind ruffled his hair as an amazing slice of coastal scenery whizzed by.

He was too keyed up to enjoy it, however.

The fingers of one hand were wound tightly around the steering-wheel as his tension grew, dreading the enforced company of his father. Worrying about how the chief would be with Jess. And hoping he could keep his temper in check for the sake of Jess and his mother, who couldn't bear any confrontation between father and son.

He glanced briefly at Jess. Why had he invited her?

Had he learnt nothing from his experience with Caroline? Did he truly want to expose her to his father's arrogance?

But a part of him couldn't bear to tackle tonight without her. He'd been surprised to realise he wanted her by his side.

Because this was their last night together.

And. She was important.

She was looking out her side of the car, her hand loosely tucked into his. Strands of blonde hair had worked free of her ponytail and whipped across her face and she seemed lost in thought as her teeth worried her bottom lip. She'd been a little quiet since the press conference and she seemed tense now too. He gave her hand a squeeze as much for his own assurance as hers.

'I'll be with you the whole time,' he said. 'You have my permission to tell him to push off if he gets too overbearing. In fact, it might be fun if you did.'

She gave him a small smile. 'I'll be fine.' And she returned to the view out her side of the car.

He felt his unease ratchet up another notch. He hoped it

was just the spectre of him leaving tomorrow. It had hung over both their heads, casting a further pall on an evening that was already fraught enough.

Unfortunately it was a looming reality. The elephant in the room that they'd avoided the last few days.

But this was his life.

His reality.

And despite two months stretching ahead without her, Adam was looking forward to getting amongst it again. These last weeks had been a nice break from his hectic schedule but he could feel the little thrill in his chest at the thought of getting back to work.

Sure, he was going to miss her but he also knew that missions were intense and exceedingly demanding of his time and focus. There wouldn't be a whole lot of time to dwell on what he was missing.

And then two months would be up before he knew it and he'd be back and she'd be waiting for him.

The best of both worlds.

And as tense as they may both be at this moment, he knew in a couple of hours, when they were alone, he'd give her a night together that would get them both through the ensuing months.

'Darling, come in.' Sylvia Carmichael greeted her son, kissing him on the cheek. 'I was glued to the TV this morning during your press conference. You did a marvellous job and that young woman…oh, my, she just looks amazing, doesn't she?'

Adam smiled. 'Thanks, Mum.'

'And this must be Jess.' She smiled at Jess. 'I've heard so much about you from Ruby.'

Jess shook her hand, trying not to let the innocent comment hurt. Of course Ruby would have spoken about her.

Why on earth would Adam talk about her? Until last week they had just been an extended fling.

She concentrated instead on the pride in Sylvia's voice.

Adam shut the ornately carved front door behind them and his mother winced as the wind caught it and slammed it harder than he'd intended.

'Mum? Have you got a migraine?'

Sylvia smiled. 'Just a little one. I'm sure it'll be gone in a jiffy.'

His mother had been plagued with migraines since as far back as Adam could remember. Often quite severe. He noticed the strained look around her eyes. 'You should have cancelled, Mum.'

'Nonsense.'

'Have you taken something for it?' he asked.

Sylvia waved her hand. 'Your father says they make me muzzy-headed.'

Adam's mouth flattened into a thin line. 'Go and sit down,' he ordered. 'I'll get you your medication.'

'Don't be silly, darling, I'm fine.'

Jess could feel the rage vibrating from Adam in waves and noticed his mother's marked pallor. 'Mrs Carmichael, why don't you show me the way to the lounge room?' Jess suggested.

'Of course, my dear,' she said. 'Where are my manners? And please call me Sylvia.'

Adam stalked into the lounge room a minute later with a glass of water and two tablets. 'Here,' he said, kneeling beside his mother.

The great Gregory entered as his wife popped the pills into her mouth. 'You still got one of those damn nuisance headaches?' he said gruffly.

Adam stood. 'Yes, how inconvenient for you.'

'Adam.' His mother's hand slipped into his and the strain in her voice was unbearable.

'Saw the press conference,' Gregory said. 'The girl looks amazing. Good repair job.'

Adam was stunned for a moment to hear such praise come from the big chief's mouth.

Unfortunately he was about thirty years too late.

'Darling, this is Jess Donaldson,' Sylvia said rising to her feet.

Jess shook Gregory's hand, shocked at how much he looked like Adam. It was positively eerie. Like looking into the future and seeing Adam as a sixty-year-old. A very handsome, very distinguished sixty-year-old.

No wonder Caroline had been a little freaked out!

But there was a haughtiness about Adam's father that hadn't been replicated in his down-to-earth son. A way of looking down his nose that was disconcerting. She felt as if she was being judged and with a quick purse of the lips found wanting.

'Pleased to meet you,' she murmured politely.

Gregory nodded as if it was perfectly obvious she should be pleased. 'Drinks, Sylvia,' he said, turning to his wife as he sat in a large white leather lounge chair that faced a wall of glass overlooking the darkening ocean. 'I'll have my usual.'

Adam noticed Jess's surprise and he glared at his father. 'I'll get them,' he said, turning to his mother. 'You should go and lie down for a while.'

Even though the prospect of being left alone with his father was grim indeed.

His mother patted his hand. 'And miss the fun?' She crossed to her husband and kissed him on the cheek. 'How was work, darling?'

Jess listened to an angry diatribe about incompetent

theatre nurses that lasted ten minutes while Adam fixed the drinks. She was pretty damn steamed herself by the time Adam passed her a glass of white wine.

Didn't he know what she did?

Adam slipped his arm around her waist and pulled her snugly into his side. 'I told you he was a bastard,' he murmured in her ear.

Jess couldn't help herself, she smiled. In fact, she had to bite her lip to stop herself from laughing.

'Think about later. About when we get home. That's what I'm doing.'

Jess felt heat bloom not only in her face but in other parts of her body.

One last night with Adam for two whole months.

The chief addressed Jess. 'Tess, is it?'

Adam's jaw clenched. 'Jess,' he corrected, his voice clipped.

'Jess. You're family are farmers, yes?'

Jess couldn't believe anyone could put emphasis on a word that denigrated it so completely. She suddenly felt like a country bumpkin.

She straightened a little. 'We have a hundred thousand acres about seven hours directly west of Sydney.'

Gregory whistled. 'What do you grow?'

'Cattle. Mainly.'

There followed a *conversation* involving the scandalous price of beef, poor farming management practices and a very ill-informed monologue on the drought.

Jess, aware of Adam growing tenser by the moment as he politely argued each point with his father, was grateful when Sylvia announced dinner was ready.

She hoped it wasn't beef.

The meal, a melt-in-your-mouth, savoury soufflé, was

divine and almost made up for Adam's father's continuing prattle.

When they were all done Sylvia stood and started to clear the dishes. 'Off you all go through to the formal lounge and I'll bring in the coffee.'

Jess stood too, picking up her plate and Adam's.

'Don't be silly, Jess. I'll do this. Off you go.'

Jess smiled at her. 'My gran would tan my hide if I didn't help after you've gone to all the trouble to cook such a beautiful meal' she said, gathering dishes. 'And with a migraine too.'

Adam heard the note of reproval aimed at his father and smiled.

'You're close to your grandmother?' Sylvia asked.

'Oh, yes,' Jess confirmed. 'I grew up in my grandparents' house. We all lived together.'

'How charming,' Gregory murmured.

The inflection on charming was slight but there nonetheless. Enough so Jess wasn't left in any doubt Adam's father thought she and her family were yokel hayseeds.

'Hey!' Adam growled. 'Back off.'

Her mother gasped. 'Adam!'

'It's okay.' Jess turned to assure him, placing a hand on his wrist, biting back the retort that had come instantly to her tongue. Instead she smiled at his father. 'Yes. We have a very charmed life.'

And they did. Jess considered herself blessed to have had the experience of growing up in an extended family like people used to do. She felt it gave her an unusual perspective.

And no one was going to make her feel ashamed of it.

'This way, dear,' Sylvia said.

Adam started to follow them but his mother shooed him away. 'Stay and talk to your father,' she said.

Adam wanted to do that about as much as he wanted to jump off the cliff the house was perched on. But her eyes implored him and he could hear the plea in his mother's voice. She hated confrontation and so wanted Adam and his father to get along.

A little late for that.

Jess followed Sylvia into the kitchen and set the dishes in the sink.

'You mustn't mind him, dear. He's does tend to speak without thinking. It's the curse of a brilliant mind.'

Jess gave a forced smiled. Adam was right. His mother was clearly besotted with his father. Totally blind to his faults—his arrogance, his condescension, his ego.

So love truly *was* blind.

They made small talk as they prepared the coffees, Sylvia talking mostly about her husband's accomplishments and Jess answering questions about the press conference.

Sylvia loaded the coffee mugs and after-dinner mints onto a tray and Jess carried it back to the lounge room.

'There you are, darling,' Sylvia said, passing Gregory his cup. 'Are you comfy? Would you like your footstool?'

Jess watched her fuss, risking a glance at Adam. His gaze met hers and she could see the frustration stirring the golden flecks in his eyes.

Jess turned away to inspect the wall of framed photos nearby. No surprises that they were all of the great Gregory. Not one of Adam or Ruby, or even husband and wife. She raised an eyebrow at some of the famous faces on display.

'Aren't they fantastic?' Sylvia said, sidling up to Jess. 'Gregory's celebrity clients just adore him. They're always so pleased with their results.'

Jess nodded, offering no comment. She came to stand

in front of a black and white print of Adam's father standing in front of the Sphinx.

'Oh, this is my favourite,' Sylvia murmured. 'It's been a lifelong ambition of mine to go to Egypt. Gregory's been several times for work things. When he retires he's going to take me. He's going to take me to all these places he's been,' she said, indicating the wall.

Jess noticed pictures from London and Italy and America.

'Adam's offered to go with me, of course, but I couldn't be away from Gregory for so long, he depends on me to be there for him. I'm happy to wait.'

Jess felt a heavy sick feeling start in the pit of her stomach. Sylvia sacrificing what she wanted to please her man.

It was eerily familiar.

She walked on to the nearby sideboard where there was one framed picture of Ruby and Adam together with their mother. Jess was struck by the similarities between Ruby and Sylvia—there was no mistaking they were mother and daughter—and she smiled at how happy they all looked.

A smaller frame, out of the way, hidden almost behind some ugly modern art sculpture, caught her eye. She picked it up.

'Oh, that one.' Sylvia laughed dismissively. 'It's just an old one of me.'

Jess stared at it. A young Sylvia in her nurse's uniform, complete with starched white veil, looked back at her. Her cheeks glowed and her eyes, so like Ruby's, sparkled with promise. 'Did you like being a nurse?' Jess asked.

Adam's mother took the frame and looked down at it. 'Oh, yes.' She smiled. 'I loved it. I was going to specialise in renal. Dialysis was in its infancy here in Australia and it was so fascinating.'

Jess watched as Sylvia absently ran a thumb over the

glass. Her face looked wistful. 'My older brother died from kidney disease in his teens.' She shrugged. 'I wanted to make a difference.'

Jess couldn't take her eyes off the image. Adam's mother holding her past in her hands. Did she regret it?

'Do you regret it?' she asked tentatively.

Sylvia held onto the frame for a few more seconds and then placed it gently back on the sideboard, pushing it back behind the sculpture.

'Of course not,' she said with a bright smile. 'Sure, I loved it but I'd fallen head over heels for Gregory and I couldn't believe he wanted me too. There were so many girls who were after him.'

She glanced over at the object of her affections and sighed. 'He didn't want his wife to work. He needed me to keep everything running and on an even keel so he could build his career. And then Adam came along.'

Jess nodded even as her head spun and she leaned against the sideboard for support.

Sylvia had spent her whole life waiting for Gregory.

Because he'd wanted her over all the others.

And when he retired, her life, what she wanted, was going to begin.

Wasn't that exactly what she'd agreed to do for Adam? *Wait.*

The chief was talking and Adam was sitting opposite him when the women rejoined them. He wondered when it would be polite to leave. Jess was quiet as she sipped her coffee and he placed his hand over hers. 'Are you okay?'

Jess was decidedly not okay. She felt like she was going to throw up any moment. But she forced a small smile to her lips.

'Just a bit tired,' she murmured.

It was all the excuse he needed. Adam put down his mug. 'It's time to go.'

Five minutes later, after a teary goodbye from his mother and a stiff *if you change your mind about private practice* from the chief, he'd popped the top up on his car and they were backing out of the driveway.

They drove in silence for five minutes before he said, 'I'm sorry. I told you it would be awful.'

Jess nodded. It had been nowhere near as awful as the slow dawning she'd experienced talking to Sylvia.

The realisation that she was on the precipice of becoming Adam's mother.

That she too, would give up everything—bend her fairy-tale—because he'd chosen her.

Over all the others.

A pain built in her chest. It pressed against her rib cage with terrifying intensity. Her heart pounded, her ears filling with the deafening thud. She sucked in a breath as she rubbed at the spot where the pain seemed to deepen with each second.

She felt as if she was suffocating in the enclosed confines of the car.

Was she having a heart attack?

Adam glanced at her as he drove. She was sitting rigidly in her seat, staring at the windscreen as if she was seeing a ghost, while she rubbed her chest. 'Are you okay?'

Jess dragged her eyes away from the road ahead and looked at him. He was so beautiful. And she loved him. So deeply it was frightening.

She shook her head. 'Stop the car.'

Adam frowned. 'What?'

'I have to…I need to get out. I can't…' She rubbed at her chest harder. 'I can't breathe.'

CHAPTER ELEVEN

A LOOKOUT loomed on the right and Adam pulled the car over into the small, deserted parking lot. The note of panic in Jess's voice and the agitated rhythm of her hands was scaring the daylights out of him.

He shut the engine off and turned in his seat to ask her to explain but she was tearing off her seat belt, clutching wildly at the door, pushing it open, leaping out.

He winced as the door slammed after her.

Damn it.

He should never have taken her to meet his father! He'd been his usual insufferably rude, condescending self and now she was understandably upset.

First Caroline and now Jess.

He watched her go, quashing the urge to go straight after her. She looked like she needed space.

He'd give her a minute or two.

Jess sucked in large gulps of the cooler night air as she walked blindly towards the rotunda perched on the cliff. The brisk sea breeze whipped her hair around and she didn't notice the full moon or the breathtaking way it illuminated the ocean and the broad sweep of the bay below.

She was blind to it all as her turbulent thoughts crashed around her head as loudly as the surf on the rocks far below. *What was she going to do?*

He was going off tomorrow on yet another jaunt overseas. One of many.

This is my life.

That's what he'd said not long ago.

And then he'd asked her to be here for him.

But how many years would he keep asking her to do that? How many years would she do it? Each time hoping this one would be his last?

Waiting to do what she wanted. Go home. Live and work in the outback with the people who needed her there.

People like her grandfather.

Get married. Have children.

Live the fairy-tale.

What had he told that reporter today? *As long as there are people who need me.*

Jess reached one of the picnic tables sheltered beneath the rotunda and hoisted herself up onto the table, placing her feet on the seat. She stared out at the horizon, at the light of a boat winking in the distance.

People were always going to need him.

How could she hope to compete with that?

By the time Adam joined her a minute later her heart rate had settled and the dreadful sick feeling had lessened as a sensation of inevitability had taken hold.

She knew what she had to do.

No point beating about the bush. That's what her grandmother had always said. And if nothing else Jess had inherited a healthy does of pragmatism from old mother Donaldson. Adam stood in front of her, his hands buried in his pockets. The wind ruffled his hair from behind and she felt a rush of love that seared her to the core. She wanted nothing more than to throw herself at him. Bring him down with her on this table and love him and never let him go.

Instead she said, 'I can't do this.'

Adam cocked an eyebrow. 'Have dinner with my father again?'

Jess gave a weak smile. 'You asked me to wait for you. To be here when you got back, and I told you I would but…I can't. Not any more.'

Adam frowned. This was *not* good news. He'd been happier these last weeks then he'd been in a long time. And when Jess had said yes to entering into a long-distance relationship with him, he'd been ecstatic.

He had the best of both worlds.

And he wasn't going to give that up without a fight.

Damn his father to hell.

'Look, I don't ever actually see my father very much, you know.'

'Oh, Adam.' Jess shook her head. 'This isn't about your father. It's about your mother.'

'My…mother?' Adam blinked. 'You don't like my mother?' *Everyone liked his mother.*

Jess sighed. 'Of course I liked your mother. It's just…' She climbed off the table and pushed past him, walking to the fenced-off edge and leaning on the railing. Adam sidled up beside her, placing his elbow next to hers. 'I'm afraid I'll turn into her.'

Adam frowned. 'Jess…you're nothing like her. You're strong and independent and you know what you want out of life and how to go about doing it. You have a career plan and I've got to tell you, the way you tried to guilt the chief tonight over my mother's headache was great. You're not going to let anyone walk over you.'

Jess wanted to bellow. Couldn't he see that *he* was walking all over her?

And she was letting him.

'But you already are, Adam.'

Adam stilled at her words. He straightened. 'I beg your pardon?'

Jess didn't want to hurt him but she needed him to see what he was doing.

'Don't you see?' she implored, turning her head to face him. 'You're doing exactly what you want and ignoring what I want, what I need deep in my heart. You want me to wait for you while you gallivant around the world. For how long? For ever? You told that reporter today that you were going to do it for as long as you were needed. Well, what about me, Adam? I have plans too and if I agree to this, if you keep asking me to wait, and I will wait, Adam, then I'll end up sacrificing everything, just like your mother waiting for your father to retire so he'll take her to bloody Egypt.'

Adam heard the contempt in her voice at the end. 'Are you saying I'm like my father?'

Jess looked back out to sea. She couldn't bear to see her home truths find their mark. 'I'm saying that I think this relationship suits you very well indeed. Just as the relationship your father has with your mother suits him very well.'

'I am *not* my father.'

Jess shook her head at Adam's stony insistence.

'No. In a lot of ways you're not. You're not a boorish pig who's insufferably arrogant with an ego the size of Sydney. And you're doing your damnedest to be the opposite, Adam, I can see that. Hell, you've spent most of your life running away from him. But you don't realise that you're making the same relationship errors. Asking me to do things that I don't want to do. Treating me like he treats your mother.'

'I'm not,' he denied.

Jess snorted. 'I'm learning to surf for you.'

Adam frowned. 'You don't like surfing?'

'Not particularly.'

He gave her an exasperated look. 'Why didn't you say so?'

Jess wanted to cry. He just didn't get it. 'Because I'll do anything for you, Adam. Just like your mum does for your dad.'

Adam looked out over the milky ocean. 'It's a good skill to have,' he said defensively. 'Great for your balance.'

Jess shook her head. 'Where the hell am I going to surf at Edwinburra?'

They were silent for a moment or two. 'The point is,' Jess sighed, 'you're asking me to put aside my needs so I can be there for you. Using my feelings for you to get what you want.'

Adam felt a wave of denial rise in him. She was wrong—it wasn't like that at all. He'd always hated the way his mother let his father walk all over her. He would never want that in his own partner.

'Well, what do you want that I'm so callously asking you to put aside?' he demanded.

'I want the fairy-tale, Adam. I hadn't realised I was giving it up until tonight. I'd been kidding myself that I was just postponing it. But my grandmother taught me to be true to myself and I'm not at the moment, Adam.'

Jess looked at the ground and absently kicked at the path for a moment before looking back at him.

'I want the fairy-tale. And that doesn't involve the prince being away for ten months of the year. I want some commitment that this is going to end at some stage. That at some point you're going to want to stop moving around and settle down. Have a family.'

Adam blanched. 'A family?'

'Yes, Adam, I want kids and a home and the father of those children around to love us.'

Adam ran his hand through his hair. He couldn't keep up with the speed of the conversation. 'I think we're getting a little ahead of ourselves. It's only been a handful of weeks.'

Jess nodded. 'For you, yes. But not for me. This is what I want. It's what I've wanted with you since the day I met you.'

Adam reeled. 'But…I…I never asked for this. For you to feel like this,' Adam said. In fact, he'd warned her not to. 'I never promised this.'

Jess turned facing the rotunda. 'I know. I'm not blaming you. Just telling you that I'm not going to settle for less any more. For some less glittery version of the fairy-tale.'

Adam turned his head. They were close and his mouth was almost at her ear. 'They need me,' he murmured.

And that was the crux of it.

She needed him too but she obviously wasn't his priority. Just like his father not making his mother a priority. That didn't make him the bad guy. If anything, his reluctance to pull away from his beloved patients made him even more noble.

She just couldn't be the one hanging around waiting for him to realise she needed him more.

That he needed her more.

Her heart shattered in a million pieces.She cleared her throat from the lump of threatening emotion. 'Of course. And they are lucky to have you. Come on,' she said, pulling away from the rail. 'Let's go. You have an early flight.'

Adam watched her walk towards the car. 'Jess,' he called after her.

'It's okay,' she threw over her shoulder. 'It's fine.'

Adam followed. It felt far from fine. It felt…empty.

He climbed into the car beside her a minute later. She was staring out her window, her face turned away from him. He wanted to touch her, to turn her face and tell her the words she wanted to hear, but, damn it, he'd never promised her those things.

This was why he only did one-night stands.

Until Jess.

He started the car and drove off and they completed the trip in silence. He switched the engine off in the garage forty-five minutes later. Jess reached for the doorhandle and he put a hand on her shoulder. 'Wait.'

This couldn't be it. He didn't want it to be over.

Jess stilled. She turned to face him. 'Its okay, Adam,' she said, giving him a sad smile, lifting her hand up to cradle his jaw. She leaned forward and dropped a soft kiss against his mouth.

Then she turned away, opened the door, made her way into the house and climbed the stairs to her bedroom.

She shut the door quietly behind her.

And for the first time since she was fourteen and her mother had told her about her grandfather's death she threw herself on the bed and sobbed like a baby.

Two days later Jess finally emerged from her room. She'd ignored all knocks on her door, including Adam's, and had only come out to use the toilet and refill her water bottle.

She hadn't eaten or showered or brushed her teeth. She hadn't answered any calls or texts. She had just lain staring at the wall or sleeping, her nose buried in her Adam-infused sheets.

Ruby, Tilly and Ellie were sitting at the table in the kitchen, eating tea together, when Jess entered. They all looked up. It was rare to have them all there without their partners and Jess was grateful not to have to put on a brave face in front of the men.

'What's for tea?' Jess asked.

The three women looked at each other. 'Noodles,' Ellie said. 'We left some for you.'

Jess nodded and helped herself to a big bowl. She was starving. She sat down next to Ruby and piled her fork high before devouring the mouthful.

'Are you okay, hon?' Tilly asked.

Jess nodded. 'I will be,' she said around her second forkful.

'He broke it off, didn't he?' Ruby fumed. 'He's my brother and I love him but really…I warned him not to hurt you.'

Jess patted Ruby's hand. 'No, it's okay, I did. I broke it off.'

All three women paused in mid-forkful and looked at her. 'You did?' Ellie said.

Jess laughed. She couldn't help herself. 'Yes.' She shrugged. 'I realised that I wanted more than he was offering. I deserve that.'

Ellie squeezed Jess's hand. 'Too right, you do.'

Tilly nodded. 'Good for you.'

Jess smiled at her friends and they all smiled back before tucking back into the noodles.

Ruby ate a bit more than said, 'I know it'll be awkward around here when Adam comes home but…you're not going to move out, are you?'

Jess shook her head. She'd thought about it and thought about it the last two days. 'Absolutely not. We're both adults, it'll be fine.'

Besides, it was his loss. She was damned if she was going to move out of her home and away from her friends to save Adam some awkwardness.

He'd have to face her every day he was home.

She only hoped it hurt him as much as it was going to hurt her.

Six weeks later Adam sat in a makeshift office with his colleagues in a sweltering village church, waiting for Lai

Ling and the other Eastern Beaches patients to arrive for their follow-ups.

He could feel the stirrings of excitement and welcomed it with open arms. It was the first time he'd felt something other than a bleak kind of emptiness that only working every hour God gave him could erase.

He'd pushed himself and everyone else around him mercilessly. To do more operations, to see more people. Anything to stop himself from thinking about Jess.

He'd rung and texted a couple of times in the beginning, convinced that time apart would change her mind, but when they hadn't been returned he'd abandoned any further plans for contact.

She'd made it clear that it was over.

And he was just going to have to respect that.

If only it was as easy to stop thinking about her.

He heard a door open and looked up to see a group of people entering the church. They were all smiling and despite his nagging gloom Adam couldn't help but smile back. The difference they'd made to these people's lives was incredible.

They'd gone from outcasts to being embraced once again by their communities.

And then he saw Lai Ling and she beamed at him and he got to his feet and met her halfway across the room. His first thought as he greeted her and shook her hand was that he couldn't wait to tell Jess all about it.

Damn it—when would that stop?

Then she started talking ten to the dozen, grinning the whole time, and Adam laughed. He didn't have a clue what she was saying but just watching her face, her beautiful complete face, as she chattered away was a truly amazing thing.

He led her over to the upturned wooden crate that he was

using as a desk. Several charts were stacked in the middle.
His phone rested on the top of them to be handy should he
need to access one of the many medical applications that
had been loaded on to it. Like Lai Ling's clinical imaging,
for example. A couple of taps of the screen and he could
pull up all her X-rays, MRIs and CT scans.

'You look good,' Adam said, smiling at Lai Ling.

'Thank you,' she said shyly in slow English.

Adam tilted her head from side to side, his finger under
her chin as he inspected her wounds with a dermascope.
Living in a village where clean, fresh water was hard to
come by and nutrition wasn't always optimal was not conducive to good healing.

But Lai Ling's scars were fading rapidly and there were
no signs of infection.

'Good. Very good,' he said to Lai Ling. 'You are a very
good patient.'

She beamed at him again. 'You very good doctor.'

Adam chuckled. It was for moments like this that he did
what he did. That justified his gypsy existence.

And the sacrifices that came along with it.

Lai Ling's gaze fell on Adam's phone. She pointed. 'You
love Jess.'

Adam looked down. Lai Ling had seen the screensaver
on his phone. It was a shot of Jess laughing at him on the
beach at Coogee. Her hair was blowing across her face and
she looked like a real Aussie beach bum.

He hadn't been able to bring himself to erase it.

He picked the phone up and opened his mouth to deny it.
It was preposterous. How could he love her? They'd been
together for such a short period of time.

But suddenly it hit him. He did love her.

He was in love with Jess.

The truth of it was so simple it was startling.

All these weeks of ignoring the ache inside, pretending it was something else. Jet lag, fatigue, lack of sleep.

Of trying to work the feelings away, bury them under as many patients and late-into-the-night surgeries as possible.

A bubble of emotion clogged in his chest. How was it that a nineteen-year-old girl in a Third World village could see the truth of it and he couldn't?

He looked at Lai Ling. 'Yes.' He nodded his head then he laughed. 'Yes, I do.'

Lai Ling beamed back at him. 'You and Jess get married?'

'Yes,' Adam repeated.

If he hadn't totally blown it.

Two hours later he pulled Dr Raylene Burr, the mission's overseer, aside. 'How soon can you get someone to replace me?' he asked.

Raylene regarded him for a moment, weighing up his mood. Should she tell him the truth or sugar-coat it? 'Pretty quickly, I imagine. Your colleagues are about to vote you off the island anyway.'

She'd never been much of a sugar-coater.

Adam frowned. 'What? Why?'

'Don't be obtuse, Adam. You've been a pain in the butt the entire mission. You're grouchy and have been biting everyone's head off. You've been like a bear with a sore head. Or worse, just like your old man.'

Ouch!

Adam felt the criticism right down to his toes. He'd spent the last six years of his life flying around the world, trying to prove he was nothing like his famous father, only to morph into him when things weren't going his way.

'Why didn't you tell me?' he demanded. Raylene had

worked with his father many years ago and had about as much love for the chief as he did.

Raylene snorted. 'And get *my* head bitten off. I don't think so.'

Adam's breath hissed out. 'Sorry. It's just… There's this woman…'

Raylene laughed. 'Oh, my God. Well, well, well. I never thought I'd see the day. Adam Carmichael the world's greatest bachelor bites the dust. She must be something else.'

Adam laughed too. It felt good. 'Hell, yeah.'

Raylene nodded. 'I'll have someone here in two days.'

It felt like an eternity.

Adam was exhausted when the taxi dropped him off at Hill St four days later. No one was home so he dumped his bag in his room and went to check the calendar. According to the yellow scrawl, Jess was on a morning shift.

He checked his watch. Another five hours.

His gaze travelled up the staircase and he smiled.

Jess was exhausted when she arrived home at three-thirty. A lot of sleepless nights had seen to that. Lying awake, thinking about Adam. Wondering where he was and what he was doing. Wondering if he was angry enough with her to have hot, sweaty revenge sex with a colleague.

None of her thoughts had been conducive to sleep.

Still, she knew that the black cloud raining inside her couldn't last for ever.

Things would get better.

She climbed the staircase, her gaze wistfully falling on Adam's door before the incline took it out of sight.

The things she'd done behind that door.

In Adam's bed.

The things he'd be back to doing with others on his return to Australia.

Her footsteps were sluggish, her heart heavy as she pushed open her door. She wished she could fast-forward to this time next year.

One year's distance.

One year's perspective.

And then a form in her bed frightened the hell out of her and she almost screamed. Her pulse sky-rocketed as she clutched her chest.

Adam.

What the hell? He wasn't due back for another two weeks.

A feeling of déjà vu rushed out at her. Followed closely by exhaustion-induced rage. Just who the hell did he think he was? Did he think he could just come back home and pick up where they'd left off? That she'd forget he'd chosen his work over her and fall back into bed with him?

Even if, once again, his gloriously naked body begged to be touched.

She marched across to the side of the bed, picked up a pillow he'd once again just tossed on the floor and hit him square in the solar plexus with it. 'Get out,' she ordered.

Adam struggled through a hundred layers of thick, sticky slumber. It had been the first decent sleep he'd had in weeks, laying amongst the aromas he remembered so vividly. The aromas of Jess.

'Hey,' he protested, grabbing her arm.

'Don't "hey" me,' Jess yelled as she wrenched her arm free and continued her assault on his abdominals. 'Get out of my bed.' *Thump.* 'You can't just come back here…' *thump* '…and expect I'm going to…' *thump* '…fall back into bed with you.'

Thump. Thump.

'You chose your job over me.' *Thump, thump, thump.* 'You...' *thump* '...moron.'

Thump, thump, thump.

Adam looked at the yelling she-devil rearing over him, wielding a cushion, her ponytail swishing madly, and laughed.

Jess thumped him three more times for good measure. 'Don't laugh at me!'

'Jess,' he said, grabbing her hand and easily removing the offending cushion. 'Enough.'

He pulled on her arm and she toppled on top of him. 'That's not the way to greet the man you love,' he murmured.

Jess pushed against his chest as her traitorous body bloomed into heat. Then he cut off the protest she was just about to launch into with a very masterful kiss.

When he pulled his mouth away she was breathing hard.

They both were.

'Now, that's a greeting.'

Jess felt tears prick the backs of her eyes. 'Let me go,' she murmured huskily.

'Jess.'

'Let me up, damn it!'

Adam took his hands off her very delectable butt and let her slide off him. She sat on the side of the bed and stared at the floor.

'What do you want, Adam?'

Adam stroked a finger up her bicep. 'You.'

Jess felt a well of despair rise in her. She turned and looked down at him. 'Why?' she demanded.

'Because I love you.'

Jess sat very still as his words came to her in slow motion. Had he just said he loved her?

No.

She must have misheard. 'What?'

Adam smiled. 'I said I love you.'

He put his hand out to stroke her arm again and she shrank from it. 'That's not funny, Adam.'

'Tell me about it.'

Jess stared at him. He had a slight smile on his mouth and sincerity shone in his lapis lazuli gaze. 'I don't understand.'

Adam sat up. 'Oh, darling, neither do I. All I know is that I've been miserable without you. And an absolute pig to work with. The chief would be very proud. Then I saw Lai Ling a few days ago and she saw your picture on my phone and she said I loved you and I knew. Suddenly, right there in that jungle, I just knew she was right. The reason I've been feeling so wretched the last six weeks is because I've been in love with you all this time and in total denial.'

Jess held her breath. Dared she hope? 'Really?'

He nodded. 'Really.'

Adam could see the battle blazing in her blue eyes. She wanted to believe him but she was wary. Still, she didn't look like she was going to slug him with a cushion again so he moved a little closer and dropped a kiss on her shoulder.

'I had a lot of time to think on the plane and I realised you were right. I was asking you to make all the commitment and not giving you any of mine. Asking you to wait around for me, thinking only of my career and ignoring your ambitions. And I don't want that. I want to be in a partnership where we both get to do what we want.'

She swayed a little closer to him and he pushed her ponytail back behind her shoulder. 'I don't know how we're going to work it out but I love you, Jess. And I want to be with you for ever. I want to marry you and have kids with you. I want to give you the fairy-tale.'

Jess couldn't believe her ears. He was saying all the things she'd fantasised about.

Maybe she was dreaming?

'Just please say you'll love me too,' he murmured as he nuzzled her shoulder.

Jess looked into his eyes and smiled. She leaned forward and laid her forehead against his. 'Of course I'll love you. I've loved you for the last three years. And I'll love you the next three hundred if I can.'

Adam groaned as he inched his mouth closer to hers. 'I've missed you.' And he pressed his mouth against hers in a kiss that was one of pure tenderness and love.

He pulled back. 'I'll quit Operation New Faces, whatever you want.'

Jess opened her eyes. The world was still spinning so she anchored her forehead against his again and clutched his biceps. 'No, Adam.' She shook her head slightly. 'I don't want you to give up what you love doing. Not straight away. Not altogether. Surely you can just cut back the number of missions you do? I know how much it means to you, how much a part of you it is.'

'I thought you wanted me to quit?'

'No, Adam. I wanted you to need me more than your work. To realise that I needed you more than they did. Knowing you love me, that you're committed to me is enough. I do want us to talk about a plan for the future, though, for us spending more time together. But it doesn't involve quitting.'

Adam's shoulder's sagged. 'Thank goodness. For an awful moment I thought you were going to suggest I go into private practice like my father. I couldn't bear that. Getting all stuffy and full of myself.'

Jess smiled. 'So don't. Go into the public system. God knows, it needs good doctors too. Or how about the bush?

Do you know what waiting lists are like out there? People need surgeons in places where there aren't any. You could do so much out there.'

Adam pulled back to look into her face properly. He smoothed his hand down her cheek. 'That's what you want to do, isn't it? Go back and work in the bush?'

She nodded. 'Yes, I do. But it doesn't have to be for ever, Adam. I know you like the beach. So we compromise. That's what love's about. It's what you do for the person you love. You compromise.'

Adam smiled at her. His practical country girl. 'I love you,' he murmured.

'Oh Adam. I adore you.'

He kissed her then. Once, twice, three times. He couldn't believe how incredibly lucky he was.

'I know something else that love's about,' he whispered against her mouth as his hands slid to the buttons of her shirt.

Jess smiled as his mouth travelled down her neck and she angled her head more to give him full access. She pulled the sheet away to reveal his beautiful male nudity. Her eyes grew large at the sight of him.

'Mutual admiration and respect?' she said huskily.

'Sure,' he said, urging her down on the bed. 'Let's call it that.'

Jess smiled at him then got lost in his kiss.

EPILOGUE

One year later...

THE murmur of conversation and clinking of cutlery filling the Edwinburra Community Hall hushed as the sound of tinkling glass grew louder. Everyone turned to face the bridal table.

'In a break from tradition,' Ruby said, 'I'll be proposing the toast to the bride and groom.'

Jess smiled at her new husband looking sublimely sexy in his tux and then up at her new sister-in-law.

Everything about today had been perfect.

The full fairy-tale.

'Firstly, I'd like to congratulate both Jess and Adam for completely ignoring every piece of sage advice I ever gave them about staying away from each other. Clearly, for the first time in my life, I was wrong.'

The wedding guests, who included the entire town of Edwinburra as well as a contingent of city folk, laughed, clapped and cheered.

As Ruby's witty speech continued Jess looked around her at the tables filled with family and friends.

Her parents and grandmother beamed at her and Adam, radiating joy and love. Their adoration of Adam was gratifying and, she noted, reflected in all the faces of

Edwinburra. They had embraced him and his long-term plans for a flying surgeon service like a prodigal son.

Adam's mother, pride and happiness glowing in her face, sat beside Jess's grandmother. The chief had had a prior engagement, some conference in the US where he was key-note speaker, and no one—not Ruby or Adam or Sylvia—cared.

In six months' time she and Adam were embarking on a two-week holiday in Egypt and had surprised Sylvia with a ticket. Jess was determined Adam's mother would see the Sphinx.

Jess's gaze found Tilly and Marcus. Tilly was trying to watch Ruby with rapt attention but with Marcus attempting to distract her by nuzzling her neck it wasn't working so well. Jess smiled as Tilly's eyelids fluttered shut briefly.

It had been a full year for them both. The Eastern Beaches obstetric unit had celebrated its first year under Marcus's directorship with amazing good-outcome/low-intervention figures. They'd almost finished the renovations on their cliff-front mansion and they were due to tie the knot in a few months.

Jess was looking forward to that wedding!

Opposite them sat blissfully married Ellie and James. A glowing Ellie sat with her back, snuggled against her husband. Her five-month-pregnant belly, already obvious on her diminutive frame, was on proud display. A doting James cradled it with his hand.

Truth be told, they were both glowing and Jess wondered who would win the battle of wills over how much longer Ellie worked. James had wanted her to stop the moment she'd found out she was pregnant but Ellie loved her work on the ortho ward and working with her husband too much to give it up before it was necessary.

The jury was still out but she had a feeling that James

enjoyed the way Ellie distracted him from his goal as much as she did.

The reception crowd laughed and Jess was drawn back to Ruby, an adoring Cort gazing up at her. They were both tanned and gorgeous, having just come back from a holiday in the wilds of Venezuela where they'd secretly got married.

Ruby was now studying and working in mental health and Cort was still senior registrar in the emergency department at Eastern Beaches. They'd moved into his beachside flat one suburb over from Coogee and Jess seemed to spend as much time there as she did at Hill St.

There was more laughter and Jess tuned back in to Ruby's speech as she realised her friend and sister-in-law had turned to face her and Adam.

'It's been an eventful year.' Ruby paused and slid a hand onto Cort's shoulder. 'A lot of us have found out that despite differences and stumbling blocks and even well-intentioned friends…' more laughter '…that true love will find a way. So if I can ask the bride and groom to be upstanding, we'll drink to that.'

Adam smiled at her, dropped a kiss on her mouth and offered her his hand. Jess took it, her heart swelling so much she felt sure it was going to punch a hole in her chest.

She rose to her feet, fussing with her skirt for a moment, still unable to believe how timeless her grandmother's cream Chantilly lace wedding dress was and how well it had endured the march of time.

Adam took her hand and smiled down at her before raising his glass. Jess followed suit.

'True love,' he announced to the packed hall. Everyone repeated the toast and took a swig of their champagne.

Adam turned to his wife. His beautiful Jess, who looked

like Cinderella, Snow White and Sleeping Beauty rolled into one.

'To fairy-tales,' he murmured, touching his glass to hers.

Jess smiled back at the man she was going to love for ever. 'To fairy-tales.'

* * * * *

A sneaky peek at next month...

Medical Romance™

CAPTIVATING MEDICAL DRAMA—WITH HEART

My wish list for next month's titles...

In stores from 4th November 2011:

❏ The Child Who Rescued Christmas – Jessica Matthews

❏ Firefighter With A Frozen Heart – Dianne Drake

❏ Mistletoe, Midwife...Miracle Baby – Anne Fraser

❏ How to Save a Marriage in a Million – Leonie Knight

❏ Swallowbrook's Winter Bride – Abigail Gordon

❏ Dynamite Doc or Christmas Dad? – Marion Lennox

Available at WHSmith, Tesco, Asda, Eason, Amazon and Apple

Just can't wait?

1011/03

MILLS & BOON® Book Club

2 Free Books!

Join the Mills & Boon Book Club

Want to read more **Medical** books?
We're offering you **2 more**
absolutely **FREE!**

We'll also treat you to these fabulous extras:

- 🌹 **Books up to 2 months ahead of shops**

- 🌹 **FREE home delivery**

- 🌹 **Bonus books with our special rewards scheme**

- 🌹 **Exclusive offers and much more!**

Get your free books now!

Visit us Online

Find out more at
www.millsandboon.co.uk/freebookoffer

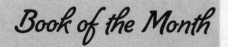

Have Your Say

You've just finished your book.
So what did you think?

We'd love to hear your thoughts on our
'Have your say' online panel
www.millsandboon.co.uk/haveyoursay

- 🌹 Easy to use
- 🌹 Short questionnaire
- 🌹 Chance to win Mills & Boon®
  goodies